CITY OF SHADOWS

To Jo,

Keep chasing your dreams, it's worth it.

THANK YOU!

JOHN NAUDI

Copyright © 2018 John Naudi
All rights reserved.
ISBN-10: 1981237313
ISBN-13: 978-1981237319

*to God and His creativity;
may this book be a reflection of it*

Acknowledgements

I would like to start by thanking my wife, Justine, who supported and encouraged me in spite of all the time this novel took me away from her. As a Beta-Reader, she was part of this very long journey almost as much as I was.

Big thanks go to Eddie Attard (renowned author of *Delitti Maltin*), Charles Said-Vassallo (owner of *maltagenealogy.com*) and the Malta Maps Society. Their help in the research has been invaluable. Special thanks also go to Joseph Sultana (owner of *visionplus.org*) without whose encouragement I would have never started this journey.

I cannot miss out on expressing my gratitude to Chris Calleja for taking the perfect photo and Michael De Giovanni for editing it brilliantly. Their skills made such an attractive exterior to this book. Thanks to Colette Cumbo for her excellent editing and proofreading skills. The support and patience of these people was without any limit.

Last and not least, I beg forgiveness from all those who were present over the course of the years and whose names I failed to mention.

John – January 2018

I have been to Rome, Paris, Prague, New York, Hong Kong and Beijing ... yet none have captivated me like Valletta

Prologue

Malta, late 19th Century

The darkness had settled now.
 The last rays of the setting sun were long past gone. The waxing gibbous loomed in the sky. At such hour, the damp streets and alleys of Valletta were no place for any stranger or local alike. No one lingered on the pavements or against the walls when the fingers of darkness came creeping in. Not even on the renowned *Strada Reale*. The street of trade and life, with its limestone buildings shining like gold under the morning sun.

But now it was so dark no gaslight from the lamp posts seemed to help. The only sound Archibald heard was that of the mare's hooves hitting the paved road. In the silence of the carriage's cabin, the horse's thuds sounded like thunder. They reminded Archibald of his childhood fear of lightning. His mind went back to how he used to crawl towards his mother. He would not fall asleep unless she waited on the rocking-chair beside his bed. It was a great relief to get tucked in, under his bed sheets, safe from the ravaging thunder and darkness outside.

Tonight, twenty years later and thousands of miles away from home, the relief he felt was pretty much the same.

He withdrew his fingers, letting the window curtain fall off. He felt he had already seen enough of the island for one evening. He hoped that all he had heard about Valletta was true, not that it would give him any comfort. He came from Britain and knew how sombre and dark a place the world was becoming. In Britain people spoke of revolution and the enlightenment, but Archibald thought differently.

Here, on this speck of land, Archibald's opinion of a lightless world seemed to strengthen. He had just set foot on Malta for the first time. But from the time he left the Grand Harbour up to now, his only impression was that this wasn't going to be much of an experience.

He was wrong.

The coach came to a halt, bringing Archibald back to his senses.

'You arrived, sir.' He heard the coachman say. 'Auberge d'Auvergne, *Strada Reale*.'

Archibald stepped out of the carriage, cautiously. The wide façade in front of him was a two-floored building with a decentralised entrance. No light came from the wooden louvered windows.

'Well, good night to you, sir,' whispered the coachman.

And with that he struck at his horse and was off without a moment's hesitation. Archibald glanced back and sighed. He made for the guarded entrance.

The Auberge reflected the style of architecture used by the Knights Hospitallers. A massive courtyard, surrounded by sixteenth-century long corridors and Romanesque arched columns. Even in this dark hour, the yellowish hue of the Maltese rock still managed to catch his eye.

The sound of approaching footsteps echoed to Archibald's left.

'Constable Whitlock? We have been waiting for your arrival,' said a man to his left. 'Good evening, I am Constable Thomson,' he added.

Archibald tipped his hat and nodded.

'Please follow me to the Superintendent's office,' instructed the constable.

The walk to the Superintendent's office was not long but to Archibald it almost felt like a long journey at sea. He got lost in admiring the architecture of the Auberge. The many paintings on the walls were a goldmine of cultural and artistic bliss.

'Wait till you've seen Castille,' exclaimed the other constable.

Archibald lowered his head from staring at the ceiling and raised an eyebrow at him.

'Your countenance gives you away, if I may be so bold,' continued Constable Thomson.

'Yes, I've often been told so,' replied

Archibald.

The constable suddenly raised a hand to indicate the door behind him. 'Superintendent Casolani is waiting.'

'Thank you, constable, I'll take it from here,' replied Archibald, making slowly for the door.

He knocked and waited.

The urge of taking another quick glance at the architectural beauty around him overcame him. The doorknob suddenly creaked and turned, and Archibald straightened. No voice came from within the room as the space between the door and the casing widened. Archibald hesitated, until a strong voice finally asked him to come in.

A fire was burning in the hearth on one side of the room, next to which stood an upholstered, two-seater maroon sofa. The floor was fully carpeted in navy blue. The intricate design on the walls gave off an aura of warmth. The Superintendent sat behind a brown-waxed desk at the far right corner of the room. He was robust and carried broad shoulders that reminded Archibald of a heavy wardrobe he had back home.

'Superintendent,' he murmured, trying hard to conceal his nervousness and intimidation.

'Constable Archibald Whitlock, finally,' replied Superintendent Casolani, stroking his chin. 'Have a seat,' he ordered, indicating the chair in front of his desk. 'I imagine you're famished and exhausted. I will be brief tonight, tomorrow we will speak in more detail.'

Archibald took his seat and thanked his superior politely.

'No need to be nervous, Constable Whitlock.' Casolani waved his hand casually. 'This is partly your homeland, after all. Am I right?'

Archibald nodded. 'Yes, Sir. My mother was Maltese, Sir. From Vittoriosa.'

Casolani got off his chair and made for the hearth. He thrust his hands forward and rubbed them against each other. He looked over his shoulder at Archibald, who was already on his feet.

'Malta is quite a peculiar place to live in,' started the Superintendent. 'Generally, not very clean, as you'll soon start to discover. But peaceful. Most of its people are kind-hearted. They're *very* religious, friendly ... and loud,' he ended with a grin.

Archibald smiled faintly.

'The situation we have in front of us, however, is something Malta has never experienced before. I, myself, am still finding it a bit hard to conceive.'

Archibald narrowed his eyes. Casolani remained silent for a while.

'In this country,' he went on. 'The average quota of murder cases is between two and three times a year, Constable Whitlock. Since last October, when the first victim related to this case was found, we've had a total of *four* murders.'

Archibald gaped. 'In Valletta?'

The Superintendent nodded. 'Yes; all in this city. The first one was in October. Male, found in Hastings – a public garden in Valletta. We thought it had been a one-off brutality, until last March. Two sailors were found dead on Saturday the 13th. Then a female, just a week later.'

March ... that's two months ago. Archibald blinked. 'And how are these four cases all related, Sir?'

Casolani sighed heavily. 'The victims were all found without their eyes. The eyeballs were missing from the crime scene - never found.'

Archibald raised his hand to his mouth. The Superintendent walked back to his desk and sat down. 'That should be enough for one evening; it is already an exception that we meet this late. You will be lodging at Morell's Hotel, during your time here. I trust you'll find it suits you fine. You are to report back here tomorrow, at eight in the morning.'

Archibald bit his tongue. *That's enough for the evening?*

Casolani waved a hand at him. 'We'll speak more about all this and the investigation required tomorrow. It is already too dark. A good night's sleep will bring light back to the world and to our petty brains. A carriage is waiting for you outside. Constable Thomson will escort you to it,' he ended dryly.

Archibald thanked the Superintendent, and made for the door.

Constable Thomson was waiting for him in the corridor. Archibald felt relieved to be finally heading to bed. But it would actually be a while before he managed to fall asleep. His superiors in London had barely briefed him on why he was needed here, save for his fluency in the Maltese language – which he felt was insignificant. His curiosity still needed to be satisfied.

'Morell's Hotel, *Strada Forni*,' announced the

cabman as the carriage came to a halt.

Arrived, already? I could've come on foot. Archibald descended from the carriage.

The cabman yelled at his horse and rode off into the darkness.

Looks big ... and dark. Archibald nodded and made for his final destination for the evening.

He hadn't even knocked when a dim light appeared from behind the door. A skinny, pale, dark-haired footman, with narrow eyes and a nervous stare greeted him.

Morell's Hotel was a manifestation of British style and architecture. A temple of modernity that instantly reminded Archibald of home. There were a good number of guests in the dimly lit main entrance. Despite the late hour, some still lingered about. One was musing lazily on a painting. Another two sat whispering over shimmering glasses of red wine. Few, if any, really cared to turn their attention to Archibald. They were – or *appeared* to be – too immersed in whatever they were discussing or worrying about. The majority were middle-class. Their accents gave them away, though. Archibald had never witnessed such a blend of nationalities before. Not in the same place at the same time, at least. Maybe what was being said, lately, in London, was true, after all. The world was indeed changing.

Not changing, really. More like becoming smaller.

'Welcome to Morell's Hotel, Mr Whitlock,' said another footman, showing Archibald to his room upstairs. 'Breakfast is at half past six, luncheon at one o'clock and dinner at seven.'

Archibald thanked the footman, then scurried inside his dull, colourless room. It reminded Archibald of the weather back home. He winced at the bleakness of the plastered wall and the shabby old furniture. The low bed was basically a mattress, more than anything else. No light came from the window to his left. The glowing light of the candle was going to be Archibald's only guide. He sighed and dragged his feet towards the bed and sank there.
    He dreamt of home.

1.

'Wake up, Archie, dear. It's time …' his mother's soft voice never ceased to be a powerful invitation to get out of bed. 'Archie, wake up, now!'

'But mother …'

Her voice suddenly turned base. 'Constable Whitlock?'

Archibald opened his eyes to the darkness around him.

'Sir, please. You need to wake up,' came a feeble voice from somewhere ahead.

'Where am … what in the name of …?' Archibald raised his head slightly, blinking into the darkness.

'Forgive me, Constable Whitlock.'

The muffled voice was coming from behind

the door. It was Constable Thomson. 'The Superintendent has requested your presence, Sir.'

'What's the time?' murmured Archibald, sitting up and rubbing his eyes.

'Nigh three o'clock, Sir. The Superintendent awaits you downstairs. He says the matter cannot wait.'

Downstairs? It's still three in the morning, heaven and earth! Archibald cleared his throat and sighed heavily. 'I'll be down as soon as I can.' He got out of bed and made for his uniform. *Was I being too hopeful for believing I could sleep till six, at least? The Superintendent said eight o'clock ...*

Downstairs, the Superintendent's silhouette waited in the main hall of the hotel.

I was down here only a few hours ago. Archibald frowned. It was a struggle to keep himself composed as he strode towards the Superintendent; a dying candle in his trembling hands.

Someone else emerged into Archibald's view next to Casolani - a thin man of average height. He looked past his thirties and carried dark eyes and hair. His thick eyebrows and moustache reminded Archibald of Ottoman canvas portraits.

'Inspector Eduardo Attard,' said the Superintendent. 'This is Constable Archibald Whitlock, from Britain. Whitlock, this is Inspector Eduardo Attard.'

They both nodded, raising their helmets politely.

'Għandi pjaċir,' said Archibald, recollecting the

Maltese formal greeting of being pleased to meet someone. Inspector Attard kind of smiled.

'Inspector Attard is one of the best local detectives we've had in the last years,' said Casolani, walking to the main exit. A doorman was already working on opening it. The two followed the Superintendent out of Morell's.

Casolani walked in the middle, with Archibald to his left and Attard to the right. The morning chill got to Archibald's bones and made him cross his arms. It was quite chilly, considering what he'd been told about the Maltese climate. Casolani led onwards, the lantern in his right hand barely shedding enough light. By this hour, the gas lamps in *Strada Reale* were all spent. The waxing gibbous was hidden behind clouds. Suddenly, Archibald started feeling the need to walk faster.

Due to the chill of course, he kept telling himself. It seemed like the darkness wanted to engulf the lantern and all three men in one go.

The Superintendent was silent. The weak light from his lantern showed a deep frown and narrowed eyes. Archibald kept looking around, hoping to spot anything indicative of their destination. He also tried to distract himself from the sense of eeriness by examining the architecture around. Valletta *had* to be a beautiful city to have reached his ears in London. But it was too dark now and it somehow felt like his eyes could not get accustomed to the darkness.

'We have just found another corpse, Sirs,' said

Casolani suddenly. 'I'm afraid we'll soon have to admit we're facing a crisis, gentlemen.'

'I wish we were actually facing whoever is doing this,' said Inspector Attard.

Another one? Archibald didn't bother to reply. He was somewhat glad they weren't silent anymore. He wished the murderer had waited, at least, one more night. *A good night's sleep is all I'm asking for, hang it all!*

'I will not brief you on the condition of the corpse. You'll see for yourself soon enough,' said Casolani, amidst the sound of their footsteps. 'I want *you* to come up with your own interpretations of whatever's happening. We're almost there,' he ended, taking a left to a downhill.

He hadn't finished speaking when Archibald noticed silhouettes of police officers. One of them was slightly bent downwards, his lantern revealing a hump on the ground. Another two shared a lantern, inspecting the vicinity. The last two were standing guard, or so it seemed.

Upon the Superintendent's arrival, one of those on watch called out in a hushed voice. After all the formal salutations and introductions were made, Casolani signalled to Archibald and Attard to examine the corpse. One of the other constables handed Attard his lantern. He started to say something in Maltese, which Archibald figured was about the discovery of the corpse.

'Corpse found less than an hour ago. Right here, *Strada Vescovo* ... ' Attard translated. 'Circa half past two, by Constable Cassar.' He pointed at the Constable who had just handed him the lantern.

Archibald took out his pocket watch. *Twenty past.*

'Body yet untouched by the police,' went on Attard. 'Constables Molinari and Lanfranco are surveying the nearby streets.'

Archibald pocketed his watch and squatted. He had seen a dead body or two in London. It was always gruesome, to say the least. The horrid smell made him cough and wince. One of the Maltese constables handed him a handkerchief. He thanked him, struggling not to lose balance. Against all his natural instincts, Archibald kneeled closer to the corpse. He almost despised the light coming from Attard's lantern.

The corpse was facing upwards and still quite intact. The eye sockets were empty. The mouth lay recklessly open. Whoever had meddled with it last, had definitely struggled to get something out, or in. A horrendous mixture of blood, arteries, all kinds of body fluids and tissue were still drying up on the broken face. Inspector Attard lowered the lantern closer to the disfigured face.

'Female. In her early twenties, give or take,' commented Archibald.

'Body already cold,' added Attard, touching the corpse's neck. 'Any sign as to how she was murdered?'

'Pass me a magnifying glass, please,' said

Archibald.

Attard walked to the other side of the corpse. He held his lantern close. Archibald thanked the constable and put on his leather gloves. He put the glass against his right eye and sunk his face against the corpse's.

'There is a tongue … only part of it, though,' he said after fingering through the mess of blood and vomit. Then he got up and went to lean against the closest wall, coughing and inhaling deeply.

'So, is there any clue as to how she was actually murdered?' insisted Casolani, walking closer to them.

'We need more light,' replied Attard, sighing heavily.

'The blood coming out the eye sockets is dry. There's blood on the temples and … there's some on the floor.' Archibald gulped and approached the corpse again, pointing at the ground. 'There, look.'

Attard got up and followed some trail with his lantern, away from the corpse. He stopped a metre or so away and straightened. 'There's blood splattered on the wall, too,' he commented, pointing at the wall, to Archibald's left.

'The lethal blow was definitely dealt around here,' added Archibald, nodding.

Attard nodded. The Superintendent waved a hand to one of the local constables. Archibald thought he heard him telling them to go and check for more blood trails down *Strada Vescovo*.

'What else, Sirs?'

Attard sighed slightly, kneeling closer to the corpse's face. 'Do you think she was moved? Before she was found, I mean.'

Archibald shrugged. 'We have to move the body to a morgue for better examination.'

Everybody turned their heads instantly to look at Archibald. Their dropped jaws, raised eyebrows and startled movements needed no deciphering.

What the deuce are they gaping at? He tried to utter something but failed.

One of the constables passed a quick comment in Maltese. The other two grinned and puffed.

'The morgue … ' Archibald turned his attention to the Superintendent. His expression was blank. 'I mean, examining the body will help us understand whatever happened here.'

The local constables looked far from convinced. One of them passed another remark about the disgrace of tampering with the bodies of the dead. The Superintendent's face was still blank.

The dark ages indeed … Archibald's mind went back to certain rumours he had heard about Malta. *These aren't religious people, they're superstitious.*

'That wouldn't be a bad idea, in fact, Constable Whitlock,' said Attard suddenly, eyeing the Superintendent.

Idea? It's necessary, heaven and earth! Archibald tapped his feet.

'Well get your hands dirty then, Caruana! And you too Mifsud, come on,' blurted out Casolani after a while. 'We don't have all night. Go get the *katalett*, and let's get this done. Take the corpse to the *Ospedale Centrale*. Doctor Galea must see this. The Inspector and Constable Whitlock can have a better look at it later today. Constable Whitlock, you may take your leave back to Morell's. In the morning, come straight to my office after the morgue. I still have to give you all the details about this mayhem. I think you've seen enough for one night.'

Archibald turned to look at the corpse. *Enough? We haven't even started.*

The Superintendent had already started on his way back to the Auberge D'Auvergne.

'I'll show you to Morell's,' Inspector Attard told Archibald.

Archibald nodded, but he still couldn't believe how religion and superstition could hold such a heavy grip on people, in the 19th Century. He followed the Inspector – not before taking one last look at the crime scene. He felt reluctant to leave in this manner. All he'd just witnessed would definitely weigh heavily on his mind, throughout the rest of the night. He was sure he wasn't going to manage to sleep easily.

He was wrong.

2.

The moonlight's rays always felt good against the skin, especially after days without. *Especially,* when someone knew the power they contained, the elation they gave, and the memories they revived.

Memories ... the Wanderer closed their eyes, and marvelled at how much the human species depended on sight. *Fools! If only they knew what one learnt after closing their eyes ...* Well, if anyone really knew, the Wanderer wouldn't be here in the first place.

The Wanderer looked down at the corpse, with its hollow eye-sockets and gaping mouth facing the sky. The scene brought back memories of the past.

Memories of the first kill.

The Wanderer would never forget how the young boy's life dissipated as his eyes were pulled out. He had looked like he was weeping, even after dying. Sometimes, it was hard to admit that no killing had been as pleasant as that first one.

The sailors got what they deserved, just like the young boy. Rosaria too, for she had played with fire. The Wanderer would never forget their faces, the empty eye sockets and gaping mouths, looking at the sky.

'You helped them see,' the Master had said.

'That's already much more than they deserved,' The Wanderer had replied.

The Wanderer closed the book. *Maybe that applies to you too*, thought the Wanderer, looking at Ms Anna's rotting body. *No one gets between us.*

Slithering into shadow, the Wanderer looked at the moon, then vanished down *Strada Vescovo.*

***

It was dark. So it was time to prepare to go to bed.

Anna was late. He was feeling tired and there was no time to wander about when you felt tired.

Wherever she was, it was none of his business; he knew that at least. She could take care of herself as much as she could take care of him, after all. He knew that too. So he washed his hands clean and made for his cold bedroom.

Well, it will start getting warmer soon. That's what

Anna always says; in May it is already warm, he thought. He walked swiftly down the corridor, hunching as he goes. The chill, spreading from his bare toes to his shoulders, made him hug himself and walk faster. Not that his bedroom was any warmer. But it always felt cosier, somehow.

Well, Anna dearest, he thought, opening the creaky wooden door to his room and glancing at the dark corridor behind him, one last time. *I'll see you tomorrow morning. But please, don't come waking me up when you arrive. You know I love my sleep.*

With that said and done, Joseph shut the door behind him and swiftly made for the tallow candles. 'Ah, lovely!' he said, lighting one of them and holding it close to his hunched shoulders. Guided by the dim light, he put on his pyjamas and scrambled into his makeshift bed. 'Good night,' he murmured, blowing out the candle.

But he couldn't sleep, not even after he recited all the bedtime stories over and over. His mind kept going back to Anna. The night got darker, colder and perfectly silent, but she didn't appear at the door to give him his goodnight kiss. Joseph's mind raced back to the fearful things he had heard the neighbours talk about, earlier this year. Anna had told Joseph they needn't worry and that she would protect him. No matter how hard he struggled to keep the fearful images out of his mind, he ended up sweating and shaking violently.

Help me, oh Lord Almighty, he prayed. *Oh Guardian Angel, who in His great mercy God has granted me for mine protection, enlighten me, guard me, guide me and protect me through this night …*

A sound outside made him jump.

It's just a rat … or a cat. He squeezed the thin blankets closer to his shivering chest.

It was cold, but the midnight chill was the least of his worries tonight. On other occasions, he would complain to Anna and she would comfort him, with her singing and bedtime stories. Oh how he loved them! Tales and songs of how the Knights, together with the brave people of Malta, had defended the islands against the Turks through a whole summer – many, many years ago. Until they finally defeated them and sent the Suleiman back to the East …

'Tell me a story, Anna,' he would ask.

'You are growing too old for stories, Joseph,' she would say at first. But then she would smile and give in. And she would tell him the story all over again, caressing him behind the ear till he fell asleep.

Not today, though. Anna was late. He felt lonely and afraid. And he couldn't sleep.

'Leave your eyes open,' she always told him. 'And after a while you'll start seeing everything, no matter how dark it is.'

But tonight the darkness kept growing and his eyes didn't seem to gain that sort of power. Maybe it belonged only to Anna and she could transfer it to him. But she was not here now. And he felt lonely and afraid, in the dark. He closed his eyes and prayed again lest the devil came and took him away.

'Wake up, Joseph. I was lost, but now I'm home.'

Joseph woke up with a start. He looked around him, heaving and sweating. It was morning. His first thought went to Anna. He flew out of his bed and rushed out of the room to greet her.

'Anna!' he yelled, rushing down the short corridor.

This was strange. Ever since they were children, Anna always said hiding was a very stupid game. Besides, they never had enough places where to hide. Joseph went to her bedroom, knocked and waited.

No answer.

'If I come in you'll scream at me, Anna. You're cheating, come out,' he said from behind the door, hopping on his bare feet. 'This is not fair. I need to go to relieve myself now. So, come out and I'll forgive you and we'll have breakfast together,' he ended.

No answer.

He decided to answer nature's call.

Then, he changed into his everyday ragged shirt and shabby trousers and walked back to knock on Anna's door.

'Come on Anna, I'm getting hungry ... and it's not fun anymore,' he grumbled. 'I'll be outside feeding the stray cats and the pigeons,' he ended, leaving without much ado.

When Joseph came back from his feeding duties, he searched every nook and cranny for Anna. His stomach grumbled noisily, until it started to hurt. Not to mention the headache. He started to scratch his grey hair and move idly about.

I need some air, he thought, making for the street once more.

It was still empty, save for some early birds who had to commute this time of day. The tall buildings of *Strada St Ursola* provided plenty of shade at the height of noon times. The neighbourhood didn't help much either. Most kept to themselves – to the little they had – and nobody really felt like asking too many questions. Not because they weren't curious; gossip was the order of the day around here. Still, Joseph's neighbours often said that God gave you a pair of ears and one mouth, so that you listen more than you talk. The recent murders were encouraging more citizens to follow this saying.

As a result, no one noticed Joseph as he hunched over a group of pigeons, cooing lazily close to his door.

'Few people ever notice us,' murmured Joseph, remembering what Anna always told him. 'We're invisible to them.' Joseph knelt closer to the birds. 'Hi, pigeons.'

The birds cooed in return, ever so used to humans in this area.

'I cannot give you anything to eat today. I'm still waiting for Anna to arrive. Did you happen to see her, by any chance? You lovely little birds.'

The birds went on their way, ignoring Joseph as much as his fellow neighbour did.

Joseph got up on his feet again, still eyeing the birds with a faint smile.

'No one's seen her,' he continued in a low voice. 'We're invisible to them all.'

His stomach protested once more and one of the pigeons instantly turned its little neck at the sound. Joseph's smile faded away as the pigeon abandoned the group and moved closer to him.

Humans can eat birds, I suppose.

3.

'Rita, wake up!'

Rita tried to open her eyes. It took her a while to remember who and where she was, until she recognised her younger sister's voice.

'You have to wake up, Rita, there's someone at the door.'

Rita opened her eyes abruptly and raised her head from the pillow. She was going to say something, when the whole room started spinning. She dropped her head backwards, shut her eyes and waited till the spinning stopped.

There was more knocking on the door.

'Where is mama?' she murmured to her sister. 'Tell her to go open the …'

'Mama works in the morning, Rita.'

Rita sighed heavily and waved her sister off. She swore in Maltese and helped herself up. 'Coming, coming!' She got off the bed, rubbing her eyes and struggling to keep them open. *At least that stopped the knocking,* she thought. *Now where the hell are my shoes!*

'Lucia, have you taken my shoes?' she shouted at her sister.

'No,' said Lucia.

'Rita …' came the voice from behind the main door. 'It's me, Maria.'

Maria was her best friend … her only one, really. Rita slipped on her gown and hurriedly made for the door, trying not to stumble over anything in the process.

'You look terrible!' was the first thing Maria said, as soon as Rita opened the door. 'And aren't you feeling cold?' She looked down at her friend's bare feet worriedly.

'Jesus! Are you going to stay out there acting as though you were my mother? Come on in …' replied Rita, making way as her friend entered.

The house was no more than three rooms next to each other; a simple parlour, the cooking room, and the dormitory. The parlour was a dingy, whitewashed room, containing a two-piece sofa and a couple of straw-hewn wooden chairs. Maria made for the comfort of the sofa, while Rita bullied her younger sister into getting them both a glass of water.

'So, what is it? Tell me.' said Rita, sitting next to her friend and turning to face her.

'Oh no,' laughed back Maria. 'First, tell me why you look so awful, barefooted as though you just fell out of bed. It's eleven in the morning, for God's sake.'

Rita didn't even smile. She turned her face away from her friend and sipped at her glass silently.

'You're not going to tell *me*?' insisted Maria, almost jumping on her seat. 'I'm your best friend, come on!'

'You're my only friend,' said Rita bleakly. She wasn't the most sociable of characters; the people of the neighbourhood weren't the friendliest. Ever since her father died, she found less solace in anyone other than herself.

'Hearing you speak like that, I don't think it's the right moment to tell you what I've come to …'

'Oh, please do,' insisted Rita, turning quickly towards her friend and grabbing her by the wrist.

'Uhm, fine. But only if you promise to tell me what happened to you last night.'

'Last night? How do you mean?' Rita asked, trying hard to conceal her shock. Maria couldn't possibly have an idea of what happened, no one must know!

'Oh, come on, sweetie. It shows all over your body and face. You either didn't sleep all night, or had a rough one.'

'Had a rough one.' Rita turned her attention back to the glass in her hand, feeling guiltier that her last reply was not exactly a complete lie.

Maria narrowed her eyes and shrugged,

ignoring her friend's stubbornness. 'Fine, keep it to yourself then. They found another corpse last night,' she said after a while. 'Rumour has it the police found it in *Strada Vescovo*. They don't seem to have any clue as to what's going on, if you ask me ...'

Rita gasped, putting her hands on her mouth. *No! Not* Strada Vescovo. *You cannot be right, please!*

'Rumours in the *Manderaggio*,' continued Maria, 'are that these murders keep getting messier. I'm pretty sure the police will be issuing some warning or something.'

'At what time was it found?' asked Rita bluntly, staring as though her friend wasn't even there.

Maria shrugged. 'Do I look like the police to you? What is the matter with you today, Rita?' You're really acting weird and it's as though you haven't slept all night. I bring the latest gossip and all you do is stare at me, as if I am a ghost.'

She was right. Rita's mind was elsewhere and she wasn't really doing a good job at hiding it.

'Well, you know what? Goodbye ... let me know whenever you feel like talking again,' ended Maria stubbornly, jumping off the sofa and making for the door.

'Maria, wait. Mar, please ...' said Rita, holding her friend by the arm.

Maria stopped, looked back, and frowned.

'I'm sorry,' said Rita, letting out a sigh.

Maria returned to her seat. 'They're not saying

anything, yet,' she said. 'But, it is definitely related to the previous murders. The victim is a woman.'

Rita huffed. 'Related? How?'

'They're all being found in such a horrible state, Rita,' said Maria. 'No one can deny it any longer. Besides, this makes it the fourth case.'

'Fourth?' Rita shook her head gently, from side to side.

'Fourth case, fifth victim, yes,' Maria nodded. 'The first case this year, in April, consisted of two men. Sailors, apparently. No great loss there, if you ask me.'

Rita bit her lips and clenched her fists. *Well, at least the police are busy ...* 'That's terrifying,' she said plainly.

Maria nodded again, got up and made for the door. 'Well, I'm off. Got a busy day ahead of me and more rumours to gather. Take good care of yourself, will you?'

Rita thanked her and nodded. For a moment, she thought of telling Maria; sharing her secret would definitely help. But her friend was out of the door before Rita blinked. *No one must know.*

Even though she trusted Maria with her life, Rita knew she wouldn't understand. Losing her only friend was the last thing she needed. If the police ever came knocking at her door, all the *Manderaggio* would learn of her sin. Eventually, her mother would come to know. And Lucia too.

No, please God, not Lucia! she prayed. *No one must know.*

Her mother arrived home a few minutes later.

'Come help me - oh dear, it's like you've seen a ghost!'

Rita raised her head slightly, eyes still blank and looking elsewhere.

'Well, are you going to help me carry this water? Or shall I call your sister to help?'

Rita blinked and pulled herself together. Silently, they carried the buckets together into the kitchen. Lucia jumped gleefully at the sight of her mother, whilst Rita started to pour the water into different buckets.

'You could have at least prepared something for lunch, my dear,' she told Rita.

'She woke up late, mama. And then Maria was here,' interrupted Lucia with a grin.

Rita glared at her sister.

Mother's face turned serious. 'At what time did you wake up, Rita?'

Rita hesitated before answering, 'Eleven, ma.'

'Eleven? I've been out and working the whole morning, while you woke up late and had a chit-chat with your friends …'

'It was just Maria, ma,' replied Rita, barely whispering and avoiding her mother's eyes.

'And where are your shoes? And why the hell do you smell like …' Her mother hesitated and looked at her younger daughter. 'Lucia, go and play outside, darling. Come back in time for lunch.'

Lucia obeyed readily, hopping out of the kitchen.

'Rita.' Her mother's tone turned stern. 'There are always less people by the water spring at around two, in the afternoon. You will go and clean yourself then. What were you up to? There's no way you could have gotten this dirty just by sleeping.'

Rita struggled not to tremble, and wished the ground would open to swallow her up. There was no way she was going to tell her own mother. 'I think it's better if I just went to the well right now.' She cut across her mother and went out of the kitchen. At the main door, she stopped and left a couple of shillings from the night before. *That's what I am doing, Ma.* And with that, she stormed out of the house.

Her mother kept yelling after her, but Rita knew disobedience was her only option. Not that she really had any. After all, it was lack of choice that led her into this depraved situation. But no one could know. It would kill her mother, and bring unspeakable demons upon Lucia, that would haunt her for the rest of her life. There was hardly any hope for her. Knowing that she could protect her twelve-year old sister, however, kept her going through this mayhem.

The narrow streets and crammed buildings of the *Manderaggio* surely offered no consolation. She just hurried along, hardly knowing where she was really going. Little did she care who noticed her. No one stopped from what they were doing to look at this young woman, running barefoot and barely dressed in the middle of the day. On other occasions, she would have cared, especially knowing how in Malta, particularly in this neighbourhood everyone seemed to know everything about everyone else.

But not today.

She had no mind for it, if that could describe it well enough.

She actually didn't know what she was feeling. Was it rage? Pride? Whatever it was, she hoped it would be over quickly. Such dark thoughts would only drag her to hell. Isn't that what they say about the seven vices?

At the mere thought of hell, her heartbeat quickened. Her body shook to the point that it was becoming difficult to keep balance. She started praying to the Almighty God in her heart; begging Him for forgiveness. The Church said Heaven's Gates were shut to people like her, but she tried hard to cling to the memory of her deceased father.

'The greatest mercy of all,' he used to tell her, wearing his unique, radiant smile, 'is that God became human and allowed man to put Him on a Cross. He died so that mercy could be found for all, my sweet child.'

Rita ran as though she was hunted. She found herself out of the *Manderaggio* and approaching the bay of *Marsamuscetto*. She stopped only when she realised she was getting close to the sea. No matter how busy and hectic the Port of *Marsamucscetto* always seemed to be, it never ceased to amaze her. The blue skies and calm sea!

The breeze of May already smelt of summer. From this month till October, Malta blessed its inhabitants with stunning, blue, cloudless skies. The sea was soothing to her eyes as it was to her very soul. Every Maltese liked the sea, being surrounded by it. But she loved it in a way words could not explain.

Undoubtedly, she had inherited this love from her father, who had spent his life serving the British Empire as a shipwright. It had been his trade and he loved it with a passion. Rita would see it in his eyes whenever he returned from *Marsamuscetto,* after a day's work. He would give her a brief explanation of how this ship got damaged, or how that boat could be repaired. No matter the damage it suffered, no ship was beyond repair. His narratives were the best bedtime stories for Rita.

'Papa,' she mumbled to herself now. 'How I wish you were here, pa. I don't know what else to do. But you would.'

He would smile at her, even now. She would confess her grave sin to him and he would scold her and get momentarily angry. But he was her "papa". He would sit down with her and ask her to explain further. He would listen, whilst she gave him her reasons; that she had to do this because he was gone. He might even put his rough finger on her dry lips and tell her that there was no need for her to explain. Then they would look at the blue skies and sea, and walk back home. He always loved her; he always understood.

'I need you, *Papà* ...' she whispered, tears trickling down her cheeks. 'Please, walk me back home.'

4.

'Come on in,' he heard the muffled voice say, from behind the door.

Inside, Constable Adami formally introduced them.

Archibald held back a grin. *Constable Whitlock … I like the sound of that.*

Superintendent Casolani nodded politely. 'You may sit down,' he told them, then rang the bell for one of the tea-boy. 'No discussion may take place before the mind is invigorated by the essence of tea.'

The tea-boy filled their cups.

'I trust you both had breakfast?'

'Yes, Sir,' Archibald and Attard said.

'Leave us.' Casolani waved a hand at the tea-boy, then turned his green eyes on them. He looked at them silently for a while, lowering his eyes only to stir the tea in his cup. It was so silent you could hear a pin drop.

'So, tell me, Whitlock,' started Casolani. 'How was your meeting with Doctor Galea?'

Archibald gulped. He rubbed his palms against his knees. 'Superintendent, Doctor Galea confirmed all victims were found with their eyes missing.'

'And?'

'We can safely assume the eyes were ripped out *after* the victims were murdered. The Doctor deduces no such feat could have taken place whilst the victims were still alive, or were conscious. Their screams would've woken up the entire city. Besides, whoever did this, is rough and definitely unskilled in any form of anatomy.'

The Superintendent nodded slightly. 'Not a doctor, then. What about the bodies? Were they killed on the same spot they were found?'

Archibald wet his lips. 'Save for the two sailors found on 13th March, yes.'

The Superintendent stroked his chin. 'Hmm … the ones found in Hastings Gardens. What about them, then, Whitlock?'

Doesn't he know all this already? 'They were found on a bench, in full uniform, sitting next to each other,' explained Archibald. 'Their heads bent backwards, as if they were looking at the sky.'

'Before their eyes were removed, of course.' The Superintendent sniggered.

Archibald nodded. 'Judging by the blood found on the scene of crime, the Doctor confirms the sailors were moved to that position *after* they were murdered.'

'What about the weapon used?' Casolani fixed his eyes on Attard.

Look at Mr Attard, sure! Why, you cannot afford to let me *tell you about the autopsy, blast you!*

Attard shot a quick look at Archibald before answering. 'Superintendent, Doctor Galea confirms his previous hypothesis. The lethal weapon must have been something blunt and heavy.'

'Confirms?' The Superintendent narrowed his eyes.

Yes, thanks to the autopsy on this morning's victim. Archibald bit his tongue and fought the urge to roll back his eyes.

'Yes, Superintendent,' said Attard. 'The ... from the examination performed on the victim found this morning ... the Doctor confirms the blow was to the temples. Quick and fatal.'

'Interesting,' said Casolani.

Interesting? If you had ordered an autopsy on the previous victims, you'd be less in the dark now. Some gratitude would be nice, at least ...

'So, another victim murdered on the spot,' went on the Superintendent. 'A quick, unclean death. Constable Whitlock, I seem to recall you observed this morning's victim had its tongue ripped out.'

So it is me again ... 'Yes Superintendent. It was.'

The Superintendent sighed and shook his head. 'This keeps getting darker and dirtier, gentlemen. Four cases, five victims. No witnesses …'

'Save for Mr Axiak, in *Strada Zecca*,' added Attard, nervously.

The Superintendent harrumphed. 'You mean that blind, old withering fellow?'

Attard nodded timidly. 'Well, he still hasn't given up his claim.'

Casolani sniggered and looked at Archibald. 'This fellow lives in *Strada Zecca*, close to Hastings Gardens. On the night of 13th March, a couple of hours before the two sailors were found dead, he heard laughter outside his home.'

'And the fluttering of wings,' added Attard, flatly.

Archibald raised an eyebrow.

'Yes, Whitlock.' Casolani was almost grinning. 'Valletta's population is just above twenty-four thousand people, with twice that number of *pigeons*.'

'I see,' replied Archibald. 'What about the victims' relatives?'

The Superintendent raised a finger. 'See, that's one of the major problems we have here, Constable. Neither relatives, nor friends have come forward, for any of the victims. Not even to help with identification.'

'Strange …' Archibald narrowed his eyes.

'You're telling us. In a country where everyone seems to know everything about everyone else ...' said Attard, with a faint smile on his face.

'That is sad,' commented Archibald, lowering his head.

'And shady,' said Casolani.

'Truth be told,' added Attard. 'We have rooted suspicions that the first victim was a member of some notorious gang in Valletta.'

'The one found in October?'

Attard and Casolani nodded.

'Valletta isn't too different from London, Whitlock,' said Casolani. 'Only smaller. The lower-class is mostly illiterate, here. And wherever there's ignorance, gangs rule.'

'Gang-fights are not rare, either,' added Attard.

A hooligan in October, two sailors in April ... with barely any serious investigation done. Let alone an autopsy! Archibald sipped at his tea. 'What about the female found in April, a week after the sailors?'

Attard sighed. 'Not much, really. No relative or friend approached the authorities. We're hoping that by examining the body of the last victim ...'

'We need more information,' interrupted the Superintendent. 'We need to find out why these particular people were chosen for the slaughter, Sirs. They don't seem related, in any fashion. We're left with no idea about the killer's motive. For months, we have tried to find witnesses, suspects ... even rumours would put us in a better position at this stage.'

You have done nothing for months. Now that the autopsy has proved useful, you don't even have the face to admit it.

'We have no clue of when the next murder will take place,' went on the Superintendent. 'For I'm pretty sure it will, eventually. This country has never seen something of this level, particularly not in such a short span of time. And what leads do we have to solving this riddle? None at all!'

Archibald nodded passively. *Well, if the victims' corpses were examined in a morgue, it would have helped. But you had to be ignorant and bury them!*

'This is why you're here, Constable Whitlock …'

Why, of course. Thank God!

'You and Inspector Attard must find the key to this riddle.' Casolani puffed and stomped violently back to his chair.

For a couple of minutes he stood there, then got up and started pacing around the office again. His heavy footsteps were the only sound in the room. Attard was rubbing at his bushy eyebrows. Archibald remained silent. He had the impression Casolani was a detonator, about to explode at the slightest intervention. He looked shocked, and tense, to say the least.

As for Archibald, he was completely lost. As a constable in Whitechapel, he had dealt with high crime before; yet this still felt different. He felt as inapt as when he first joined the police force, five years ago. Even worse, the Superintendent seemed so stubborn and foolish. Archibald was sure the autopsy would help, just like those being performed in London in the last years. But Malta really seemed to be a whole new world. Archibald recalled the vision from earlier on this morning, in *Strada Vescovo* and the examination beneath the waxing moon. The local constables had all dropped their jaws because he recommended taking the body to a morgue for examination.

I think I would've received more praise had I recommended an exorcism. Archibald fought the urge to smile at his own thoughts.

Well, the constables were constables – though that still didn't wholly justify their ignorance. But this was the bloody Superintendent! It totally frustrated Archibald when people were this ignorant and reluctant to welcome new ideas. Change was inevitable, particularly now, in this century.

'Meanwhile,' Casolani was by the window, rubbing his chin and examining the sunny façade. 'We have to acquire whatever information we can about the last victim.' He turned to look at them. 'I'll issue a post by this evening,' he said, staring blankly as if talking to himself. 'We'll double the patrols, too. Anyone providing useful information will be listened to and given protection if necessary. But we must act fast.'

Attard and Archibald both nodded.

The Superintendent turned his attention to them. 'I don't need to remind you of the importance and urgency of this case, of course. I'll write you all the necessary authority to enter anywhere and question anyone, as you deem fit. Speak to the people, listen to details in their rumours … you know how this is done, both of you. Don't come back without anything useful, Sirs. Any questions?'

'No, Sir,' they replied dutifully.

'You're dismissed.'

Finally, no more time wasted. Archibald clenched his fists.

The two made for the door; Archibald suddenly realised he had not finished his tea, yet.

'And one more thing,' added Casolani, when both Attard and Archibald were almost at the door. 'Do not wear those uniforms anymore, not for now. The last thing we need is citizens shutting their doors and being overwhelmed by paranoia as soon as they see you. We need to help them feel at ease, remember that. We need information. Now go and leave me in peace!'

The rays of sunshine greeted Archibald as soon as he stepped out of the Auberge d'Auvergne. They helped massively against the heavy mood inside. The warm strokes of sunlight against his pale cheeks lifted his spirits, like a pretty lady's smile. It was only mid-May, but already warmer than any British Summer he had ever known.

Strada Reale was as busy as a beehive. Everywhere you looked, gentlemen in their cutaway morning coats and derby-style hats crossed each other, hurriedly. Occasionally, one slowed their pace upon recognising an acquaintance. But only to raise their hat slightly, smile politely and move on. The fine and intricately dressed ladies walked mostly in groups. They held hands and giggled at passers-by, or walked hastily around, their pretty faces hidden beneath their delicate hats. At certain spots, small groups of people would gather for a chat. Men to talk business, women to gossip. In the darker and narrower alleys, the lower-class went on with their lives and errands. They appeared alien to the bliss around them. As someone who grew bored, or too accustomed to a spectacle they witnessed all their life.

Archibald couldn't help noticing Inspector Attard's relief.

'You must know I never fancied uniforms, Constable Whitlock,' said the Maltese Inspector, smiling slightly and eyeing his colleague. 'They're called *mantilla*,' he explained, noticing how Archibald was staring at a woman across the street. She was wearing a black hooded shawl, which covered her head and shoulders. 'Or what the Sicilians call the Maltese *faldetta*. It's called *għonnella* in Maltese; worn by most of the women here and on the sister-island of Gozo. It makes even the ugly look beautiful, if you ask me.' He winked.

'It gives her face an enthralling radiance,' replied Archibald, poetically.

Attard chuckled slightly.

'Never seen them anywhere before.'

'Hmm. Walk with me, Constable,' he said, heading left.

Archibald nodded and followed.

The flow of people was overwhelming. Most were going against their direction, pushing them away in haste. Archibald started to realise the Superintendent might've been right, after all. London was usually hectic, to say the least. Valletta was just as busy and noisier.

'I must admit, Valletta looks very different from last night, Inspector,' he told Attard, as they hustled through the crowds around them. *It's as if there wasn't any murder ... do they even care?*

'It is calmer in the afternoons. On Sundays, it's as silent as a graveyard. And the spacious *Piazza San Giorgio* helps,' answered Attard, indicating the location a couple of yards ahead.

'I see. Yet at night, it has a ...'

'Magical effect, if you ask me.'

'Oh,' replied Archibald, taken aback. 'I was going to say *eerie*.'

Attard shrugged back. 'Well, they say London is constantly covered in fog.'

Archibald nodded. 'That is true. It's because of the number of factories surrounding it. I was in no way drawing a comparison, however. Forgive me.'

'Oh, come now, Whitlock! Who said anything

about comparison? There's nothing to forgive. Look, the *pastizzi* vendor!'

Archibald jerked his head in the direction his colleague had just indicated. On the side of the street, a short, roughly-dressed man was carrying a cane basket. He shouted something in Maltese. Archibald followed Attard, who rushed through the crowd as though he just spotted an old friend. They spoke in Maltese for a while, until the man handed him a wrapped piece of white cloth. The Inspector gave him some shillings from his side-pocket.

'Maltese *pastizzi*,' he told Archibald. 'I don't know what to call them in English. Come, the *Piazza* is close.'

Archibald had just caught his breath.

'You just wait and see, Whitlock. Once you've tasted these, you will have to resist the urge to buy some more,' he chuckled.

They walked on. Archibald turned his head from one side to the other, absorbing all he could of this beehive of a city. *It's really like there wasn't a murder last night ... how can they remain so indifferent?*

Piazza San Giorgio was to their left. The Governor's Palace standing majestically opposite; a massive building manifesting Renaissance Mannerist architecture.

'That was designed by a Maltese architect, did you know?' said Attard, noticing Archibald's fixed stare on the Palace.

'During the time of the Knights, right?' replied

Archibald.

'Yes, in the era of the Knights of the Order of St John. Cassar – can't quite remember his first name exactly. Many prominent buildings in Valletta were commissioned by the Knights of St John, and designed by Cassar. The Auberge D'Auvergne too, for instance,' he ended.

'And this must be *Piazza San Giorgio* …' said Archibald.

The inspector nodded. 'St George's Square, yes. The French used to call it the Square of Liberty. They had shot a group of people, here, once, during the siege of eighteen hundred, when the Maltese wanted to hand over Valletta to the British.'

Archibald raised an eyebrow.

'It is now the scene of numerous festivities, such as Carnival in February,' he ended with a smile.

Archibald almost smiled back, sliding his finger between the collar and his neck. *What is it like in August, if it's already this hot now?*

Attard took off his gloves and was unwrapping the cloth off the *pastizzi*. 'Here, take one,' he said.

Archibald took off his gloves and obeyed. His taste buds were suddenly overwhelmed by a myriad of flavours. The pastry was undoubtedly fresh, with a mouth-watering savoury taste. Archibald had to control himself from rudely devouring the entire thing in just two gulps.

'Delicious, right?' commented Attard, noticing

the Englishman's expression. 'I'm sorry you get to taste only the *ricotta* one. The vendor already ran out of the other ones.'

'The other ones?' asked Archibald between a mouthful and another.

Attard nodded. '*Pastizzi* come with two different fillings. *Ricotta* or peas. They're both delicious, if you ask me.'

'They're delightful!' exclaimed Archibald, wiping his mouth on a handkerchief. 'Thanks, Inspector Attard. If I eat another two of these, I would have to skip lunch.'

They both chortled heartily.

'What do you make of all this, anyway?'

Attard wiped his greasy hands on a handkerchief, then put his gloves back on. He raised an eyebrow, looking confused.

Archibald lifted a finger at *Strada Vescovo*, which crossed *Strada Reale* at the other end of the square.

'Ah,' sighed Attard, stroking his cheek. 'From my experience of murders in this country, it is definitely something personal. The Maltese are very friendly and good-hearted, Whitlock. But we also get offended easily. Unfortunately, we tend to take things to heart. From the little we yet know of this, I say we'll soon discover it has to do with jealousy, or pride, or … you name it.'

'Or money?'

Attard shrugged. 'Maybe. What about you, Whitlock. Are you forming any opinion yet?'

'I believe the autopsy helped.' He let that sink

in, before continuing. 'The removal of the eyes is recurrent in all cases. And the fact that the eyes have never been found, irritates me at best. I mean, have you been in contact with any taxidermists, yet?'

'Not really, no. That would be a good idea, actually. Though well, I can hardly picture anyone collecting eyeballs for sport.'

'You'd be surprised … Have you considered the possibility of some sort of superstitious ritual being performed here, maybe? I heard the Maltese are very religious.'

Attard looked at his colleague. 'Constable? I understand your scepticism of my religion, as we do have many rites, but I cannot see how Roman Catholicism could possibly inspire such atrocities.'

'I was thinking more on the lines of the occult, like Satanism, Mr Attard,' replied Archibald.

Attard pursed his lips. 'Granted. Devil worshippers have been around for many, many years. That's because they were never foolish enough to leave a trail of corpses behind, I suppose.' He shrugged. 'I do not know, but it lacks motive and organisation. Don't you think?'

Archibald nodded. 'I agree. The thing I find difficult to understand is the lack of witnesses. Is it possible some witnesses could have been bribed? I mean, all the victims were killed then left to rot outside.'

Attard nodded. 'Besides, gouging the eyes surely requires the aid of some tool, despite how gory. And it must take a couple of minutes, I presume.'

'And *no one* saw or heard anything? All victims were found by the police, right?'

Attard nodded. 'Constables on night patrol, whom we have questioned. Didn't lead to anything, unfortunately.'

Archibald turned his gaze towards *Strada Vescovo* again. He wondered whether the police could be somehow involved, here. It was a scandalous notion, to say the least. Yet back in London, constables had occasionally been bribed to ignore important clues, or overlook evidence. 'Well, in London …' he started, but then hesitated.

Maybe it was better to keep his thoughts to himself. More talk of London could raise questions related to his past – which he wished to keep to himself as much as possible. He noticed Attard was still looking at him with those bushy eyebrows and narrow eyes. 'It is a heavy case,' he said, removing his hat and scratching at his dark hair.

Attard sighed. 'My theory is we're dealing with a sick mind. Our killer needs to be put in an asylum.'

Archibald narrowed his eyes. 'A fugitive, maybe?'

'Hmm, that was one of my very first thoughts on this matter. But there have been no breakouts, recently. The lack of discipline and pattern makes me believe this is the work of a rotting mind.'

'I'm afraid I have to agree. On what days of the week were the victims found, do you remember?'

Attard nodded. 'The first three cases were all found between a Saturday night and early morning Sunday. That looked promising, until today's victim ...'

'Tuesday, early morning.' Archibald nodded. 'Do you remember what they wore?'

Attard raised his eyes in thought. 'The sailors were in uniform, as the Superintendent mentioned earlier. The others ... well, nothing out of the ordinary. Definitely lower-class, also explains the lack of witnesses coming forward. No one seems to care enough, unfortunately.'

Archibald sighed heavily. 'Unfortunately indeed. Doctor Galea told me the last victim wasn't dead for too long, a couple of hours at most. That would mean the victim, whoever she was, was out late. The others ... we'll never know.'

Attard looked sad, but unaffected by Archibald's comment. 'No wonder no one showed up as a witness. As the Maltese saying goes, he who plays with fire is bound to get burnt ...'

'Yes, we have that saying too.' Archibald leaned forward, resting his elbows on his knees. 'It seems like we're up against some lunatic, then. It feels like there's little we can do to predict his next move and it's so frustrating.'

Attard nodded and made to move on. 'Shall we walk to Morell's? I'm finding this discussion interesting, but my mind needs nourishment. And it's been a while since I had lunch at Morell's. I'm famished.'

Archibald was already on his feet, when he saw Constable Molinari running towards them.

'Inspector Attard,' he said, heaving. 'The last victim … we have her name.'

'Well spit it out, Molinari!'

Molinari straightened and took a deep breath. 'Ms Anna Sultana. She lived in *Strada St Ursola* and has a brother.'

5.

The Falcon's Perch was as loud and as busy as ever. Like every other evening, the British sailors returning from their morning shifts opened their stinking mouths to sing like buoyant maniacs. Their Maltese colleagues never protested, joining in with their local songs; competing for attention as though they were trained opera singers. Those who did not participate in this merriment, sat languidly in some dark corner to observe the revels of a sottish society. Others made their way out as stealthily as they came. Complaints were never an issue at The Falcon's Perch.

Actually, complaints were the least of concerns for the property owners of *Strada Stretta*. The few who complained were taken care of, in some way or another. In the morning, *Strada Stretta* was no different from the other streets of Valletta. But at night, it turned into a spectacle of entertainment and modern noise. It housed pleasure for any man – particularly men - if they were courageous enough to venture through the darkness. They would find themselves here, where their thirst could be quenched – in both the literal and symbolic meaning of the term.

It was through this bedlam that she raced, as fast as her legs could go. She only stopped when she reached the entrance of The Falcon's Perch. The singing had calmed down, though not completely ceased. Some old chap was playing the guitar to a Maltese melody, accompanied by a few drunken locals who sat and sang with harsh voices. She looked for the clock from beneath her hood, but someone – or something – had knocked it off the wall tonight. She sighed nervously, and scanned the inn.

He was seated at the usual table, right across. Spotting her, he gestured with his hand for her to get closer. 'You're late,' he said as soon as she took the opposite chair. 'You know that irritates me. Isabella? That's your name, right?'

She nodded.

'Liar!' He spat into the empty bowl in front of him. 'You thought you could trick *me*?' He landed his elbow on the table, pointing his index finger at her. 'I know you, *Rita.* You're still *not* twenty-one!'

Rita couldn't conceal her shock. She suddenly

felt dizzy, clutching at the table in front of her. She knew she would faint soon. *Don't ask, don't beg*.

'Well now, we *do* seem to have a problem,' he continued, mockingly, toying with his black moustache.

'Please ...' she started, unable to contain herself.

'Your secret is safe with me,' he said ironically, smirking.

Rita's eyes dropped. She barely ever looked him in the eye, let alone when he grinned and revealed his almost toothless mouth.

'I won't say a word about your age, my dear. Though, well, we might need to go over that little arrangement of ours. That's why we're meeting, isn't it? You comply and your name will remain Isabella. Your age ... well, our sailors don't really care about that, now, do they?'

'Please, I am already ...'

'No, no. None of that begging. You will do as I say.'

Rita lifted her head slightly, staring blankly at his chest and avoiding the wild grin on his dark face.

'Please, I cannot.'

'Of course you can, dear. You're good at this,' he continued, opening his arms and shrugging. 'You're such a natural, *Isabella*. Natural beauty, natural liar. You must also be naturally skilled at ...'

'Please, Mr Calleja,' she pleaded, looking

hesitantly around.

'You have it right here,' he whispered, brandishing a metallic token between his thumb and middle finger. That badge was her protection, her salvation, her permission. Basically, it was a mask if the police ever came looking.

'This is what you need, right?' He moved his dark hairy hand closer to her delicate face.

No one must know, she thought, taking the coin-sized token. Her head started swirling, and she felt like the whole world was collapsing. The cheer and gaiety around her seemed muffled, her vision got blurry and dark. She told herself to get up, but found herself leaning backwards instead. Mr Calleja was blabbering and making threats to secure his ownership on her. Rita forced her body forward, but the spinning didn't stop. Suddenly, she felt his tight grip around her tender wrist.

'Sit down.' His voice terrified her. 'Or I'll kill you right here!'

She tried with all her might to pull his hand away, but managed only to sink back down to her seat. She heard him asking politely for a glass of water. It was brought.

'Isabella, Isabella …' he said, in a melodic tone. 'You keep disappointing me, even though I am so willing to treat you well. Here, drink.'

He put the glass close to her mouth.

'Drink, I say!' he blurted out. 'That was the last time I will ever *ask* you to do something. Drink.'

Rita took the glass and sipped at it reluctantly.

'I need my money. You need your life and this secret kept safe, *Isabella*. You'll be starting from tomorrow. With a salary.'

Rita failed to hide her disappointment. A salary meant her earning would be controlled, and restricted. No commission, no chance for her to make the money she really needed to save her family from their miserable fate.

Mr Calleja read her expression and shook his head. 'A salary,' he insisted, pausing slightly. 'And you should thank God for it, my dear. You know what you have to do and where you have to be. Now, stick that token to your bosom, and be gone. I've more important deals to look into tonight.'

'Mr Calleja, please …'

He shook his head. 'Salary. You gave me a false name. You lied to *me*. You should thank God you're still alive. Now, get your pretty arse out of here, you bloody whore. And don't return before tomorrow,' he ended.

Mr Calleja didn't move. He kept glaring at her until she downed the water, got off the chair, covered her head and walked out of the inn.

The darkness outside engulfed her like a shadow swallows the light off a wall. Sobbing and trembling, she rushed through *Strada Stretta*. She was hardly aware of where she was going, and didn't really care if anyone noticed. She wished she could hide from the rest of the world. If only she could just disappear, like a shadow affronted by light … because the light was no place for people like her.

I belong where no hope exists, she thought, taking a right into *Strada St Lucia*.

Her worn out sandals against the gravel echoed through the dark street. For a moment, she thought she heard a sudden thud, right behind her. She quickened her pace and didn't look back. She was sure she heard footsteps following, but kept going until she reached the part where the street crossed *Strada Zecca*. There, she stopped abruptly and turned to face her follower.

For a moment, she could swear a figure was standing under the lantern, in a corner to her left. But there was nobody, wherever she turned or looked. The *Manderaggio* was straight ahead; a cluster of buildings atop of each other, lurking ominously on whoever approached. Rita walked towards the corner, under the lantern. She leaned slightly against the limestone wall and caught her breath, her eyes still on her surroundings. Her heart was thumping so heavily she felt her chest was about to burst open. She fought the urge to close her eyes and lean backwards.

'Good evening, missy.'

Rita jolted. *'Kristu!'*

There stood a constable, only a few paces away.

'Good evening Constable,' she mumbled, trying hard to conceal her surprise.

'Is there a problem here, missy?' he demanded, scanning the narrow alley in front of him.

'Oh, no Sir. Of course not. I live here, close by. Thanks, but everything's fine.'

The constable narrowed his eyes and eyed Rita from head to toe. He shot a quick glare towards *Strada Stretta* before looking back at her.

'Then be on your way. This isn't the right time for anyone to go walking around, let alone young ladies such as yourself,' he said in Maltese.

Good, at least he doesn't think I'm a Brit looking for trouble ... Rita pretended as though she was on her way, then hesitated, momentarily. She appreciated the safety of standing close to the light, under the lamp-post, against the corner.

'Well, miss? I won't ask you twice.' The constable's face was stern.

Rita smiled faintly and went on her way. Losing herself in the dark constricted lanes of the *Manderaggio,* she was glad she was heading back home.

6.

The door of the house in front of them creaked open and a low mumbling voice allowed them inside. The stuffy air hit Archibald's nostrils as soon as he walked through the door. It was very damp and a smell of mould filled the air. Attard followed, asking the host whether anyone else lived in the house. Archibald had doubts whether this could actually be considered a house.

When his eyes settled to the darkness inside, he started observing his meagre surroundings. The general structure was poor, the plaster on the wall was faded. He second-guessed the room must've been built by an inept builder, or a hasty owner. The only furniture in the room was a worn, low, wooden table in the centre and a chest of drawers in the corner, on top of which stood a messy heap of unused tallow candles.

The host was in such a state, as though to blend in with the environment. A tall, skinny man with hunched shoulders and unkempt grey hair. His bulging, faded, green eyes reminded Archibald of vultures from a book of illustrations he had, when he was still a child. Those pair of eyes seemed to follow him and Attard's every move, with intent precision.

'Please, sit down,' said the host, sitting on the ruined floor.

Archibald raised an eyebrow, but his colleague nudged him politely. Attard obeyed, and Archibald followed, reluctantly, after scanning the spot as though it were a crime scene. He regretted the Superintendent's decision to not wear their uniforms. He'd rather not ruin his afternoon attire.

For an awkward minute or so, the host simply smiled and stared at them attentively. Archibald couldn't discern whether the poor lad was really smiling, or whether it was just an expression of naivety. One thing was sure - it was disturbing. Although he was physically in the room with them, his mind seemed to be miles away.

'Good morning, Sir,' started Attard in Maltese, taking out a small pencil and notebook. 'I'm Mr Attard and this is my colleague, Mr Whitlock. He's from Britain, the land of gentlemen.' They still abided by the Superintendent's command of not mentioning they were the police, of course.

The host nodded. 'My name is Joseph. Hi,' he said, in Maltese.

'Good. It's you we need to talk to,' continued Attard in a gentle tone, though to Archibald the Maltese language always sounded very harsh.

'Have you by any chance seen my sister, Anna?'

Attard and Archibald glanced at each other.

'That's why we're here, Mr Joseph,' said Attard. 'We need you to help us. When was the last time you saw your sister, Anna?'

Archibald leaned slightly forward, careful not to get too close to the scratched and dusty table. From what he could gather, Joseph was telling Attard that the last time he had seen Anna was on Tuesday. *Yesterday* ... He rubbed his nose. Joseph's accent was very raw and much harsher than Archibald was used to. He couldn't help noticing the man's strange mannerisms. This Mr Joseph was either a simpleton, or very good at acting like one.

'What did she do, Joseph?' asked Attard, ever so gently.

Joseph shrugged and tilted his head slightly sideways. 'She went out during the day, then returned back home, precisely at seven, in the evening. She took care of me. Prepared dinner and helped me go to sleep – because I am always hungry and very tired.' He said the last few words in a mimicking and high-pitched tone.

Archibald figured he might be quoting his sister. 'You're not so dumb after all,' said

Archibald coldly.

Attard shot a glare at his colleague, but Joseph's expression remained blank. Apparently, he didn't speak English.

'Mr Joseph, was Anna ever late, at all?' insisted Attard, turning to face their host.

Joseph shook his head fervently, as though answering the questions was rewarding in itself. 'Only last night. I think she got lost, not late. That's what she told me, when she woke me up.'

Attard and Archibald raised their eyebrows.

'Woke you up? How do you mean?' said Attard.

'At night, sir. I heard her voice. She told me she had got lost,' Mr Joseph replied, matter-of-factly. 'Then she told me she found her way home again. I woke up then, but still couldn't find her anywhere.'

'So did you see her again since last night?'

Joseph shook his head.

'I see.' Attard sighed heavily.

Come on man, you have to give us some useful information. Archibald folded his arms nervously, leaning uncomfortably on his thighs. The broken tile beneath his buttocks was driving him insane. No matter what position he took, the edges of the tile kept sticking into his behind, interrupting his train of thought and concentration. Not to mention the chill slowly creeping up his spine.

Joseph's facial and bodily movements weren't helping either. The way this guy's straw-like, grey hair and oval head bounced at each nod made Archibald nervous. His thin, shrunken chest and shoulders, gave him shivers. Not to mention the way his mouth twitched whenever he smiled; revealing yellow teeth. And those fixed eyes, protruding like orbs out of his vulture-like face. It was by now quite obvious that Mr Joseph was not all there. Archibald's little patience was nearing its limit.

'Did Anna have any friends, Joseph?' Attard seemed oblivious to his colleague's evident and growing restlessness.

'You seem pleasant enough to me. I thought you were going to tell me where Anna is.'

Archibald muttered something in his mother tongue, shaking his head in dismay.

'Hmm, I see. But we need each other, here, Mr Joseph,' said Attard, ignoring his colleague's obvious reactions. 'What about Anna? Did she ever talk to you about her job? Her life? Any arguments she might've had with …'

'No, not really. She was always out, leaving me here, alone. And when she came back and I asked where she had been …'

Archibald's interest rekindled. Mr Joseph's voice suddenly turned anxious.

'… she would tell me she was too tired to talk. *I worked all day for you, is what I did*, that's what she would say. Then she would smile and expect me to smile back. When I didn't, she would simply give me a hug, kiss me on the cheek and promise to tell me a story. *But first I have to cook dinner, Joseph, dear.*'

Attard shifted slightly in his position. Archibald couldn't help notice how Mr Joseph's voice carried a kind of anger, or resentment. All the previous blankness and innocence of expression had almost vanished.

'… and now I'm here left alone. Hungry and tired. No more bedtime stories about the knights for me. Anna's gone and found somebody else to take care of. She always said I was getting too old, anyway.'

His eyes weren't set on either of them anymore. Mr Joseph seemed lost in some other realm, where he blabbered and argued with himself. Attard and Archibald eyed each other. The inspector indicated he might be needing a little bit of assistance in dealing with this odd character.

If you haven't managed in Maltese, I cannot imagine what I can do in English. Archibald narrowed his eyes.

According to the very short briefing from Constable Molinari on their way here, an old couple had approached the police, earlier in the morning. They said Anna bought their bread and delivered it to their house, daily. By morning, the couple had already heard about the corpse found in *Strada Vescovo* and their concern for Anna sparked the moment she failed to show up. Apparently, according to the same couple, Joseph and Anna's parents had vanished at sea many years ago. No other relative ever appeared since. Unfortunately, the couple's resourcefulness was limited – or so they claimed. Still, Archibald was grateful.

He got up from the ground, dusted off his gloves, took out his pocket watch and frowned. 'Are you happy, Mr Joseph, that your sister is gone? Because you seem to be quite … *undecided*, shall I say?' he asked, in the little Maltese tongue he could master.

Attard stood up reluctantly and started pacing around the small room. Mr Joseph didn't move. He bent his neck slightly and looked up at them.

'So, Mr Joseph, are you glad your sister is missing? Or do you want to see her again?' insisted Archibald, his voice getting sterner.

Mr Joseph nodded with vigour.

To which question are you actually nodding, you half-wit fool! 'Why? Why would you want her back? She keeps forcing you to smile, kiss her, and hug her … and keeps reminding you what a burden you are to …'

'Mr Whitlock, please!' interrupted Attard in English. He stopped pacing around.

Archibald returned an ironic grin, to which Attard simply shook his head solemnly.

'If you won't help us, Mr Joseph, we'll be taking our leave straight away …'

'No!' Mr Joseph was on his feet. 'First you tell me where Anna is. Then you may leave. That was our agreement.' He was glaring, particularly at Archibald.

Archibald stealthily made for the pistol beneath his coat. *I never imagined I'd have to use it here.* 'Did he say *agreement*?' he whispered to Attard, in English.

Joseph's eyes moved nervously between the two of them. Attard was about to speak, when a knock at the door startled them all.

A thin voice came from behind the door.

'Come in,' replied Joseph in Maltese.

No one moved as a priest walked into the room. His gait was calm, as though the whole world could wait. He was of average height, strongly built, with dark complexion. He passed between the police officers and walked closer to the host. He was dressed in Dominican robes and lowered his hood. Attard lowered his head, then walked to the priest and kissed his hand. Archibald gaped.

'Is everything alright here, Inspector Attard?' asked the priest, as Mr Joseph kneeled.

Attard nodded nervously. Archibald's eyes widened.

'This is Constable Whitlock,' started Attard, reluctance evident in his voice.

Archibald winced. *Seriously? You're blowing the cover just like this?* He looked at Mr Joseph, who seemed totally unperturbed by the revelation.

'We're here on investigation, assigned by the Superintendent Casolani,' Attard went on.

Archibald had to stop himself from slapping his colleague in the back of the head. *What the hell is wrong with you, man?* He looked at Mr Joseph again. The fellow was either an adept actor, or a genuine idiot.

'Hmm ...' The priest turned his eyes to Archibald. 'I'm Don Lorenzo. Lorenzo Testaferrata. Dominican of Our Lady of *Porto Salvo* – Fair Havens – and St. Dominic's Basilica,' he said in English. 'Are you from Britain then, Mr Whitlock?'

'Yes.'

'I'm here on behalf of the Roman Catholic Church, Mother to us all. I protect and take care of all the flock of St Dominic's parish.' The priest looked at Mr Joseph. 'Particularly during such times as these. We're being struck by the devil's arm, gentlemen.'

'If it were the devil we were after, your help would be greatly appreciated. But this matter is the ill fruit of man, unfortunately,' replied Archibald, without any effort to conceal irony in his voice.

'Hmm ... of course it is.' Don Lorenzo started walking towards Mr Joseph.

Attard cleared his throat as the priest's white tunic brushed by. Mr Joseph raised his head to smile at the approaching Lorenzo.

'We were just speaking to Mr Joseph here, because ...'

'Joseph is pure and free of the devil's snare, Inspector Attard,' interrupted Don Lorenzo. 'I can vouch for that myself.'

Archibald's eyes widened. 'Then we would gladly have a conversation with *you*. You could prove to be quite helpful.' *Heaven and earth, Mr Attard ... why do you look like the sacrificial lamb?*

The priest shrugged, smiling faintly. 'Why, sure. But Mr Joseph's need for a priest is dire, at the moment. I'm sure you understand. We can set an appointment at St Dominic's, however. Whenever you want.'

What are you going to do, tame the poor fellow? Archibald clenched his fists and frowned.

'We were in fact just about to take our leave,' replied Attard, nodding to the priest and putting on his hat. He shot an indicative glance to Archibald and led them both outside.

'Good day to you both, then. May God bless you.' Don Lorenzo shut the door behind them.

7.

*C*afé *de la Reine* was pleasant, with its seats beneath the orange-trees and with a fountain splashing fresh water. Still, it could give Archibald no calm. Not this evening, at least. His tea went cold. Sipping at it to avoid Attard's stare was irritating. The Maltese Inspector wouldn't stop trying to have a conversation with him. He had explained the dampness in the weather, pointed out almost every shop beneath the arcades surrounding them, narrated the petty history of how the statue of Grand Master de Vilhena had been moved from Fort Manoel to this square …

But Archibald kept avoiding eye contact. He kept glaring at his pocket-watch, as if it would make time fly. It was almost seven. *A couple more minutes and I can take my leave for dinner at Morell's. Thank God!*

They had been sitting here for almost an hour. Sunlight would soon abandon Valletta to the meagre light of gas-lamps.

'Do you play cards, Mr Whitlock?' Attard wasn't giving up, yet.

'I certainly don't lick boots,' replied Archibald languidly, whiffing on his cigar. *At least these are pleasant.*

Attard sighed. 'Whatever do you mean, Whitlock?'

Archibald shrugged indifferently and looked at his pocket-watch again. Attard crossed his legs and started to light up his cigar, then enthusiastically helped himself to another cup of tea. Archibald glanced at the teapot lying on the table between them.

'Tea?'

Archibald didn't even stir.

'I've never heard of an Englishman with such a poor appetite for tea.'

'And I've never heard of an Inspector cringing at a member of the Catholic Church …'

'That's because you're still young and inexperienced. Is that what you want me to say?' Attard's voice was now stern. So stern, in fact, that it finally grabbed Archibald's attention.

'Inexperienced!' the Constable was finally looking at his colleague.

Attard shrugged.

'I'm from London.'

'Then why are you *here*, Whitlock?'

Archibald's shock couldn't be concealed.

'I was sent here to help with this bloody investigation. An investigation you all seem so intent on ruining. First the constables and the Superintendent - now you!'

'I ask you to calm yourself, Whitlock. What are you on about, really?'

'Why in God's name did you tell the Dominican that we are the police?'

'Whatever I did back there,' replied Attard, calmly. 'Was to safeguard our reputation.' He inhaled deeply on his cigar.

Archibald raised an eyebrow and sniggered.

'I don't know what's the situation in London,' continued Attard. 'But the authority exercised by the Catholic Church in Malta is strong. And some of its members are more influential than others.'

'Authority! Then what do *we* have? We're the bloody police! *We* are the authority, hang it all!'

Attard gave a quick look around them, then nodded. 'Granted, Whitlock. I am in no way denying that. I'm as much a police officer as you are. Only with more local experience, that's all.' He winked, smiling slightly. 'I *know* that people such as Don Lorenzo have influence, here.'

Archibald took his eyes off his colleague. He leaned forward to stub out his cigar, then dived back grumpily into his chair. Attard didn't look away, but sipped at his tea, passionately.

'This very morning, we sat there,' started Archibald after a while. He was pointing at *Piazza*

San Giorgio ahead. 'And we were of the same opinion, that there's some crazy disturbed mind behind these murders.'

Attard nodded.

'Shortly afterwards, we find ourselves knocking at the door of Mr Joseph's house,' Archibald went on, furiously, 'the *brother* of Anna, the last victim of this messy case. I think we both agree Mr Joseph isn't quite straight in the head.'

Attard grimaced, but nodded.

'We had a suspect – our *first* suspect. Something you didn't have for months. Then a bloody priest walks in and you let him take it all away with a whiff of his tongue. You let him dismiss you!'

Attard looked at his teacup for a while, before answering. He seemed to be concentrating on some inner thoughts. Archibald assumed he was constructing some form of reply or defence.

'I agree with you. Mr Joseph is a suspect. I think you didn't fail to notice how he spoke about his sister for a moment. His attitude shifted instantaneously like *this*,' he said with a snap of his fingers. 'He's so mad, I think he honestly believes his sister is still alive.'

Archibald's dark brown eyes didn't leave Attard's. The Maltese Inspector had just raised an interesting point for discussion. The Englishman made a mental note to get back to Don Lorenzo later.

'It seems so. Unless *he* murdered her, of

course,' said Archibald. 'He mentioned something about hearing Anna talk to him. In the middle of last night? That's when she was … well, being murdered.'

'He did. But I'm sure he was referring to when he saw her last, yesterday evening.'

'It could be. But I think I remember him saying she woke him *at night*, then he looked for her, to no avail.'

Attard shrugged. 'Well, if that is the case, he was either dreaming or else he's hearing voices. He could've killed her and doesn't remember.' He raised his palms towards the sky. 'I don't know.'

'We definitely need to talk to him, again,' suggested Archibald, narrowing his eyes.

'I agree. I'll speak to Don Lorenzo.'

'Don Lorenzo? Bah!' said Archibald, straightening in his seat.

'Yes. We'll see what he thinks about it.'

'What the deuce are you talking about, man? The man's a *priest*, heaven and earth! We're the police. Why should we care about whatever a cloaked man thinks about this?'

Attard stretched his arm, palm facing downwards. 'We already discussed this, Whitlock. He's an important figure in Valletta …'

'I don't bloody care!' said Archibald, his arms wide open.

A group of men at another table looked at them. Archibald glared back. 'Don't you think we ought to answer solely to the Superintendent?' he said in a lower voice. 'What's the Catholic Church got to do with this?'

'A lot. Now keep your calm, and hear me out,' replied Attard, in a measured tone. 'We answer solely to the Superintendent on this, no doubt about that. I've been in the police force since I was eighteen. I know what we must do and to whom we must speak. But this is also a matter of being cunning ... of playing the role.'

'What role? Speak clearly, it seems like I'm still *young* for all this game talk,' he hinted sarcastically.

'You leave it to me.'

'Leave it to ... you can't be serious!'

Attard nodded.

'I cannot agree, I'm sorry. We're a team. Explain yourself Inspector. I have all evening.' Archibald immediately regretted saying that. *Morell's exquisite dinner will have to wait for another time.*

'It is my opinion,' Attard rested his elbows on the arms of the chair, 'that we must be wary. Whatever you do, in this country, you're better off having the Church on your side. Always. I know you might tell me we're doing our job, and that we should find no interference, but the Church is a very powerful ally to have, here in Malta. That's how things work over here, whether you like it or not. Besides, the Church would have definitely involved itself, sooner or later. You wouldn't want It against you, trust me. Not in this country.

'All we've had so far is a good number of unhelpful neighbours and witnesses hiding in the dark. On the other hand, Don Lorenzo is in the know. He visits people, speaks to them and listens to rumours and gossip ... some of which can be *facts*. His visit to Mr Joseph means he's interested in these murders. I'm sure he wasn't just visiting the poor fellow out of the goodness of his heart.'

Archibald sniggered.

'I'm no fool, Whitlock,' went on Attard. 'Let's give the priest some time.'

Archibald's only reply was a sigh. His stare fixed on something far ahead.

'We know nothing of the first four victims,' continued Attard. 'I don't think we ever will. If the first victim was really part of some gang, I'm sure his comrades will do anything but approach the police. The poor sailors we found in Hastings don't even have relatives who mourn for them, as far as we know. The female we found a week later, might as well be a whore from *Strada Stretta*. That's not promising. Our killer likes to target the loneliest of society.' Attard's voice turned solemn and he lowered his eyes.

Archibald sighed, nodding slightly. 'Anna and her brother ... we were lucky, finally. I only wanted to stress the importance of how we cannot let this one go.'

Attard nodded. 'I know. And I agree with you.' He sipped at his tea. 'Meanwhile, we can visit a taxidermist, as you suggested this morning. Worth a try, while Don Lorenzo gathers the information we need. There's a certain Mr Bonavia. He owns a shop here, in Valletta.'

For a short while the two of them sipped at their tea in silence.

'This Mr Bonavia is an elderly, nice fellow,' added Attard, shortly. 'We must approach him with caution, though. We don't need him to think we regard him as a suspect.'

'No uniforms, thank God!' Archibald smiled faintly.

Attard stubbed out his cigar in the tray and stretched his legs. 'I think I'll be off then. Another long day awaits us tomorrow, and I don't …'

'Inspector Attard, Constable Whitlock,' said a voice from behind Archibald, so sudden it made them both jump.

It was Constable Molinari again. He was shaking and struggling not to drop his lantern.

'*Kristu*, Molinari!'

'The Superintendent has just sent for you,' said Molinari.

Archibald and Attard jumped to their feet. Their faces a perfect depiction of alarm and apprehension.

'Your presence is urgently requested at Mr Joseph's house, *Strada St Ursola*. The Superintendent will meet you there.'

Archibald could swear he heard voices in the howling wind.

8.

Emmanuel cupped his hands to catch some fresh water and splashed it on his face. He looked in the mirror. His face was pale, his eyes faded, his stark black hair unkempt. He shut his eyes, and tried to banish the dream from his inner eye.

'Lel,' came the sweet soft voice of his beloved wife.

She was standing by the door jamb. Her delicate beauty never failed to make him smile.

'You look troubled, dear.' She laid her hand lightly on his back.

Emmanuel turned towards her, grabbing her fine face gently. 'Had a bad dream, that's all,' he said, kissing her.

She kissed him back. 'What about it?'

'You don't have to worry, darling,' he replied, backing away slightly.

'I don't have to. But I do,' she replied, sighing. 'I'll just go and prepare breakfast then,' she added, when it became clear her husband wasn't in a talkative mood.

On his way out of the bathroom, Emmanuel stopped as soon as he crossed another mirror. This morning, looking too much into his own eyes was something he wanted to avoid. *I was just a boy*, he told himself, scurrying to the wardrobe. He made for his neatest pair of trousers and shirt.

His wife had just started faffing in the kitchen.

'Sshh!' she said, putting her forefinger over her lips.

'Are they still asleep?' he asked in a whisper.

'Yes, let them sleep just a little while longer, it's Saturday,' she said.

Emmanuel walked closer, hugging her passionately.

'I have to prepare breakfast, Lel …'

'I just wanted to tell you that I love you,' he whispered in her ear, not retreating but caressing her delicate face. 'You know that, right?'

Catherine turned to face him, holding his hands in hers. 'Is anything wrong, honey?'

'Of course not, dear,' he lied.

'Are you sure you feel like taking this trip, Lel? The capital will be as busy as a beehive. You could always just write back and ask him to meet another day.'

'I'm fine, Cat. And besides, Don Lorenzo's

always been like a friend to me, and it's been quite a while.'

'I know, dear,' she insisted, raising her delicate hands to her husband's face. 'Do you know what it's all about?'

Emmanuel shrugged, not willing to share his troubles yet. Catherine knew his story. He had never concealed anything from her. But it was still too early to share today's fears, lest they were as unreal as they were unfounded. The priest might just want to see him in order to catch up, after all these years. Emmanuel had to admit he was quite looking forward to the meeting himself. 'His letter didn't mention anything in particular, no.'

'Here,' she continued, handing him some fresh bread. 'At least take this with you.'

'I should be back in time for lunch. Wake up the children by seven,' he said reassuringly, kissing her one last time before making for the door.

'Emmanuel,' she said, holding him slightly back by the arm. Their eyes met. 'I love you too.'

Strada San Domenico was surprisingly quiet. Well, as quiet as it gets on a Saturday morning. A flock of pigeons cooed lazily in the shade of the Basilica. The rattling sound of an approaching *karozzin* made them take flight. Don Lorenzo appeared out of St Dominic's Friary as soon as Emmanuel descended the single-horse drawn carriage.

'Don Lorenzo!' Emmanuel paid the cabman and walked towards the priest.

'Mr Speranza!' exclaimed the priest, as Emmanuel lowered his hat and kneeled to kiss his hand. 'I see you look very well.'

Emmanuel nodded.

'Come inside,' continued Don Lorenzo, smiling. 'We have so much to talk about, you and I.'

Emmanuel nodded again, and followed the Dominican into the Dominican Friary. The ceilings were high, the structure old but well-maintained. Emmanuel liked that scent, common to all old and spacious buildings. A long stark corridor eventually led to the convent's humble parlour.

The priest asked Emmanuel to sit. 'Would you like a glass of water, perhaps?'

'I am inclined to accept. It's scorching out there,' replied Emmanuel, shyly.

'And it's still May. Imagine what August will bring.' Don Lorenzo wiped his brow with a handkerchief, then rang a small bell.

When the water was brought and both men had sipped at it for a while, it was Don Lorenzo who spoke first. 'How are your wife and children? Catherine, right? Remind me the names …'

'They're doing well, thank you, Father. Yes; it is Catherine. Then there's Michele, John, Elizabeth and Luca. They grow up so fast,' explained Emmanuel, a smile appearing on his face.

The priest smiled. 'Michele! I remember you always loved St Michael, protector of the faithful from the wicked one. A really good name for a boy. And Luca is the youngest then?'

Emmanuel noticed a flicker in the priest's eyes. He hoped it was purely innocent and not related to the past.

'Yes,' he replied plainly. 'Sliema is wonderful. We're …'

'Reminds me why I wanted to see you, my dear friend,' said the priest, ignoring Emmanuel's attempt to change the subject.

Emmanuel sighed faintly.

'I am sure you remember Luca, my dear Emmanuel. Such good friends are rarely found, and even more rarely forgotten. Particularly when they've gone to rest and dwell with Our Lord too early. It is not my intention to trouble you with the past … not unless it were truly necessary. But these times are proving to be so.'

Emmanuel's eyes narrowed, though the worried look didn't fade. 'These times?'

The priest rubbed his palms against his knees. 'Haven't you heard anything about what's happening here, in Valletta?'

'Recently, you mean?'

'We've had, or shall I say *been having* a series of murders.'

Emmanuel nodded slightly. 'I remember reading something in the papers, around two months ago, yes.'

The priest sighed. 'Actually, it all started in October, last year. There were another two in March, a week apart.' Don Lorenzo looked at Emmanuel. 'And the last one was *this* month. Last Tuesday night, to be exact.'

Emmanuel gaped. 'That's ... that's terrible, Father.' He crossed himself, to which the priest sighed.

'Yes, only the Almighty can spare us, I'm afraid,' he said. 'Now I wouldn't have brought you all the way from Sliema and away from your dear family, had I not deemed it so important. Now, what I'm about to tell you ... I have confirmed with my most trusted sources, more than once. See, these murders have been gruesome, to say the least. There's the hand of the devil in this, I'm sure.'

'Don Lorenzo?' Emmanuel leaned forward on his seat.

'The victims. They had ... they were all found with their eyes torn out.'

If Emmanuel looked shocked before, now he was aghast. The young man's jaw dropped and his eyes widened.

'Are you sure of this, Father?' he muttered after a while, his voice almost trembling.

The priest nodded.

Emmanuel made to stand up and leave. 'Father ... I have to go back to my family. This is ...'

'Emmanuel, you need to sit down.' Don Lorenzo's commanding tone made the man stop for a while, at least.

'Now listen to me. When you confided your thoughts and fears in me that night so long ago, I admit I didn't give you much credit. You were only a boy. But never did I speak a word of your fears to anyone. So rest assured, you and your family are safe. You don't even exist to whoever might be doing this. Worst case scenario would be, you're remembered as one of the closest friends of Lord Manduca's son. Still, that was ten years ago. Your two families were not related in any way, save for your friendship with Luca. No one is after you.'

'Then why am I here? What do you need?' asked his visitor impatiently.

'You're here because there is a link between these murders and Luca's, ten years ago. If not by the same person, but surely some friend or follower of theirs who is so intent on leaving a message. Well, at least judging by the way they're murdering these poor victims. And you're one of the few links I can trust.'

Emmanuel was breathing heavily. His eyes focussed on the priest, who took this to mean he could go on with the conversation.

'The police are following this case, of course. There's a constable from London too, along with one of Malta's best: Inspector Eduardo Attard. Reasonable enough, for a country which has never seen such a high rate of crime in such a short time span …'

'And what do the police have to say to this?'

The priest sighed. 'Another reason why I need you, Emmanuel. From what I heard, the British constable only arrived last Tuesday night.'

'Isn't that the same night of the latest murder?'

Don Lorenzo nodded. 'They have either found something crucially ill, or they have found nothing at all. Still, you know how the police are. They want to control everything, know everything, and hide it from the rest of the world. They want to play God, but there's only one God.'

'But, Father ...'

'I must protect my flock, Emmanuel. I cannot let it die like cattle ready for the slaughter without doing anything. I am their shepherd.'

'And in what way do you think I could possibly help you?'

Don Lorenzo fidgeted with his cup for a while. His eyes darted from left to right, then he got up and walked around the parlour. 'I need you to start by telling me everything you remember of that dreadful night. Anything you remember about Luca. *Anything* that comes to mind, Emmanuel.'

'That's ten years ago, Father. I was just a boy,' said Emmanuel, his gaze following the priest around the room.

'It is those who are like children that will enter the Kingdom of Heaven. And you weren't *that* young; about fourteen, right? Now tell me, Emmanuel. Tell me everything you remember, and then you can go back home with my blessing before the sun has even began to set.'

Emmanuel hesitated for a while; he was trembling and closed his eyes. He buried his head in the palms of his hands and leaned forward on his knees. His fears were materialising. It was not merely a childhood memory. It was a bad experience *not* so long ago; the loss of the closest friend he ever had. Emmanuel was afraid for his family, no matter what the priest said. Malta was a tiny bit of land in the Mediterranean. People knew each other and had contacts all around.

He trusted the priest, as much as he trusted the word of God. That's why he had confided solely in him ten years ago, when Luca Manduca was found dead. Luca was the son of one of the most well-known noble families in Mdina; the family of Pietro and Francisca Manduca. At the time, he was Emmanuel's best and only friend. That night, ten years ago, Luca had been found dead in his own bed. His eyes gouged. His elder sister, Maria Isabella Manduca, had been abducted, never to be seen again. Both siblings gone in one night!

Emmanuel downed his glass of water, wiping sweat off his brow with his left arm. 'There's nothing to say, really,' he started, while Don Lorenzo paced around. 'They were a good family. No enemies that I can recall. I remember his sister, really, Maria Isabella.' He was blushing. 'I used to like her, though she was not my age, nor was she my type … she was a bit bossy.'

Don Lorenzo nodded. 'Understandable, my dear friend. She was older than Luca, right?'

'Yes. Twelve years,' continued Emmanuel, with a sigh. 'They were a nice family ... I'm sorry, Don Lorenzo. I do not think I have anything else to say.'

The priest stopped walking and narrowed his eyes. 'Tell me what you remember from the night of the murder,' he said.

Emmanuel sighed and went on. 'I don't know, Father. Like everyone else, I was fast asleep in the safety of my home, that night ... like Luca and Maria Isabella,' he ended sadly.

'Some days after the tragedy, you told me something else, Emmanuel.' The priest's face was now stern.

'The dream?' Emmanuel rolled his eyes and raised his arms helplessly. 'I was just a boy ...'

'Yes, and you spoke your mind, as all children do. You confided in *me*. And I disregarded you, back then. I am not doing that mistake again. Not now.'

Emmanuel didn't move or make a sound.

'Well?' the priest sat down in front of him.

'Luca was my best friend. And I was still a boy.'

'I know,' said the priest. 'But it might prove helpful in our investigation.'

'*Our* investigation?'

'I must protect my flock, Emmanuel. Now tell me about the dream again. I am ready to believe whatever you have to say. Speak your mind, friend.'

Emmanuel sighed and looked at the floor. 'I

was young. And I needed to blame someone for Luca's horrible death ... for the sudden loss, do you know what I mean? You cannot possibly think the devil murdered them,' he ended, looking at the priest with a ghastly countenance.

'The devil is cunning. You saw him, on the night Luca was murdered and Maria Isabella taken.'

'I didn't see him. I dreamt about him. It's different. And I was still a boy. So I blamed him for killing my best friend, and stealing his beautiful bossy sister,' insisted Emmanuel.

The priest frowned.

Emmanuel tried to say something but failed. He simply rolled his eyes at the priest.

'People are being killed in Valletta, Emmanuel, with their eyes plucked out of their sockets. Just like Luca. The devil is at work again, my friend.'

'What do you want me to say, Father? That I saw the devil in my room? That it was a terrible winged creature, with black holes instead of eyes? And a giant orb, as white as the moon, held by the horns on his head?' He raised his arms at the priest, then sighed. 'It was a dream, for Heaven's sake!'

'A vivid one, apparently. And definitely not a one off.'

'How do you mean?'

'You had this dream again since then, several times. Didn't you?' The priest was pointing his index finger at Emmanuel.

Emmanuel looked downwards and shook his head.

'Look at me, Emmanuel.' The priest's eyes were fixed on him. 'And tell me the truth.'

'Yes, I did have the same dream again. It is the most terrible event of my life, Father. Surely, you do not expect me to forget it that easily, do you? The dream is just a constant reminder of what happened, that's all. When I have that dream, it is like living the event all over again.'

'But what if it is not just a mere dream?'

Emmanuel raised an eyebrow.

Don Lorenzo didn't move.

Emmanuel looked away and got up. 'It's time for me to go, Father. I'm very sorry. My family needs me.'

The priest didn't move. 'Go home, think it through. We'll meet again soon.'

'I don't wish to leave my family alone again, now that I know what's happening in the capital,' said Emmanuel, stopping at the doorway. 'But you are more than welcome in Sliema, whenever you want, Father.'

'Your family is safe, my dear friend.'

'Fine. But I'm not leaving Sliema for this. I trust you understand.'

'Only a little, Mr Speranza,' added the priest in an insistent tone.

'Then I wish you, and Valletta's citizens, the best of luck in solving these murders. But this is my family. I must not leave my family.'

The priest nodded sadly, but Emmanuel had

already disappeared out of the door.

A servant immediately appeared. The priest asked for a drink and a jug of fresh water was brought to the table immediately. Lorenzo downed a glass and scurried out of the parlour, to his cell. He kneeled down and crossed himself.

His first link to the past didn't look like it was going to bear any fruit. Emmanuel had become too secular. Lorenzo closed his eyes and prayed to the Almighty that his second link would be more promising.

9.

It was close to midnight. The waxing gibbous was barely visible amidst the thick and damp air. The heat typical of mid-May, was enough to have discouraged most men from getting out and seeking nocturnal adventures. The wilder ones had apparently already found whatever it was they had set out for. *Strada Stretta* was quiet for a Saturday night.

Rita stood at the entrance to The Falcon's Perch, waving her hand-held fan and enjoying the solitude. Giuseppe had long left. Finally, she was alone. Instinctively, her thoughts still turned to prayer and she asked Heaven not to send anyone else. *Foolish girl*. She frowned at the thought that Heaven's Gates were shut to people like her. Her only hope were the stars which were barely visible tonight.

The sudden sound of footsteps made her start. A lone figure was approaching. Rita let out a sigh of relief as she realised this fellow was not targeting her. He was mumbling and, apparently, talking to himself. The guy just staggered and burped, before collapsing some metres away. Rita thought she heard the sound of coins hitting the ground in the dark. Tightening her grip on her tallow candle, she courageously approached the fallen drunkard.

'I wouldn't.'

Rita jolted, dropping and losing her only source of light. She turned to face the speaker. The faint light from his lantern revealed a young man, clad in barkeep's fashion. His facial features looked Maltese. His face was clean-shaven, dark complexion complimenting darker hair. Rita found herself staring into his very curious eyes.

'Stealing is a sin,' he continued in English. 'But I assume you've committed worse than theft already, missy. There are no rules in the dark.' His eyes moved to her spent candle on the ground.

How judgemental! 'Very impolite of you, sir, to speak to a lady in such a …'

'You're no more a Lady than I am a Baron,' came his prompt reply. 'By the looks of it, you're exactly what I need tonight.' His eyes took her all in.

Rita gave up on the stars and faked a smile. She approached the young man, despite the tension running through her spine. 'So …' she started, throwing her right arm over his shoulders. 'Are you not going to buy me a drink, then?'

The man raised his head at the dimly lit sign. 'Uhm … well, sure! Missy. I sure do need some company.'

Against all her instincts, Rita leaned against his chest. 'Why, I'm the best you can get.'

The young man fidgeted in his pocket. Rita started caressing his face. *It is smooth, at least … he cannot be more than twenty-five.*

'Here's your payment,' he said flatly, letting the coins drop.

Rita picked them up and felt his hand grabbing her behind.

'A lady of the night who knows how to count. Impressive!'

Rita fought the urge to frown. That title always felt like a dagger going through her chest.

The boy pressed his index finger to her lips. 'How about skipping the drink, shall we, missy?'

Self-righteous and *presumptuous! The night cannot get any worse.* Rita took him by the arm and gently led him into The Falcon's Perch.

A couple of drinks later, the nightmare started. The dreadful reality which Rita had to succumb to, almost every night. The terrible nightmare she lost hope of ever waking up from. No, this wasn't like when she was a child; when she would wake up from a bad dream and call her papa in the middle of the night. This was *Strada Stretta*. This was the only way she could feed the mouths of the ones she loved. She had yielded to the pressure. At first, she made herself believe she was in control.

From then on, it was all lies. The way her chest heaved up and down, the way she closed her eyes and bit her lips, the way she moaned and groaned. Lies … it was all lies! She almost started to believe she was really good at this, as they grabbed and pulled firmly at her dark, black hair. Men really seemed to take pleasure in doing this sort of thing. She was learning and discovering many other things about men. All their strength vanished when confronted by her bodily movements and sounds. *Just like metal*, she thought. *Strong metal which melts as soon as it is stroked by fire.*

And then she would instantly feel powerful again. She would really begin to understand what she was doing. In the darkness of 'her' room, at The Falcon's Perch, men lost their pride the moment they undressed to have her. They came from every walk of life: politicians, lawyers, merchants, farmers, seamen. These were the same men who bullied and yelled at each other, out there in the streets. But that happened during their daily routines. Now here, it was night. On her bed, their greatest weakness was revealed and they were hers for the taking.

The young lad got off the bed and made for his trousers, whilst Rita wiped semen off her thighs.

'When I was young,' he started, with his back to her 'A priest in my village used to say that this – what we just did – is a grave sin. I once asked him how one deciphers what is a sin and what is not? Do you know what he answered me?'

Rita shook her head without looking at him.

'He told me that whenever we sin, we feel a deep sadness inside. That sadness is the result of sin, he said. I didn't believe him. What do you think?'

Rita took a small step backwards. *Me?*

The fellow must've read her thoughts. He turned to look at her. 'Yes, I'm asking you.'

Rita shrugged timidly, raising her robes to cover her bare breasts. Those hazel eyes seemed to pierce her soul.

'I'm diverting from the subject, forgive me ... missy.'

Rita closed her legs. *Now why don't you go away?*

'You don't have to blush, missy.' His voice was rather soothing. 'Have you ever wondered why God created carnal pleasures? The Church says it is a sin. What we did tonight, together. Do you believe it's a sin, missy?'

Rita didn't answer. She was still trying to figure out how a young man could be so talkative.

'My name is Filippo, by the way. You're not much into conversing, are you? It seems like you've had enough of me, for tonight. Well, if I had to speak my mind out, I'd say it is a sin.'

He paused, as if waiting for Rita's reaction.

'That's our little secret, though. Is that agreed?' He winked.

Those hazel eyes ... Rita, what are you doing? She made to get off the bed.

'May I ask you a terrible question?'

What would make a question terrible? Rita failed to hide her bewilderment.

Filippo flashed a grin. 'I take that as yes. Aren't you afraid, to roam the night? I mean, in light of what's been happening in Valletta, recently?'

Rita didn't move.

The other girls spoke about the murders, almost all the time. Everyone did, really; especially since the latest corpse was found in *Strada Vescovo,* four nights ago. The Falcon's Perch was making good money out of it and Mr Calleja's aggressive attitude was tamed – at least for a while. Maltese, British and foreign - they all loved to gossip - as long as they had a table and a few drinks to share.

'I admire you.' Filippo was smiling.

Me? Rita blinked.

'I don't understand why God allows innocent people to suffer at the hands of the wicked,' he went on.

This guy should be in a seminary, not in a brothel. Rita couldn't quite comprehend what he was up to. She feared he might be trying to win her sympathy, so she got off the bed. Maybe if she concealed her body, it would help.

'You have a nice body,' he said. 'I can't help

wonder how beautiful your soul must be.'

Rita froze. *Are you mocking me?* She bit her tongue, though all her instincts told her to lash out and hit him. But she remained put, standing as he looked through her. She wanted to scream at him and then she wanted him to stay. That sudden confusion caught her unprepared and she shivered. *No, Rita. Stop. You're beyond any kind of hope.* This Filippo was too sentimental for this environment and Mr Calleja would certainly not be pleased.

'Please, sir,' she started, with all the courage she could master. 'I must go back downstairs.' She thought she saw sadness in his eyes. *Grow up, Rita. You're not his first and definitely not his last. Since when do you fall for empty words ... and beautiful eyes.*

Filippo did not move.

'Sir, please. It was fun and I shall never forget this night,' she said. 'But please, I need you to leave. You must leave.'

Filippo sighed heavily, shaking his head.

Good, I need you to give up on me. 'Thank you, sir. Please understand.'

'I do,' he said, finally walking towards the door. 'Goodnight.'

Rita let out a sigh of relief as he turned the doorknob, opened the door and stepped out of the room. That done, she made for her clothes and prepared herself for the rest of the night. She looked at herself in the small mirror, tidying her hair and pushing up her bosom, beneath the clothes.

Why am I shaking? She put on her sandals and went stealthily down the stairs. The Falcon's Perch slumbered. An abandoned glass of water on the bar attracted her attention. *Stealing is a sin.* She held her breath and tiptoed to the bar. Scanning her surroundings, she downed the water before her conscience could tell her otherwise.

The night had turned quite chilly, at least. Rita knew that come summer, any form of cold would just be a memory and humidity a nightmare. *Strada Stretta* was like a graveyard. The drunkard was still lying on the exact spot where she had left him. Rita leaned against the wall, next to the entrance. Filippo's hazel eyes appeared in her mind's eye. Rita blinked and shook her head guiltily.

As the sun's faint rays started to show, she wrapped her arms around her and headed for home. Hiding her face behind her hair, she rushed through the dimly lit alleys of Valletta, hoping not to come across any police patrol. A drizzle of rain ... Rita smiled faintly, grateful for anything that concealed her passage through the dark lanes of the *Manderaggio* and home.

A white figure at the door made her falter. She turned pale and felt her body hair stand on end. She froze as soon as she realised it was her mother.

No, God, please no. She trembled violently. Instinctively, her mouth tried to form words and her mind raced wildly. She had never seen her mother so grave, not even when she received the very bad news of her husband's tragic death.

'Where were you?' Her mother's voice echoed above the rain. Her face depicted utter disgust.

'Let's go inside and discuss this, mother.'

'No,' her mother said. 'You're not putting one foot inside my house. Tell me where you've been tonight, last night, and the one before last. And every other *night* before that.'

Rita felt like she had lost her ability to speak. *God, please. No!* 'Ma, let's talk inside,' she whispered, eyeing their surroundings.

'No. You're not my daughter.'

That hit like thunder.

'Ma, please. I'm …' Her tongue froze.

Despite the rain, she could hear the sound of silence. Her legs were trembling - not because of the rain. Her mother raised her right arm, slowly, pointing towards the wet street, in the fading darkness.

'At least let me explain, Ma,' she said, with tears in her eyes.

'A lady of the night has nothing to explain to me. Just leave,' her mother ended firmly.

No! 'A lady of … Ma, it's me, Rita!' she begged, slightly approaching her mother; her soaked hands clutching at her chest.

'I won't say it again. Leave my sight, right now!'

'I'm doing this for you and for Lucia …'

The door to her home was closed before she

could finish. Rita was left out there, in the rain, like a drenched and tattered curtain, flapping in the doorway of an ancient ruin. She turned her head around in panic. *Where will I go?*

She couldn't control her breathing. Everything around her seemed to be folding in on itself and was ready to engulf her. Each raindrop felt like a bucket of ice being thrown at her. Tears wouldn't just stop streaming down her frozen cheek. Rita hurried through the alleyways of the *Manderaggio* without really knowing where she was going. She was physically lost and mentally shattered. Spiritually, she felt as dead as though she had never even been born at all. And then, a tempting thought occurred to her; like a flash which comes and hopefully does not stay. God, was she born to be made to suffer so much? Rita dwelled on that thought as she ran out of the *Manderaggio,* disappearing into the morning blanket that was covering Valletta.

10.

Archibald was used to London, with its mists like ghosts. But the darkness in *Strada St Ursola* seemed to be more than the mere absence of gaslight. The waxing gibbous was as ineffective as Constable Molinari's lantern. The darkness seemed to swallow them whole. Archibald kept looking over his shoulders, as he and Inspector Attard followed the constable to Ms Anna and Mr Joseph's house.

The darkness hadn't encouraged the citizens of *Strada St Ursola* to mind their own business, however. Some were outside, watching Mr Joseph's house from a safe distance. Others were less courageous, but just as curious; watching from behind their louvered or glass windows.

'For a moment, I thought she had returned

from the dead ...' said one of the onlookers.

'Returned? She'd more readily sell her soul to the devil, than return to her brother,' said another woman.

'I'd bet she isn't dead. She just left ... isn't that what she wanted to do all along?'

Two constables were keeping back the crowd from getting closer to Mr Joseph's house. 'Show's over, folks. Go back to your homes ...'

The wind had increased, Archibald was thankful for his evening clothes. *Where did all these people come from?*

The Superintendent stood beside the entrance, holding a lantern. He spotted them coming and signalled for them to go closer. 'Molinari, stay here with the others. Whitlock, Attard, come in.' He moved his head slightly sideways indicating they go in and the two followed him into Mr Joseph's house.

Strada St Ursola was dark, but Archibald had to find new words to describe the blackness in here. It was like a presence, nagging at his consciousness. It took time for his eyes to adjust. A constable's silhouette was the only thing he could make out; the light of his lantern glowing in the dark.

'Just in time, gentlemen,' said Superintendent Casolani. 'We need to search the house.'

'Where is Mr Joseph?' asked Attard in between heavy breaths.

'He's either hiding in here, somewhere, or else he's just gone, ran away,' the Superintendent whispered, shaking his head. 'He woke the entire neighbourhood up, calling for his sister, Anna. Some of his neighbours tried to talk with him, calm him down. But the fellow's crazy. He went back inside, eventually ... but *not* quietly.'

Archibald gaped.

'Gone where?' asked Attard.

The Superintendent huffed. 'Would we still be standing here, if I knew?'

Archibald preferred not to ask any questions, just yet. Casolani looked like he was ready to explode.

'The man's dangerous. We've got a murderer on the run,' said the silhouetted constable.

'No one asked your advice, Mifsud,' blurted Casolani.

Archibald narrowed his eyes. The darkness was almost overwhelming. He couldn't see the end of his own arm. He tapped his foot to make sure it was still there.

'For all we know, Mr Joseph could still be lurking in the shadows of his own home,' went on the Superintendent. 'Mifsud, give that bloody lantern to Constable Whitlock and follow me outside.'

Archibald reached for the lantern like a baby for his mother's breast, but Attard beat him to it.

'You have a good look in this house,' continued Casolani, stopping briefly on his way out. 'Speak to me tomorrow morning, *if* you discover anything useful.' He stormed out into *St Ursola*.

Attard raised the lantern to look at his colleague. 'Shall we, Constable Whitlock?'

Archibald could barely make out his face in the dim light of the lantern. Everything else was pitch black. Archibald nodded and followed him into the darkness, the lantern in Attard's hand like a beacon of hope.

They stepped over wobbly tiles, and crouched unsteadily against walls. Archibald wished he had taken more mental notes of the house, when they were here earlier this morning. He remembered the room they were in was a small hall, which led to another room through a corridor. He was also aware there was a flight of stairs in the same corridor, but preferred to keep following Attard's lantern. Shadows danced around them - forming one moment, disappearing the next. Their very own shadows bounced in rhythm with the lantern in Attard's right hand. The shadows stretched, then they bent, forcing Archibald to keep looking over his shoulders.

Both rooms held very little furniture; everywhere was dusty and bare. A few open drawers revealed tallow candles and some moth-eaten books. Bulky, worn out curtains hung on the walls, covering closed windows which neither of them was keen on opening.

Not with that howling wind outside! Archibald shivered.

The kitchen at the far end of this floor – judging by the unpleasant smell of stale left-overs

– was no better than the first room.

'Let's try the second floor,' suggested Attard almost in a whisper, whilst heading towards the stairs.

The shadows followed like pests in a swamp, ready to engulf the dim light.

Archibald thought he felt fingertips caressing his spine. *Your brain's playing tricks on you, fool!* He cleared this throat, heaving like he had run a mile.

Attard noticed his disquiet and grinned slightly.

What's so funny? Archibald bent slightly to catch his breath.

They reached the landing on the first floor. A tile shifted under Attard's foot, almost making him lose his balance.

'*Ostja!*' The Maltese inspector instinctively reached out in the dark, trying to clutch at the closest object and dropping his lantern.

Archibald held back a snigger, then walked to his colleague and helped him out of a stinking pile of heavy and dusty garments.

'It's only a bunch of rags,' said Attard, getting up hastily.

It's not like anyone's watching. Archibald's grin faded. *Well ...* he made for the lantern, which luckily hadn't died out with the blow. 'If Mr Joseph were here, he might have something to tell you about the mess you just made ...' he joked.

'If Mr Joseph *was* here, he'd surely have run out after all this noise,' replied Attard dryly, straightening himself and dusting his derby-style hat. He raised his bushy eyebrows and turned to move on. Archibald blinked and tried to look beyond the lantern, trying to think about something else as the journey into the darkness resumed.

The landing joining the only two rooms on this floor was furniture full of ragged clothes, tallow candles and books.

'Anna must've been literate,' commented Archibald.

'Books everywhere but not one single bed in sight,' said Attard in a serious tone whilst pointing down at a mixed pile of cloth and wool.

A creaking sound which came from the other room made them both jump. Archibald stepped closer to Attard, who stood as still as a statue.

'Give me that lantern,' whispered the Inspector.

Archibald hesitated. 'This silence is killing me, man.' He bit his lips and handed their only source of light to his colleague.

Attard crossed the landing and Archibald followed, his hand on the pistol beneath his coat. The short walk to the opposite room, across the corridor, seemed to last a lifetime. Their footsteps echoed like bells and their panting was not dissimilar to the howling wind outside. Archibald's mind went back to the lifeless curtains downstairs and hoped they were as still as they had left them. The pistol slid against his sweaty palm and he fought his trembling hand.

Attard was glaring at him. 'Really?' He

mouthed, eyeing the pistol.

Archibald replied with furrowed brows. Attard rolled his eyes and moved on.

The room was no different than the rest of the house. Dark and stark. This window, however, was open. The curtains flowed heavily with the draft. Once again, tallow candles lay scattered everywhere. A makeshift bed looked like someone had flown out of it in a rush. Sheets of paper from a torn book swirled around on the floor, one piece leaving the circular rotation and landing against Archibald's shin. He picked it up.

'Close that window,' said Attard.

Archibald obeyed, warily returning his pistol back to its pocket.

'If Mr Joseph escaped through this window, he was wearing clean shoes.' Attard was studying the floor beneath the windowsill. 'There are no footprints here.'

Archibald pocketed the piece of paper, then turned his attention to his colleague. 'Or no shoes at all, judging by all this poverty,' he added, waving his hands around.

They went through all the house once more. Attard gave up lantern-holding and Archibald was more than eager to accept the new role. The second search proved no more fruitful, however. There were no signs of intruders, struggle or any form of forced entry. Even worse, there was no sign of Mr Joseph anywhere.

Almost two hours later, the Inspector and the constable emerged from the house. *Strada St*

Ursola was empty, save for Constable Molinari – who had been left to watch the main entrance.

'The crowd lost interest and returned to the comfort of their homes, Inspector,' he said, lantern raised. 'The Superintendent will speak to you tomorrow.' He locked the door to the house behind them.

Archibald and Attard thanked him and Molinari with his lantern were swallowed by darkness.

'Well, the Superintendent won't be pleased,' said Attard, eyeing the lantern in Archibald's hand.

Archibald sighed heavily. 'Tomorrow is a day I do not look forward to.'

Attard sniggered. 'I look forward to my bed. Come, let me walk you to Morell's. I will need that lantern to get home in this darkness.'

Archibald nodded faintly.

The march to *Strada Forni* was sombre and silent. Archibald kept fidgeting with the paper inside the pocket of his trousers. He wasn't too keen on sharing this, yet. And besides, his colleague seemed in quite a hurry to get to bed. Archibald didn't blame him. In a couple of hours, they'd be on their feet and facing the Superintendent. They both needed the silence and company of their own thoughts, while it lasted.

'Goodnight, Whitlock,' whispered Attard, when they reached the entrance to Morell's.

Archibald handed him the lantern before

going inside. He was about to ask Attard how far he had to walk to get home. *Another time, mate. I'm too tired.* 'Goodnight, Inspector.'

Back in his room at Morell's, Archibald lay on his bed, staring at the ceiling above. With Mr Joseph now gone, he suspected the investigation was only going to get harder. He frowned, then reached for the piece of paper he had found in the house. It had brushed against his shin, in that room upstairs. Momentarily fascinated by the style of handwriting it contained, he had decided to keep it. Just before coming up to his room, however, he had asked a footman to translate it to English.

'Sure, sir, of course,' the footman had said, smiling and looking at the piece of paper. 'This says: I'm very sorry. But she left me no choice, Joseph.'

11.

Lorenzo buried his heavy head in the palms of his hands, taking a break from scanning the text in front of him. He sighed and closed his eyes for a moment, stroking his dark hair tediously. His lips were parched, his tea had gone cold. He puffed nervously and looked away from the book in front of him. *Enough of this.* He rubbed his eyes and forehead, as though it would cure his headache.

He had been at *The Imitation of Christ* all morning, hoping it could get his mind off the murders. Sighing, he pulled the book right under his nose. He could smell dust on the book and could see the tiny particles of the paper, intertwined seamlessly under the morning light. 'I can't think,' he told Don Roberto across his desk. *My fault. Why am I doing this here?*

The other priest took his eyes off whatever he was reading.

'I think I need some fresh air,' said Lorenzo, getting off his chair in frustration. He left the library like the devil himself was chasing. Don Roberto followed.

Lorenzo raised his hand. 'I'll be fine, Roberto, thanks.' He tried to keep a passive tone. 'Just need some time alone with the Lord. And besides, I've some errands out of the city.'

Don Roberto was from the younger generation ...

Fervent and dumb. Lorenzo made for the exit, before the young priest could irritate him further.

Valletta was in its usual state of morning energy and life - hustle and bustle everywhere. Sunlight caressed the limestone buildings, despite the atrocities the city had witnessed in the last five months. Valletta was like a beacon of light amidst a world threatened by wars, plagues and the harsh struggles of daily life. *Strada Reale* was in no less blossom and grandeur, but it wasn't on Lorenzo's morning agenda. He hurried towards *Porta Reale* to take the *karozzin*. The small carriage was more private, and quieter than that long piece of modern, metallic junk of a railway train. The English boasted about it, but Lorenzo found it constraining, dirty and loud.

The priest froze.

Almost instinctively, he found himself looking over his shoulders. Then it was gone in a flash.

He frowned. He felt convinced someone was watching him. 'Lord be with me,' he mumbled, moving on. His mind raced back to today's mission. This was what he was called for. This was his mission - to protect God's treasured souls from eternal damnation. This morning was all about the citizens of Valletta. The people of Malta.

It's for their sake, after all, he thought, climbing the *karozzin.*

Città Notabile had barely changed over time. It was less crowded than the capital and the people were mostly of a high class. They had an air of calm too, pacing around like they were floating on air; their backs straight and their chins raised. Unlike Valletta, Mdina didn't reek of shops, bars, or a hectic populace. It was much smaller and its alleys narrower. Lorenzo winced at the sudden realisation of how much he had missed this small city on the hill. This jewel was the old capital, which for many years had protected the Christian noblemen from the Muslim infidels.

'Don Lorenzo?'

Lorenzo turned his head and looked behind him. An old couple walked slowly towards him. 'Mr and Mrs Xuereb?' he said, squinting his eyes.

The couple nodded and bowed respectfully.

'How good to see you!' said Lorenzo, smiling.

'Good to see *you*,' replied Mr Xuereb, bowing and kissing the priest's hand.

His wife followed.

'You seem happy and in good health, the Lord be praised,' commented Lorenzo, to which the couple smiled.

'We are, thanks be to God,' replied Mr Xuereb, looking at his wife and smiling. 'The Almighty has blessed Maria, our daughter, with her seventh child last January, Father; a baby girl.'

'Oh! That's great news! She and her husband must be jumping for joy!'

'They are indeed, Father. They've moved out to Rabat a couple of months ago.'

Rabat was the suburb of Mdina.

'What brings you here, anyway?' Mrs Xuereb asked, curiosity evident in her tone.

'It's not a sin to ask,' replied Lorenzo, noticing how Mr Xuereb glared at his wife. The priest bit his lips and forced his brain to think fast. 'I came to see a friend. And besides, I still miss Mdina sometimes. So, I'm hitting two birds with one stone, as the Brits would say.'

'We would love to invite you over, for a cup of tea, Father. But we were on our way to visit Maria and …'

'Do not let your hearts be troubled,' Lorenzo said, mastering his pious voice and resting a hand on Mr Xuereb's shoulder. 'I won't be staying too long. I have to return to the capital by sunset. But thanks, you have my gratitude and my blessings.'

The couple nodded humbly. 'Thank you, Don Lorenzo!'

'Take care of each other, now. You have a new niece. A miracle that brings forth more blessings from the Lord Himself.' The priest smiled and nodded one last time.

As soon as they had their backs on him, Lorenzo turned back to his destination. He felt a tinge of guilt as he took off. He really did wish to spend some time with old friends like Mr and Mrs Xuereb. The years he had spent in the Dominican Seminary in Rabat, had given birth to a special relationship towards Mdina and its flock. And it was all coming back to him now. *My flock is in Valletta now.* He turned the last corner to the Manducas' *Palazzo.*

He knocked on the door, and waited.

'Good morning … Father?' A servant in his mid-forties and liveried clothing opened the door, wincing and shading his eyes from the sun.

'Good morning. I'm Don Lorenzo. Are Lord and Lady Manduca at home?'

The servant cleared his throat. 'Do you have an appointment with Lord Manduca?'

Lorenzo bit his tongue and sighed politely. 'Unfortunately not. But I am an old friend.'

'I'm sorry, Father, but I …' he started, then hesitated. 'Please, do come in and wait inside, while I check with Lord Manduca, himself.'

Lorenzo thanked him and walked in. The mansion hadn't changed from how he remembered it. Classical ornaments and paintings everywhere. A testimony to the wealth of the Manducas.

Much darker than I remember it, though.

Before long, another servant came asking him

to follow. Lorenzo nodded and obeyed. He was led through arched corridors and rooms covered in all kinds of intricate design and architecture. The silence, however, was almost disturbing. The priest tried his best not to show how awkward he felt, hearing the sound of his own footsteps.

At last, the servant leading Lorenzo stopped and indicated a door. 'Lord Manduca awaits you inside.' She smiled faintly and opened the door.

Lorenzo thanked her and walked inside.

Pietro Manduca, Lord of this *Palazzo*, sat behind a round table, across the parlour.

Lorenzo fought the instinctive urge to wince. 'Good morning, Lord Manduca,' he croaked.

'Don Lorenzo.' The lord looked almost ancient. He carried too few strands of white hair. His face was like weathered stone and his eyes seemed to have lost the sharpness Lorenzo remembered him to possess.

The priest forced a smile. This was supposed to be one of the rooms where the Lord and Lady welcomed their guests but it made Lorenzo cringe. It was so dark and cold. For a moment the priest had to remind himself the sun was shining outside.

'God bless you,' started the priest, hardly aware that he hadn't taken a single step closer to Lord Manduca. 'You look well and in good health.'

'Are you here to mock me?' His voice was harsh, like a wagon wheel threading on dry and coarse rock.

The priest cleared his throat. *God, help me.* 'Mock you? No, surely not, Lord Manduca.'

'Then why are you here?'

Lorenzo bit his lips and clasped his hands in front of him. 'I … I thought of paying you a visit, like …'

'But you're serving in Valletta now. So what brings you here, Don Lorenzo?'

Lorenzo rubbed his sweaty palms together. *Where is Lady Manduca?*

Lord Pietro Manduca had never really been the friendliest amongst his fellow noblemen, but *this* attitude was far from what Lorenzo expected. Together with his Lady, Francisca, they had been amongst the first noble houses to welcome the priest to Mdina. They had also raised two very healthy and beautiful children: Maria Isabella and Luca … until that tragic night, ten years ago. Evidently, that night had changed Lord Manduca for the worse.

'I miss the parishioners and their kindness.' Lorenzo kept smiling against all his instincts. *You could've at least offered me a seat, Pietro. For good, old times' sake, if for nothing else.*

'Are the parishioners not kind enough in the capital?' The lord sniggered.

Lorenzo feinted a worried look. 'Well, Valletta is under attack,' he said in a heavy tone.

The lord raised an eyebrow.

Finally, I got your interest … The priest sighed profoundly. 'The city is stricken.'

'Stricken?'

Good ... Lorenzo put on a helpless face. 'Crime, it seems. Horrendous terrible murders.'

The lord clicked his tongue. 'So the papers weren't making it all up.'

Seriously? You heard and you couldn't care less. 'I'm afraid not so, Lord Manduca. The victims ... uh!' He raised his eyes dramatically. 'They have suffered greatly.' Lorenzo paused, hoping it would sink in.

'Murder is man's worst weapon against himself,' went on the lord, matter-of-factly.

Come on, ask me. Make me tell you! Lorenzo nodded. 'There's more than mere man behind this, I'm afraid.' Lorenzo took a step forward. 'This is the devil's work. We're witnessing his hand ... directly.'

'The devil is always behind such atrocity, the Lord save us all.'

Lorenzo sighed heavily. 'What's hitting Valletta is a host of demons, I'm afraid. I have seen it once, before. It is terrible. I have hope in our Lord, no doubt. But these murders are horrendous. I've never prayed so hard in all my life.'

The lord leaned slightly forward. 'How so?'

'The victims ... forgive me, Lord Manduca ...' Lorenzo shook his head. 'I would be too bold to speak further.' He lowered his eyes. Inside, he felt like grinning.

'You didn't come all the way here to tell me *it would be too bold to speak further*!'

'They are Valletta's problems and I should not

trouble you with them.'

The lord's seat creaked. 'I said … tell me.'

'As you wish, Lord Manduca,' replied the priest. He cleared his throat and straightened. Despite the fact that he had managed to get Pietro to ask him what he wanted, it still wasn't easy to say it to his face. 'The victims … Well, they were all found without their … without eyes.'

The silence was terrifying.

Lord Manduca's eyes were fixed on him. Lorenzo said a small prayer in his heart and fought the urge to look away.

'So that is why you're here,' Manduca said.

'The capital is in terrible danger, Lord Manduca. I must protect my flock.'

'I don't care what state Valletta is in!' His voice wasn't flat anymore, his left arm was raised.

You won't send me off yet. Not that easily. Not before you prove useful. Then you can die, for all I care.
'God has ordered me to come and speak to you, Pietro.'

'How dare you!' Manduca was on his feet. Lorenzo instinctively took a step backwards. 'And what did the Lord ask you to tell me?'

Lorenzo tried to speak, but failed.

'Have you lost your tongue?' Manduca took a step forward and coughed.

'Lord Manduca,' said Lorenzo, finding his courage. 'Please, calm yourself. I am your ally in this endeavour.'

Manduca coughed violently again, almost crouching. A servant came in to assist him but he shoved her away. 'I'm fine, I'm fine.' The lord coughed again, then turned back to his seat.

Lorenzo didn't move.

'Jane, get the priest a chair,' he mumbled, diving into his.

The servant nodded and hurried out of the room.

'Thank you, Lord Manduca,' said Lorenzo, as politely as he could. *Finally, now sit down and do yourself a favour.*

'Speak plainly. You've already wasted a lot of my time,' said Manduca, leaning heavily on his left side.

A wooden chair was brought for Lorenzo. He sat down slowly. He couldn't let Manduca see through him. *God guide my words ...*

The old lord was glaring at him.

'I'm ... I'm sorry, Lord Manduca. I am terribly sorry for having returned with the darkness of the past.'

Manduca raised his hand idly. 'Enough of that. Do you have any clue of whoever is behind these murders, or not?'

Lorenzo nodded slightly. 'The Lord has been guiding me.'

'Who murdered my son, Lorenzo?' Manduca's stark eyes were on the priest.

'I suspect it was no one but the devil himself,' replied Lorenzo, plainly.

The lord narrowed his eyes.

'Lord Manduca. On the night your Luca was ... murdered and Maria Isabella abducted,' the priest crossed himself. 'Did you notice anything strange?'

'Like what? What do you mean?'

'Like the devil himself. An evil presence.'

'So you are not speaking symbolically?' The lord raised an eyebrow.

The priest shook his head confidently.

'Are you telling me the devil is killing and abducting people now?' Manduca's voice contained a hint of mockery.

You too have fallen from Grace, even here? Lorenzo had gotten used to this type of mentality, through his recent years in Valletta. The people in the city were adopting such a profane mentality. Their love of materialism, wealth and politics was driving them away from the truth. It was the mentality of the new world. Lorenzo used to think it was too far to even reach the Maltese islands and taint them. Life in Valletta was proving him wrong, however. It seemed Mdina was none the better. 'Yes, that's what I'm saying,' he said in a sad tone. He really felt sad, this time.

The nobleman grumbled something to himself. 'After ten years, you come all this way to tell me that the culprit of my son's and daughter's murder is the devil? They were *my* children, they were pure and kind to everybody. The devil could not touch them.' He pointed a bony finger at the priest. '*You* know this, Lorenzo. You remember them well.'

The priest nodded.

'Then you're wasting your time and mine,' he

said. 'I *was* strong once; powerful and wealthy. I believed that would help me bring justice to Luca's killer. I was confident it would help me find my daughter and bring her back. I went out to Rabat and *Boschetto*, that very night. I was convinced I could track down that bastard myself.' Manduca waved a hand and leaned slightly backwards, his expression still blank. 'Bah! All in vain. I found nothing. And nowadays I'm a widower with no heirs.'

So the Lady is resting with Our Lord. This is the very last thing I needed to hear. 'I'm sorry to hear about Lady Manduca.'

Manduca didn't even budge. 'You don't have to be. There's nothing you could've done. The devilish fever took her. You weren't here.'

Lorenzo felt those last three words were said intentionally. He chose to ignore the lord's hint, however. 'You can still do the Lord's work, Lord Manduca. God needs you.'

'What do *you* need, Lorenzo?' Manduca narrowed his eyes. 'My wife was a saint, my children walked in the light. I will rest only when I join them. I cannot help you,' he ended, helplessly.

'Maybe you can. Tell me about Luca, about Maria Isabella,' insisted Lorenzo. 'Did they ever tell you, maybe, that they saw the devil? Lucifer himself? That he appeared to them?'

Manduca shook his head and let out a chuckle.

Lorenzo paled. 'Lord Manduca …'

'Have you lost your mind? Get out of my

house,' said Manduca, dryly. 'No one taints the memory of my son or daughter with false accusations.'

'Lord Manduca, what I'm saying is that ...'

Lord Manduca's stern eyes were fixed on the priest's. He was almost standing again. 'Wilfred! Show Don Lorenzo out, please.'

The footman came rushing in.

Lorenzo looked at the footman nervously, then back at Manduca. 'I've never doubted your children walked in the light, Pietro.' *I have to say something to make me stay ...* 'Lucifer tempts all the children of God. I know him, he ...'

'If you know the devil so much, then go and ask him why he killed my children. Go back whence you came, there's nothing left for you or the devil here. He took everything from me.'

The footman took a step closer to Lorenzo. The priest shot him a glare.

Manduca let out a sigh and leaned heavily backwards. He was not looking at the priest anymore. 'Luca was twelve years old. Maria Isabella had just turned twenty-four,' he whispered without lifting his eyes. 'I dream about his hollow eye sockets, every night. We looked for Maria Isabella for days without end.'

'I remember. It was dreadful and I'm sorry.' Lorenzo lowered his eyes. 'The devil murdered your son and took your daughter with him.'

Lorenzo's mind took him back to that night. The first screams, the first light coming from the windows. It was like Mdina was on fire. The authorities had, as usual, proven useless in finding Maria Isabella or the culprit over the following days. Days turned to weeks and months, until Lorenzo had started to realise they had all been tricked. It hadn't been a man who took Manduca's daughter and butchered his son. It was Lucifer and there was no catching the most cunning and intelligent creation in the universe.

Lorenzo raised his head hopelessly at Lord Manduca. The old nobleman wasn't looking at him. The footman awaited.

'Why are you still here, Lorenzo?' Manduca was stroking one of his eyebrows.

The nervous footman approached the priest.

Lorenzo sighed and shook his head. 'I know the way out, Mr Wilfred, thank you.'

The footman nodded, but followed him out of the parlour nonetheless.

Just as they were going to descend the last stairway, before the exit, another servant came rushing at them. She was old and her face familiar.

'I'll take him from here, Mr Wilfred,' she told the footman in a commanding tone.

Wilfred nodded and returned to his post.

Lorenzo thanked them both, and descended the stairs.

'Before you leave,' whispered the servant, as soon as they reached the exit. She was holding Lorenzo by the hem of his sleeve. The priest was already half way into scolding her. But her face … it had endured many harsh seasons and allowed for no questioning or opposition. Lorenzo held his tongue.

'What I'm about to tell you, is only for Maria Isabella and Luca's sake,' she said, in such a blunt Maltese accent. 'And for the great respect I've always had for my Lord and Lady.'

Lorenzo blinked. He didn't know what to say.

'Look for Luigi.'

Lorenzo raised an eyebrow.

The old servant looked over her shoulders, in case the devil himself was watching. 'Luigi.'

'Who …?'

She jumped at the sound of the opening of a door. 'Find Luigi and you might find your answers, Father. Be very careful,' she ended, pressing at Lorenzo's arm one last time before hurrying back up the stairs.

12.

The Falcon's Perch wasn't the most illuminated inn in *Strada Stretta*, but Rita could read him from miles away now. No matter how dark, loud or crowded the inn was, she was getting used to his mannerisms in a way not even she could explain. She had no trace of doubt: tonight, Mr Calleja was on the edge.

The gentleman sharing his table was composed, as always. His elegant clothes were a contrast to this place of debauchery. Rita knew better than to believe he was visiting The Falcon's Perch solely for entertainment reasons. His visits were infrequent, but constant. He was mysterious, to say the least. Rita always made sure to keep herself busy, and as far from him as possible. But she liked it when he came. She loved it, because she got to see Mr Calleja subdued and afraid.

Tonight's visit, like all the others, involved the gentleman gesturing Mr Calleja into submission. Mr Calleja was like a rabid dog, ready to pounce. But the gentleman held the leash, and he told the dog to sit and wait. And Mr Calleja, the dog, obeyed.

The gentleman got off his chair, calmly. Rita sighed, her moment of peace was over. She gazed into the glass of wine on her table, and downed it to prepare herself for the night.

'Where are my clients, Isabella?' Mr Calleja made her jolt. He liked calling her with her false name.

Rita got up. *How did he get here so fast?* She gave a quick look around. The gentleman was gone. Mr Calleja was glaring at her, his ugly dark face almost touching her. She lowered her head and made to cross him, but he grabbed her by the arm.

'You do not ignore *me*, Isabella,' he said.

Her arm hurt. Rita gave a quick nod. 'Forgive me, Mr Calleja. It won't happen again.'

'That's what you said yesterday evening. Look at me when I speak to you!' he squeezed her chin and raised her head.

Rita tried to shake her head. His grasp was firm. Her jawbone hurt. 'I'm sorry,' she whispered.

'That won't help much now, will it?' he said, releasing his grasp.

Rita found the courage to take a step towards

her room.

'I'm not done with you, whore. Come here.' Mr Calleja pulled her so hard she almost lost her balance. 'You have been terrible, and disrespected some of our clients.'

A common client passed by them. Mr Calleja flashed a smile at him, and the client kept going.

'And I know you've been sleeping in that room, Isabella,' he continued, pressing harder on her arm. 'Do you expect me to provide you with a roof now, too?' he said mocking her.

Since when do you care? Rita avoided his eyes.

'Well, you can forget it if you keep treating our clients this bad.'

'But, Mr Calleja…'

'The only butt which I'll accept is *this*.' He smirked, spanking her behind. 'Now go get it working in there. Work it hard, or else get out. If I get even a rumour of your idling about and disappointing our clients, I'll finish you with my own two hands. Am I clear?' He clenched his fists in front of her pale face.

'Yes, Mr Calleja.'

'Good. Now get out of my sight,' he ended, turning his attention to an approaching client with a smile.

If I don't do this right, I might end up dead, she thought.

Seeing Mr Calleja's unusual reactions to that gentleman had made her forget reality for a while. But it never lasted too long. She knew Mr Calleja could kill her. His threats were no joke, and Rita had never underestimated him. He often boasted of being able to do whatever he wanted, and she wasn't willing to put him to the test. The gentleman might have a subduing effect on him, somehow. But she was Rita Formosa, and no one would notice her disappearance. Her very own mother had disowned her, just two nights ago. There was no place to escape. Thoughts of ending her own life had crossed her mind countless times in the last two days. Till now, she had managed to push them down by thinking of Lucia, her little sister. *I have to survive this, for her*, she thought, climbing the stairs to get prepared for the long night.

Her mother could come to terms with what Rita was doing, some day. Yet Rita's worry wasn't so much about money anymore. Her heart kept telling her Lucia would need her older sister soon. With these thoughts in mind, she prepared herself for the guests downstairs. Her fringe kept falling in front of her eyes. She huffed and walked out of the room.

The hall downstairs was packed. Mr Calleja was outside, welcoming guests with that ridiculous grin of his. Rita descended the stairs, swaggering and smiling as well as she could. Tempting men wasn't difficult for someone like her. She knew she was attractive beyond the average female. Well, judging by how easily a good number of men fell for her fake smiles and poses. They often praised her for her dark hair, slightly curled at the tips, which complimented her pale skin. Her jade green eyes had helped many a man forget his earthly troubles. She didn't even need to take some of them to the room, luckily for her. Their drunkenness made sure they never remembered what *didn't* happen.

But this is sinful. God has bestowed beauty upon me, and I'm using it to send his own children to hell, she thought, beaming at Giuseppe.

He was a regular local at The Falcon's Perch, and she was one of his favourites. Giuseppe had laid eyes on her like a blind fool, and she had used him to convince Mr Calleja to employ her. That was about three weeks ago, when the devil's voice had convinced her of the only way to save her family. A lady of the night. No amount of regret could change the mess she was in, now. She dragged her feet towards Giuseppe by the bar. He already stank of alcohol. *Whiskey, for a change.* 'Will you not buy me a drink, my dear Giuseppe?' she said, leaning on his shoulder.

It was useless, really. In *Strada Stretta,* ladies of the night usually agreed with their employers on a commission for every drink they managed to make their clients buy. Others, mostly the older generation or less beautiful, reverted to a fixed, very low salary. Rita was stunning, but legally under age. Mr Calleja had taken that as an opportunity to give her no option but the one that suited him best: salary.

Giuseppe blinked. His eyes could barely stay open. 'Isabella, my beautiful!' he exclaimed, raising an empty glass.

Rita pushed slightly against him to stop him from falling off his stool. '*Come stai, stasera?*' She knew he loved it when she spoke Italian.

'I will buy you a drink? I will buy the whole pub for you, *bellissima mia*,' he said, raising his hand.

If only you could buy my freedom, you fool.

One of the barwomen winked at Rita as she took Giuseppe's order and money.

Is she mocking me? Haven't I already told her it's useless with those drinks?

The next couple of minutes consisted of Rita smiling and caressing the poor fellow, whilst trying hard not to vomit right in his dirty face. Her mind kept reminding her she couldn't afford to disappoint Mr Calleja again. That held her from striking Giuseppe right in the face.

'I'd like to have a bit of that, *cara mia*,' said Giuseppe, putting his hand beneath Rita's skirt.

She forced a smile. 'Let's go upstairs,' she said, grabbing Giuseppe's arm.

As she turned, she noticed a stranger watching them. He was right at the foot of the stairs. Rita avoided eye contact and moved on; Giuseppe trailing behind her like a thirsty tramp.

'You're in the way,' said the stranger, who was now blocking the way upstairs.

'Beg your pardon, sir. Can't you see I already…'

'I wasn't talking to you. But to *him*.' He was pointing at Giuseppe.

Rita raised her head just a little. His face was

familiar. It took a while for Giuseppe to realise his journey to paradise had been interrupted. He murmured something, to which Rita nodded. The stranger remained as still as stone.

Come on, please, move! This was… Rita started. *Those hazel eyes…* 'Filippo?'

The stranger nodded. 'You remember my name. Lovely! Can we have a quick word, please, missy?'

A quick word? Rita raised an eyebrow. She pretended to ignore him, but Filippo stayed put. Rita frowned. 'You must wait, sir. I already have a client.'

Filippo shrugged. 'If you wish so, missy,' he said, waving a hand coolly. 'I'll count to a hundred as soon as I see *him* coming down. Then I'll come up. Does that suit your pleasure?'

Rita wasn't too sure whether he was ridiculing her or being serious. No one had agreed or submitted themselves to *her* requests for weeks. She stared at Filippo, blankly. Filippo nodded again, moving out of her way. He patted the drunkard slightly on the shoulder and wished him good luck.

'I'll be right here,' he told Rita, sitting at the closest table.

Rita led Giuseppe up to the room. Filippo was watching her, carrying such an oddly serene face she wanted to scream.

Her room was dark. She always tried to keep it so. Giuseppe sank into the bed. She took out a bottle of whiskey and a small glass, filled it, and walked silently to the bed.

'Here, handsome,' she told Giuseppe, handing him the glass.

Giuseppe downed it in one gulp. Rita began to undress, trying with all her mind to imagine no one was watching her. The darkness in the room always helped, as long as the clients didn't complain. At least she didn't see how his eyes were scanning her, or how his mouth drooled, or his member hardened. She could feel his breath close to her slit. His hand shortly followed. Rita shut her eyes and made fake noises.

In a couple of minutes, the nightmare was over. Luckily, Giuseppe was on one of his drunkest nights, so he was done quickly. He thanked her and staggered out of the room, while Rita wiped semen off her thighs.

She wanted to cry. She knew she wouldn't hold for much longer. Every night was like this. Filippo would soon be at the door, so she couldn't afford to disappoint another client. Mr Calleja would kill her.

'Good morning, missy.'

Rita jumped, raising a hand to her breasts. She heard Filippo walk in and close the door behind him, and she prayed it could be morning soon.

'Is everything fine, missy? You look like you've just seen a ghost...'

Rita shook her head and turned to face him.

'You *are* beautiful,' he said. 'You make me believe in God.'

It's going to be this religious nonsense again... She

walked slowly towards him, letting go of the blankets covering her bosom.

'You know I cannot say no... to *that*,' he said, his hazel eyes almost flaring.

'You have nice hair.' She caressed his dark brown hair, and pressed her bare breasts against his chest.

Filippo grabbed her behind, lifted her, and threw her on the bed.

Another nightmare's over, Rita told herself, getting up and making for her dresser table. She had to admit sinning with Filippo felt different... somehow. She had felt it the first time too. She blushed.

'I really had a good time, missy,' said Filippo, breaking the awkward silence and sitting up on the bed. 'May I also have your name?' he asked.

'Isabella.' Lying was becoming almost natural to her now. *If that's what it takes to keep me alive ...*

Filippo sniggered. Rita turned to look at him.

'Light up that lamp,' he demanded.

Rita raised an eyebrow.

Filippo bobbed his head at kerosene lamp on her dresser. 'Go on. Do it,' he insisted.

'But it's soon dawn, sir.'

Filippo's stare made her wonder whether he would ask nicely again. She obeyed, but reverted to studying her face in the mirror.

'What is your name, missy?'

What a pest! She started playing with a strand of hair. 'Isabella,' she replied flatly. She could see him glaring at her through the mirror though.

'Why are you lying to me?' he said.

Rita froze.

'It takes a good liar to recognise another,' he explained, matter-of-factly.

'So... you're a liar too?' she asked, pretending to be interested in his game. *If I tease him, he might leave me in peace.*

He didn't answer, but leaned backwards on his outstretched arms instead. Despite his odd character, Rita kept finding it hard not to look at him through the mirror. His alluring face, hazel eyes and complimentary chestnut hair... 'I have enjoyed my time with you, sir. But it is time for you to leave. Please.'

Filippo grinned. 'Don't you ever get tired?'

Rita avoided his eyes. 'Tired of what, sir?'

'Of all the lies,' he replied, bluntly.

'Do you always talk so much about yourself, all the time?' Rita dared, in a sarcastic tone.

'I'm more interested in you, frankly,' he replied.

'Me? Don't you have any friends?' *Whatever is your game, man?*

He shrugged. 'It's not friendship I'm seeking.'

Oh my... he's crazy, and romantic. Rita stood up. Despite everything, she thought she felt something for this young man. Maybe it was pity, or just pure curiosity. Was it compassion? He did look a bit lonely.

'You're not very talkative,' he said again. 'And you still haven't told me your real name.'

I just wish to sleep ... Rita harrumphed.

Filippo raised his arms. 'Fine. I think I understand,' he ended, getting off the bed. He was going to say something else, and then stopped abruptly.

For a brief moment she thought she saw his face grow tense. Then it was gone, faster than it had come. He stood still, like he was trying to hear a sound which was not there. Rita could hear Mr Calleja's voice amidst the noise downstairs. He was yelling at one of the bartenders.

For a change. Rita bit her lips.

'Until our next meeting then, Isabella,' said Filippo suddenly, making for the exit.

Rita gaped, but then sighed in relief. She ran a hand through her dark hair. 'Finally!' She was still trembling.

It wasn't the first time that a client of The Falcon's Perch had sought her out for a second or third nightly visit – apart from Giuseppe, of course. Despite how desperate she was, and how much she hated what she was doing, Rita knew she was attractive to most men. She was getting used to all the possible ways to give them pleasure, unfortunately. But Filippo made her feel something different; made her feel *something*. She wasn't too sure what it was. He was childish, in a way. Like a young boy behaving well only because his mother would give him sweets. At the very least, he had earned her curiosity.

She shook her head, hoping it would shake off such thoughts. The greatest love of all, her mother's, had recently been the one to condemn her. Rita was far from ready to go through anything as close to that experience again. Besides, for all she knew, Filippo could be trying to lure her into some form of trap. He was after all, a man. And all men seemed to want was to squeeze her breasts, split her legs open and find relief inside her.

Rita froze.

She used to believe she could always be better. She used to believe in goodness, and in good people. Despite how things had turned out for her family after her father's tragic death, Rita had always held to some kind of hope. Until her mother had made sure that hope diminished; like a bucket of water thrown on an already weak flame.

You're not my daughter… a lady of the night has got nothing to explain to me…

Her mother's words, from two nights before, still echoed in Rita's head as she descended the steps to the main hall. They would continue to echo until the day Rita joined her maker - of that she was sure.

Any hope of returning to her mother and Lucia was suddenly gone.

13.

He had heard about Malta before his journey here. But most of the British rumours described it as either gloomy, or very dirty. His mother – a Maltese national – had run away from home with his British father. That had started a romantic tale, which later led to the forming of Archibald's family. These facts, however, never really helped him improve his opinion of Malta. What Inspector Attard told him about the view from here, however, was true. It was fantastic, to say the least!

Memories of his mother immediately made Archibald reach for the crucifix against his chest. 'Keep it close to you, Archie, all the time,' she used to tell him, kissing him on the forehead.

'It will protect you from all evil…' he said

now, murmuring his mother's words out of memory.

Archibald had very little memories of him being innocent. Ever since he was a boy, he always felt he was too intelligent for his own good. He would continuously inquire about the nature of this and that, wondering why humans behaved in this way or the other. His father ignored his questions most of the time, ever so lost in politics. His mother had always been the listener. Her answers, though, always revolved around her faith. He never completely understood the way she recurred to it; like someone taking cover under a shield to protect them from flaming arrows.

It had not, however, protected her from the monster of cholera. His father changed after that. Actually, they all changed. George and William immersed themselves in their studies of economics and banking. Jane found refuge in love. Their father had become thinner, sterner, and as silent as the grave of his late wife. Archibald had tried to leave Police school then. He had even attempted a furtive journey home once, which utterly failed. Luckily, his superiors had shown some empathy during those tough times, and he was re-admitted under a watchful eye. He smiled slightly at the folly of his youth now, as though it weren't only some years ago.

Manoel Island fell deeper into shadow as the sun set behind him. A soft spring breeze caressed his face, and Archibald decided he had enough solitude for one evening. He came here to think about this past week's events. The investigation into Ms Anna's murder returned no further results. The police scoured Valletta for Mr Joseph, since his sudden frantic disappearance five nights ago. The Superintendent was furious, of course, and didn't want to see Archibald's or Attard's faces until they had something concrete. Archibald still had the piece of paper he had found in Mr Joseph's house, but he wasn't too sure how sound it was to share it, yet.

What astonished him the most, however, was the people's reaction to these murders. He didn't know whether it was courage in disguise, or plain indifference. One thing seemed certain, however: life in Valletta seemed hardly affected.

Archibald sighed heavily. Tonight's walk hadn't helped him arrive to any conclusion, save that his half-Maltese blood might finally be discovering its roots. Hastings Gardens were beautiful, and Valletta he was also growing fond of. These evening strolls through its dimly lit streets and narrow lanes were relaxing. The capital was gloomy, yes, but in a mysterious way, which Archibald found impressively attractive. Maybe it was due to the yellowish limestone buildings, or because of the way in which the massive architecture of the Knights towered above everything else. Whatever it was, Archibald felt that the more he succumbed to it, the easier it became for his senses and soul to feast upon it.

Close to the Governor's Palace, he stopped. This was one of the most satiating structures to his eyes. Even now, in this creeping darkness, he could still picture it in detail in his inner eye. Tall and proud, amidst the open *Piazza San Giorgio,* and opposite the Main Guard. It never ceased to amaze Archibald how such locations could be so lively and bright during daytime, and then fall into a deep and soundless slumber at night. He didn't know which to love more. The energy of population and light made him feel alive. The sense of transcendence and mystery appertaining to the night, allowed him to reach deep inside his soul and find purpose. What kind of purpose, he didn't exactly know.

He shook his head and blinked in order to avoid getting lost inside his own mind. Fidgeting nervously with his lantern, he raised it right in front of his face the moment the wick caught light. His eyes fell on a small gap across *Piazza San Giorgio*, which he recognised as *Strada Vescovo*. His curiosity took hold of him. He scanned his surroundings for any passers-by, and then made towards the narrow street. This was where he had examined Ms Anna's corpse, on his first night to the island. *You're a grown man, don't act like a child, and you'll be fine. It's just a little dark, cannot kill you...* He tried to focus on the sound of his boots against the moist cobblestones, as he crossed *Piazza San Giorgio*. He avoided looking at the dancing shadows emanating from his portable light.

Strada Vescovo was as dark and silent as a week ago. The only difference now was the corpse was not here, obviously. From this location, Archibald could almost see the silhouette of the horizon down ahead. He took a deep breath, and took *Strada Vescovo,* downhill. His hearing sharpened, his hand's grip tightened around the lantern's handle. His left was ready to reach for his pistol. *As if they'd be that foolish to thread close to here again….* Archibald stopped on the exact spot where Ms Anna's body was found. He could still picture her empty eye sockets, and ravished face. The bloodstains were hardly visible. He struck the ground idly, as if this would reveal something he had missed a week ago. 'I hope this taxidermist proves useful, tomorrow,' he whispered to himself.

His feet moved him onwards, even though his shoulders trembled. They led him from one narrow street to the other, now downhill then uphill. His arms did shake a little, but they still had enough strength to raise the lantern and guide Archibald through the darkness. He gazed at the street names attached to the limestone walls. From one constricted lane to another, Archibald got lost in the narrow lanes that promised to swallow him and his lantern whole. He visited *Strada San Giovanni* again, where the third victim was found on 20th March, a week after the sailors in Hastings.

This nocturnal trip, however, wasn't proving to be any different from the previous ones. His knees ached, and he couldn't stop yawning. Eventually, his mind started to drift across various images he could not entirely grasp. Whether they were recollections of the past, fears of the future, or insecurities of the present, Archibald couldn't quite exactly figure them out. He kept stopping to rub his eyes, until even the light coming from his own lamp started to hurt him. Resignedly, he dragged himself back to Morell's.

Inside his room, he sat down to start removing his shoes. Before he knew it, he fell backwards and was snoring like a trumpet. He dreamt of the victims. In the dreams, however, their eyes shone silver like the moon. They spoke to him in a language he failed to understand; even Ms Anna, with her appalling face and missing tongue. Their mouths opened and closed, drenching the foul air with their fouler breaths. He tried to shout at them, but their distorted faces silenced him…

Waking up next morning was neither easy nor pleasant. Inspector Attard had managed to get them a meeting with a taxidermist this morning. *It might prove useful… hopefully.*

Attard was waiting outside as soon he stepped outside Morell's.

'They do have a spectacular breakfast, here,' commented Archibald, nodding to Attard and tapping his stomach slightly. *Something feels like home, at least.* 'Have you ever been to another country, Inspector Attard?'

Attard shook his. 'Mr Bonavia's office is this way. Come.'

They headed left, taking a corner uphill to *Strada Teatro*. The street was in its early-Tuesday-morning state of tranquillity. A few pigeons cooed here, one shabbily dressed man cut across them there. They crossed *Strada Stretta*, and *Piazza San Giorgio* came into view. The bustle of *Strada Reale* hit Archibald's senses.

'Inspector Attard,' he murmured.

The Maltese glanced over his shoulder at his colleague.

'Would you happen to know from where I could purchase a cane?'

'A cane?' Attard raised an eyebrow.

'Yes. Why, do you find it funny?'

'Oh no, Whitlock. Who said anything about finding it funny?' Attard shot a quick glance at the pocket watch in his hand. 'You just remind me of my earlier days as an Inspector, sometimes.'

Archibald huffed and looked around. It was close to eight o'clock, but the square was already full of life and blazing sunlight. This sunny climate needed getting used to.

'It will be another couple of minutes before Mr Bonavia opens,' started Attard. 'There is a shop, on the way to the taxidermist's, in *Strada Mercanti*. Might as well stop there and get you that cane then, shall we? You can then christen it on our way to Mr Bonavia's. It's not that far,' he pocketed his watch and took off towards the

Governor's Palace.

Archibald followed, trying hard to conceal his sudden eagerness. *You go buying a cane, first thing in the morning.* He was assigned the task of vanquishing the horrors striking Valletta and its people. He felt a tinge of guilt.

Inspector Attard led on towards *Strada Teatro*. 'That's the Malta Public Library,' he said, pointing at a neoclassical building to his right.

'Isn't this *Tesoreria* square, where we had coffee last Wednesday?' Archibald loved the sweet scent of citrus emanating from the orange trees in the square.

Attard nodded and quickened his step. 'The gentleman's shop is just around this corner. It's called *Ta' Michele*,' he said, taking a right onto *Strada Mercanti*.

Ta' Michele was beyond what Archibald had expected. The shop was another testimony to how much he had underestimated Valletta. His jaw dropped the moment he stepped inside. In front of him lay a myriad of the finest coats, hats, gloves, and all attire a man could delight in. Colours and material ranged from the finest to the rarest, and Archibald felt like crying as he caressed them with his fingers.

'Come, Whitlock,' said Attard, noticing the Englishman's awe. 'You still have to see the inner section. Try not to faint though,' he ended in a chortle.

'Good morning, sirs.' They were greeted by a gentleman, dressed in the finest selection from the shop itself. He looked like he was in his forties, but his demeanour was experienced and elegant.

Attard and Archibald removed their hats.

'Inspector Attard, how good to see you again!' he yelled suddenly.

'Good to see you too, Mr Apap,' replied Attard, indicating his colleague. 'This is my friend, Constable Whitlock, from London.'

Archibald nodded politely. *So much for concealing our profession. This city is too small. How does the Superintendent expect people not to know Attard is an Inspector?*

'A friend of yours is a friend of ours,' continued Mr Apap, fervently. 'How may I be of service on this fine morning?'

'I am looking for a fine cane,' answered Archibald.

'A fine cane, sure! What make?'

Archibald muttered nervously.

'I see,' said Mr Apap, unperturbed. 'You're still undecided. Not to worry. Come now, follow me, if you please.'

Archibald and Attard followed him into the accessories section. Once again, Archibald failed to conceal his astonishment as he found himself inside a gentleman's emporium.

'Choosing a fine cane is not an easy decision. It's like choosing a lady, if you ask me,' he joked, skimming through his products. 'We have defence canes, automaton… everything a gentleman like you could ask for. What is your budget, if I may be so bold, Mr Whitlock?'

Archibald cleared his throat and rubbed at his back. Attard shot him a quick glance, raising his bushy eyebrows.

Mr Apap smiled. 'Don't worry, sir,' he said confidently, scanning the Briton from head to toe. 'Just give me a minute.' He started rummaging through his wares.

Archibald nodded timidly, tapping his right foot. Attard remained motionless, expression blank.

'Here, do try this,' came Mr Apap's intense voice again, thrusting a dark wooden walking stick at Archibald. 'This is right what you need. Go ahead, sir. Try it.'

Archibald grabbed the cane and raised it in front of his face. It was a marvellous, sturdy, black-painted hardwood staff with a chrome trim and a faceted glass handle. It felt comfortably light. Archibald walked around with it in his right hand.

'It sparkles and shines as soon as it catches the light, sir. Glimmers like silver, sir. And silver matches everything, and attracts the ladies.'

'I'll take it,' said Archibald, to which both Attard and Mr Apap raised their brows.

'Then it is yours!'

After all the necessary arrangements of payment were made, the two thanked Mr Apap and made for the exit. Archibald looked at his new cane, and smiled. Attard was behind him.

'The Apaps have always treated us well,' he said, noticing Archibald's facial expression. 'Now, Whitlock, to business. Come, follow me...'

Archibald lowered his cane, grinning as its lower tip tapped the ground.

'Watch it!' he heard Attard saying.

He had barely turned his head, when he suddenly felt his cane leaving his hands. A young boy had just brushed past him, and was running away for his life.

'Halt!' yelled Archibald. 'Halt! Thief, stop that thief!' Archibald took off after the lad before Attard could stop him. He didn't even hear him shout or remind him about their original destination at the taxidermist's. All that mattered was the running boy, who had just cut across into *Strada Teatro*. Archibald kept his eyes on him, cutting recklessly through the crowd and ignoring the alarmed curses thrown at him. 'Stop that vermin!'

At the point where *Strada Teatro* crossed *Strada Reale*, the boy sped left like a rabbit on the run. Archibald followed, throwing his hat carelessly away. But the boy ran even faster, taking another swift turn rightward. Chased and chaser sped downhill. The distance between them increased, as did Archibald's gasps for breath. His leg yelled in pain, and his heart felt as though it would explode soon. He took one deep breath, blinked... and the boy was suddenly gone.

'Damn you, damn you!' he groaned, never stopping.

The boy was nowhere to be seen.

Eventually, his knees gave way and he found himself leaning and panting heavily. He wiped his brow and looked around. It was hot... scorching hot, like he was on fire. He realised he was no longer wearing his coat. 'Goddamn you.' He stomped his foot. 'I had just bought it. Goddamn you!'

A passer-by looked at him, shock evident all over his face. Luckily, wherever he was now was a less frequented street. Archibald shut his eyes and tried to catch his breath again. He was already straightening up when the sound of hurried footsteps caught his attention. He stood still and listened. The footsteps came from the street around the corner to his left. He tried to hold his breath and listen. The footsteps weren't getting any closer, so he tiptoed downhill.

Strada Stretta... he took a mental note of the street sign, and peeped around the corner. A middle-aged man walked into a building through its backdoor. The building looked humble, but busy; Archibald's nostrils took in the pleasant scent of fresh baking. He had found a bakery, but he had lost the boy and his new cane. He shook his head desperately, and walked into *Strada Stretta* like he was going to a funeral.

The sound of conversation caught his attention. The whispers came from a narrow street to his left, right opposite the bakery.

'What are you doing?'

'Waiting for you of course.'

Archibald got closer, making sure he couldn't be seen or heard. Judging from the shadows, one leaned against the wall. The other's shadow was lost amidst the buildings. They spoke in Maltese.

'Of course you are.'

Both male, approximately my age. Archibald thanked his deceased mother for having taught him this weird tongue. By their tone of voice, they seemed on friendly terms with each other.

'Did you come alone?' This one's voice sounded younger and thinner.

Archibald leaned stealthily against the wall. *This looks interesting!* Besides, he couldn't just step out of the corner now that he was eavesdropping.

'I'm always alone.' This one's voice was more reserved, and baser.

'Not a good idea, in times like these,' the younger voice sniggered.

Archibald narrowed his eyes, making sure to grasp as much of the Maltese slang as he could. He peeped at the shadows on the ground again. The one who had initially been leaning against the wall, was now standing. The other one's shadow was still invisible.

'I've no one to be afraid of,' went on the reserved voice. 'I hope you have news about Calleja.'

'He's not as passive as we hoped.' He sounded eager, like it was the main reason he had come to this meeting. 'He's asking questions, unfortunately.'

Archibald held his breath.

'What type of questions?' The baser voice said, evidently interested.

'He's meeting with a gentleman, frequently.'

'What gentleman? Where?'

'Why, at The Falcon's Perch, of course.'

'At The Falcon's Perch?' The reserved one sounded surprised.

'This gentleman… well, he looks like he's someone important, or powerful.'

A short silence, then, 'And…?'

Archibald closed his eyes and bit his lips. His heartbeat felt loud.

'I've never seen Calleja silenced, Pawlu. Not like this,' went on the younger one, in a form of a statement. 'This gentleman speaks to Calleja like his father or older brother would. Don't look at me like that. I know what I saw.'

Pawlu? Calleja? The Falcon's Perch? Archibald blinked, fighting the urge to wipe his brow. Standing still made the heat feel ten times worse; he thanked his past self for getting rid of his coat during the chase.

'This gentleman,' said the reserved one. 'Is he helping Calleja? It sounds more like he's threatening him, to me.'

Archibald saw a hand's shadow waving.

'I think this gentleman's some kind of lawyer, or similar.'

'Are you telling me Calleja is walking down the legal route?' The reserved one, Pawlu apparently, sounded surprised again.

'Whatever he is doing, I fear he's got us on his

trail, Pawlu. This gentleman, he knows things. I bet it won't be too long before we see him or Calleja on our doorstep.'

Pawlu chuckled lightly. 'I hardly think he would, yet.' He also sounded very confident and sure of himself. 'Calleja could've come for us months ago, when his brother died.'

'And what tells you he hasn't already? How do you think *she* got killed?'

Archibald raised an eyebrow. *Heaven and earth...* He leaned very slightly forward. *If they see you, Archie...* He needed to get an idea of the reserved one's build, just in case. But only the younger one's shadow was visible.

The bakery's backdoor was still closed. No one walked in the street around him. This was getting interestingly informative, but he knew there was only so much time he could remain here. Attard would be looking for him; it would be highly embarrassing if his colleague found him eavesdropping, like a lady. Then again, he wasn't ready for another run, of that he was sure.

'You're getting ahead of yourself, my friend,' the reserved one said.

'You asked me to…'

'I know what I told you to do.' Pawlu's voice grew impatient. 'And that never involved being afraid of Calleja… nor his minions.'

'Fine. I'll keep an eye on him then,' ended the younger one, stubbornly.

'Yes, *and* on this gentleman, or lawyer… whoever he is. But let's not jump to conclusions yet, shall we?'

Archibald heard a pair of footsteps getting fainter. He looked at the ground. The shadows indicated the younger one was walking away.

Pawlu, Falcon's Perch, Calleja and this gentleman… His mind raced. *Wait, Archie! Wait for one of them to leave, at least.* He let out a heavy sigh.

'Who's there?' came the sudden voice of Pawlu.

Archibald held his breath, biting his tongue to stop himself from swearing. *Eavesdropping, what were you even thinking?* He bent his head downwards and walked into the street. 'I'm terribly sorry to cut across you, sir. But…'

He faltered.

The street went uphill, but there was no one. Archibald gasped.

The closest door was barred, and the next visible street was a bit too far to run to so swiftly. A shadow and the sound of flapping wings made Archibald jump.

He raised his head and wished he could fly, just like those pigeons. *Strada Carri*.

It was empty and quiet.

All the physical efforts he had endured suddenly took hold of him. His knees ached, his chest burnt, his face felt like a teapot. He remembered the cane, and felt sad. *It could be a blessing in disguise,* he told himself. The conversation he had just stumbled upon was suspicious, to say the least. He needed to discuss it with Inspector Attard, who would after all want to know what happened. Nevertheless, the mere thought of narrating the last events made Archibald blush. Word could spread fast. He could already picture the local constables, laughing at the tale of how the British Constable was robbed and outrun by a street urchin.

Sombrely, Archibald made for the darkest and narrowest alleys of Valletta. Some walking minutes later, he finally found himself back on *Strada Reale*. Taking a left to the Auberge, he pondered on the conversation between Pawlu and his friend. From the little he knew about Malta, Pawlu was as common a name as John, George, and William back in Britain. Not for the first time, he wished he were back home.

14.

Lorenzo wiped his face dry. Cold water usually helped him wake up and prepare for the day. He looked at himself in the mirror, and uttered a prayer. His eyes immediately raced back to his small desk, in the corner of his cell. It wasn't much, but enough for every Dominican.

'Heaven and earth...' He sat at the desk and unlocked a small drawer. He took out the letter he had received yesterday, and read it again. Read it for around the hundredth time now, like it was the Divine Office or the Holy Bible itself. *Mr Emmanuel Speranza's hand, without any doubt. God help me...* he winced.

In Lorenzo's dreams, Mr Speranza would write back, asking for forgiveness and offering to help. Together, they would solve the crisis that had taken over Valletta.

This letter, however, told exactly the opposite.

In less than two lines, Mr Speranza had plainly told Lorenzo to leave him in peace. The priest didn't know how he hadn't put it to the fire yet. He had come across many hard-headed men and women, particularly during Confession. But Mr Speranza's stubbornness was proving to be of unique ranking.

Who in God's name does he think he is! He fought the urge to crumple the paper. *Maybe I should write back to confirm I received his letter, at least.* He had tried to scribble something yesterday. But all attempts failed. Now, he felt more like taking a carriage straight to Sliema, knock at Mr Speranza's door and shake him by the collar. That might help the creature get some sense back into that empty head of his.

These murders were taking a heavy toll on the Dominican, and not just spiritually. He felt cornered, in a maze where he just lost all his keys to the exit. Emmanuel and the Manducas were Lorenzo's first hope at solving this riddle. Their past was the closest link to Valletta's present and its gruesome reality. It touched them on a personal level. Their passive reaction to the present situation was what frustrated the priest most.

All Lorenzo was left with was this mysterious fellow, Luigi. From all the shop owners, family members, friends and other acquaintances he knew in Valletta and Mdina... the priest knew no one by that name.

You don't even know his surname. Lorenzo sighed desperately, sitting down and burying his head in the palms of his hands. *Cannot stop trying. Not yet.* Valletta needed him. Malta needed him. His flock needed him. And he would rather die than give up.

A knock at the door of his cell made him jump with a start.

Lorenzo put the letter back inside the drawer and locked it. 'Who's there?'

'Lorenzo? It's Roberto.'

Lorenzo raised his eyes. *Oh God, now's no time for this one.* 'You may come in.'

Don Roberto came in, carrying a folded newspaper. He went straight to Lorenzo's bed and sat down. The older priest raised an eyebrow.

'Good morning, Father Lorenzo,' he said, smiling slightly and unfolding the newspaper on his lap.

Lorenzo's eyes followed. 'Good morning,' he murmured.

Don Roberto gasped like he had just found something he was looking for. 'There,' he said, handing the newspaper to his fellow priest.

Lorenzo took the newspaper. *Fede ed Azione* always carried a slight scent of wet ink, most probably due to this morning's dew. He flinched, remembering how wet parchments gave him a tingling feeling of dirt and disorder. He didn't understand why, but ever since he was a little boy, damp paper made him cringe. His siblings would make fun of him, and he would cry. On some occasions he wouldn't stop, unless his mother took the dank paper away. As he grew older, he got over this weird obsession. However, in rare instances such as right now, the priest remembered he was not entirely free from this obsession yet.

'Another article about the murders,' he said dryly, handing the newspaper back to Don Roberto. He leaned forward, resting his elbows against his knees.

Don Roberto sighed. 'Do you think the devil is punishing us?'

Lorenzo narrowed his eyes. *It is too early to discuss such matter. Why can't you leave me in peace?* He shrugged.

'Well, the police don't seem to be having much luck…' Don Roberto trailed off.

Lorenzo sat up straight. 'When did the police deserve any recognition or authority in the eyes of God? No one is above the Almighty. And no one should try to be,' he said sternly. 'Besides, did you know they got a British officer helping them? A Protestant, to make it even worse.'

Don Roberto crossed himself and gaped. 'The devil is right on our doorstep.'

Lorenzo nodded slightly.

'What about witnesses?'

Lorenzo sighed heavily. 'No one is willing to help,' he said flatly. His mind went straight to Mr

Speranza.

'You can't blame them. The devil's claw has lashed out violently at us,' said Don Roberto, shook his head in anguish.

Lorenzo said nothing. He didn't even bother to look at the younger priest. He was feeling tired, as though he did not sleep at all.

'Well,' the young priest went on. 'Four murder scenes. I still can't believe nobody saw anything. We have to remind the flock that omission against evil is as much of a sin as committing it.'

You won't be the one reminding them. Why can't you just go back to your books and leave me in peace, damn you! Lorenzo nodded faintly, still not looking at Don Roberto.

'Do you think the police know more than the papers?'

Lorenzo glared back. 'How do you mean?'

'I mean. Do you think they could be hiding something?'

'That's what the police do, Don Roberto. God will punish them for their insolence and pride...' *But not before I solve these mysterious murders.*

'And what is your opinion on the matter? I'm curious.'

Persistently. 'How do you mean?' *Why can't you just go back to your cell and speak to the wall?* Lorenzo got up and made for his desk. Fidgeting with the paper, with his back to the priest might make Don Roberto take the hint and leave.

'Who do you think is behind the murders, I mean?'

What a stupid question! Can't you just leave? 'Why, the devil, of course.' Lorenzo didn't turn to look at him.

Don Roberto nodded and sighed. He sounded sad. 'Well, see you later, Don Lorenzo.' He got off the bed and exited Lorenzo's cell.

Finally! Lorenzo looked at the door of his cell. It was closed. He opened the drawer and took Mr Speranza's letter. 'Regretfully, I won't be able to help you further…' he read. His stomach rumbled.

During breakfast, he kept mostly to himself. Even nodding to some of his fellow Dominicans was an effort. Apparently, it was evident on his face.

'No, I'm just feeling a bit dizzy,' he told an old and insisting Don Gianni.

His was not completely out of luck, though. He managed to avoid Don Roberto at least and their Prior, Don Massimo Gauci, who was out on some errands, this morning. Lorenzo didn't feel he would've managed to avoid those stark, hollow black eyes - not this morning.

When breakfast was finally over, he hurried to his cell. Rarely was he so eager to pray and meditate in the solitude of his room. Going up the stairs, he came across Don Gianni, who was descending.

'Ah, Lorenzo…'

Can't hope for some peace and quiet too soon. Lorenzo paused.

'A little urchin was asking for you, this

morning.'

Lorenzo almost tripped. 'Beg your pardon?'

The old monk nodded and cleared his throat. 'A young boy. This morning, when I went out to pick mail. He asked for you. Forgive me, but I asked him what was the matter. He said he had to deliver something, but only to you.'

Lorenzo raised an eyebrow. 'I mean no offence, Don Gianni. But are you sure he was looking for *me*?'

The old Dominican nodded again. 'Yes, Lorenzo, he said he had something to be delivered only to you. I suggested he comes inside and wait; I almost pitied him… poor creature. But he refused. Seemed in quite a rush, if you ask me. He said he'll come back tomorrow.'

And when were you planning to tell me this? Lorenzo bit his tongue. 'Do you know what it is he wanted to … to give me?'

The old priest shook his head. 'He ran away and said he'll return tomorrow. First thing after dawn, he said.'

Very organised and busy, for a street urchin. Lorenzo wished to ask Don Gianni if anyone else had been with him, or around. *I don't want to seem too keen. There must be some mistake.* Lorenzo shrugged. 'Well, I'll see to it tomorrow. Thank you.' *Did this little creature give you a name, perhaps?*

'*Kun imbierek*' Don Gianni ended, coughing and resuming his descent.

But Lorenzo was already at the top of the

stairs. He rushed into his cell and closed the door behind him. His mind was racing. His heart was pounding. Rarely had he felt so crushed by curiosity. The street children of Valletta were mostly orphans, or children of the lower-class. They roamed the city, begging or offering their shoe-shine services. Most of them, unfortunately, made their real pennies by delivering news to specific locations, or individuals… unofficially. This was an ill portent.

There must be some kind of mistake. Lorenzo slid into his cell, closing the door behind him. He started feeling dizzy. The cell spun, and he heard himself coughing. The wait till tomorrow was going to be long, and unpleasant. Lorenzo couldn't help wondering what old Don Gianni thought about a street urchin asking for him. He only prayed he didn't spread the word. Keeping himself calm and composed in front of his fellow priests was going to be a challenge. He already found it hard not to punch some of them in the face, under normal circumstances. And these weren't normal circumstances.

Delivered by a street boy… Lorenzo walked to his desk and sat down, leaning on his elbow. *Just wait till tomorrow.* He wiped his brow with a handkerchief and shut his eyes, wincing.

An image flashed in front of his inner eye.

'Don Roberto,' he said to himself, in a low voice. If the slightest rumour of this reached Don Roberto's ears, it would spread like wildfire. Lorenzo rushed out of his cell, his chest heaving and his legs shaking. The young priest spent most of his free time reading books. Lorenzo prayed, and ran to the priory's library like the devil was at his heels.

The Dominican library was a humble but cosy place. Lorenzo visited often, for the tranquillity it provided. Not this morning, however. He stepped in as calmly as he could. Two priests sat at different desks, scrutinising some sacred text.

He's not in here… Saint Anthony please, help me find him.

This morning, peace would only come once he lay hands on Don Roberto – hopefully not killing him in the process. *Wait. Just calm yourself, and wait.* Lorenzo caught his breath. He couldn't afford having anyone tell Don Roberto he was looking for him. It would eventually lead the young priest to seek him out, and Lorenzo would need to come up with some valid excuse. It was still too early for that.

Dinner with his brethren was business as usual. First, the noise of screeching cutlery accompanied by the occasional harsh cough of Don Gianni. Then, as plates were emptied and stomachs filled, discussions on the hottest topics of Church and State. Currently, there was the papal appointment of Monsignor Buhagiar as Apostolic Administrator of the Diocese of Malta, some months ago. Don Tumas Zarb, the Parish Priest for Valletta, had recently visited them and confirmed this piece of news. Lorenzo rolled his eyes at another priest who was airing his view on the matter. The whole table listened, as though he was inspired by the Divine.

'Seems like I am not the only one who's not intrigued by these arguments,' Don Roberto told Lorenzo. He was sitting right next to him, just like during lunch.

Lorenzo nodded. Just like during lunch, he was failing to find the right words or means to discover whether the young priest knew anything about the messenger boy. None of the other priests had looked twice at Lorenzo, so far. That was a good sign, but he couldn't rely solely on speculation.

Dear God, let it be that nobody knows.

'Are you feeling well?' Don Roberto was looking at him with that curious look of his.

Like you really care... 'Of course I am, Don Roberto. Thank you for your concern.' *God, guide me, please.*

'You look like you've seen a ghost. And you barely touched your plate.'

Lorenzo looked down at his plate. 'I'm not that hungry, no.'

Don Gianni coughed in the distance.

'You barely touched your plate at lunch,' went on the young priest.

You're too intelligent for your own good, Don Roberto. Lorenzo rubbed the palms of his hands against his knees. 'I'm just...'

'... The street urchins, I mean. They're increasing. How can you not have noticed?'

Lorenzo almost jolted.

The loud-voiced Don Salvu, three seats across, was speaking with Don Gianni – who was actually drowsing.

'Funny that you mention it,' jumped in Lorenzo. 'I did notice it, yes.' He made sure Don Salvu heard him.

Don Roberto gasped. He had surely noticed the oddity of his sudden interest in another conversation across the table. But Lorenzo could not lose the opportunity, it was a God-sent.

'Why, thank you Don Lorenzo.' Don Salvu looked at Lorenzo, who nodded back.

Lorenzo glanced at Don Roberto and said, 'The government doesn't seem too willing to help the church anymore.' God had just shown him how to get Don Roberto involved in this conversation. He fixed his eyes on Don Salvu again. 'Without the government's help, there's only so much we can do. Don't you think?'

'I don't think the government can really do anything about this,' joined in Don Roberto.

Lorenzo held back a grin. *Thank you, Lord, thank you!*

'Of course he cannot,' replied Don Salvu, sarcastically. 'That's nobody's duty but ours.'

Don Gianni was in the land of nod, his head bobbing. *This* was the right moment. God had heard Lorenzo's prayers, He was by his side. It was now or never. *Carpe diem*, as the Latin saying went. 'The streets of Valletta are filled with urchins, of late. Poor creatures...' he started.

Don Salvu was nodding fervently.

'It's been ages since I came across one,' said Don Roberto.

Lorenzo looked at him. The young priest was lost in the heated discussion, which probably meant he was speaking the truth. The dark clouds inside Lorenzo's mind suddenly dissipated. He wanted to just stand up, sing and dance. He couldn't help but sigh in relief. The risk he had taken proved worth it. Don Roberto knew nothing about the street boy.

'I'll be off, brothers,' said Lorenzo, getting up in as much a composed manner as he possibly could. 'I'm enjoying the topic, but my eyes are heavy.' He wished them all a good night, and took off for the peace of his cell.

Inside, he closed the door and leaned against it. *Thank you, Lord.* He said the Vespers and laid his body and heart to sleep.

Lorenzo opened his eyes.

'First thing after dawn...' the voice inside his head was still saying.

He recognised it. Don Gianni had told him yesterday morning, when quoting the street boy. Lorenzo looked at the small window of his cell. It was clearly morning, but the sun's rays were still weak. He flew off his bed, washed his face, and then rushed downstairs. Don Anthony was coming up the stairs, carrying mail.

Not Don Gianni... oh dear God, thank you! Lorenzo nodded to the priest and rushed outside.

God was on his side, guiding and protecting him. This was a clear sign that He had an important mission for Lorenzo. The priest folded his arms and waited. As long as God was with him, he could wait all day.

Not for too long, apparently.

A young boy, no more than ten years old, was running towards him. Lorenzo looked around. *Strada San Domenico* was as silent as a graveyard.

'Don Lorenzo Testaferrata?'

Lorenzo flashed a warm smile, despite the morning chill. 'I am,' he whispered.

'This is for you.' The boy handed him a piece of paper.

'God bless you, child.'

The boy was out of sight before Lorenzo finished making the sign of the Cross to bless him.

Dark indeed… He unfolded the piece of paper, hands almost shaking.

The handwriting was neat.

Don Lorenzo read. Don Lorenzo gaped. His whole body was shaking now, not just his hands.

Father Lorenzo Testaferrata,

You cannot save Valletta, just like you couldn't Mdina 10 years ago.

But for old times' sake, I'm willing to give you a chance.

Come to the Chapel of the Bones, this Friday, eleven o'clock in the evening.

L.

15.

They were at Mr Bonavia's shop, the taxidermist in *Strada Mercanti*. Archibald looked down at what he was holding in his left hand. 'My cane!'

Attard shot him a glare, his bushy eyebrows haunting. Archibald excused himself, and they both turned their attention back to the taxidermist.

'I can't help but wonder,' said the old taxidermist, coughing without covering his mouth. He walked towards Archibald. 'Where did you get that cane from? I think it is mine.'

Attard rolled his eyes. Archibald took a step back.

A quacking sound blared right behind him. He turned to look at an embalmed duck staring at him. It quacked again.

How in the name of ...?

'Mr Bonavia, please.' Attard cleared his throat, loudly.

Mr Bonavia turned back to the Maltese Inspector, and nodded. 'Yes. I'm pretty sure that walking stick's mine. Sorry, why were you here, again?'

'We're investigating the recent murders in Valletta. And the gouging of the eyes,' repeated Attard, excitedly.

Mr Attard losing his patience? Archibald lowered his gaze to look at his left hand once more. He held the shiny cane right within his firm fist. *No, this is not how it happened.*

'... Yes of course, I would be willing to testify to that. It is impossible for someone to perform such a gruesome act in the middle of the night. Yes sure. Not unless they were so keen on gaining attention. Of course, sure, yes, I can testify...'

Archibald forced himself to look at Mr Bonavia. He was sure he remembered him saying that already. He had lost his cane *before* they came here, however. The old taxidermist leaned on one of his side desks, and coughed violently. Archibald noticed how ugly this poor creature was; like a withered tree, wrinkled and trembling all over.

'You can barely hold your arm straight, let alone pluck eyes out of their socket,' he heard himself saying, before he could stop himself.

Attard's eyes almost popped out of his head.

No! Archibald was sure he had not said that when they were here before. *Before?*

There was a kind of haziness to the atmosphere. Everything felt like they had been smoking opium. Funnily enough, it was barely bothering him. He found himself struggling to hold back laughter. *What a waste of time!* He looked down at his left hand. The cane was gone.

All of a sudden, he was alone in a very dark room. The moon's rays barely made it through the louvered window. The curtains were torn, drifting slightly with the soft breeze. They looked like a hag, or some kind of beggar, reaching out to the empty room.

Archibald looked at the piece of paper in his left hand. *What is this?* He took out a weird round glass out of his breast pocket. It was silvery white, just like the moon. *How in the name of…?* He turned to the small parchment in his left hand. He could read it somehow, even though the handwriting was a mess – and in Maltese.

'I'm very sorry. But she left me no choice, Joseph,' Archibald read. 'Now what is that supposed to mean?'

The ground shook suddenly, and the piece of paper slipped from his fingers. Archibald swore and tried to grasp it.

He stopped. There was fresh blood on his hands. He gasped for breath.

The ground shook again. Archibald lost his footing and fell backwards.

He felt himself sitting up again and heard

himself yelping.

He opened his eyes.

He was back on his bed in the darkness of his room, at Morell's. He was heaving and sweating. The candle on his bedside table was spent. He gave his eyes a moment to settle to the darkness.

Jesus! What was that? Felt so real…

He fidgeted with the candle, and lit the wick again. It reminded him of the moon-like orb in the dream. He made for his pocket watch beside the candle. *Three o'clock…*

Everything was so quiet! A slight breeze from the window reminded him of the haunting curtains from the dream. He sighed and rubbed his eyes, then let his head fall back on the pillow. His thoughts drifted back to what he just dreamt. He smiled at how vivid the duck appeared. A slight bitterness came over him when he remembered the cane. The moon-like orb still fascinated him. He did have a creative brain; it helped colour much of his childhood. It took him back to the dark room in Mr Joseph and Anna's house… and the piece of paper. He sighed anxiously.

Following the eavesdropping experience, Archibald had desperately returned to *Ta' Michele*'s shop in *Strada Mercanti.* Luckily, Inspector Attard had met with an acquaintance and Archibald found him still there. He winced now, remembering how irritated Attard had sounded – despite his composed voice. Together they had walked to Mr Bonavia's, the taxidermist of Valletta. Archibald sighed heavily at the reminder of how fruitless their visit had been. Come morning, he had to meet Attard to discuss it further.

As if there is anything else to discuss…

It was eight days since they found Ms Anna's wretched body in *Strada Vescovo*. Yet they were no closer to a solution to whatever was going on. The investigation was literally going nowhere. This meant that he had to share his piece of information. The conversation between Pawlu and his friend could still be unrelated to the case – though very suspicious. Yet the contents of the letter he had found at Mr Joseph's house… that deserved more attention, to say the very least.

Attard should know. Archibald didn't know what held him back, really. He had just followed his gut feeling, initially. He stretched towards his bedside table and opened the drawer, careful not to shake the candle too much.

'I'm very sorry. But she left me no choice, Joseph,' he read the English translation on the back.

Who had written this? The 'Joseph' after a comma meant it was either signed by Joseph himself, or else the letter was for Joseph. Archibald doubted Mr Joseph was even literate.

If only we had more time to discover that… He winced, remembering Don Lorenzo's grand entrance at Mr Joseph's house. Whoever had written the letter, referred to 'she' like she was some kind of threat. Archibald deduced that 'she' was Ms Anna. According to the old couple, who claimed to know the siblings, Anna was anything but a threat. Nobody else came forward to assert that opinion, however. So, as far as he was concerned, Ms Anna might've been playing with fire and got burnt.

His heart told him otherwise, however. Ms Anna was another victim to this lunatic murderer who plagued Valletta, and she deserved justice. As for her brother, Archibald's heart told him he had not killed his sister. He wouldn't have caused so much havoc and noise if he had wanted to escape Valletta stealthily. Someone or something scared him off.

Archibald nodded. *Mr Attard needs to know.*

Familiar faces from Britain suddenly appeared, scolding him for not being able to work in a team. He heard himself arguing in favour of his great skills and performance results. He blew out the candle and shut his eyes, before memories of the past returned to haunt him. In no time, he was in a dreamless sleep.

'I can't believe it,' Attard was saying.
'Well, it doesn't make much sense,' replied Archibald, shaking his head slightly.

As he had correctly assumed, Attard wanted to discuss the visit at the taxidermist's. What Archibald hadn't predicted, however, was a knock at his door as early as half-past six in the morning. One of the hotel's servants came to tell him his colleague was waiting for him in the breakfast hall downstairs.

Morell's breakfast chamber was empty of guests, save for the two of them and the servants on the morning shift. Archibald couldn't help notice how, despite the early hour, the sun's rays were already bright.

'This is becoming even more difficult, every day,' Attard went on, wiping his mouth on a napkin.

'I have to admit,' Archibald said, fidgeting with the piece of paper in his pocket. 'I'm clueless. Mr Bonavia is too weak to have performed any of those atrocities. I mean, did you see how his hands tremble?'

Attard nodded, his eyes distant. 'It could've been an act, too.'

Archibald let out a long sigh, shaking his head. 'How do you mean?'

'If I were in his position, but also guilty, I'd put on an act in front of the police.'

Archibald shrugged. 'The poor creature's in his late fifties… God bless him to have made it this far!' Archibald frowned. 'Even if he had some crazy reason to want to kill someone… why now? I see no motive.' *Why are you so intent on blaming the poor man?* To him, the old taxidermist was definitely not who they were looking for. But Attard seemed so adamant in finding him guilty. Archibald thought his colleague was in denial. He could not admit they were failing. Maybe the piece of paper had to wait… for now.

How can I say this politely? God help me… 'I think

we've failed, Inspector Attard…'

Attard raised an eyebrow and looked at Archibald. 'Failed?'

Archibald bit his lips, nodding.

'Shall I go tell the Superintendent this case is closed?' he said mockingly.

Archibald frowned. *You're really not making this any easier.*

Attard shook his head, blinking. 'Then don't speak such nonsense!'

Archibald fought the urge to get off his chair and storm out of Morell's. Instead, he inhaled deeply, drumming his fingers on the table and looking away. He crumpled the paper in his fingers inside his pocket. *Not today. Sorry, Mr Attard, but I don't think you're ready.* 'I just … I don't think Mr Bonavia is our man,' he said, as calmly as he could. He heard Attard sigh.

'I understand. But my thoughts differ,' replied Attard in a low voice.

Fine! Archibald turned to look at his colleague again. 'On what grounds… pray, tell me? You say Mr Bonavia was putting on an act, because that's what you said you would do. So that makes him guilty… and you think *that* is enough for the Superintendent?'

Attard's expression remained blank.

'I thought so,' Archibald ended, standing up, picking up his hat and storming out of the hall. He went to his room, almost running up the stairs.

Peace and quiet was all he needed, right now.

He shut the door behind him and made for the small desk in the corner of his room. *I need to think.* He took out the piece of paper from his pocket; flattening it and putting it back safely in the drawer. He drew another piece of paper from the small stack provided by the hotel. *Mr Joseph*, he thought, taking out his personal slate pencil and scribbling the name down.

Ms Anna, Don Lorenzo, Pawlu, Falcon's Perch… victims without eyeballs…

Archibald let his mind run wild. It took him through all the people he had met since setting foot here. He wrote them down. Every single one of them. His mind immediately took him back to yesterday morning's mishap: the cane. Remembering how he was robbed made him frown.

Pawlu and his friend… He knew too little, and could only make baseless assumptions. 'They sounded on friendly terms. Of that I'm certain,' he whispered to himself. Then wrote down the word 'gang' next to their names.

Valletta and London had a number of traits in common. From what he'd heard, gangs were one of them. Archibald knew that, unfortunately, this type of people always had more access to whatever went on in a town or city. Those who locked themselves up in the chambers of authoritative and bureaucratised lives were usually more alienated, and blind to see the truth.

'Gangs…' he said, resting his open palms on the desk and leaning on his arms. 'We've looked for acquaintances and neighbours of the victims. But gangs...'

Following the Superintendent's orders, they wore no uniforms during the entire investigation. But Valletta was too small. By now, Archibald suspected most of the city already knew about Constable Whitlock from Britain. As for Inspector Attard, he was certainly one of Malta's best officers and could not be a stranger to anyone. There was no way they could approach Pawlu's gang, or *any g*ang in Valletta, without causing havoc or unrest. Besides, getting involved with gangs was too lowly.

Unless...

Archibald raised an eyebrow. After gangs, the best source of information was... he frowned. *Attard was right.* Don Lorenzo could prove useful. He wrote 'gangs of Valletta' next to Pawlu's name, then drew a short horizontal line to the right and wrote 'Don Lorenzo' next to it. *'M'hemmx x'taghmel,'* he told himself, remembering the Maltese saying when one had few options.

Unfortunately, Don Lorenzo was the best and only link they had. The irony was almost tragic. Archibald had to accept that, or else he might as well give up the investigation. He harrumphed, bothered by the realisation that Attard was actually right.

16.

Something about *Strada Stretta* was strange, this evening. It was quiet. The silence beneath her balcony reminded her of a graveyard.

A graveyard, where all the dead go to rest.

But not her. She did not even deserve such a place. The deepest pits of Hell were reserved for souls like hers.

This is the best way. Rita took a step forward, careful not to slip off the window ledge. At least she still wanted to end it with some kind of dignity, ironically enough. *Strada Stretta* waited below. It reminded her what drove her to this point.

Following her dear father's death, and her mother's hopeless salary, *Strada Stretta* had promised her some hope. Only because she was foolish enough to believe the stories, of course. '*Strada Stretta* is easy money…' people in the *Manderaggio* would say. Her mother and those old friends of hers, however, always spoke the opposite. They would say it was the devil's den; Lucifer's own pit. Rita should have listened to them more. But as the Maltese saying goes, everyone is wiser after the event.

She still remembered how Mr Calleja had smiled at her, on that first night three weeks ago. *Strada Stretta* had been like a goddess, and Mr Calleja its priest. Rita was so foolish! He had not smiled at her beautiful eyes or soul. That much she was certain, now. He only looked at her body like a relic; a means to an end - to summon more believers to his temple. In a matter of days, the true intent of Mr Calleja had come to light, and Rita's blindfold came off. He was a man, not a priest. And her mother and her withering friends had been right all along: *Strada Stretta* was not a temple, but the underworld. It devoured souls. Rita was one of its most essential and powerful servants. Chained, till the day her own soul dissipated into the nothingness she became.

It ends here… No one would witness her final act. Only the full moon, with its silver rays striking at everything they touched. She shut her eyes. A harsh dry breeze swept past her and she found herself clasping the jambs by her side. Despite her decision, her body still followed its basic instincts, and fought for survival. *It ends here.*

She took another step forward, releasing her grip from the left-hand side of the window. She thought she could already hear the demons and the souls of the damned, calling her from Hell. *At least, I won't be alone anymore.* Rita unclasped all her fingers from the right-hand jamb. *Now, I'm like one of papà's boats, adrift with the wind.*

This, her final act, was the only hope she had to save her younger sister, Lucia, from eventually following the same path. This was going to save Lucia, so Rita was more than willing to do it.

'Heaven and earth!' a distant voice said.

'I'm beyond any of those, now,' Rita heard herself saying.

'*Kristu!*' the voice said again, panicking.

Rita smiled slightly. She had known panic once. It had controlled her for days and nights. *Not anymore.* She took a deep breath, then pushed herself slightly forward.

Something swiftly hit her beneath the belly. A grip so strong it almost made her gasp for breath. It pulled her backwards, pulsing and warm, and Rita felt herself falling backwards.

Instinctively, she opened her eyes. *I'm… where…* She blinked.

Her back hurt a little. A man was on top of her, on his knees. His face was familiar, and he was smiling.

'Missy…' he said.

Rita craned her neck slightly.

'Missy, what under heaven and earth were

you doing?' he asked.

'Filippo?' Rita mumbled, rubbing her nape.

He nodded, his face suddenly beaming.

'Am I ... are you dead too?'

Filippo raised an eyebrow. 'No. You were standing on the window ledge and ...' he said, pointing to the aperture behind him. 'Missy. Whatever were you thinking?'

Rita frowned. 'How dare you?' she bellowed, pushing him away and standing up.

The room started spinning. Everything turned blurry. Rita raised a shaking hand to her forehead, and felt herself drifting. She thought she saw Filippo come between her and the floor of her bedroom. Then everything went dark.

'Come, sit on the bed, missy. You must be unwell,' said Filippo.

Rita felt his firm grip again, dragging her to the bed. She sat but wouldn't lie down. Not in this state, and with a stranger next to her.

'Do you have any water here?' Filippo kneeled in front of her, by the bedside.

Rita waved her hand, hoping to also push him away in the process. 'Just leave me alone, please. Don't you know it's impolite to enter a lady's room without invitation?'

She heard him laugh.

'You still talk a lot, considering the terrible state you're in,' he said in a light tone.

What is so funny? Her head hurt and she could barely open her eyes. It was still dark outside.

How long have I been out?

A knock at the door made her jump.

'What in God's name do you think you're doing, Isabella!'

That terrible voice! She had to stop living, now, or else… Her eyes bulged out. She got off the bed as though the sheets were on fire.

'I'm sorry, Mr Calleja, he's just a …' she paused and blinked. 'Mr Calleja?' Rita rubbed her eyes. There was no one else but Filippo kneeling in front of her, signalling her to stay quiet.

'Missy?'

Rita raised her hand to her head, and fell back on the bed. 'What is the matter with me?'

'It's going to be alright, missy. It's just us in here. You hit your head when you fell, and you need to rest.'

Rita glared at him. He flashed a smile and winked at her.

'How did you… what are you doing?' she asked, eyeing him. *How does he manage to keep that smile?*

Filippo shrugged. 'I could ask you the same question.'

'That's none of your business, sir.'

He chuckled. 'Sir? So we're back to fake politeness then, missy?' He put on a melancholic expression. 'I must admit, you're even more attractive when you're angry.'

Rita shrugged, and gave him her back.

'Unless you want to talk about it, of course…'

Rita paused. She sighed and shook her head,

then walked to her bed and sat in front of the mirror.

'I never understood why people did... that kind of thing,' he went on.

Rita tugged at a braid in her hair, pretending to ignore him.

'Until, one day, I felt like that too. It's... ' he sighed heavily, sitting at the foot of the bed.

Rita stopped fidgeting with her hair. 'You've no idea, sir. Please, just leave,' she said.

A knock at the door. Rita looked at Filippo, who looked slightly pale, all of a sudden.

'Tell them you're occupied, missy.'

Rita raised an eyebrow. *So I didn't just imagine this one, too.* 'Occupied, dear,' she yelled at the door, then narrowed her eyes. 'So that *was* the door, now?' *What's he so afraid of?*

'Yes, it was. And thank you, missy,' he said, smiling and getting off the bed.

Rita's gaze followed him as he walked to the door and turned the knob slowly. He looked at her, raised his index finger to his lips and took a peep outside. A whiff of stale food and alcohol crept inside, but no sound. The Falcon's Perch slumbered.

Rita looked at the window, still open. *It is dawn soon...* 'Are you hiding from someone, sir?' she asked, flatly.

Filippo shut the door behind him, and shrugged coolly. 'Me, hiding? Of course not, missy. I just want to make sure no one comes in. Want to spend the rest of the night with you, that's all.'

Is he mocking me? 'As long as you behave,' she heard herself saying. *Rita!* She blushed, stopping herself from raising her hand to her mouth.

Filippo flashed a smile. 'I will not move from here,' he replied, sitting on the stool beside her chest of drawers. 'Unless I see you approaching that window again, of course. There's no way in heaven I can let you do *that*.'

She shot a glare at him. 'Why would you care?'

'Missy… why would someone as beautiful as you want to end their life?'

'That's none of your business.' She walked to her bed, sat down and gave him her back. Somehow, she didn't feel tired.

'What are you running from, missy?'

'I could ask you the same question, sir. But you promised to behave and stay quiet. So please do.'

Filippo sniggered. 'You've got quite a nerve. I like that. Go ahead, ask me. I'll answer any of your questions, if you do the same.'

Rita fought the urge to look at him. 'Why are you here?'

'I'm staying as far away from Mr Calleja as I possibly can.'

Rita turned to look at him before she could control herself. 'Well, if that is the case, this is the last place you should be in, sir.'

He raised his hands, palms facing the ceiling.

'Why are you here, really? Don't you know The Falcon's Perch is Mr Calleja's?'

He smiled. 'I'm not dumb, missy. Yet, it is now

my turn to ask a question.'

How arrogant! Rita looked away, turning her eyes to the window in front of her. 'You seem to take things very lightly. Why should I discuss anything with you?' She started untying her hair. 'I need to sleep soon. You must leave.'

He shook his head, and raised his index finger. 'Why missy, I already answered a question. Now it's my turn to ask. We can stop this immediately after that, if you like.'

What is he up to? Running from Mr Calleja, and hiding inside my room?

'What could bring such a beautiful lady as yourself to attempt jumping out of a window?'

Rita rolled her eyes and shrugged.

'How did you end up here?' he insisted, waving his hand at the darkness around them.

'I have to help the people I love,' she murmured. 'Satisfied?'

Filippo raised an eyebrow. 'We share something in common then, it seems. And apparently we both don't have much choice, but to stay…'

'Who are *you* helping?'

He didn't answer.

Rita looked at him teasingly. 'It's your turn to answer, sir.'

Filippo smiled. She liked the way his hazel eyes shone when he smiled. Something about his scruffy dark hair also made it easier to look at him without shaking.

'It is my turn indeed. Why am I here? I like

your company.' His eyes were fixed on hers.

Rita didn't look away this time. *He just sat there. Is this some kind of new game - trying to attract me?*

'My turn, missy.' He winked. 'Are you afraid of Mr Calleja?'

For a while, Rita kept her silence. 'He was very nice to me, on the first few nights, of course. Then he started to show his true colours. He's outrageous, scary… ugly. I believe he's a dangerous man. He has threatened me many a time since I first came here.' She turned her eyes to the window in front of her, and clasped her hands in each other. 'I never really bothered much. But two nights ago, he scared me indeed. He stank of alcohol, and came waving his belt-knife in my face, saying he'd ruin it if I ever tried to escape.' Rita found herself weeping and heaving. *Rita, you cannot let him he see you cry!* 'Sir, you really don't need to hear this.'

Filippo walked to the window, and sat right on the sill opposite her. He was still smiling faintly.

Rita looked up at him. *Why is he being so kind?* 'Please sir, you must leave.'

Filippo raised his left hand, palm facing her, and said nothing.

'You've been coming here, to this room, despite all the dangers of facing Mr Calleja,' she added. 'You've been using me. Is that it?'

Filippo sighed resignedly. 'At first I was, yes.'

Honest, at least. 'I'm afraid,' she said before she

could stop herself.

Filippo looked moved. 'Missy…'

'He tells me that a lot of those who spend the night with me… he…' *Rita, what in heaven's name are you saying!*

'Missy, jumping out of the window was not going to help put things right.'

Rita looked away. 'Once I'm gone, Mr Calleja cannot threaten me anymore. And Lucia… my sister will be safe.'

'You're just confused, missy.'

'Why are you doing this, anyway?'

'What?'

Rita puffed. 'Pretending to care.'

'Why is it so hard to believe someone cares, Isabella?'

'My name's Rita.' She gasped and raised her hand to her mouth. *Oh God!* She flew off the bed as if he had just thrown a bucket of ice at her. 'Please, just leave. I'm tired,' she whispered, walking away and trembling.

'That's a nice name, missy.'

She sighed heavily. 'Sir. You're a good man,' she sat down on the opposite side of bed, giving him her back. 'Whatever you believed you could find in this room, isn't here. You deserve better.'

'As do you, missy. What makes you think otherwise?'

'You don't know me, sir. Please, just leave.'

'I know your name now. And that you only stepped into this rut to help the ones you love. You do not have to worry; your secrets are safe with me.'

Why can't he just go away? She wished she could scream at him, but was afraid it would wake the whole inn. She was crying again.

'I want to help you.'

She fought the urge to look at him, with tears in her eyes. 'Just leave, sir, before I get Mr Calleja for you.'

Filippo sighed. 'That's not fair, missy. And it would only get us *both* in trouble.'

'Leave,' she ended flatly.

Something convinced him. Filippo shook his head, and submissively made for the door. Rita didn't budge. She heard him sigh and close the door behind him.

The breeze died down; very typical of the last days of May. It would soon start to be so hot that no open windows or drawn curtains would kill the heat. Come August, Malta would be like hell's very own stove. No wonder its rock was yellow.

With such sombre thoughts, Filippo darted out The Falcon's Perch. He kept looking over his shoulder as he made his way home. The first light of dawn emerged from behind the dull-coloured, limestone inns and brothels of *Strada Stretta.* While Valletta slowly woke up to another sunny, bustling Friday, this was the only street that slumbered. Of course, it was up all night; fulfilling dreams and desires like no other place would. *Strada Stretta* was home to Jazz, binging, and all the new pleasures the 19th century promised to provide.

Even God rested on the seventh day of providence, when He created the world ... Filippo staggered. He wasn't drunk. He was confused. Bumping into Mr Calleja wouldn't be ideal right now.

Rita was proving to be quite stubborn, and it made him sad. Still, she was different to the others. Filippo looked around warily. He was sure he heard footsteps. The street was empty. *I need to rest, or I'll soon be imagining Calleja… or the devil himself.*

He wished his brain would conjure the image of Rita, instead of these sounds that made him jump every couple of metres. Why did the brain always have to bring up images of one's fears, rather than desires? It frustrated Filippo. Pondering on such thoughts, he resumed his way home.

17.

The room was cold, damp and inhospitable. *And it's still bloody May*, Archibald thought, scowling at the structure of Don Lorenzo's cell. He found it odd how the priest had preferred they speak in the privacy of his cell. *I hope you have something useful.* Archibald glared at him. *You could have at least offered us a glass of water.*

The priest was blabbering about Valletta, Attard listened and nodded at intervals. Archibald bobbed his head every now and then, hoping the priest didn't direct any question at him.

'The devil decided to strike hard at us,' said Attard in a solemn tone.

Archibald hoped his colleague's dramatic

attitude was only to please Don Lorenzo. He understood his tactic, yet still found it hard to speak rubbish himself.

'God is punishing Valletta,' replied the priest.

Archibald fought hard not to roll his eyes. He sighed and nodded slightly, instead. *How does Attard manage to fake all that interest?* He forced a grim frown, even though he felt like laughing at the priest's tragic zealousness. 'Indeed,' he said, as gravely as he could muster.

The priest eyed him. 'There is a lot of sin in our midst. This is the purging, unfortunately for all of us.'

Archibald raised an eyebrow, stiffening on his seat. 'And how would you go about *purging* the city, if I may have your thoughts?' he asked, narrowing his eyes.

Attard nodded nervously at his colleague's question, and cleared his throat.

'I have continuously been urging our dear parishioners to hold on to prayer and fasting. It gives glory to Our Lord to see His people's devotion reignited.'

'So are you saying God is doing this?'

Attard didn't look too happy.

The priest's expression was blank. 'It is thanks to harsh and difficult times, that the lost flock reunites and sets about to discover God again,' he replied piously.

'Father,' started Attard in his usual calm tone – only after having shot Archibald a glare - 'We have come seeking your guidance.'

Don Lorenzo lifted his head, and smiled faintly at the inspector. 'If the Lord grants me wisdom, for I am His humble servant.'

Right! Archibald covered his mouth with his hand, pretending to be leaning on his elbow. He didn't know whether the priest had seen him grinning. He wasn't sure he cared, either. He kept reminding himself of why they were here, and the little to no other choices they had. Attard was explaining how the police force was doing its best to find the culprit behind the murders. He told Don Lorenzo how they had spoken to anyone related – by blood or contact – to all the victims.

And unfortunately, you're the only link we've got left…

'It is a good idea you don't wear those uniforms of yours, when questioning people,' said the priest.

As if that were up to you to decide. Archibald frowned.

'So, do you think someone from the lower classes could be behind all this?' asked the priest, eyeing Attard.

Attard nodded slightly. 'We do not know from where to begin, however.'

'The disappearances of Mr Joseph and his sister worry me greatly,' said Don Lorenzo. 'His sister, dear Ms Anna, was very gentle and kind-hearted. It saddens me, and I pray for her soul every day.'

Better pray for the living… Archibald sighed.

'What about her brother, Mr Joseph?' asked

Mr Attard.

Don Lorenzo turned his eyes on him. 'He was a simpleton. He didn't deserve this.'

'*Was*?' Archibald fixed his eyes on the priest.

Don Lorenzo shrugged. 'I pray every day for him to be still alive. But the poor creature could barely take care of himself.'

Attard cleared his throat. 'Would he have had any reason to kill his sister, do you think?'

The priest looked shocked.

Archibald flexed his fingers. *I'm very sorry. But she left me no choice, Joseph…* The words from the letter to Mr Joseph. He was grateful his colleague and Don Lorenzo were too focused on each other to notice his discomfort. A little voice inside his head scolded him once again. Seeing Don Lorenzo tense, however, was worth it.

'What makes you think Mr Joseph would do such a foul thing?'

It was Mr Attard's turn to shrug. 'He ran away from his own household, Father. Would you have any idea where he could've run to, perhaps?'

Don Lorenzo shook his head and leaned slightly backwards.

'So, you had no further contact with him since the morning of the 12th?'

The priest sighed. 'I wish I had,' he said, sombrely. 'The poor fellow and his sister didn't deserve this.'

'Our task is to find the person responsible for these murders. What else can you tell us about Ms Anna?'

The priest locked his eyes on Archibald for a while, wetting his lips. 'Despite the harsh life she endured, Ms Anna was amongst the most exemplary of my parishioners.'

Their silence was enough indication for the priest to go on. He got off his chair and walked next to the window of his cell. The sun stroked his dark skin, and his brown eyes seemed to shine for a moment. His hands were clasped behind his back, and he just stood there for a while, in silence.

'Ms Anna was always a good catholic,' he started saying. 'Taking care of Mr Joseph ever since their parents died, some years ago. She attended Mass daily, and confession regularly. She confided in me, quite often.'

Attard and Archibald glanced at each other.

He's hiding something. 'But…?' Archibald moved on his seat.

Don Lorenzo sighed heavily and gave them his back again. 'But things changed… recently.'

'Recently?'

'Yes. She became more distant over the last few weeks, before she was killed. She stopped coming for confession, and didn't come to Mass any more. Not even on Sunday! When I visited their home for the ritual blessings, after Easter, she wasn't even at home. Mr Joseph had no idea of her whereabouts, of course. From what I managed to gather, however, she had found a new job, and was making new friends. The bad kind.'

Attard narrowed his eyes. 'How do you mean?'

The priest glanced at them over his shoulders. 'What I'm about to tell you are just rumours. But they might prove helpful.'

Anything at this point,' said Attard, keenly.

'I think Anna was seeing someone, a few weeks before her murder.'

'Name?'

The priest shook his head. 'I wish I knew, Constable Whitlock. I never laid eyes on the fellow myself.'

'Is this the man you meant by *the bad kind*?' inquired Attard.

Don Lorenzo nodded. 'Again, this is all according to what I heard through the grapevine. It might not be true, but I heard this man was some poor bastard, who got lucky.'

'Got lucky?'

'Yes, Inspector Attard. It seems he inherited something valuable. Not by blood, however. These are just rumours, unfortunately. I tried to get something out of Mr Joseph before he disappeared, but the poor creature had literally no idea of what happened to his sister.' The priest took back his seat.

Attard stroked his chin.

Archibald stared like he was reading into something which was not there. *A cup of tea would be nice, Don Lorenzo.* He buried his head in his hands.

'On Sunday, 9th of May, I saw her at Mass

again,' said Don Lorenzo, almost making them jump.

Archibald looked at him. *Maybe you're not as evil as I thought...*

'That's the Sunday before she was murdered, right?' added the Inspector.

The priest nodded, and a faint smile appeared on his face. 'I was so happy to see her back at church.'

'I can imagine,' said Attard, smiling slightly.

'I say unto you,' Lorenzo said in a pious tone. 'That likewise joy shall be in heaven over one sinner that repenteth, more than over ninety and nine just persons, which need no repentance.'

'Luke, chapter fifteen,' said Archibald. *If we're really going to quote the Holy Bible...*

Attard's expression was blank.

'You know the Bible well, Constable Whitlock.'

Certainly more than you do. Archibald nodded. 'Was she accompanied by this lucky gentleman, maybe? Did you speak to her? That Sunday, I mean.'

The priest's face turned sombre again. 'No. She was with Mr Joseph, as usual. But they were on a seat at the back of the basilica. Definitely not usual for Ms Anna. But at least she was there. I tried to speak to her, yes, immediately after Mass, but they were both gone.'

'That's two days before she was found dead,' noted Attard, gaping slightly.

'Yes,' ended Don Lorenzo, nodding slowly

and clasping his hands together.

A short silence followed.

Archibald frowned. *If Ms Anna's seeing somebody were just a rumour, why did you even bother mentioning it to us?*

'So you did not have any further contact with Ms Anna, or Mr Joseph, after that. Right?' Attard broke the silence.

Don Lorenzo sighed profoundly. 'Unfortunately not. I only spoke to Mr Joseph on the morning of the 12th.'

The first time we met… Archibald rubbed at his right temple. *This priest's heart is in the right place, despite all that self-righteousness and piety. Attard was bloody right…*

'One thing is certain,' went on the priest, looking down at his feet. 'On that Sunday, Ms Anna looked troubled.'

'Troubled?' Attard narrowed his eyes.

The priest sighed. 'I do not know what changed her. Her life was never easy, to be fair. But before all this, she was different. She always had faith.'

You're blaming Ms Anna's newfound love for it, despite how much you said it was just a rumour. Archibald sensed regret in the priest's voice. He looked at his colleague, who seemed lost in thought. His mind raced back to the piece of paper inside his room, at Morell's. Attard was looking at him.

'She took her life, and her relationship with the Lord, very seriously.'

Archibald leaned slightly forward.

'So why, and how, she so suddenly sold her soul to the devil… I do not know.'

You could've at least not given up on her so easily… Archibald grimaced. *Despite all that, you've proved to be quite helpful.* Archibald suppressed a frown. It wasn't easy to admit Attard had been right. This man of the cloth, this *catholic*, had so far proved to be their most fruitful contact in all this cursed and clueless investigation. 'Thank you… Father,' he whispered.

Attard turned to look at him, but Archibald avoided his eyes.

Don Lorenzo smiled a little. 'It is a sad story,' he ended.

Attard and Archibald both nodded.

'We have already taken too much of your time,' said the Maltese inspector, politely getting off his chair. 'Unless there's anything else…'

'Unfortunately not, Inspector,' said the priest, sighing and shaking his head. 'It would be nice to say a short prayer for Ms Anna and Mr Joseph.'

Attard took his seat again.

Archibald commanded his whole body to stay still as the priest stood up, opened his arms, and uttered a prayer. Attard replied in almost perfect unison. Archibald simply nodded every now and then, avoiding the priest's eyes.

'Go in peace,' ended Don Lorenzo, making the sign of the Cross and waving his hands at them.

'He could have at least given us something to drink,' said Archibald in a light tone.

They were heading back to Morell's. Attard had walked in silence, but now he was looking at Archibald.

'It is evident Don Lorenzo believes Ms Anna's death came about as a result of her secret relationship with this mysterious man,' he said.

Archibald nodded and sniggered. 'I cannot understand why all the hesitance to admit it was *not* a rumour, however.'

Attard looked at his feet. 'The answer to that question requires thought and discussion, Constable Whitlock. We need to replenish our energies. I'm famished.'

'And thirsty,' added Archibald, wincing under the sun. He took out his pocket watch. It was almost noon. He wiped his brow and frowned.

'Is there something bothering you, constable?'

Archibald returned the watch to its pocket. *Does it show so much?* 'It's Don Lorenzo,' he lied. 'He has…'

'Surprised us?' Attard was smiling.

'I…' Archibald sighed and looked away. His mind couldn't stop picturing the thing inside his cabinet, in the room. It was not easy to admit Attard was right. 'Yes, he did indeed.'

Attard was still smiling. 'He surprised me too, you know? I wasn't expecting him to be helpful.'

'You did well. You're good at it,' joked Archibald, chuckling nervously.

Attard nodded.

I'm very sorry. But she left me no choice, Joseph. The words from the letter echoed in his head. Archibald cleared his throat. 'Inspector Attard, there's… something. Something you might want to… *need* to see. There's something I must show you.' He flexed his fingers.

'Oh?'

'We need to discuss it. Over lunch, please, because I'm famished. If you do not mind, of course,' said Archibald, voice slightly trembling.

'Sure, constable.' He narrowed his eyes and gave a quick look around. 'Let's meet in Morell's parlour, after dinner. I have some other errands to run in the city. And both our minds need some time to rest and think. Besides, it's quieter then.'

'The less chance of eavesdropping, the better.' Archibald nodded.

'Yes. See you this evening, Morell's parlour. Have a good afternoon,' ended Attard, tipping his top hat and setting off.

Archibald nodded and smiled faintly. He sighed and headed for Morell's. *I'm very sorry. But she left me no choice, Joseph…* He couldn't get the words out of his head.

Hopefully, lunch and a good nap might shed some light on how he had to proceed.

18.

Lorenzo shut the door. He leaned with his back against it, and took a deep breath in. Inspector Attard and the English constable had just left his cell. It wasn't easy, but he did it. It wasn't a morning he would ever look back and smile at, of that he was certain. Still, he would remember it as the day he managed to get the police off his trail.

They'll leave me in peace, finally. Lorenzo smiled slightly. He walked to his desk and dived into his chair, looking at the two empty chairs that held them for almost the entire morning. They felt almost haunting, even now.

Lorenzo's mind went back to the conversation he had just had. He felt a sudden tinge of guilt as Ms Anna's face crept in front of his inner eye.

Beautiful Ms Anna, with her flowing black hair, and dark green eyes. She possessed a simple yet powerful approach towards life, such as Lorenzo had never seen.

Until she decided to give her soul to the devil… Lorenzo frowned. *Dragging her brother behind her, poor creature.* Lorenzo would never know what she had gotten herself into. But nothing ever went well for those who dealt with the devil, anyway. He could never preach enough. Ms Anna had played with fire and got severely burnt, that was sure. Whether it had anything to do with love or anything else, Lorenzo felt sorry for her. *It was all for the greater good, in the end…*

The siblings' stories were tragic, but they had served a purpose. Now that the energies of the police force were focused elsewhere, he could finally turn his attention to what really mattered. The letter was locked inside his drawer. *That* would save Valletta from this horror, the police might as well be damned. Lorenzo read it for the hundredth time.

Father Lorenzo Testaferrata,

You cannot save Valletta, just like you couldn't Mdina, 10 years ago.

But for old times' sake, I'm willing to give you a chance.

Come to the Chapel of the Bones, this Friday, eleven o'clock in the evening.

L.

Lorenzo gulped and sat down, his hands trembling. He had barely slept last night, pondering on the four lines of text. The meeting was tonight; he wished he had more time to think. This was Luigi, he had not doubt. Lorenzo had visited Lord Manduca in Mdina on Monday, and the little urchin came to deliver this letter on Wednesday.

Two days… There's only one way Luigi could've known I was looking for him… Lorenzo wiped his forehead. *The devil is behind this, I knew it from the start.* 'God be my light and protection,' he prayed, looking at the letter again, without touching it. He closed his eyes and travelled back in time, to Mdina, ten years ago. *Luigi… Luigi…* The name brought no particular memories.

He could always go back to Mdina, physically, and knock on Manduca's door to request a word with that scruffy maid. But just thinking about it made him gasp for breath. God knows what Manduca's reply would be. Noblemen were similar to the police, and liked to believe they were gods. Even if Lord Manduca allowed such a meeting, Lorenzo could easily become Mdina's new subject of discussion. No, he didn't want that.

Luigi…

It wasn't common for him to forget names, even though ten years wasn't a short time. To the contrary, however, Luigi seemed to have no problem remembering *him.* The priest drummed his fingers on the desk; it was not easy admitting he was scared. He wished he could at least recognise the handwriting, which was strangely elegant.

Considering a servant of Lucifer wrote it. He got up and looked out of the window. Valletta buzzed like a beehive below. *The Chapel of Bones…*

The Chapel of Nibbia was its proper name; dedicated to Our Lady of Mercy. It was renowned for its crypt full of bleached bones of the deceased patients from the *Sacra Infermeria*.

Lorenzo sighed at Luigi's ingenuity. 'Tonight it is, then, Luigi,' he whispered, leaving his cell for lunch with his brethren.

***

The Wanderer flexed their fingers and bit at their lips, looking at the sky. Tonight was about Don Lorenzo.

The incompetent fool. The Wanderer grinned in the darkness.

The priest was not going to like this. The Wanderer kept conjuring images in their mind, of how the priest was going to react. He would gape for sure, and make the sign of the Cross; like he did five days ago when the Wanderer watched him rushing out of Valletta. He would make the sign of the Cross, like he did on that night ten years ago, in Mdina.

The night of the first kill.

Incompetent fool.

Their Master was right. People like Don Lorenzo were hypocrites. They spoke about things they knew nothing of; preached about realities they didn't really believe existed – not deep down, at least.

'Belief,' the Master always said. 'Belief is a strong thing.'

Maybe that's how Nikola managed to see us running out of Mdina, ten years ago - despite the Veiling... No! The Wanderer couldn't get such thoughts into their head! Wincing, they laid their eyes on the Chapel of Bones, now visible in the moonlight.

Don Lorenzo was there.

What a fool! The Wanderer could almost sense the priest's fear and hear him trembling. Not that they blamed him. It was dark, save for the light of the full moon. Without the Veiling, one logically felt exposed.

Time to teach you a lesson. The Wanderer grinned and reached for the trophy inside their side pocket.

***

The full moon watched over Valletta like a sentinel, shedding silver rays onto the slumbering city. Lorenzo was grateful for it, because he did not bring any light out with him. It wouldn't be ideal if someone recognised the pious Dominican, roaming through the city in the middle of the night. Still, the priest had made sure to pass through the narrowest and most confined streets, just in case.

At the top of *Strada Ospedale,* he stopped;

panting and wiping his brow. It was hot, and the *mozzetta* wasn't helping. To his right, the *Sacra Infermeria;* everywhere else, lay shrouded in an eerie silence. The Chapel of Bones waited further down, at the end of the street, to his left. From here, he could not see its frontage. It felt like watching a stealthy beast waiting to pounce on its prey, silhouetted in the darkness of the hunting ground. Despite the heat, Lorenzo felt a slight chill. He crossed himself and scampered down the street, wincing at the clack of his own footsteps.

The Chapel was closed, as he expected. Its frontage dimly illuminated by two small hanging lanterns.

Where are you, Luigi? He looked around him, but there was no piercing this darkness. The moon itself seemed to shy away. *The devil is coming…* Lorenzo clasped his sweaty hands and uttered another prayer. The Dominicans were God's elite warriors in the epic battle against the devil and his servants. He couldn't leave just yet.

He jolted, waving his head frantically around. That eerie feeling he had felt on his way out of Valletta, last Monday, touched his consciousness again. He was being watched. *Even though I walk through the valley of death, I will fear no evil,* he prayed. *Thou art with me; Thy rod and Thy staff, they comfort me…*

The full moon shifted in the night sky. Lorenzo paced around, clutching at his rosary beads like his life depended on it. No one appeared. He lost track of time, and his knees and ankles starting to ache.

I cannot give in…

A sudden thought occurred to him, and he stopped. His prayers were keeping the devil away, hence why Luigi did not appear. Reluctantly, the priest put his rosary beads away but nothing changed.

He tapped his feet and frowned. *You're nothing but a coward, Luigi,* he thought, grabbing the rosary beads and walking back the way he'd come. 'Good Lord!'

He hadn't taken ten steps, when an object hit the chapel's stonework, right behind him. He could see the small object's silhouette, by the foot of the barred doors.

What in heaven's name…? Lorenzo looked around warily, scanning the darkness. *Where are you Luigi?* 'Come out, you coward,' he heard himself saying.

Perfect silence was the only reply.

The priest took one daring step towards the chapel. *God, please help me…* He focused on the thing that waited at the doors. Two very small round objects, untidily bound together. Lorenzo kneeled, grabbing them from the floor, and…

He froze.

'Good God!' He had prayed hard all night to avoid seeing the devil. Now, he felt like weeping and begging for the Lord's mercy as a pair of rotting eyeballs stared at him.

19.

The candle flickered.
Archibald tilted his head slightly upwards. No sign of a breeze, even though he opened the window as soon as he entered his room. The heat and humidity almost made Archibald sick. During dinner, he overheard some locals saying this heat was to be expected for the time of year – but that didn't help him feel any better.

So he wrote it down. He liked doing this sometimes, scribbling down his thoughts and worries in his diary. It felt like his irritation seeped out of him. It made him feel less tense. Archibald's deepest irritation, however, came from the piece of paper to his right.

He won't like this. For sure he won't, he thought,

moving the piece of paper closer to the candlelight. He liked Maltese script, even though he couldn't read it. It amazed him how a language of Semitic origin could be written in the Roman alphabet. *I'm very sorry. But she left me no choice, Joseph.* Archibald read the English translation so many times, he knew it by heart now.

He stroked his forehead. There was something odd to the original handwriting; the one in Maltese. Archibald could almost sense it, though he couldn't explain it. Initially he had told himself it was because he wasn't used to the Maltese hand. But the more he looked at those words, the more he was convinced that whoever wrote it was… confused. His mind raced back to the events of the day, particularly their morning meeting with Don Lorenzo.

He took out his pocket watch. *Ten minutes to ten.* He grabbed the piece of paper, stood up from his desk, then pressed his ear to the door and waited. According to Inspector Attard, curiosity in the Maltese was easily aroused by anything or anyone. He couldn't risk letting anyone know what he was up to, walking out of his hotel room at such a late hour. As soon as Archibald was sure no sound came from behind the door, he put out the candle, donned his top hat, and sped out of his room.

The candles on the walls were dim. There was no time for his eyes to settle to the subdued light. Archibald crossed the corridor as fast, yet as silently as he could. He descended the stairs. The soft thud of his boots made him flinch. He gave a quick look around the main hall. Down here, the candles and lanterns were almost spent. He turned his eyes towards the hotel parlour, and lowered the brim of his top hat. Muttering a quick prayer in his heart, he stealthily made for the parlour.

'Too hot to sleep, sir?'

Archibald stopped. 'Yes,' he whispered, barely raising his head. He faked a smile, just in case and made to move on.

'It is indeed,' said the voice from behind the front desk. The gentleman was Maltese, judging by his accent. 'It's only going to get hotter.'

Archibald cleared his throat and nodded slightly. He lowered his top hat till his forehead hurt, and took another step forward.

'Going anywhere nice, sir?'

Since when has it become anyone's business? Archibald released a frown. 'Just the parlour,' he replied flatly.

The Superintendent was right: the Maltese were too talkative. Archibald had never really minded it, though… until now. The gentleman said something else, but Archibald was already out of earshot.

Once inside the parlour, he took out his pocket watch. *Almost ten*. He sighed heavily and, out of habit, took a seat in a dark corner by one of the glass windows.

Outside, it was pitch black. He blinked and

looked away. He had been here for just over a week, but had gone on a number of strolls around the city. The small capital was more relaxing than he cared to admit, particularly when it slept. In fact, he was growing quite fond of Valletta, despite its narrow and sloping alleys. He recalled Attard telling him Valletta had been built in haste.

'Because, following their Great Siege victory in 1564,' Attard had told him. 'The Order of the Knights of St John feared the Ottomans would launch another attack on Malta…'

Eventually, the Suleiman got busy conquering other lands and they left Malta and the Knights in peace. Archibald blinked and looked around the parlour.

Come on Mr Attard… what's taking you so long? He turned to gaze at the darkness beyond the window again. It reminded him of the monster he was chasing and the horrifying mess these murders had left behind. *Victims without eyes… no witnesses.* He sighed. In all these years as a police detective, he still couldn't understand how any human being could commit such atrocities. His mind raced back to Britain. *Come now, you've seen worse than this. Much worse.* An inner voice challenged him, however. He *had* been sure Malta could never provide a worse criminal scenario than London. That was before he arrived here, ten days ago. He wasn't entirely sure anymore. The victims of Valletta, with their gory eyeless faces, had by now visited him almost every night.

It made him feel helpless, like a child. He hated it.

Footsteps through the parlour's doorway made him almost jump off the sofa. The silhouette of a man approached him. Archibald recognised him and sighed in relief.

'Inspector Attard,' he said, standing up politely and tipping his top hat.

'This is certainly not very British of me, forgive my lateness,' whispered Attard, eyeing his pocket watch.

'Why, you're not British. So there's nothing to forgive.' Archibald smiled slightly.

'Shall we sit, then?' Attard sat on the sofa with his back to the window. 'Have you rested, constable?'

Archibald nodded, and returned to his seat. He paused and cleared his throat. 'Did you come alone?'

Attard raised an eyebrow. 'Why wouldn't I?'

'Just wanted to be sure, that's all. What I want to discuss is of an urgent and confidential nature.'

'I sure hope it is, Whitlock. I'm seldom out this late, and definitely not in my evening clothes.' Attard chuckled lightly.

Archibald shot a quick look around. The parlour was empty save for the two of them, and a footman standing by the door. He reached for his side pocket and handed a piece of paper to his colleague. Attard raised it to his face and winced. A short silence followed, during which Archibald prayed in his heart.

'How did… where did you…?' Attard cleared his throat. 'Do you know what this says?'

Archibald nodded. 'Turn it over.'

Attard obeyed.

'I had it translated.'

The inspector bit his lips. 'Where did you find this, Whitlock?' He still looked calm, and composed.

Archibald rubbed his nape and lowered his head. *Compose yourself, come on, Archie, be a man.* 'Mr Joseph's house.'

Attard gaped. 'When did you…? Oh, that night… when we went to investigate Mr Joseph's and Ms Anna's house.' He wasn't asking.

Archibald nodded faintly. He was glad the parlour lights were very dim.

Attard sighed. 'And you had it translated… when?'

'That same night, by a footman.'

'The same… Jesus! What does it say? Tell me.' His voice was not stern, but flat. His expression blank.

'I'm very sorry. But she left me no choice, Joseph,' he whispered.

'Is this what you said I *needed* to see?' Attard's voice was still in a whisper.

Archibald nodded.

'You told me this meeting was confidential. Doesn't anybody else know about this piece of paper, then?'

Archibald shook his head. 'Nobody else.'

Attard inhaled deeply. 'I could ask you what

took you so long, Whitlock.' His tone was calm. 'To be frank, though, I'm more interested in knowing what made you share it with me *now* - after more than a week!'

This was the part Archibald dreaded; the hardest part. He sniffed and sighed heavily, lifting his chin with what little pride he could muster. 'You were right,' he said in a whisper.

'About what?'

'About the priest… I mean. You were right, about what you said about Don Lorenzo.'

'I say a lot of things. Please, explain yourself further.'

I can't believe I'm saying this. 'He's helped us in this investigation.' Archibald gulped before continuing. 'You said Don Lorenzo could be useful in the investigation. I agree. You were right.'

'By what means, do you think?' His voice was still flat.

Please… why are you making it so hard! 'Because he was very helpful, of course. And on our side, it seems.' Archibald felt like belching. 'He has given us a way forward.'

Attard stroked his chin with his free hand. His eyes left Archibald for a second. 'But what does this piece of paper have got to do with Don Lorenzo? Do you think we should show it to him too, Whitlock?'

Archibald wasn't sure whether Attard was mocking him or being serious. 'No.'

'Then… are you showing it to me because you

finally trust me?'

Archibald tapped his foot. 'It's not that I didn't… bah! What can I say?'

'You don't like working in a team. Is that so?'

Archibald looked at his feet, and nodded.

Attard looked back at the piece of paper. For a moment, Archibald was sure he could hear his own heart beating like a drum, wanting to pop out of his body.

'I imagine you want to know what I think about this?'

Heaven and earth… hold your tongue, Archie. You're only getting what you deserve. 'Yes, I do. Inspector, I'm just…'

Attard sighed faintly. Archibald thought he saw him smile, but it was too dark to tell – and too good to be true, truth be told.

'This piece of paper could confirm the rumours about Ms Anna seeing somebody,' said Attard in his ever-calm voice. He eyed Archibald worriedly, then shot a quick glare around them and signalled the footman. 'But before that… I need a good cup of tea,' he said with a smile.

The footman approached, and Attard ordered tea and all the utensils it entailed.

I just told him I've been withholding important information for over a week… how does he remain so calm? Archibald forced a smile, but Attard was already lost in thought. The parlour was empty and dark; the dimmed lanterns giving barely enough light. It all reminded him of a graveyard, made even worse by how the cutlery rattled like bones.

'What really strikes me about this note, is how *personal* it sounds,' said Attard, at last.

Archibald narrowed his eyes. 'Oh?'

'Whoever wrote it, used the word *ħafna*, which means they're *very* sorry. While in your tongue it is quite common to say I'm very sorry, in Maltese we just say *I'm sorry*.'

Archibald nodded and sipped his tea.

'In addition to that, the writer knows Mr Joseph's name…'

'Unless it was Mr Joseph himself who wrote it,' said Archibald, timidly.

Attard raised an eyebrow. 'The comma in the English version, the one *you* wrote down, might suggest that. But the Maltese version, the original, has no comma before the name Joseph.'

He really has no intention to scold me. Archibald nodded. 'I am of the same view. But it is better to look at all the possibilities. I do not think Mr Joseph wrote this. I don't think he killed his sister, either.'

Attard nodded back. 'If he had, why would he even write this note?'

'The writer is either a fool, or he wants to help us find him…' Archibald clasped his hands, and fought the urge to look at his feet again.

'Help us?' Attard pursed his lips.

'I know it sounds silly. But maybe, without even knowing it, the writer wants to get caught,' explained Archibald. 'Maybe he feels guilty for having killed Ms Anna, judging by what he wrote. Getting caught would be his redemption, so to speak.'

Attard returned to stroking his chin. 'What you said about him feeling guilty… makes sense, actually. Unless he's mocking Mr Joseph, of course. Still, how would someone who killed five people in less than a year, suddenly feel guilty?'

'It is sick,' insisted Archibald. 'Yet you yourself said you're of the opinion that the note is personal.'

Attard looked away, nodding slightly. 'I said so. But why did he feel guilty after his *fifth* victim?'

Archibald straightened, and took out his notepad. He tore a sheet, and put it next to the candlelight on the low table between him and Attard. He scribbled *letter to Mr Joseph*, and drew a circle around it. 'So far, we agree that the writer murdered Ms Anna. And he's somehow feeling guilty. He must've known them… or Mr Joseph, at least.' He wrote *writer is murderer, writer feeling guilty,* and *writer knows Mr Joseph and/or Ms Anna* on the sheet from the notepad.

Attard watched him for a while, then looked back at the piece of paper in his hand. 'Why would you leave a letter at the house of one of your victims, and address it to her brother?'

Archibald raised his head from the notebook. 'Even more reason to believe the murderer felt guilty.'

Attard shook his head. 'Yes, Mr Whitlock. But if the murderer knew Mr Joseph for the simpleton that he is, why write him a letter in the first place? I don't think Mr Joseph is literate.'

'I wouldn't judge a book by its cover. The man told us his sister read him a lot of stories. So *she* was literate, for sure. That doesn't make *him* literate, I know. But why else would he write a letter to Mr Joseph if he knew he couldn't read it?'

Attard sighed heavily. 'Too many questions. Besides that, *when* did the murderer deliver this letter?'

Archibald cleared his throat and looked at his knees. 'I found the note upstairs.'

Attard raised an eyebrow. 'It had to fly to get up there.'

'It *was* windy that night, truth be told. And most windows were open, if I recall correctly.'

Attard nodded slightly, then looked at Archibald's notes. 'If the murderer and Mr Joseph knew each other, then Mr Joseph would've allowed him inside. I highly doubt this was delivered by anyone other than the writer himself.'

Archibald nodded. 'I agree.'

'That could explain how the it ended up drifting in the room upstairs, apart from the wind,' continued Attard. 'Say the two men had a friendly chat, till the murderer revealed his true intentions, at some point.'

'Makes perfect sense, Inspector Attard,' said Archibald, raising his head but not looking at his colleague. 'The neighbours did, after all, report Mr Joseph going into a frenzy before he disappeared.'

'And there were clearly no signs of violence in the house…'

'Which means that the murderer didn't approach Mr Joseph violently. That sustains the theory that he felt guilty for killing his sister.'

'So he tried to find redemption by speaking to her brother,' ended Attard, his index finger raised and his eyes bulging.

'Still,' said Archibald, leaning slightly backwards. 'Why write a letter to Mr Joseph if you plan to talk to him face to face?'

Attard took a sip from his cup. 'What if talking to Mr Joseph was *not* part of the murderer's plan?'

Archibald narrowed his eyes.

'The murderer felt guilty,' went on Attard, putting the cup on the low table between them. 'So, he sought redemption. He wrote the note, then went to deliver it to Mr Joseph's house, late in the evening. Secretly, of course…'

'Then someone saw him,' said Archibald, straightening in his seat. 'Or something happened which he hadn't planned. So the murderer had to get *inside* the house.'

'Could be,' said Attard, waving his index finger. 'Mr Joseph would've let him in, if they knew each other. They spoke for a while, maybe Mr Joseph was given the letter at some point too. Whatever happened, the murderer eventually told him he had killed his sister, or Mr Joseph understood it.'

'And all hell broke loose,' ended Archibald, his eyes bulging out of his face.

Attard leaned back and sighed like he had just finished a race. He leaned slightly to his right against the sofa, and stroked his chin. Archibald was gaping and looking at his own notes.

'Incredible, Inspector! I mean, it's just theory, of course. But it follows.'

'It does, constable Whitlock. One question still bothers me, though. How does someone kill five people in less than a year, then suddenly start to feel guilty after the fifth one?'

'It is strange. But, what if it isn't about the fifth one, or the fourth, or the first? Maybe it is about Ms Anna, and who she was. It is personal, like you said.'

Attard narrowed his eyes and looked at his colleague. 'Go on.'

'The note says Ms Anna left him no choice. So, whatever twisted plan or pattern this sick bastard is following, she might not have initially been part of it. She became a threat. A potential witness, maybe?'

'I would agree to that… if we hadn't found Ms Anna in the same state as we found the other victims.'

'With her eyes ripped out of her face you mean?'

'Broadly speaking, yes. It didn't look like he killed her only because he didn't have a choice. Maybe he felt sorry afterwards. But that brings us back to the mystery of *why* and *what* the bloody hell made him feel so sorry so suddenly.'

'You're right,' replied Archibald, lifting his hands, palms facing upward.

'I don't know,' said Attard, shaking his head and biting his lips. 'We built a good theory of what happened in that house, that night. Apparently, Ms Anna was a threat to our killer, and she was killed for that reason. Unfortunately, this gets us nowhere closer to finding *who* the murderer is,' he ended, re-filling his cup.

Archibald leaned forward for the piece of paper. He skimmed through the Maltese script, then turned to his own handwriting.

'This leaves us with Don Lorenzo's rumours only,' said Attard, reclining in his seat.

Archibald looked at his colleague, and back at the piece of paper in his hands. 'If only the priest had a name for the person of that rumour,' he said, putting the paper back on the table, beside his half-full cup. *It's too hot for tea here,* he thought, noticing the cup's dancing shadow caressing the paper. *Shadows…* His eyes almost popped out. *All I could see was one of their shadows…* he found himself standing.

'What is the matter?' Attard looked bewildered.

Damn… Archibald's memory couldn't have been triggered at a more unsuitable moment. He had to tell Attard, unless he found a better way to explain why he was suddenly on his feet. He *had* eavesdropped on a private conversation, after all. The rational part of his brain raced to find the best way to get to the point. Attard's surprised stare waited…

'This could very well *not* be a one man show, Inspector,' he heard himself saying, remembering why he had decided to give Don Lorenzo a go. *Gangs of Valletta…* 'What if there's a gang behind all this. A member of a gang, maybe, who is having guilt feelings for the transgression against Ms Anna.'

Attard blinked and wet his lips. 'That was one of the main reasons why we agreed we needed Don Lorenzo. He has contacts and…'

It is now or never, Archie… He returned to his seat. 'Besides that,' he told his colleague, raising a hand. 'It would make sense, theoretically, that all these crimes were committed by a group of individuals. The bodies were killed on the spot, and not dragged into the streets, for instance. No single man could perform such a feat all by himself, right?'

'Granted. But we've already been over this. That's why we went to Don Lorenzo. We got some rumours, that's all. So, the problem remains: where do we start looking?'

Archibald inhaled deeply, resting his hands on his knees. *God help me, please…* 'Last Monday. When that little scoundrel stole my cane. Jesus! I chased him like a hare on wheels. I came upon…' Archibald fought the urge to stop. This was embarrassing.

'Constable?'

This was no time for sticking to his pride. Not

now. Archibald took another deep breath; it felt like he was running. 'Last Monday... that boy who stole my cane. I chased that cursed little creature all through Valletta... I lost him, as I told you. But... on my way back, I stumbled upon a private conversation. It was in Maltese, so I didn't understand everything that was being said. It was between two young men. They...'

'You were eavesdropping?' Attard's eyes were almost out of their sockets, his jaw almost touched the floor.

'Just listen, please,' insisted Archibald, glad it was too dark for his colleague to see he was blushing. 'I didn't see their faces. But I know they were two men, by their voices. I could only see the shadow of one of them, anyway... they kept talking about a place; The Falcon's Perch. One of them was called Pawlu. They kept referring to a certain Mr Callus – or Calleja, I'm not entirely sure, now... and a girl, who apparently got killed in relation to this Callus... or Calleja.'

Attard didn't move. Archibald lowered his eyes, shyly.

'Were you planning on telling me this next year?'

Archibald sighed. 'It didn't seem important at the time ...'

'A girl got killed.' Attard harrumphed slightly. 'How is that not important?'

'Forgive me,' whispered Archibald.

'I might as well go to The Falcon's Perch all by myself, get the information I need, walk out, and do not share anything else with you.' Attard's tone was as calm as ever, but definitely irritated. 'What's wrong with you, Constable Whitlock?'

Archibald looked away. 'You're right. I should've told you sooner. Is that what you wish to hear?'

'First the note, now this. What I wish to *see* is us working as a team!'

'You're right.'

'Yes, of course. You keep saying that. Is there anything else you've been keeping to yourself that you wish to share?'

'You don't have to mock me. I'm just...'

'I'm not mocking you.' There was a certain serenity and care to his tone, considering the circumstances. 'I only want to solve this case. And I need your help just as much as you need mine. I only want to make sure if we're going out that door to investigate further, we're doing it as a team,' he ended, pointing at the parlour's exit.

Archibald nodded, still looking at his feet, his hands clasped. He heard Attard sigh and felt the tension ease off slightly.

'The Falcon's Perch is an inn. Number 67, in *Strada Stretta*,' said Attard, grabbing the pot to refill his teacup. 'Considering we've got nothing to lose, and almost no other clue how to proceed on this investigation... I'd say The Falcon's Perch is the best way forward. I can arrange a meeting with Mr Calleja. He's the owner of the inn. It won't be pleasant, but it is necessary.'

Archibald felt like he had just run a mile.

'Better than appearing before the Superintendent without any clue of what to say,' he attempted, smiling slightly to the floor.

'Oh, that's a face I don't want to see just yet,' said Attard, chuckling.

Archibald glanced at Attard and back to his own feet. *I deserve to be sent back to England and get flogged. This man's a saint.* He made to get up.

'Where do you think you're going now, Whitlock? Sit down. We still have to discuss how under heaven are we're going to visit The Falcon's Perch without causing havoc and paranoia. That's a harder and longer discussion than the one we just had. We'll need that bloody notepad of yours.' He sighed and looked around the parlour. 'And I need more tea…'

20.

Rita peeped out of her window, glancing at the full moon and expecting it to melt at any moment. The heat was unbearable. She looked down at *Strada Stretta*, narrowing her eyes as though it would help her to see better. The street was still loud, despite the time of night and the fact that it was a Saturday. Maybe because Mr Calleja was away.

Enjoying himself at some brothel, other than his own. Rita pursed her lips. *Then why did Filippo still turn up in my bedroom, tonight?* She could answer that another time.

Tonight's questions were more urgent. She shook her head, focusing again on the street below her little balcony. People chattered and sang, while others touched each other. Anything that would help them forget their daily troubles, really. Filippo appeared the moment Rita almost gave up looking out for him. She bounced on her toes as she watched him merging into the alienated crowd. Rita returned inside, closed the window, put on her shoes and sprang out of the room as though the ceiling was about to collapse.

What's with all these people tonight? Don't they have a home to go to? She thought, pushing through the mass outside The Falcon's Perch.

She raised her head above the crowd, and spotted Filippo heading east. Between one 'excuse me' and another, Rita slithered through the alienated crowd and got out unscathed. She saw Filippo's silhouette stopping momentarily at the crossing with *Strada Vescovo*.

What are you looking for?

Filippo moved on. Rita followed, wishing she had something to cover her head with, despite the heat. She was grateful for the narrowness of *Strada Stretta*. At least it shielded her from the rays of the full moon. Sometimes, Rita wondered what had been on the mind of the Knights when they planned *Strada Stretta,* during Valletta's construction. Maybe it had always been intended to offer shelter to whoever wanted to hide. A haven, destined to protect all those who the evolving, dynamic world would not accept.

Whatever Filippo was hiding from, she hoped to discover soon. There was a story behind every man who visited her bedroom. Filippo's, she wanted to discover. She had asked herself why many times. Even tonight, before setting out on this perilous adventure into the night; she had asked herself a thousand times. She almost wanted to slap herself back into reason, because she couldn't find the answer. Nevertheless, she was here, chasing a man into the dark narrow alleyways that the Order of the Knights of St John had planned for them both... so many years before.

Filippo stopped again, so abruptly Rita almost lost her footing.

Kristu! Rita bit her tongue.

He was at the crossing with *Strada San Cristoforo*. He looked on either side of him, in front and also behind him, sniffing the air like a dog would. Rita instinctively uttered a prayer in her heart, wishing she was invisible. Fortunately for her, Filippo walked further down *Strada Stretta*, and turned into a door of a shabby-looking inn. Rita followed, advancing towards the crossing with *Strada San Cristoforo*. A left-hand turn went downhill and a right went uphill. The street looked dull, dark and empty. Not like *Strada Stretta* ahead and the dimly lit entrance which just swallowed Filippo.

Rita frowned. *Another brothel...* She remained by the corner and watched the monstrous building from afar.

People scurried in and out of the place, pretty much like they did at The Falcon's Perch. Like The Falcon's Perch's clientele, they were mostly lower-class. They all seemed less drunk, however, and there were almost as much ladies as there were men. The façade was slightly wider than that of The Falcon's Perch, having two floors and a couple of balconies. Rita looked at *Strada San Cristoforo* to her left and right. The street was too open and bare; she fought the urge to cross it.

Besides, why would you want to get any closer to another brothel? She tugged at her hair and blinked, fighting dirty images of Filippo forming in her mind. She could not allow herself to make up these images. Not because it was a sin; she was already beyond salvation. Such images would, however, force her to answer questions she would rather not tackle yet. *I have to get back.* Yet she remained there, watching the entrance of the inn, like a lighthouse in the middle of a dark and desolate sea. The full moon hovered high above, the stars dimming as the sky turned violet. But the crowd coming in and out of the inn didn't diminish.

I have to get back... Rita was just about to turn back, when she recognised his voice. She jumped and fixed her eyes on the entrance. Filippo emerged, his chestnut curls and bobbing head towering above the crowd. A figure with dark hair was following him. Rita bit at her fingernails as the two men walked away from the entrance, and closer to *Strada San Cristoforo.* She pressed herself against the wall, away from the corner, tugging at her black hair. *What are you up to, Filippo?*

When the two men got closer, out of the

crowd's bustle, she could see Filippo's hazel eyes. He seemed restless. The other fellow scanned the surroundings. Filippo was taller, and of a slimmer build. The other fellow carried dark features, a thick beard covering almost all his neck. They stopped at the corner with *Strada San Cristoforo*.

'I think I know what he's looking for,' Filippo started saying, turning to look at his companion. 'But first, I need to ask you something. And I need you to be honest with me.'

Rita bit at her fingernails.

The shorter one frowned. 'Filippo, this must…'

Filippo raised his hands. 'Listen to me, Pawlu!'

'No, Filippo. Listen to *me*,' replied the shorter one, shaking his head feverishly. He looked impatient. 'He's in there, right now.' He was pointing at the inn.

Filippo grimaced. 'Who?'

'Calleja!'

Rita's heart almost skipped a beat.

A booming sound erupted from inside the inn. People were running out and away, scattering unevenly into *Strada Stretta* and *Strada San Cristoforo*. Perturbed faces peeped out of the neighbouring bars and balconies. Filippo and his friend were looking at the entrance, seemingly undisturbed. Rita cowered, grateful for the good number of people who fled the bedlam, all running her way. *Mr Calleja!*

Mr Calleja had a firearm raised in his right

hand. 'You!'

Filippo and his companion were already sprinting down *San Cristoforo*, with Mr Calleja in hot pursuit.

Kristu! Rita legged it after Mr Calleja the moment he gave her his back.

Running downhill wasn't as easy as she'd thought. Though, truth be told, she hadn't really thought about this. Her brain kept sending warnings, but her body ignored them. Her eyes focused solely on Filippo, as he and his companion sprinted onwards like leaders in a race. Mr Calleja heralded their presence, bellowing and cursing at almost every step. He was fast, and too far ahead to even hear her following. Uphill, downhill, and around the four corners of Valletta they went. Keeping up was becoming an effort, and the heat wasn't helping.

Il-Kristu! Rita held back a scream, as her toes hit something hard. Spasms of pain shot up her foot and she slowed down to look. *Bloody pavements.* She lifted her head and faltered. Mr Calleja had stopped at a crossroads, almost within arm's reach. He was still with his back to her, and was looking from left to right, like a fox on the prowl.

Rita held her breath. She had only looked down for a second. *Few more steps and you would've ended right in Mr Calleja's arms, you fool!* She didn't move.

'They're not here,' a voice to Mr Calleja's left said.

Mr Calleja harrumphed and vanished uphill, into the dark street.

Rita released a sigh. Her chest heaved, her clothes were soaked in sweat, her right foot in excruciating pain. She hopped to a barred door, close by, and pressed herself behind the jamb. *Please...* She shut her eyes and prayed in the darkness. She listened.

'I've seen that boy in my inn before. Find them both, and give them a good beating. Don't kill them yet,' Mr Calleja said under his breath.

Rita knew that voice when she heard it. It carried a signature she recognised from a mile away. She trembled, despite the sweat trickling down her neck and between her breasts. *Where am I?* The Manoel Theatre stood a couple of metres behind her, across the street, like a slumbering beast. Rita looked at the spot where Mr Calleja had just been. She could hear the echoes of *Strada Stretta*, behind the building where she stood now. *Strada Forni, then.*

But where was Filippo? He was being hunted by Mr Calleja himself. That was not good. Filippo was playing with fire. Filippo was a fool. Filippo almost deserved the beating from Mr Calleja. Filippo should... Her foot throbbed. Rita raised it and started rubbing her toes. *I have to get back and take care of this.* She lifted her head. The sky was turning to a hue of light pink. She was grateful The Falcon's Perch was almost around the corner, up *Strada Teatro* and then a left turn.

As soon as she turned onto *Strada Stretta*, she

almost bumped into a man.

'I'm very sorry, sir,' she said. *Look at my breasts, of course...* She held back a frown.

He was in evening clothes. His shirt was untucked, his collar open, and his moustache ruffled. Rita recognised when a man was just out of a brothel, nowadays. He didn't even look at her, but staggered on down *Strada Teatro*. She lowered her head and moved on.

At the entrance to The Falcon's Perch, she stumbled upon another gentleman. This one didn't look at her bosom. He was short, wearing his evening clothes. His eyes were fixed on hers.

'Well, excuse me, lady,' he said in a posh English accent. He removed his top hat, revealing rich auburn hair and moved out of her way. His square face was familiar, but she was too tired to think. He was neatly dressed, carried a cane and...

Mr Calleja appeared right behind him. Rita cowered, looked at her feet and scurried into The Falcon's Perch. Mr Calleja made way slightly, without even a second glance.

That's strange...

He always harrumphed or sniggered, whenever she crossed him. Sometimes he grabbed her so tightly from the wrist it hurt. Rita suddenly remembered where she had seen the finely dressed gentleman before. He was the one who made Mr Calleja as tame as a sheep ... the only one. He was still looking at her. Those dark narrow eyes contrasted his pale skin and red hair.

Rita shuddered. She forgot her injured foot and took off in a quick pace.

Victoria, the nosy barmaid, came between Rita and her room. 'Rita, where have you been?'

She forced a smile. 'Working, of course.'

'Come and have a drink with me, my dearest. You deserve a break,' said Victoria, tapping her on the shoulder and dragging her to the bar.

I deserve a bed. That's all I want... Rita looked over her shoulders; the gentleman wasn't looking at her anymore. She sighed in relief, taking a place beside Victoria.

'So, I saw Elisabeth yesterday...' started Victoria.

Rita nodded idly, as the middle-aged wench blabbered on about some other barmaid who worked in The Falcon's Perch. That was how she delighted herself, this Victoria, most of the time; gossiping about other people as if it were any of her business. Rita didn't mind her, usually. However, it was morning soon and she desperately needed some sleep. Besides, Mr Calleja and his scary friend had just returned and were walking closer to the bar.

'It's late, so I won't be long,' the dark-eyed gentleman told Mr Calleja, putting his top hat on the bar. He spoke in English and in an accent which was not going to be easy for Rita to understand.

'Yes, of course,' Rita told Victoria in Maltese, nodding to her colleague's chatter and giving the men her back.

'You attracted too much attention to yourself, tonight,' went on the gentleman, in a scolding voice. 'It will all be yours soon, Calleja. I've got them cornered. But no more fire and noise. I thought we had agreed to stop doing that. From now onwards, we proceed in silence. Is that understood?'

Apart from the astonishing fact that he spoke to Mr Calleja as one would to a child, this man's voice carried a peculiar tone. It was cold and welcoming at the same time. Whatever effect he had on Mr Calleja, it was powerful. This man was dangerous, to say the least. Rita thought of the murders and the victims. Creative images of what she had heard crept through her mind and she gulped.

Victoria was still gossiping. Rita wanted to slap her straight in the face. Unfortunately, she needed her, if she were going to find out who Filippo was up against.

'I've almost found what we're looking for. But I need you to behave,' continued the gentleman. '*Don't* do anything foolish, Calleja. You can kill whoever you want, once I'm done.'

Kristu! For a moment, Rita regretted her knowledge of the English language. She tried to focus on Victoria's stupid babbling, lest she faints on the spot. The gentleman picked up his hat and left. Throughout the whole conversation, Mr Calleja hadn't said one single word. If this gentleman didn't possess some sort of power, then Rita didn't know who else did.

Filippo!

He was in grave danger. Despite how much she believed a good beating would help the young man grow up, he needed to know who he was up against.

He deserves to know, at least. Somebody has *to tell him.* Rita stifled a yawn. She nodded to Victoria and bid her good night. As she crossed Mr Calleja, he seemed to ignore her. Rita took the opportunity to rush to her room.

Her bed waited. That wretched thing she had so vilely tainted with her sins. It reminded her of all those men and of how she had condemned them to eternal damnation. This bed was one of hell's fiery pits, and Rita its most loyal servant. She still had nightmares almost every night. She would have them, she was sure, for as long as she served the devil and his evil purpose.

Her foot throbbed. 'Damn you,' she told the bed. For the first time in three weeks, she longed to dive and drown into it. She lit her small lamp and walked to her bed.

She froze.

A wooden box lay on her pillow.

Rita glanced at the door and the window. Both were closed. She set the lamp on her bedside table, and grabbed the box carefully, as though it contained gunpowder. It was about the size of her forearm, but very light. Something was engraved on the lid.

Pity I cannot read, she thought sadly, laying the box on the bed and opening it.

Her heartbeat quickened, her eyes bulged out, and her hands trembled.

She was looking at a beautiful red rose.

Rita lifted the box to her face and sniffed. The rose's sharp smell caressed her nostrils. Somehow, it reminded her of sunny days spent with her father by the sea, at *Marsamuscetto*. Images of Filippo flashed through her mind. She tried to shake them away, but felt the hair on her skin stand on end. *The boy's a young fool, but he deserves to know what he's up against, at least.*

Despite everything, she was smiling.

21.

The Basilica was empty, dark, and cold.

Wherever he looked, it felt like he was seeing it through a piece of black cloth. Everything was so colourless, and smudged. Narrowing his eyes or blinking didn't seem to help. Silence surrounded him like a presence. He couldn't hear himself breathing. His heart was racing, he had no doubt. But even that sound was blocked by the presence surrounding him. He had resisted the cold for a while. Until he tried folding his arms on his chest, and realised he could not even move. That had set off the shaking. And so, for the first time after many years, Lorenzo wept. Even the tears trickling down his cheeks were cold.

Please just take me, Lord. I'm ready, my Lord. Your

servant awaits, he prayed, for the hundredth time since waking here.

A wicked laughter echoed in the Basilica. For an instant, Lorenzo felt relieved; anything was better than the horrifying silence. But the laughter didn't stop. The ground shook, and the Basilica trembled.

A pair of eyes appeared suddenly in front of him.

Lorenzo tried to scream, but all he heard was that harrowing laughter. He closed his eyes, but those two eyeballs were waiting in the darkness. The laughter was tearing through his being, the rotting eyeballs stared back at him.

Lord, please. I'm ready, get me out of here, I beg you. I… his thoughts paused. *How did I even get here?*

Suddenly he felt it. A part of his being was coming back to consciousness. He had completely forgotten all about it, during this terrible sojourn; like it had never even existed. *How did I get here?* Now it was back, and he couldn't help wondering how he hadn't felt its absence before. *How did I get here?* He was finally whole again.

Lorenzo opened his eyes. He was in a dark room where the only illumination was the moonlight coming through the window. The bed was comfortable, though he would've preferred a softer pillow. He tried to move his head, and almost wept at the success.

Where am I?

The room spun a little, but he was glad to see his own body.

'I'm alive,' he whispered to himself. He had never been so happy to hear his own voice, despite how hoarse it was.

Someone snored, and Lorenzo scanned his environment. There were another three beds; an empty one to his left, the other two across the room. He was the only one awake.

Ospedale Centrale … He fought an instant surge of panic. Resting his head back against the pillow, he let out a sigh of relief. *How did I get here?* The events from the supposed nocturnal meeting at the Chapel of the Bones dashed in front of his inner eye. Lorenzo winced and frowned and groaned. *The eyeballs*, he thought as heavy sleep took over.

He was in a dark place again; not the Basilica, this time. There seemed to be no up or down, no left nor right. A light mist stroked at his feet, leaving a dreadful chill wherever it touched. Lorenzo was alone.

At first.

A tall, slender silhouette appeared right in front of him. It was fully robed and hooded, with long hands and legs. It had no eyes, but Lorenzo knew it was looking at him.

'Who are you?' he asked, his voice echoing slightly in the void.

The figure let out a shrieking laugh.

Lorenzo cowered and raised his hands to his ears. *No, please. Not that again. Anything but that, please. Lord, save me!*

'The Lord abandons the wicked and the corrupt, Lorenzo.' The figure's voice was like thousands speaking all at once. 'You do not have true faith.'

This is just another bad dream. You have to wake up, Lorenzo. Wake up, Lorenzo!

'Don Lorenzo?'

He woke up with a start. He was back in his bed, at the *Ospedale Centrale*. The rays of the sun bounced off Don Roberto, who was standing beside the bed.

'He's up, Sister!'

A young woman appeared shortly. Lorenzo blushed as she leaned closer, checking his pulse, eyes, and all the other things these people claimed to know. Thankfully, the nurses at the *Ospedale Centrale* were all nuns; not that it helped him feel more at ease. Don Roberto's look was blank.

'God bless you, Father,' she said in Italian. 'You should be good to go back to *San Domenico* by tomorrow morning. The Lord is indeed with you,' she ended, straightening.

Lorenzo nodded, and glanced at Don Roberto.

'How do you feel, Don Lorenzo?' he asked, in Italian.

The nurse looked away.

Trying to impress the nurse now, aren't we? 'I'm fine,' he replied, frowning.

'I'm Sister Ursola, Ward Mistress. I'll be just outside the room, should you need anything, Father,' said the nurse, bowing and smiling slightly.

'Thank you, Sister.' Lorenzo waited for her to leave, then shot Don Roberto a quick glance.

He pursed his lips. 'You were found two nights ago,' he started in a whisper. 'Near the *Sacra Infermeria*.'

Lorenzo scowled.

'You were by the door of the Chapel of the Bones. Knocked out, apparently. So they brought you here.'

Lorenzo blinked, shutting the image of those dreadful eyeballs from his mind. 'They?'

Don Roberto nodded slightly. 'Two fishermen found you, on their way to work, before dawn. They rushed to the *Sacra Infermeria*, and brought the *Katalett*. I don't know who carried you, however. Sorry.'

Lorenzo moved uncomfortably in the bed. *So I lost consciousness. What about the eyeballs?*

The fishermen must have noticed the horrendous trophy. No matter how dark, their foul stench couldn't go unnoticed. Don Roberto didn't look like he was withholding any information… or he was hiding it well.

'Two nights ago, you said? That makes…'

'You slept all throughout,' replied the young priest.

I wonder who else of the brethren came to visit. It was irrelevant, really. Two nights and a whole day were more than enough, unfortunately. By now, the whole Dominican priory would know what transpired. Lorenzo had no doubt.

'Well,' said Don Roberto, smiling faintly. 'You need to rest and recover. We need you at the priory, Don Lorenzo. I'll leave, with your blessing.'

I need to get out of this bed, right now! Lorenzo nodded, and blessed him. 'Thank you for your visit, Don Roberto,' he ended.

With the young priest gone, he could finally think again. He wished he was out of this bed, and inside his own cell. He pondered about escaping the hospital for a while. *Don't be stupid. One fool is already more than enough*, he told himself, thinking of Don Roberto.

As much as he needed to return to his cell, running away would make him look insane. Being locked in the lunatic asylum was the last thing he needed. Valletta could wait another night for him to recover, he hoped.

Just one night … Lorenzo's inner eye took him back to the experience of two nights ago. The eyeballs, wherever they were, belonged to the devil. The murderer of Valletta had tried to put him under a sleeping curse. But God brought him back, for a plan. He grimaced and looked at the window. He couldn't see outside. One more night, and he could return to hunt down this murderer. Luigi, the coward who hadn't showed up. He had definitely been watching him that night, and not from afar. Someone *had* thrown those eyeballs. *But why leave me there? Why not kill me, or offer me as sacrifice to Lucifer?* Lorenzo shuddered at the thought.

Luigi needed him. Why, Lorenzo didn't know yet. Maybe not even Luigi himself did. This wasn't simply a game of cat and mouse, this was a cry for aid.

If he wanted to kill me, he had the right opportunity two nights ago.

Whatever it was, he had to face it. God was on his side. Valletta needed him. Maybe even Luigi did. For now, it was enough knowing that he had to get out of this bed, and back out there. He pushed himself upwards. The whole room whirled. Lorenzo frowned, falling back onto the pillow.

I have to get back out there…

Sleep took over him.

Lorenzo sighed, leaning against the closed door.

'Finally,' he whispered, opening his eyes and scanning the room.

He had never felt this grateful to be back in his cell, even though it stank of stuffiness. The priest walked to the window, allowing some more light and air inside. Then he turned to look at the closed door, frowning. He had been given a light breakfast before leaving the hospital, so the world outside his cell could wait.

God, help me, he prayed, thinking of all the curious faces and inquisitive questions that awaited him beyond that door. He didn't blame them. If he were in their place, he was very likely to react in the same way. No one ever left the priory so late in the evening, unless they had some form of consent. Lorenzo shook. He needed to come up with a solid explanation soon. He ran his hand through his dark hair. 'What am I doing?' He sighed heavily, and walked to his bed.

The Lord had freed him from the sleeping curse, but he could still feel its lingering effects. *Lucifer's servant is trying to break my resolve …*

A knock at the door startled him.

'Don Lorenzo, may I come in?'

A bit longer … all I ask is some time to think! 'I'm resting. Who is it?'

'The Prior wants a word. At his office, now.' The muffled voice was almost demeaning.

Lorenzo felt like he just got hit in the stomach. 'I'll be down straight away. Thank you.' He was expecting this, though not as quickly. Fr Massimo Gauci, their Prior, was not usually this hasty. Unfortunately, it seemed all the odds were against his favour, lately. He got off his bed, making for the rosary beads on his desk. Outside his cell, the corridor was empty and quiet. He closed the door as silently as he could, and took off before any fellow brother came out of their cell.

'Come in,' said Fr Massimo.

Lorenzo walked in, head bowed and already sweating. The Prior sat behind his desk, scribbling on some leather-bound register.

'Good morning, Lorenzo. Please, sit down.'

You could at least look at me… 'Good morning,' he replied, taking a seat and fighting the need to wipe his brow.

Prior Massimo closed the register, putting it inside some drawer beneath his desk. 'Very well.' He looked at Lorenzo, clasping his hands together and leaning slightly forward. 'In the light of recent events, is there something you wish to tell me, Lorenzo?'

Lorenzo swallowed. 'Prior,' he started, as solemnly as he could. 'Lucifer's hand has struck at us, fiercely.'

'Lorenzo.' The Prior sighed, raising his clasped hands to his chin. 'Do you understand why I summoned you?' He looked honestly concerned.

Lorenzo nodded, fingering with the rosary beads inside his pocket. This was not the type of Prior you beat around the bush with.

'Lorenzo. You represent the Dominican community. And not just that of Valletta.'

'I know.'

'Do you? You're one of our most esteemed, and experienced. What's going on?'

Lorenzo sighed heavily. 'Valletta is in danger, Prior.'

'You're referring to the murders.'

Lorenzo nodded.

'We have the police taking care of that.'

How could you! Really, how could you possibly even listen to yourself saying that? Lorenzo clenched his fists, and looked at his feet.

'Did I just say something to offend you?'

Lorenzo shook his head.

'Look at me, Lorenzo.'

The priest raised his head, but didn't keep his eyes on the Prior's for long.

'I do not believe I have to tell you how important our reputation is. You're not a novice.'

Lorenzo nodded humbly.

'My intention is to keep this meeting short. But I need you to tell me the truth.'

I told you that already. There's a city to save, and you're ready to abandon it to the hands of the police…

'What were you doing at the Chapel of Nibbia, in the middle of the night?'

You're still direct, at least. Even though you've lost your mind. Lorenzo bit his lips, and sighed again. *I have to think fast.* He stroked the rosary beads again. 'I was meeting a witness. Unfortunately, they failed to show up,' he lied. *Lord, forgive my trespassing, as I forgive those who trespass against me.*

'A witness?' The Prior narrowed his eyes.

Lorenzo nodded, fixing his eyes on the Prior and struggling to keep them there. 'A witness who claims to have crucial information which could help with the investigation.'

'What investigation, Lorenzo?' The Prior lowered his clasped hands, but raised his voice. 'We are not the police,' he said, matter-of-factly.

Lorenzo waited for a second, before replying. 'Of course we aren't. But how would I tell that to my witness, Prior?' He kept his voice as composed as he could, transferring his anger into his clenched fists.

'You could refer them to the police, Lorenzo. Our mission is with the soul, not ...'

Lorenzo wanted to shake his head in disagreement. The Prior was rambling about duty. Lorenzo was sure he was losing his mind.

He's most likely on Lucifer's side, and they're trying to get me off from discovering the truth. There's a city to save, and he's holding me here with all this false preaching! Lorenzo remained put. 'You're right. It won't happen again,' he said, when the Prior had finished.

The Prior raised an eyebrow.

You weren't expecting that, were you? You old devil. 'Forgive me,' he said in a humble tone, looking down at his feet. *Lucifer may be strong, but I'm guided by the light of the Lord, and St Michael's sword.*

Prior Massimo leaned back in his armchair. 'At least come to me first, next time,' he said in a calm tone.

Lorenzo nodded. *I'd rather go through seven hundred thousand years of purgatory, you traitor!* 'Yes, Prior. Thank you.'

'*Kun imbierek.*' The Prior made the sign of the cross and dismissed him.

I don't want anything from you anymore. Lorenzo almost shuddered. He got off his chair and walked to the door.

'Lorenzo …'

Lorenzo paused, and turned slightly to face

his superior.

'Tell your witness to go to the police. And don't make me summon you again. Not on this case,' he ended, in a commanding tone.

'Yes, Prior.' *I need some fresh air ...*

With that said and done, he closed the Prior's office door behind him and scurried downstairs. His collar felt threatening, his robes were almost squeezing his soul out. *I'm out of that madman's eyesight, and unscathed.*

Outside, the heat wasn't helping Lorenzo feel any better. He looked at the sky, and thanked God for assisting him. The trial with Prior Massimo hadn't been an easy one. Nevertheless, all went well for those who trusted in the Lord, as St Paul said.

I need to get to the Chapel of the Bones. He took a step forward, then stopped. From now on, he had to be very wary - keeping seven eyes open, as the Maltese saying goes. If the Prior was watching him, Lorenzo had to appear compliant. The Chapel could wait a while longer.

'Don Lorenzo?'

The priest almost jumped. A young and dirty boy was looking at him with dark brown eyes. *From where did you...?*

'This is for you,' said the street urchin, handing him a folded piece of paper.

Lorenzo took it. The boy was gone before the priest had even finished blinking.

22.

The Falcon's Perch was not an inn. It was the right place for committing all wrongdoing; the safest haven for the most dangerous. It was a temple of all that was profane. It stank of men, opium, and sex. Shadows danced everywhere, covering everyone and everything. To be fair, though, the Jazz *was* soothing. It caressed his soul like a woman's touch. The people seemed jolly, somehow, and so undisturbed by his and Inspector Attard's presence. Thankfully, Mr Calleja had preferred they speak in the privacy of 'his office', and away from this mayhem.

'Please sit,' he said, closing the door behind him.

They took a chair in front of what looked like

a desk. This 'office' was relatively quiet, though Archibald didn't mind the soft hum of the jazz from the room next door.

'So, how can I be of service? Inspector Attard and…?' asked Mr Calleja, in Maltese.

'Constable Whitlock, from London,' said Attard, raising his arm to indicate Archibald, who nodded.

'I can speak some English… I think!' Mr Calleja grinned, then lounged onto the chair behind his desk. 'No drink? You sure?'

They shook their heads and removed their hats.

'We're investigating the murders happening in Valletta,' started Attard, in his ever-so-calm voice.

'That's good. Valletta surely needs some help. And I'm here to help,' said Mr Calleja, smiling and sipping at his alcoholic concoction.

'Excellent!' said Attard. 'We're here because we know you can help us.'

Archibald moved uncomfortably in his seat. Attard's idea was to tackle Mr Calleja tactically, after they realised there was no way they could go in unnoticed. He believed Mr Calleja could give them the information they required, if dealt with warily. Archibald agreed it was worth a try. In truth, however, he felt Attard was reluctant to antagonise the owner of The Falcon's Perch. He didn't quite understand why. Attard himself had told him the police occasionally raided The Falcon's Perch. In most cases, the raids followed reports of unruly brawls, drug abuse, and suchlike petty crimes.

'Whatever it is you need?' asked Calleja.

'We have reason to believe these murders are being committed by a group of people,' started Attard. 'Gangs.'

Calleja leaned slightly backwards. 'Might be.'

'Would you know of any trouble around here, recently?'

Calleja rubbed at his right ear. 'Trouble Inspector?'

Attard nodded. 'In The Falcon's Perch, *Strada Stretta*, or thereabouts.'

Calleja shook his head, smirking slightly. 'The Falcon's Perch is surely no holy place, but we don't have any serious trouble here. I don't allow it, Inspector. As for the rest of *Strada Stretta* … that's beyond my control.'

For an instant, Archibald thought he glimpsed worry on Calleja's face. Then it was gone.

'Did you know any of the victims, Mr Calleja?'

Calleja raised an eyebrow. 'I heard they were a bunch of lonely, stray people. Poor creatures,' he sighed resignedly. 'The murderer's a coward, if you ask me.'

Archibald looked in Calleja's eyes. He was definitely hiding something, despite how well he played the act.

'He may be a coward, yet dangerous nonetheless. One of the cases involved two male victims,' went on Attard.

Archibald held his tongue. *What are you doing,*

Attard? He had agreed to an anti-antagonising tactic. Yet this stank of hesitation from Attard's end. *We have to bully him, not share our findings with him.*

'Two men killed in a single night. That's almost admirable,' joked Calleja.

Attard's expression didn't change. 'It's sad, really. And definitely not the work of one man alone,' he ended flatly, letting it sink in.

Sure, why don't you ask him to join us on the investigation next!

'How do you mean?' Calleja leaned forward.

'Murderers are always cowards, Mr Calleja. But that doesn't make them any less dangerous,' replied Attard. 'There is more than one pair of hands behind these murders.'

Calleja chuckled. 'Should I be scared?'

'You seem to know quite enough about the victims. What other information can you share?'

'Know quite enough?' Calleja grinned, leaning slightly on his side. 'In life, nothing comes for free, Inspector.'

Attard sighed. 'What do you have in mind?'

Seriously? Archibald tapped his foot and bit his fingernails.

'It would be nice if you told your men to leave The Falcon's Perch be. We would all benefit from some peace and quiet. Wouldn't we, Inspector Attard?'

Archibald straightened. 'I thought you said you had everything under control.'

They both looked at him, Calleja with raised

eyebrows.

'Well, I do, actually. Lock. But…'

Archibald cleared his throat. 'It's Whitlock. *Constable* Whitlock.'

'Whitlock, forgive me,' said Calleja, snickering. 'I do have everything under control… at The Falcon's Perch.'

That worried look again! 'What do you know about Pawlu?'

It was Attard's turn to raise his eyebrows.

Calleja's face was blank. 'That it is a common name,' he said, shrugging and retiring to his seat.

From the corner of his eye, Archibald saw Attard glaring at him. He avoided those stern eyes. His colleague would have to be dealt with later. Right now, he had to focus on Calleja, who looked taken aback.

'You didn't answer my question, Mr Calleja.'

Calleja shrugged coolly. 'What do you want me to tell you? I run this inn. It's a common name.' He looked away.

Archibald stood up, slowly. 'What do you know about Pawlu, Mr Calleja? I won't ask again.'

Calleja leaned forward, waving his index finger at them. 'You come knocking at my door, and I let you in. I offer to help you solve *your* petty crimes. Then you start threatening me and implying that…'

Attard was shaking his head. 'Nobody's threatening you, Mr …'

'You disappoint me, Inspector Attard,' he

went on, scowling at Attard. 'Why did you have to bring a *Brit* into this room?' He said in Maltese.

'This is not about *me*,' Archibald yelled back, in English. 'We came here out of courtesy. Not that you deserve any of it, evidently enough.' He thought he heard Attard telling him to calm down. 'I'm an officer of the law, and now I demand you sit your arse down and answer my question.'

Attard raised his hand to his forehead, sighing heavily.

Calleja was on his feet. 'You *demand*, Mr bloody Lock? Or whatever the shit your name is!'

'Yes, I demand…'

'*Mur ħudu f'sormok!*' bellowed Calleja, brandishing the middle-finger at Archibald.

Attard was on his feet.

'Why don't you try saying that again, in English,' replied Archibald.

'Ask your Maltese mother to translate it for you,' Calleja added, in English.

Archibald had to fight against all his instincts to leap over the table and hit him, straight in the face. Luckily, Attard was already standing between them.

'Shut your mouths, both of you!' he said in a commanding tone.

Archibald was pointing a finger at Calleja. 'That won't go unanswered…'

Attard glared at him. 'Sit down, Constable Whitlock.'

Archibald walked away from Calleja and went

back to his chair. He didn't sit down.

Attard turned to Calleja, who still carried a wide grin. 'Mr Calleja, I recommend you do exactly …'

A scream made them all freeze.

A knock at the door followed. Mr Calleja ran to open it, sounds of panic and alarm flushing into the room. A huge, shabbily-dressed man blocked the entire door way.

'There's someone who's just been murdered,' he shouted to Calleja, above the noise.

23.

The Falcon's Perch was a mess.

Not that there ever was anything orderly about this place. It was home to the derelict and the hopeless, so one couldn't expect much. The clientele was dressed as casually as usual; their gaiety and merriment as dramatic as every other evening. Tonight, however, Rita felt as though there was something amiss. She couldn't explain why.

I need a drink, she thought, descending the stairs and making for the bar.

'Giuseppe, as usual?' Victoria poured her a glass of whiskey.

Rita nodded, fingering the rim of her glass. Only Giuseppe had visited her this evening and that was unusual, even for a Monday. Not that she felt sorry, of course. 'Where's Mr Calleja?' she whispered.

Victoria bobbed her head at Mr Calleja's private room.

Rita sighed in relief. 'Is he with that Gentleman fellow again?'

Victoria shook her head, and leaned closer to Rita. 'I wasn't here when they came, but I hear he's with the police.'

Rita almost jolted.

Victoria nodded. 'It must be about the murders. There was that local Inspector … whatever the hell his name is, and a constable who, they say, is from Britain.'

Rita narrowed her eyes.

Victoria shook her head again. 'Haven't you heard? There's a constable from Britain, helping with solving these murder cases.'

I need to get out of here. Rita downed the whiskey. This was an unusual evening; even alcohol seemed to have lost its usual power. 'I need some air.' She got up and walked to the inn's entrance.

Strada Stretta was far from quiet. At least, that followed the usual pattern. People lay everywhere and around, staggering and kissing and drowning in each other's idle flattery. The full moon shone brightly, the stars blinking in the vast emptiness above. Her father used to tell her the moon didn't emit its own light. It was a stark, gigantic heavenly body which reflected the rays of the sun. He would tell her people could shine in the same way, if they allowed the power of Christ to enter into their lives. They could serve as beacons to all those in the dark.

'Oh papà,' she whispered, taking a deep breath. If there existed something in the universe that could swallow up light, she would compare herself to that. 'I have only disappointed you, pa.' If he were here, he would most probably tell her that wasn't true. 'There can be no shadow, without light,' she whispered, quoting him.

The stars blinked. She thought of Filippo, and the events from two nights ago. The young rascal had either played with fire, or strayed close enough to it. Mr Calleja and his friend weren't after him for no reason. Rita felt like slapping herself, as she remembered the red rose in the room upstairs. *Wake up Rita, you can't even read what's on that box.* She didn't know what kept her from throwing it, rose and all, away. Victoria, or somebody from the inn, might be able to read the inscription on the box. Maybe ... if it were in Maltese. Rita sighed. It could well be in Italian, for all she knew.

She peeped back inside. Whilst she was lost in thought out here, a couple of people had come in and gone out of The Falcon's Perch.

The other inn… Rita bit her lips. The one she had followed Filippo to, two nights ago… that was only a few minutes' walk away. Filippo needed to be warned, and she needed to be far away from the police.

With that in mind, she took off into *Strada*

Stretta like a swift shadow escaping the light. Despite the thick crowd, her feet didn't falter, and her soul didn't budge. At the intersection with *Strada San Cristoforo,* however, she stopped. This was where she had watched Filippo enter the inn. She moved to the exact same spot, as if just standing there could make her relive the memory. *I'm only here because somebody needs to warn him.* Rita moved on, crossing *San Cristoforo.*

Unlike two nights ago, the inn was quiet. No one walked in or out. A dim light glowed from behind its half-open, red door and louvered windows. Standing this close, Rita felt a peculiar feeling she hadn't felt last time; something about the inn felt familiar. A woman suddenly appeared from within the entrance, and Rita jolted. The woman barely noticed her, and seemed in quite a hurry. She looked like she was in her thirties; something about her stride was almost noble. With beautiful black, long hair, and dark round eyes.

'If you'd excuse me,' asked Rita in Maltese, and as politely as she could muster.

The woman slowed but didn't stop. 'Yes?' She barely turned her head to look at her.

'Could you tell me what is the name of this inn, please?'

The woman paused and sighed, eyeing her thoroughly. Rita blushed, suddenly reminded of her faded, red skirt and ragged, white blouse. She looked at her feet.

'It's The Grand Mariner,' the woman

answered flatly.

Rita thanked her, but the lady had already vanished into *Strada San Cristoforo.* She sighed, and turned to face the inn. 'The Grand Mariner,' she whispered, gazing at the inn's sign like she could read it. It sounded familiar too, but *Strada Stretta* was too full of bars and inns. Remembering all the names was impractical and futile.

Rita focused on the task at hand. *You're being foolish.* She tugged at a braid in her hair, taking a step backward. Filippo could come out of the inn, anytime. If he found her here, he'd easily think she was following him. Men were like that, very often; conceited, and firm believers that the whole world revolved around them. Then again, *she* had come here. *She* was waiting outside The Grand Mariner and fighting the urge to walk inside. *It's only because somebody needs to warn him of Mr Calleja and the Gentleman.* She paced around nervously, tugging at her hair and biting her lips till it hurt. *No, I don't like him. Even if I did, it would be childish. I'm sure Filippo knows better than to fall ...*

Rita jumped as another silhouette emerged from The Grand Mariner. This one reminded her of Giuseppe. Drunk, ugly and with a horrid smell lingering after his every step. 'They've no places for the night,' he mumbled, without lifting his head.

She nodded, grateful that he was already staggering his way down *San Cristoforo. This*

Grand Mariner is most probably just a bar, then. There was only one way to find out. *It would be nice meeting Filippo away from the Falcon's ...* Rita trembled. *I'm only doing this because somebody needs to warn him. No other reason.* She knew better than to trust her emotions, right now. They had only led her into this mess and away from her home. She didn't even know how she was still alive. Luckily, Filippo had come into her room before she ...

Her heart skipped a beat. He had saved her, after all. And not just on the night she was about to jump out of the window. Ever since *that* night, she couldn't remember ever contemplating suicide again. She stopped pacing around. *He saved me ...* Filippo deserved to get burnt by the fire he got himself into, maybe. Still, he had saved her life.

I owe him that much, at least. She took a step forward, and fixed her eyes on the entrance to The Grand Mariner. *No ... I'm allowing my emotions to take over, again!* Rita stopped and frowned.

The love for her mother and sister had made her take horrible decisions. She couldn't allow history to repeat itself. She had to use her brain, and let her heart be. Her spirit could cry as loud as it wanted. *I have to ignore it.* The red rose appeared in front of her inner eye, and she blinked. *You're not here because Filippo is in danger.* She blushed. Her legs felt like jelly and her breasts heaved. *No I can't ... he would see right through me; read it in my eyes.* She sighed heavily, looked at The Grand Mariner, and walked away.

As soon as the intersection with *Strada Vescovo* came into view, she stopped. Not because she changed her mind. The crowd suddenly got denser and louder; with their backs to her. They were looking at something on the ground, right where *Vescovo* intersected *Strada Stretta*. Then things suddenly happened so quickly.

A woman turned to look at her. '*Alla jiskansana!*'

Rita lowered her head and made to move on.

A young boy walked with the woman, scowling at Rita with dark eyes.

She was already halfway through smiling at the young boy, when she saw what people were looking at.

A dark shape lay on the ground. It looked familiar.

Rita narrowed her eyes. It was a body.

It didn't move. It gaped upwards, towards the sky.

But it wasn't looking at anything ... because it had no eyes.

Rita's eyes widened, and she screamed her soul out.

The people around the corpse almost cowered as Rita ran towards the lifeless body. Kneeling beside it, she tried to lift the lifeless head yet couldn't feel her own hands.

Filippo's eyeless face stared at her.

The world was spinning, and everything

turned as black and empty as Filippo's eye sockets.

***

The Wanderer grinned. It felt good to be covered in shadow and caressed by the full moon's rays at the same time.

Fools! The Wanderer narrowed their eyes at the crowd in front of them. *I just saved you all from seeing what you weren't yet prepared to see.*

But that was the way with people and the world, apparently. They never understood. Not even when you were doing it to save them.

'Not everyone is ready for the truth,' the Master always told the Wanderer.

He was right. But that was only their *secondary* reason for killing Filippo. The Wanderer grinned, remembering the last conversation they had with Filippo, here, less than an hour ago.

'I'm only trying to help you,' Filippo had said.

'You're a spy, and nothing but a traitor. And you're scared ... I can see it in your eyes.'

Then he had straightened and fixed his eyes on theirs. 'Is that why you brought me here? You're going to kill me.' Those last words had not been a question.

'I'm only doing you a favour.'

The Wanderer would never forget how his eyes remained fixed on theirs ... till they plucked them out, of course. He had an inner strength - the Wanderer had to give him that much. The Master might've liked him.

'No one gets between us, Filippo,' the Wanderer whispered now, glaring at the rotting corpse.

'Call the police,' someone shouted.

There was a young woman beside Filippo's corpse, wailing and banging her fists against the ground. She was a lady of the night; her clothes gave her away. For a moment, the Wanderer almost pitied her.

You'd better keep your place, woman, or you'll end up like he did.

The sound of whistles almost made the Wanderer jump. The police were on their way.

'Good luck with that,' the Wanderer whispered, slithering away from the crowd, out of *Strada Vescovo* and into the shadows.

24.

The mass of people pushed and pulled at each other and against the constables. Their tired but curious faces lingered on the eyeless corpse staring at the night sky. *Strada Vescovo* had surely never seen this many people at the same time. And surely not this late, even though this street crossed *Strada Stretta*.

'No one gets past this line,' Inspector Attard shouted to one of the constables holding the crowd. He leaned down, chalking a wide circle between the crowd and the corpse. 'Show's over, ladies and gentlemen. Go home.'

Archibald sighed heavily. The scene was sad. The raised eyebrows and bulging eyes within the crowd somehow made him think of purgatory. 'We need to know who found him,' he whispered to Attard, pointing at the corpse.

'The Superintendent should arrive soon,' replied his colleague.

'That makes our search even more urgent,' said Archibald, taking the dim lantern from Attard's hand. He glared at another constable with his back to the crowd, struggling to keep everyone in check. 'We need more light, constable. *Better* light.'

The constable pursed his lips, and shot a glance to another constable to his left. 'Caruana, we need more light.'

Archibald shook his head and huffed. He spotted Mr Calleja in the crowd.

I'm not done with you yet... He walked to one of the constables holding the crowd out of Attard's white circle. 'Constable Mifsud, right?'

'Yes.'

'Don't lose that man from your sight,' he whispered, indicating Mr Calleja.

'Yes, Constable Whitlock.'

Then he turned to Attard, who had just crouched beside the corpse.

'Nothing new, from what I can gather,' said the Maltese Inspector, grimacing in the dark. 'Eyes horrifically torn out, and nowhere on the scene. No real signs of struggle …'

Archibald took out his pocket watch, and frowned. *Twelve past midnight.* 'What about the murder weapon?' He knelt close to the corpse's head with the lantern in his right hand.

Attard narrowed his eyes and followed

Archibald's gaze. 'Nowhere to be found. But once again, a lethal single blow to the temples. Look.'

Archibald nodded. He felt like throwing up. The victim looked young, maybe in his twenties. His clothes were definitely lower-class, yet they had a different feel to them. It seemed as though the lad was a librarian, or an academic of some sort. He moved the lantern over the rest of the body, Attard's eyes followed. 'It's useless, the both of us examining this.' He glared at his colleague. 'Please, Inspector Attard. We need to find the person who found the corpse.'

Attard raised his bushy eyebrows. 'I've sent Constable Molinari to do that.'

'Molinari was here *before* the Superintendent? How efficient of him,' said Archibald, mockingly. The guy was a lazy, uncommitted fellow who appeared only when the Superintendent was around. 'Never you mind.' He shook his head and got up, walking closer to the pushing crowd. *There's hardly any choice left.* He wet his lips. 'Ladies and gentlemen,' he yelled at the crowd, in English. 'We need to speak with the person who found the victim. In the name of justice, please come forward …' He stopped.

Most of the people shifted their gaze slightly uphill.

Archibald turned. *Heaven and earth!*

'Can you tell me what's going on here?' The Superintendent Casolani entered the circle and walked towards Attard and the corpse. Constable Molinari followed him like a shadow, bright lantern in hand.

Molinari, right! Aren't you supposed to be looking for whoever found this dead bloke? Archibald approached the Superintendent, making sure not to get too close.

'We've another murder, Superintendent,' said Attard, standing up.

'Yes, I can see that. The poor fellow lost his eyes, but I haven't,' replied the Superintendent, in his rough tone. 'Molinari, get rid of this crowd.'

By the time the constable crossed Archibald, the crowd was already almost fully dispersed into the darkness of *Stretta* and *Vescovo*. Not to Constable Molinari's credit though; no one liked being close to the Superintendent's scrutiny.

That helps, thought Archibald, taking a deep breath. *God help us with the rest ...* 'Morning, Superintendent,' he said, tipping his hat.

Casolani glared back. 'What do we have here, gentlemen?'

Attard cleared his throat. 'We have ...'

'A lot of witnesses, I sure hope,' interrupted Casolani, frowning at Attard and waving his hand at the scattering crowd. 'It's a miracle we have no one from the Press yet. Where's the guy who found this poor fellow?'

Archibald was already half way through a sigh, and Attard was already looking at his feet.

'No one's come forward, Superintendent,' said Constable Molinari.

Archibald and Attard turned; Molinari stood upright and straight.

Archibald clenched his fists. *Why doesn't the devil take you, Molinari!*

'No one's come forward … in *Strada Stretta*.' Casolani sniggered. 'We need a name, or a face you could recognise.'

'Superintendent, from what I hear tell,' insisted Molinari, crossing Attard and Archibald with his head held high. 'Whoever it was ran away.'

'*Ran away*, constable?'

Molinari nodded. 'From what I hear tell, Superintendent. I assume they … they must've gotten scared, maybe? Superintendent. You know, people, nowadays.'

Casolani raised his eyebrows. 'I asked a simple question, Molinari.'

Archibald couldn't help notice how the constable fidgeted with his fingers. *You wanted to be noticed, Molinari? Bah!* He held back a grin, and looked at Attard. It was too dark, but he could see his colleague was not pleased. *That's what you get for sending Molinari.*

'Idiot!' The Superintendent waved his hand at the shaking constable. 'Do us all a favour, Molinari, and go around *Stretta* and down *Vescovo*. I don't want to see your ugly face unless you find me what I need.'

The constable nodded submissively. 'Yes, Superintendent. As you command.'

'Where do you think you're going?' The Superintendent chuckled. 'Hand me that lantern, we need it here.'

Scurrying in the dark was the last thing anyone would want to do right after a murder. Archibald almost pitied the constable. The Superintendent ordered the rest of the constables to their other duties, glaring at the corpse at every pace.

'Now, Inspector Attard, Constable Whitlock,' he said when they were finally alone 'The *Katalett* is on its way. Doctor Galea will need to look at this. While we wait, tell me what you've gathered.' He raised the lantern, and walked towards the corpse.

'Starting from similarities to the previous cases,' started Attard. 'Body is facing upwards. Eyes gouged, and not anywhere on the scene. Hit on the temples, though Doctor Galea needs to confirm this.'

Casolani stopped right beside the corpse. 'A male. That makes …? Remind me.' He handed Attard his lantern.

'This is the fifth case. Sixth victim,' replied Attard.

'Bah, right! Because the second case involved two victims. The sailors.'

Attard and Archibald both nodded.

'Superintendent, if I may. The last victim was also found very close to this spot. A few paces further up this very same street,' noted Archibald. He had actually just realised it. 'Two weeks ago, at around three in the morning,' he added, taking another glimpse at his pocket watch. 'Now it's only almost twenty minutes to one.'

Casolani rubbed at his chin. 'This could be just coincidence.'

Archibald nodded.

'This is just too chaotic.' Attard sighed. He was looking at the corpse.

'Explain yourself better, Attard,' said the Superintendent.

'Well, Superintendent.' He laid the lantern beside the corpse. 'We fail to see any pattern.'

Archibald flinched. *Now's definitely not the right time to say that, Attard.*

'First a male. Then two males. Then a female, another female, now a male,' went on the Maltese Inspector. 'Age groups differ. Locations of murder pretty much as well, if one had to dismiss this one …'

'Are you telling me you made no progress in two weeks, then?' Casolani's eyebrows were almost on the moon.

'Superintendent,' jumped in Archibald, clearing his throat. 'What Inspector Attard is trying to say …'

'I *know* what Attard is saying, Whitlock. You two have got no clue what the hell is going on in this city.'

No way! 'Superintendent, if I may be so bold. That's not an entirely correct assumption.'

'Then enlighten me, if you will, Whitlock.'

Archibald blinked, and fought the urge to look at his feet. His arms felt like a burden he never had to consider before. 'Yes, Superintendent.' He wanted to just disappear. But if Attard couldn't speak up, he had to. *So much for being wise and tactical, Inspector Attard. It would be nice if you manned up just a little.* 'The situation is chaotic. The pattern is indiscernible, to say the least. That is why we believe there is more than a single pair of hands to these murders.'

'That's so good to hear. What else?'

Why don't you shut your hole for a second? 'We've reason to believe … actually, we deduced that this could be the work of a street gang.'

Attard nodded.

Nod ahead, if that's the best you can do …

Casolani was still rubbing at his chin. 'Go on,' he said, narrowing his eyes.

Do we have to discuss this right here, in the middle of the night? God knows who else could be listening. 'Yes,' said Archibald, walking towards the corpse. It was time to portray some form of confidence, or else their superior would go on bullying them till the *Katalett* arrived, or until sunrise. 'Look at this poor fellow, right here.' He lowered his lantern closer to the corpse. 'Eyes torn out. If Doctor Galea is right, this was not done by any professional doctor or surgeon. Still, irrespective of what Doctor Galea claims, plucking out those eyeballs takes *time*. Time which the killers had, even on the previous occasion, in this same street; most probably because it was later, and quieter. But this time, they made a mistake. They committed the same atrocity at a time when this location is full of people. In so doing, they left us a clear sign that their atrocities are not committed by a single pair of hands. Because they cannot. Not before midnight, and not if you don't want to get caught.'

'Fair enough, Whitlock. It's some street gang, as you say. But what do you think is driving them?'

Archibald almost raised his eyebrows. Not because of what the Superintendent had just said, but because of the way he said it. Had he, Archibald Whitlock, finally found a way to tame this beast of a Superintendent? *Don't be hasty.* He straightened and paced around. It was still too early to bring Mr Calleja to Casolani's attention. Leaders often had the tendency to dip their fingers a little bit too much into everything. It kind of gave them a sense of control over everything they managed. He had seen this happen in Britain, as well. He didn't mind it, usually. But his gut feeling told him it was still too early to inform Casolani of their suspicions about Mr Calleja. Archibald stopped pacing and looked at the Superintendent. 'That is why we have to find out who this victim is. It would be very helpful.'

'And how do you plan to do that?'

Archibald wet his lips. *Some help would be nice, Attard…* 'I'd say we start by…'

The three of them turned at the sound of hurried footsteps from *Strada Stretta.*

'Constable Whitlock, Inspector Attard …'

Constable Caruana blinked, then froze. He was panting, and leaning against the corner. 'Superintendent, I … I didn't know …'

'Caruana?' Casolani raised his eyebrows.

Constable Caruana was not in his uniform, save for the trousers. His eyes were fixed on Archibald. 'I follow that man, as you request, Whitlock. He's Mr Calleja, of The Falcon's Perch.'

Archibald didn't have time to worry about the Superintendent's reaction. 'I know that … and?'

'I watch Mr Calleja for … for some time. I mean, I had go inside,' he answered, lowering his eyes when they met the Superintendent's.

'Inside … *where*?' said Archibald.

'The Falcon's Perch, forgive my bad English, Constable Whitlock,' answered the constable, his eyes almost watering. 'You hurry, I think it's better. Mr Calleja, he talk with this gentleman ... I couldn't hear all, but I … I can tell if some man is escaping.'

'Who was escaping?' said Attard.

'Mr Calleja, and the Gentleman.'

'What gentleman?' said Archibald.

Constable Caruana took a deep breath, and shrugged. 'I not know. I say what I see. But hurry, or Calleja and the Gentleman is not there soon.'

The rumbling sound of wheels on paved road suddenly echoed through *Strada Vescovo.*

'The *Katalett* is here,' said Casolani. 'Caruana, wait with me. Attard, Whitlock …' He sighed, fixing a long glare on Archibald. 'Go get Calleja and his friend into custody. I don't need you here.

Doctor Galea will see to the rest. I'll keep you informed if there's anything else.'

Archibald looked at the corpse, then shot a quick glance at the Superintendent. He didn't know what helped with Casolani to let them go. One thing was sure, however, it wouldn't last for long. With that in mind, he thanked God – *and* Constable Caruana – nodded to Attard, then hastened towards The Falcon's Perch like a ship on good wind.

25.

Archibald stopped running.

The crowd of people trying to get in or out blocked the entrance to The Falcon's Perch. The situation was chaotic. It was like nobody knew whether they preferred the shelter of the inn, or to be as far away as possible.

'Make way, it's the police!'

Archibald noticed Attard glaring at the person who had just shouted. The flow of people did disperse a little as they passed. Whether announcing their arrival was a good thing or not, Archibald didn't care. One thing mattered - laying hands on Calleja. He fixed his eyes on the entrance to the inn, and pushed through the crowd.

'We need to split up, in case ...' Attard had

started saying.

The noise hit Archibald's ears like the defining sound of church bells. The crowd cowered; most of them deciding lingering there was the least rational option. Archibald looked above their heads.

'Calleja, stop!' Attard yelled.

Mr Calleja emerged from The Falcon's Perch, followed by a finely dressed, short fellow.

The Gentleman … Archibald grimaced.

For a split second, Mr Calleja and the 'Gentleman' behind him glared at them. Then they took off into the opposite direction like the inn was on fire.

Archibald's feet sprang off the gravelled ground of *Strada Stretta* before he had even blinked. 'It's the police! Stop those two men,' he shouted.

And so, once again, he found himself chasing a target around the streets of Valletta. Two of them, this time. He could hear Attard right behind him. *I can't lose sight of them. Not this time*, he told himself, remembering his failure from a week ago. At a certain crossroad, Mr Calleja turned left, and uphill.

'I'll take the other one,' said Attard between heavy gasps.

Archibald nodded. He had just turned, when a sharp whistling sound went past his ears again. He cowered slightly, narrowing his eyes at Calleja's silhouette.

'He's armed.' Archibald stopped and looked

back at his colleague. 'He just ...'

Attard was on the ground, wincing and groaning in the dirt.

'Inspector Attard!' Archibald scampered towards his comrade.

'Go, Whitlock. Just catch the bloody murderer.' Attard's hand was on top of the left side of his chest. 'Go … go Whitlock. I'll be fine.' His hand was crimson.

Archibald kneeled beside him. 'You've been hit, Inspector Attard. I cannot just leave you,' he insisted, heaving.

Attard craned his neck to look at him. 'I said *go!*'

Archibald glanced back uphill. Calleja's silhouette was getting smaller. He looked around. A young man was running towards them.

'I heard … I heard the shots, and called for the *Katalett*. I …'

'Good, thank you,' replied Archibald.

'Whitlock!'

Archibald almost raised his eyebrows. Attard's voice was strong in spite of having just been hit by a bullet and lying face upwards in the dirt.

'The boy can stay with me, till the *Katalett* arrives. Can't you, boy?'

The young man nodded. He carried dark eyes, and a darker thick beard.

Hardly a boy, but anyway … Archibald looked down at Attard. 'Don't close your eyes.' He looked at the bearded man. 'Don't let him sleep or doze off.'

The young man nodded.

'I can remain alive, damn you. Now go, Whitlock!'

Archibald got up, sighed heavily, then took off uphill without looking back.

He got used to the dark, narrow lanes of Valletta, yet he still thanked God for the full moon. 'And please, help me find that murderer,' he prayed, whispering.

The two criminals had separated at the crossing of *Strada Stretta* with *Strada San Giovanni*. Yes, his last chase through Valletta had taught Archibald to keep an eye out for the street names. Luckily, this city had them signposted at almost every corner.

Where the bloody hell are you, Calleja? Archibald found himself out in the wider *Strada Mercanti*, panting and sweating. He slowed down, raising his hand through his dark hair. He had, once again, dropped his hat while on the run. Compared to the chase under the scorching sun last week, however, tonight's full moon was a blessing.

Where would I go, if I were Calleja? He narrowed his eyes, and tried to scan the darkness, to his left and right. A moment of panic gripped him as images of Attard's bloody hand crossed his mind. *The Gentleman would have left Valletta, by now*. Archibald frowned. He couldn't lose track of Calleja too. Attard had been hit by a bullet, and he had to make it count. *I've just killed again, and shot an Inspector... where would I go?*

Strada Mercanti was as dark and quiet as a graveyard. Not even the full moon seemed to suffice. Archibald knew *Porta Reale,* Valletta's main exit and entrance, was downhill, to his right. If he turns left, he would eventually go deeper into the city, and *Strada Vescovo* where... Attard's voice rang in his ears. *The murderer felt guilty. So he sought redemption.* Archibald took off to the left.

It had been quite a heated discussion at Morell's, a week and a half ago. Attard couldn't quite comprehend the idea of a murderer with a guilty conscience, at first. On the other hand, Archibald had been pretty sure it could be the case. Calleja had had all the time to escape Valletta before, but didn't. Why would he do it now? Archibald bet anything that Calleja's sense of guilt was greater than that of survival. This was the time - he either proves their theory or lose everything.

The sudden blow to the side of his head shook all the thoughts and theories out. He heard his nose crack, he gasped for air because his breath was failing. The dirt was like ash on his lips; smashing his face on the ground sent spasms through his entire body. That metallic scent of blood followed. He heard footsteps scrambling beside his throbbing head. Instinctively, he transferred his sapping strength to his arms and legs. Luckily, they responded effectively.

'Calleja…' Archibald was on his feet.

Calleja didn't blink, but came charging at him like a bull at the *matador*. Archibald prepared his muscles for impact. Calleja's head and shoulders went through his arms and straight into his abdomen. Archibald ignored the pain, before it could take over his senses. He rooted his feet to the paved road, elbowing his enemy in the back and nape. He had been in street battles before, but this Maltese thug was heavy *and* fast. Knocking his back hard on the wall behind him sent spasms through his spine, but he refused to give in. He raised his knee, hoping it would hit Calleja's stomach. The thug's grip faltered slightly. Archibald took the opportunity to try and slip out from being corned between Calleja and the wall behind him. His success was short-lived. Calleja straightened and bulldozed at him again. Archibald was prepared, this time. He raised his right leg. Calleja winced and cursed.

No time for my pistol… Archibald took one step forward, and raised his right arm at the cowered thug.

It was Calleja's turn to retaliate. He blocked the blow with his left and shouldered the constable, who lost his footing. Calleja grinned, and advanced on him. Archibald crawled backwards, kicking at will. The thug caught one of Archibald's legs and he heard himself swearing as he was propelled to the other ride of the road. It took him a while to realise the cocking sound was Calleja loading his pistol.

I'm going to end up worse than Inspector Attard, he thought, fighting with all his might to get back on his feet. *Strada Mercanti* swirled, and he heard Calleja approaching. *This cannot be how it ends.* He reached for his pistol, and heard Calleja's laughter.

The Maltese thug grabbed him by the collar and lifted his face to his. Archibald fastened his grip on the pistol and dealt Calleja a heavy blow on his temples. It didn't loosen the thug's grip on his collar but it definitely made him grimace and cower.

No other choice ... Archibald threw his head backwards, closed his eyes, and head-butted his enemy with all the strength left in him.

Calleja shouted and cursed and finally let go of him. The constable landed on his wobbly legs.

'Enough Calleja,' he yelled. 'You're under arrest for the murder of six people and shooting at an Inspector.' He hoped his legs wouldn't give in now. Calleja was rubbing his forehead with his left hand. Blood oozed from his left temple and down his cheek. His left eye was bloody and turning black. The other one glared at the constable.

'Why don't you come closer and manacle me then, you bloody Englishman?' Calleja chuckled.

Archibald picked up his pistol. He had a sudden urge to look around him, as if he were being watched. *You're being paranoid, just focus on not dropping this again.* It was getting harder to keep a steady hand.

'Unlike your Attard friend, it will take more than *that* to stop me.'

'I'm not like you, Calleja.' Archibald wiped blood off his nose. 'Now, raise your hands to your head…'

'The devil take you! I'm not going anywhere with you.'

The weird feeling of being watched crept up Archibald's spine again. He struggled not to follow his instinct, fixing his eyes on the real danger instead. 'You should've thought about that before killing those people.'

'I did not kill them!'

'Then you have nothing to fear. Justice will prevail …'

Calleja wasn't ready to give in. Archibald ducked just in time, wincing at the thug's body odour. He raised his pistol, but Calleja's next jab knocked him straight off his feet. Pain shot from his jawbone and through his bloody face; yet again he was made to taste the dust in *Strada Mercanti*.

'I did not kill those people. Go back to your country, Valletta does not need you,' yelled Calleja.

If Archibald had any strength left in his face, he would've raised his eyebrows. He was expecting more mockery and ridicule, at this point. He looked up at his enemy. *One last look at the murderer, before I become his next victim…*

Yet Calleja's attention was elsewhere. He was glaring around, as if expecting to see somebody lurk from the shadows. He looked as though he was challenging a mysterious onlooker to come forward. Archibald tried to get up. His arms trembled, and he didn't want to attract Calleja's attention again so quickly. He tried to look around, but his neck sent painful shock waves down his spine.

Calleja looked down at him, and spat. 'Don't try to find me again, or I'll kill *you* next time,' he said, disappearing down *Strada Mercanti.*

Archibald turned onto his back, slowly. He felt as though a train had just passed over him. The stench of his own blood made him want to throw up. The lack of sensation in his legs and arms made him pray to God. His ears throbbed, and his head pounded louder than his heart. In fact, he wondered whether his heart was still beating.

A faint thud reached his ears.

Get up Archie… Attard took a bloody bullet, and you were beaten like a dog. He turned on his side, wiping his brow and scanning the darkness. Momentarily, he realised he couldn't recall hearing Calleja get away. *Good God, what's that?*

A lump was on the ground, in the same direction Calleja had fled.

That's hardly ten paces away. Archibald shivered. His curiosity gave strength to the muscles in his limbs. He made for his pistol and cocked it, then staggered towards the body lying in the middle of *Strada Mercanti.* He pointed his weapon at the body on the ground. *What kind of sick joke is this?*

It was Calleja, and he was not moving. He was face downwards, but still breathing. Archibald looked around, still holding his pistol in an unsteady hand. The silence was terrifying, and that mysterious feeling of being watched returned.

'Who's there? Reveal yourself, stranger. This is the police. You have nothing to fear.'

Nothing but shadows on the limestone walls and barred doors.

No wonder no one witnesses anything, in this bloody city. Archibald looked down at Calleja's motionless body. 'Looks like it's just us then,' he whispered, cautiously nudging at the thug's shoulder with his pistol.

'Constable Whitlock?'

Archibald jumped and turned.

'Don't shoot! Please, it's Constable Caruana.'

Archibald lowered his pistol, hoping the darkness concealed his unsteady hand.

Constable Caruana narrowed his eyes at the lump behind Archibald. 'Alright, constable?'

Archibald nodded. 'Yes, Constable, I…'

'You got Mr Calleja!'

Archibald cleared his throat. 'Yes, I… Sure, of course, Constable. Help me cuff him.'

Caruana obeyed. 'You shoot him?'

'Shot him? No. I… He's just knocked out, Constable.'

As soon as they handcuffed the brute, Caruana stepped backwards like Calleja had the plague. 'Over here! Over here,' he shouted, waving to the dark *Strada Vescovo* behind him. 'Constable Whitlock, you look … I mean, Constables Mifsud and Lanfranco coming, sir… I mean, Constable,' he said, smiling faintly. 'Forgive my bad English. Good job.'

God… He looked at the sky and the full moon. *God, please forgive me.* He hoped either Mifsud or Lanfranco spoke better English; the situation was already difficult. The constables emerged from *Strada Vescovo* shortly, panting and wiping their brows. They stopped at the sight of Calleja's still frame.

'He is dead?' Constable Lanfranco widened his eyes.

'Mela ħsibtni ommok?'

Everyone jolted. Archibald turned and took out his firearm. Calleja moved and cursed in the dirt.

'Mr Calleja,' he started in the firmest tone of voice he could muster. 'You're under arrest for the murder of six people and shooting a police officer.' He wished the constables weren't looking at him with their jaws wide open.

Caruana glared at Mifsud and Lanfranco. 'Take Mr Calleja to the Police Station.'

The constables obeyed, hesitantly.

Calleja cursed and spat at them as they dragged him down *Strada Vescovo.* 'Yours is a grave mistake,' he said in Maltese. He then turned to Archibald, 'Remove these manacles so we can fight like men. If you win, I'll walk to the Police Station and give myself in.' There was something else in his eyes, besides rage.

Is he afraid? 'You're a fool, Calleja.' He nodded at the constables, and they dragged the thug onwards. Archibald walked towards one of the constables. 'How is Inspector Attard?' he whispered. Keeping a steady voice was a struggle on its own.

Caruana sighed and shook his head. 'I cannot say a lot.' He sounded miserable. 'We heard shooting. We all came to help. We found Inspector Attard lying on the ground. A young man was helping him, and he say he called the *katalett*. Inspector Attard told us you running after Calleja. Inspector Attard, he … ' Caruana faltered. 'I'm sorry. He looked … how you say? He was not in good state. He was shaking and a lot of blood from his … here.' Caruana indicated to his own chest.

Archibald raised his hand to his forehead.

Caruana went on. 'We must to find Calleja, and the other one. Superintendent and Molinari went down *San Giovanni.* Mifsud, Lanfranco and I come up here. Superintendent Casolani ask citizen stay with Inspector Attard, wait for the *katalett.* Citizen say yes, so we police could find the killers.'

Archibald was nodding.

'How are you, Constable Whitlock?'

'Me? Oh, I'm great. Thank you, Caruana,' he lied, faking a smile. *I need some peace and quiet.* 'You should go and find the Superintendent. They might need help.'

Caruana narrowed his eyes. 'I think better stay with you, sir … I mean, Constable.'

Archibald shook his hand. 'No, please. I mean it. You can go. I'll walk to the Police Station.'

'I think you must rest. Nose is …'

'Constable.' Archibald fixed his eyes on Caruana's. 'I'm fine. Find the Superintendent.'

'Yes sir.' Caruana nodded and made for *Strada Vescovo*.

'Constable Caruana … be careful, please.'

'Yes sir. Goodnight sir … I mean, goodnight Constable.'

'Goodnight.'

His whole body hurt. He glanced behind himself. *Strada Mercanti* was as silent as a graveyard; it was as though there hadn't just been a brawl. In the last couple of hours, the limestone walls of Valletta saw murder, chaos and a police officer getting shot. There was enough happening to drive any law-abiding citizen crazy.

And not a single witness came forward, so far. Archibald still couldn't fathom how anyone could remain so indifferent in such a crisis. But that wasn't what worried him most. Calleja's sudden collapse … how could someone so strong weaken so suddenly? He had hit the thug a couple of times, true. Yet Calleja was the victor. By the end of their fierce brawl, the thug had almost beaten him to death. Archibald had been at his mercy.

The guy must suffer from some illness or curse, he thought, shooting one last glance at the dark street. *He must have a weakness, after all.* He had longed to interrogate a suspect since his first night here, two weeks ago. Now, he almost wished he wouldn't make it to the Police Station, at the Auberge. Archibald limped down *Strada Vescovo*, biting his lips and wiping sweat off his brow. He *needed* to find Calleja's weakness, or else he'd rather not face him at all.

26.

Rita woke up with a start.

'It's over, dear. It's over; you're safe now. Calm down, please. You're safe now.'

The room was dark. Rita tried to get up, but the room spun.

'For God's sake, Rita. You need to lie down.'

'Victoria?'

'Yes, dear. I'm here. You're in my bed at The Falcon's Perch. You're safe now.'

'But … where … Filippo. Where's Filippo?'

Victoria put her pointer finger gently against Rita's lips. 'Keep your voice down, Rita.'

Rita looked around, heaving and sweating. The weak light from the oil lamp, by the bedside, hit Victoria's face. She looked worried.

'What am I doing here? I need to be with …'

Victoria pushed her firmly down against the mattress, then glanced around warily. 'Keep your voice down, dear.'

Rita followed her gaze. Victoria was looking at the door, which looked closed. This room didn't have a balcony, and the window was too small.

'I need to get up. Help me, Vic …'

'No! You need to listen to me, Rita dear,' she insisted. 'Just be quiet.'

Rita was about to speak, but stopped. *I mentioned Filippo … in front of her? Who else knows?* 'Sorry, Vic, I really cannot be here.'

'You *must*, Rita.' Victoria pressed her gently against the bed again.

Rita rolled her eyes and looked away. The shadows seemed ready to devour the entire room. 'What happened?'

Victoria sighed, slightly releasing her hold on Rita's chest. 'You fainted, dear. There … in *Strada Vescovo*. I carried you all the way here …'

'I remember parts of it,' Rita whispered, raising her right hand to her forehead. 'What day is it?'

Victoria sighed. 'It's Tuesday morning, still early. But you can stay here till you recover, dear.'

I've got my own room. She turned and fixed her eyes on Victoria's. 'You've already done more than enough, Vic. Thank you.' She got up, clenching her fists on the mattress.

Victoria raised a hand. 'Where do you think you're going? It's still dark outside.'

Rita ignored her, and fumbled for her sandals.

'The police were here, immediately after the murder,' said Victoria.

Rita paused.

'They came looking for Mr Calleja, and that Gentleman friend of his. The pair were expecting the police, apparently. A few minutes before the police arrived, they were quarrelling in Mr Calleja's room.'

'And this happened right … right after …?' *Don't say his name … you just pretend you don't know him.*

It was Victoria's turn to pause. She cleared her throat, and nodded. 'After the murder, yes. Mr Calleja and the Gentleman were on their way out when the police arrived. Just in time, it seems. The officers, they chased them through *Strada Stretta*. I saw more than enough for one night, so I came back to tend to your needs.'

How nice of you to avoid being in the centre of drama … to help me? Rita suppressed a frown. *How come, I wonder?*

'Some said they heard gunshots,' went on Victoria. 'Salvina said the Inspector was shot. All we know for certain is neither Mr Calleja nor the *Gentleman* returned here since.'

Oh, and you missed all that just to stay with me and tend to my wounds? What a pity! How nice of you … what do you want, Vic? Rita's feet found the sandals, and she got off the bed.

'Rita, be careful.'

She gulped. 'Thank you, Vic. I will,' she ended,

making for the door.

'Rita …'

Rita stopped and rolled her eyes, thankful for the darkness. She didn't turn to face her.

'Did you know him?'

You had to ask that … didn't you? 'Know who?' Rita was thankful for the darkness.

'The last victim, Rita.'

Rita felt like running back to Victoria and choking her. *Why, oh God … why?* Wherever she went she kept coming across impertinent people who wanted to pry into her personal affairs. Why couldn't people simply mind their own business, for God's sake?

'Know him?' She heard Victoria getting up from her chair.

'I'm just worried about you, Rita dearest,' said Victoria, creeping closer.

Of course you are! Rita turned slightly to face her. 'I'm fine, Vic. Thank you. I just need to go out for some fresh air, now.'

Victoria put a hand on her shoulder. 'It happens to all of us, sometimes. You know …'

The light came from behind Victoria, so Rita couldn't see her face. Yet she was certain the woman was wearing her usual mask of care and affection.

'Feeling those things for a client,' Victoria went on. 'Don't mistake it for love, honey.'

Feeling those things? Rita avoided Victoria's eyes, and shrugged. The woman wasn't much older than she was. *What could you possibly know about love, anyway? Just let me be.*

'Despite being victims, these people must've been involved in some kind of sinister dealings, if you ask me. And he who plays with fire gets burnt, my dear.'

Before she knew it, Rita had removed Victoria's hand from her shoulder. 'Could you just stop, please? I don't know what you're talking about.'

Victoria narrowed her eyes. 'Filippo. That was his name, right?' Her voice was suddenly stern.

'Was?'

Victoria sighed heavily, shaking her head. 'Rita, dearest. His eyes were gouged out of his face, just like the others. Do you expect him to live?'

'I know what I saw, and I don't need you to remind me. I was there, remember?'

'Rita, please. Calm down. I'm only trying to …'

Rita raised her arms and took a step backwards. 'I don't need any help! When will anyone understand that? Look … listen, Victoria. Thank you for your time and help. I wouldn't have made it back here without your aid. But now, I just … I have to leave. May I?'

Victoria shrugged. 'Fine, go ahead. The best of luck with finding any help elsewhere.'

Rita huffed. 'Fine then. You want to play the good Samaritan. What do you ask in return?'

'Excuse me?'

Rita closed her eyes and inhaled deeply.

'Forget that. What do you want to know, Victoria? He was a client. He just didn't treat me as badly. That's all. But he came, paid, and left. Just like the others. I'm sorry if you were misled by love, in the past. But that was *your* story. Mine has no love in it. Is that clear? Is that enough? What else do you want to know?'

Victoria was so silent Rita thought she could hear the flickering flame of the lamp die out.

'Get out of my room. Just leave.'

Isn't that what I have been trying to do all along? Rita sighed and walked out of the door. 'Thank you for helping me. I'm forever …'

'Get out, Rita.'

Rita trotted briskly, closing the door behind her.

Her room was in the same state she had left it. Flooded by the sunlight from behind the curtains. Rita closed the door and glanced at the rose on the chest of drawers. She ran to her bedside, opened the drawer, and sighed in relief. The wooden box in her hand was like a golden ornament. Even though she couldn't read what Filippo had inscribed on its lid, the engraved script looked professional.

I need some fresh air, she thought, suppressing tears and putting the wooden box back in the drawer. She rushed to the door, her heart beating and her chest heaving.

The Falcon's Perch hallway didn't help Rita's mood. Someone was snoring, and two old men flicked their deck of cards. A barmaid, whose name Rita couldn't recall, fidgeted with unclean dishes. The rest were gone; they were more sensible than to linger at an inn the police had just raided. Rita made for the exit. She needed to know for how long she was unconscious.

Compared to the dullness inside, *Strada Stretta* shone in the approaching daylight. Still, she frowned. By this time, the police would've taken Filippo's body to God knows where. She closed her eyes, and saw Filippo's eyeless face gaping at the sky. No amount of time will ever erase that image from her mind. She opened her eyes, and found herself fighting tears, again. *I was so close … How did I not even hear him shout, or …?* She shook her head. Blaming herself for Filippo's terrible fate was useless. It would not get her anywhere. She fixed her eyes eastwards, towards *Strada Vescovo.*

Reliving the moment was going to hurt.

At the intersection of *Stretta* with *Vescovo*, Rita started gasping for breath. Her feet felt like jelly, and she wasn't sure she could feel her arms. Her inner eye, however, worked like never before. It evoked memories of Filippo's corpse, right in front of her. His eyeless face staring at the sky above. Now, he wasn't surrounded by any crowd; not even by the police. She blinked and rubbed her eyes … and Filippo was gone. Only a white circle on the ground remained.

Why did I have to lose my senses? Rita felt like banging her head against the wall behind her. She had missed her last moments with Filippo by fainting right on the spot. In his last moments, when he might've still been feeling her presence despite his blindness, she had left him. She had allowed the curious, cold crowd – and the police – to trample all over his dignity.

She wept.

Why did you have to end up here, like this, oh Filippo? What were you ...? Rita blinked, and pushed her sullen accusations away. Blaming Filippo for his tragic death was not going to bring him back. Along with the wooden box inside her room, the memory of Filippo was all she had left. While the others had already forgotten all about him, she would not. She could not. Despite what she would *never* tell the world, she owed Filippo her life. More than that, she owed him justice.

Mr Calleja's grim face suddenly appeared before her mind's eye. She hadn't made it in time to save Filippo from Calleja and that cunning *Gentleman*, friend of his. She could waste the rest of her days crying, regretting, or she could do something about it. She glanced eastwards, deeper into *Strada Stretta.* Filippo and his friend had come out from that bar, The Grand Mariner, two nights ago. *Pawlu and Filippo ...* when Mr Calleja came out cursing and charging at them, like a bull. *It's only on the next block*. Rita glanced at the murder spot one last time, said a little prayer for the repose of Filippo's soul, then dragged herself deeper into *Strada Stretta.*

Unlike all the other streets in the city, this one slumbered in the morning. Like a satisfied beast after a wild, successful hunt. Its narrowness and high buildings protected Rita from any disruption. Not that she bothered about any onlookers, at this stage. The red door of The Grand Mariner was open. Rita took a deep breath and walked inside.

The feeling of familiarity she got from this place two nights ago, now made sense. The bar on the left, the staircase opposite the main entrance leading upstairs … The whole layout was almost identical to The Falcon's Perch. Only the room space for Mr Calleja's office was missing. Instead, there stood an old, dusty piano hiding the imperfect angle where the walls met. A good number of ladies and gentlemen already hung around the main hall. They looked more awake, sober and composed than the ones back at The Falcon's Perch.

'Good morning,' said a female voice from behind the bar.

Rita jolted slightly. 'Good morning,' she replied, clasping her hands in front of herself. It was the same woman she had crossed last night, right outside this place before … before … She straightened. 'I …'

'Yes, this is The Grand Mariner,' said the woman, giggling slightly.

Rita blushed. *She recognised me.* She looked around warily, but no one else seemed bothered by her entrance. *Well you can't just stand here.* She moved forward towards the bar, her stomach growling. 'A glass of water would do just fine,' she said.

The woman behind the bar raised an eyebrow. Then waved a black fringe from in front of her eyes, and nodded. Rita followed her as the woman got a clean glass and filled it.

'Thank you,' she said when the woman put the glass in front of her.

'You're Maltese, the first one's free,' replied the woman in a light tone.

'Oh, no. Please …'

'If I wanted your opinion on the matter, I would've asked for it. It's scorching hot outside and it's not even eight o'clock. Here, drink.'

Ġesù! Rita looked down and sipped at her drink. *I was only being polite.*

Something was noble in the way this woman spoke. Rita had observed this attitude in the woman's stride too, last night. She sighed, and gave another look at the tables behind her. An old man walked to the bar, eyeing Rita from top to bottom before having a seat. As far as she remembered, Pawlu was much younger; of average height, with dark hair and eyes. He was quite muscular too, and wore a thick black beard. A profile that almost covered the entire Maltese population, to be fair.

Rita stood with her back to the old man and looked at the barmaid. 'I'm looking for …' she started, then faltered. 'I'm looking for a room,' she lied.

'The Grand Mariner doesn't provide any, sorry,' replied the woman, without even a glance.

Damn ... Rita bit her lip and fidgeted with her glass. She couldn't just ask about Filippo on her first appearance here. 'That's a nice piano,' she added, smiling slightly.

The woman shot her a glance. 'Thank you,' she said, narrowing her eyes.

Rita wasn't lying, this time. She had always dreamt of playing the piano. Her family had never afforded something so extravagant, of course. Rita smiled faintly, remembering how her father would constantly remind her not to give up on her dreams.

'With God by our side everything is possible Rita, my dear,' he would tell her with his eyes shining and his smile never fading.

That was before he went to meet God, of course; leaving his family struggling with life's challenges on their own. Rita shook her head and blinked. The past was called so for a reason. She faced new challenges now and drowning in the past was not going to help her achieve any of goals. She deserved the mess she was currently in; she had abandoned God, walked in the devil's footsteps and condemned her own soul in the process. Yet, for as long as she had a pair of feet, hands, eyes and a brain, she would not give up. To start with, she needed to find Pawlu. He was her best and only hope if she wanted to do justice to Filippo. More clients joined her at the bar. She could sense the old man was still eyeing her. Unfortunately, the woman behind the bar didn't seem too fond of conversation.

Strange, for a woman and *a barmaid.* 'Thank you for the water,' she said.

The woman behind the bar grabbed the glass, but didn't look at her.

You must be a little curious about a new customer showing up at the bar. What kind of woman are you? 'This heat is killing me,' remarked Rita.

'It will pass,' replied the woman, flatly. 'Like everything else.'

Rita raised an eyebrow. *Fine. You're not the talkative type. Maybe you should meet with Victoria.* She suppressed a grin, and looked behind her again. A thin, weathered man was about to leave his table.

'Thank you, Luciana,' he shouted to the woman behind the bar, leaving some coins on the table. 'Good service, as always.'

The woman behind the bar nodded and waved vaguely.

Ah, so you have a name, at least. 'It's nice when customers appreciate good service,' Rita fixed her eyes on Luciana, who barely nodded. 'I mean, during times like these. It helps a lot.'

Luciana looked at her and nodded.

'How impolite of me ... forgive me! I'm Isabella,' she said, dramatically.

'Beautiful name.' Luciana sounded genuine, for the first time this morning.

Rita smiled. 'Thank you. So's yours.' *What an odd creature!*

'You're a barmaid … where?'

Rita cleared her throat. 'The Falcon's Perch,'

she whispered, looking down at the bar.

Luciana raised an eyebrow. 'Interesting! What do you reckon is going to happen there, now that Mr Calleja's been caught?'

Rita looked up. 'Mr Calleja's been caught?'

Luciana's dark, orb-like eyes were fixed on Rita. 'Yes sure, this very morning – or night, whatever. The police caught him. He was the culprit behind all these murders, presumably. If so, it will be only a matter of time before he's prosecuted and sentenced to death.'

Rita gaped. Mr Calleja's capture would mean justice for Filippo … and a very swift one at that. Yet, somehow, it felt as though it wasn't enough. 'Are you sure?'

Luciana giggled slightly. 'Well, as a barmaid at The Falcon's Perch it's strange that *you* aren't aware. It will be in today's newspapers, I guess.'

Rita sighed, leaning slightly backwards. 'Today's newspapers … right.'

'Where were you last night, then?'

Rita blinked. 'Excuse me?'

Luciana raised her arms, palms facing the ceiling. 'The Falcon's Perch was raided by the police, and the proprietor ran away. But you … were you drunk or what?'

I was unconscious, while Filippo was left alone in the dark.

'There was quite a chase. A police officer was shot. Eventually, Mr Calleja was caught.'

Rita stared blankly. She wanted justice for all of Valletta, of course but more so for Filippo. This was what she had longed to hear. Justice for Filippo is what brought her to this inn, after all. Then why was she feeling upset by this news? Why didn't this news feel adequate enough to her? She blinked. 'How do you know all this?'

Luciana tilted her head sideways. 'You work at The Falcon's Perch ... I'm more surprised how you *don't* know anything. Besides, this is Valletta, dear. Everyone knows, by now.'

'Yes, I was at The Falcon's Perch,' lied Rita. 'I know what happened. But how do you know Mr Calleja was caught?'

Luciana twisted her lips. 'Are you sure you're feeling well? You look pale, suddenly.'

Rita nodded slightly. 'It's been a long night.' She forced a smile. 'It's good that Valletta can finally breathe again. Pity Mr Calleja had to kill one more person before he was brought down.'

'Pity indeed,' said Luciana.

'Did you know him, then?'

'Mr Calleja? Of course not.'

'No, the last victim, I mean.'

Luciana paused. 'He frequented this bar. But we never spoke, no,' she whispered.

It took her awhile to resume the conversation, no wonder! Rita sighed.

The old man was still looking at her, and he wasn't blinking. She returned a flat stare, then looked behind her. Unlike mornings at The Falcon's Perch, the clientele here increased. Rita thanked Luciana, wished her a good day, and climbed down from her stool. The sound of another stool scratching the tiles followed. She didn't need to look back to realise the old fellow was following her. Most of the time, when it came to lust, old men were the worst. She quickened her pace, hoping this ugly creature found something else to look at, by the time she reached the exit. *Finally*, she closed The Grand Mariner's red door behind her and headed towards *Strada Stretta.*

'Missy.'

Rita almost jumped. The man was *old*, crooked, and missing his right leg. His grey, scruffy hair and dark brown, slit-like eyes made her shudder.

'Missy,' he croaked, standing at the door and signalling her to come closer.

Rita fought the urge to shake her head and run away. *Come on, you've faced worse than this. You can always outrun him, with that wooden leg.* She approached, cautiously.

'Thanks missy,' he started, flashing a terrible smile. 'For I'm old. My voice is weak. I cannot shout.'

Rita frowned. 'What is it?' He smelled of sour cream and onions.

'If you want to know about Filippo, better try to have a word with the proprietor here,' he whispered, looking around warily.

She pursed her lips. 'The proprietor?'

'Yes, Pawlu. He's the proprietor of The Grand Mariner,' he said, looking around warily. 'Come in the evening. *Late* in the evening,' he ended, coughing and limping back inside The Grand Mariner.

Rita gaped and almost lost her balance. She looked up at the blue sky, her stomach grumbling. She still had some time before that sky turned dark purple. For the first time in many days, however, she wished it was already dark.

27.

Lorenzo turned in his bed. Despite the dark, he scanned almost every nook and cranny of his cell. The oil lamp had long been spent; not that he needed it anymore, really. He knew the words by heart now.

Father Lorenzo Testaferrata,
Your presence at the Chapel of the Bones has proven your commitment to the cause.
But can I say the same about your ability to save Valletta?
Beneath Michael, find the Murderer's Mark and your next clue.
L.

He was exhausted, but his mind kept drawing his attention to the words like a moth to a flame.

He had barely touched any food all day. Out of worry, mostly - though a little bit of fasting could grant him the Lord's favour - something he needed dearly, right now.

Luigi is literate, Lorenzo turned in his bed again.

Few could write in English with no mistakes. Not to mention the elegant handwriting. He could've gotten help, of course. But this wasn't the type of letter one asked another to write in their stead. Luigi was literate, which meant he was also intelligent. *And ten times more dangerous.* Lorenzo shuddered. *God, help me …*

He held his breath. As much as he hated to admit it, the priest was starting to lose hope. His Saviour had apparently decided to leave him wading through this murky sea alone. *God works in mysterious ways …* He scowled. That was what he told his flock on a regular Sunday homily, or when the most afflicted visited him for counsel. It was Tuesday; nothing was ordinary about it. Lorenzo thought his saying wasn't going to help him much, for too long. He shut his eyes. *Why, oh Lord, have you abandoned me?*

He doubted whether quoting the Holy Bible worked anymore. Who was Michael? And how was he supposed to look beneath this fellow to find a clue? The Murderer's Mark? It was all so vague and scary. *It must be morning, by now.* Lorenzo glared at the window. The sky was dark violet and devoid of anything celestial. The Lord wasn't listening anymore. Lorenzo felt like swearing at Him.

No! Lord, forgive me. He clenched his fists and bit his lips. *It was a fleeting thought. No more than that ... please forgive me,* he prayed, opening his eyes and scanning the room frantically. There was nobody in the room. But his heart pound as if it was about to leave his chest. Doubting his faith could summon the Lucifer. *Oh, St Michael! Oh glorious Archangel St Michael, Prince of the heavenly host!* Lorenzo closed his eyes again, and tried to relax. *Defend us in battle and in the struggle which is ours against the Principalities and Powers ...*

His heart missed a beat.

Oh, of course ... that *Michael!* He opened his eyes. *Beneath St Michael.* He frowned in the darkness. He couldn't even see the ceiling. *What's beneath St Michael?* The Archangel was God's mightiest and strongest warrior. A lot of celestial beings were beneath him, in rank. If the next clue were in the hands of an angel ... Lorenzo sniggered. The only angel who would ever deal with one as low as Luigi, would be the Fallen One himself. The priest shuddered at the thought. Knowing he was up against one of Lucifer's agents was one thing but having to confront the devil directly ...

He made for the lamp beside his bed. The dim light made him wince - but it sure felt comforting. Lorenzo tried to ignore the shadows forming on the walls and dancing on the ceiling. He grabbed the letter again.

The murderer's mark ... why is it written like it

were an official name for something? Lorenzo sighed heavily. Luigi was the murderer; his mark had to be something he left on all the victims. Judging by the rumours the priest had gathered about the murders, that would be the gouging of the eyeballs. He looked at the letter again. *Beneath Michael, find the Murderer's Mark and your next clue.*

For now, he could assume Michael referred to the mighty Archangel. Somewhere, beneath him was the murderer's mark. Luigi's mark, whatever that was. The priest's mind flashed back to all the mental images of St Michael. In all the drawings and statues, the Archangel was always portrayed standing on the devil, brandishing his glorious sword. *Beneath St Michael ... is Lucifer! Find the Murderer's Mark ...* Lorenzo couldn't recall noticing any particular mark in any portrayal. He wished he was still at his childhood home in Vittoriosa. Looking at those biblical books and statues his parents would use to teach him religion.

He gasped.

There was a statue of St Michael in Valletta, where *Strada St Ursola* crossed *Strada Vescovo*. He glanced at the window again, and smiled faintly. The Lord had protected him from the night and its shadows, despite his momentary fury. It was now dawn. The priest jumped out of bed and made for his Dominican robes. But the room spun and suddenly, everything was turning dark and dull again. He leaned back against the chair of his desk and closed his eyes. He thought he heard the bed calling his name. *Lord, this cannot wait. I need to save Your flock. Please, grant me the strength.*

A sound of movement and cutlery came from downstairs. His stomach rumbled; Lorenzo couldn't even remember the last time he'd eaten. Rushing out without joining his brethren for breakfast would draw too much unwanted attention. Prior Massimo's face was the last thing he wanted to see anytime soon. Nonetheless, the priest put on his robes, uttered a prayer and headed straight for the refectory.

Mr Axiak was laying out the cutlery. Lorenzo asked him for some bread and water and the servant obeyed without question. 'I've put in some butter and salt,' he said, humbly.

No one's down yet. Lorenzo didn't know whether this was luck, or whether God was on his side again. '*Kun imbierek,*' he told the servant, and rushed out of the refectory without a moment's hesitation.

'Don Lorenzo, good morning!'

Lorenzo's previous hope – that his luck or favour with the Lord had returned – vanished instantly.

'Good morning, Don Roberto.' He tried to smile, but it hurt.

'Well, how are you! We haven't seen you for …'

'Yes, forgive me. I still have not fully recovered from my injury,' he lied. *And you're in the way.*

'That's sad to hear, brother.' Don Roberto looked at the loaf in Lorenzo's hand. 'I see your appetite is returning,' he said, flashing a warm smile.

Lorenzo winced slightly. 'Yes, brother. Slowly. The nurses at *Ospedale Centrale* discharged me on condition that I drink a lot of water.' *Satisfied? Now get out of my way!* He peeped at an arch leading out of the hallway.

'Were you going somewhere?'

Why don't you just ask me why I'm not breaking fast with you and let us both be done with it. Lorenzo suppressed an instinctive frown, sighing instead. 'Yes, you caught me,' he said, snickering lightly. 'I was thinking of going for a quiet morning stroll, truth be told. It looks like it's going to be a beautiful day.'

The young priest shrugged. 'Well, I sure hope so. Though, I don't think enough sun can obliterate last night's terrible events,' he reflected, crossing Lorenzo and making his way towards the refectory.

Lorenzo narrowed his eyes. 'What terrible event?'

Don Roberto slowed down and looked back at the priest. 'Why, I assumed you'd have heard by now. They found another body last night, and …'

Lorenzo struggled to keep his balance. *Heaven and earth … can it get any worse?* 'What? Where?'

The young priest pointed at the direction of the parlour. 'I read it in *Fede ed Azione* this morning. But it's also in the *Corriere Mercantile di*

Malta.' He raised his eyes, like he was recalling something. '*Strada Vescovo* again. None of the papers have photographs, unfortunately. Apparently, the police aren't allowing any photos to be taken. The public has to know how dangerous this killer is, if you ask me. Rumour also has it that …'

Lorenzo found himself walking idly towards the end of the hallway and out of the Priory. The young priest followed him for the first few steps, until his hunger won over his curiosity and he left Lorenzo in peace.

'Good Lord,' whispered Lorenzo, once he was out in *Strada San Domenico.* 'Luigi, why are you doing this to my city … why?' He gasped for breath; the street almost felt too narrow.

Out in *Strada Mercanti*, the sun hit his face. Despite the early hour, he found himself wincing. He tried to shield his eyes with his arm; that was when he realised he could barely feel it. His legs wobbled too and his stomach groaned again. His mouth felt dry. Before he knew it, his unsteady legs took him back inside and up to his cell. He hadn't yet finished devouring Mr Axiak's bread when he plunged into his bed. It rarely felt this comfortable and welcoming. Lorenzo shut his eyes and slept.

It was dark when Lorenzo woke up. *I lost precious time …* He winced.

Sloth had conquered him; he'd have to remember this during his next confession.

Lorenzo got off his bed and fumbled for the oil lamp in the dark. At least the room didn't spin this time. He lit the lamp, the flickering flame barely hitting his face. The shadows of his cell came to life. Despite the heat, he shivered. *Ten minutes to three,* the small clock read. *But the Lord's work cannot wait.* Luckily, he found his sandals quite quickly. Uttering a prayer, he made for the door.

Then stopped.

Not a good idea. He glared at the lamp in his hand, and pursed his lips. *Better face the dark than Prior Massimo or someone from his fellow brethren …* He walked back to his desk and laid the lamp there. Darkness engulfed him as soon as he blew out the flickering light.

It's dark here, let alone outside, he thought, closing the door of his cell behind him. He wiped sweat off his brow and fumbled for the rosary beads inside the left pocket of his robes. Murmuring another prayer, he headed towards the stairs.

The waning gibbous loomed over Valletta, its decreasing light shrouding *Strada San Domenico* in darkness. Lorenzo wiped his brow, then narrowed his eyes. The statue of St Michael was a couple of minutes' walk away but he would rather cross the Atlantic right now. Luigi had to have some nerve to get close to St Michael's statue and leave a clue there.

This could all be in vain, after all, thought the priest, dragging his feet onwards and looking over his shoulders. Unfortunately, he had to get to the statue to find out. Avoiding the openness of *Strada Mercanti*, he proceeded down *Strada San Domenico*, murmuring and fiddling with the rosary beads inside his pocket. He turned onto *Strada San Paolo*, wincing at the sound of his own footsteps. *Though I walk through the valley of the shadow of death, I will fear no evil: for thou art with me …*

At the intersection with *Strada Vescovo*, he paused. The statue was down the street, around the corner, to his left. He blinked, swallowed and glanced around the corner as though a little imp was about to pounce onto him. For the first time this evening, he wished he was not alone. 'Lord walk with me,' he whispered, taking a step forward. St Michael loomed over the crossing between *Strada San Paolo* and *Strada St Ursola*, guarding the four corners from nocturnal terrors. The statue was a recent addition to the many others, scattered across different street corners of Valletta. The building behind the statue belonged to the Fraternity of St Michael. Lorenzo couldn't remember the sculptor's name.

'Oh glorious Archangel St Michael,' he started, avoiding to look at Lucifer beneath the Archangel's feet. 'Defend us in …'

The priest paused, and blinked. He took a step back, narrowed his eyes and looked again. The moon's reflection hit something on the wall, right beneath the statue.

Good Lord… He approached the wall,

cautiously.

It was too dark to spot the colour, but it looked like fresh paint. Lorenzo frowned as the familiar smell of metal and rust hit his nostrils. His legs suddenly trembling, he almost dropped the lamp. *Blood!* Against every instinct, he leaned closer to the sign on the wall. The symbol looked like an inverted letter F. And while the standard F had one stroke in the middle, this one had two.

Beneath Michael, find the Murderer's Mark, and your next clue ... Lorenzo straightened and closed his eyes. This had to be the Murderer's Mark, even though it had not been found on any of the victims. That, or the rumours were weaker than Lorenzo gave them credit for. Whatever it was, the next clue had to be right here, according to Luigi.

Beneath Michael, find the Murderer's Mark ... and your next clue. Lorenzo gulped and set his eyes on Lucifer. Looking at the devil was never easy, let alone after having smelled fresh blood. He scowled at the realisation and raised his head closer to Lucifer's.

And there it was.

A piece of paper was crumpled inside the devil's twisted mouth. Lorenzo inhaled deeply. Most probably, this was what he was looking for. This was what Luigi brought him out here to find. He felt dizzy, numb and wanted to cry. *Lord, forgive me*, he prayed. He looked around him one last time, then reached for the devil's mouth and pulled out the paper. A great part of himself suddenly wished it was darker, so he wouldn't be able to read.

Fr Lorenzo Testaferrata

My Master deems your faith unworthy and that I should kill you.

Your reaching this stage, however, proves you might have what it takes to save Valletta.

Come to Hastings Gardens this Friday, at the witching hour.

L.

28.

Archibald stared at the ceiling. The flame on the bedside table had long been burnt out. Lighting another candle was pointless; the darkness, somehow, helped him think. The last couple of hours had been amongst the wildest and most shocking of his life - apart from his years in London, but of course, he didn't want to think about those. The ceiling was conjuring up his Superiors' scolding faces every time he thought about his recent experiences. Superintendent Casolani, here in Malta, had given him more than enough to worry about.

He raised his watch closer to his face. *Ten to five*. He shut his eyes and, for the umpteenth time, pondered tonight's events. Back at the Auberge D'Auvergne, he had insisted Mr Calleja be interrogated urgently. Casolani disallowed it, claiming a night inside a cell would help Mr Calleja think well about his next decisions.

'Besides,' the Superintendent had said. 'You look terrible, Whitlock. Go get some rest.'

Archibald winced now. *How do you expect me to rest?* His back was in excruciating pain, his jaw hurt and he wasn't sure whether he felt his legs. He thought of Attard again …

'We'll know more in the morning,' Casolani had said, when Archibald asked about his partner. 'For now, it suffices to know he's alive. Go to Morell's and rest, Whitlock. It's an order. We'll speak in the morning. Eight, in my office.'

The Superintendent was different, somehow. Though Archibald couldn't quite exactly understand what it was. Something odd about his voice and stern look puzzled Archibald. Something was amiss; it reminded him of his superiors back in London. Archibald frowned. *Please God, don't let it be same here*, he prayed.

Sleep took hold of him, eventually. Not one of those undisturbed slumbers, unfortunately. A horrendous number of faces kept haunting him, scolding him. Some were like the Superintendent's, others resembled his Superiors' from Britain. A few of them had silver orbs instead of eyes and their eye sockets were filled with blood.

Waking up in the morning was far from easy. He made his way down the stairs aching all over, crossed Morell's parlour and emerged onto *Strada Forni.* The day was bright, the sun scorching.

Incredible! He put on his hat. *Not one cloudy day since I came here*, he thought. Even the morning sunshine brought sunny days in London to shame. English sunny days were dull compared to these bright mornings. He wished he had time for a stroll, it would definitely help his mood. He dragged himself to the Auberge. Constable Molinari was waiting at the entrance. Archibald suppressed a frown. *Why am I not surprised?*

'The Superintendent awaits you in his office. Follow me, please.'

Archibald released his frown. *Follow you? Does the Superintendent think I cannot find my way?*

The corridors and rooms along the way were full of the usual hustle and bustle one finds in a governmental establishment. Archibald had only been here twice before, but the building reminded him of those modern farming machines he saw in books. They processed, trampled and scrambled anything in their path. He hoped he would not be ravaged in the same way.

'Come in.' The muffled voice of Casolani made him almost wince.

Archibald thanked Molinari, then stepped inside. The Superintendent sat behind his desk. Another man, in his early twenties, sat in front of him. The young man stood up and nodded.

'Inspector Ġio Felice Inglott,' said Casolani,

indicating the man sitting in front of his desk. 'Inspector Felice Inglott, this is Constable Archibald Whitlock, from Britain.'

'Pleasure to make your acquaintance.' The Inspector had brown eyes and hair and the beardless face of a man who's just come out of his teens.

Archibald forced a smile. 'Pleasure all mine,' he murmured, removing his hat.

'Sit, both of you.' The Superintendent wasn't smiling.

They did as they were told. Casolani leaned forward, resting his elbows on the desk. He eyed them both in silence, for a while. 'Very well gentlemen. We need to discuss the way forward in this investigation. There were several mistakes done which you cannot afford to repeat.'

Mistakes? Archibald held back a frown.

'Inspector Felice Inglott will be replacing Inspector Eduardo Attard.' The Superintendent had his green eyes fixed on Archibald, who nodded.

'How's Inspector Att...?'

'He's at the *Ospedale Centrale*.' Casolani turned his eyes on the Maltese Inspector. 'Inglott, you're in charge of the team now.'

Inglott nodded. 'Yes sir.'

Archibald almost gaped. *So that's why you sounded perturbed, last night! That's what felt amiss.* His cheek bones hurt from suppressing all the frowns and scowls. He clasped his hands in front of him and looked at the ceiling.

'Now with that cleared ... Whitlock, I briefed Inspector Felice Inglott on the basics. Would you kindly fill him in on the past two weeks?'

Of course! Archibald suppressed a smirk, and nodded instead. 'Yes sir.' He reached for his notebook inside his coat. 'We have … Inspector Attard and I arrested Mr Calleja on …'

'Mr Calleja of The Falcon's Perch, *Strada Stretta.*' The Superintendent dug his chin in his clasped hands.

Archibald inhaled. 'Correctly so.' He looked at the Inspector. 'We suspect Calleja is involved in these murders. From what we gathered …'

'Why, pray, tell me?' Casolani's eyes were on him.

Archibald almost gasped. *Why … what?* 'Beg your pardon, Sir?'

'It's a simple question, Whitlock. On what grounds did you arrest Mr Calleja, the owner of The Falcon's Perch?'

If you'd let me finish … 'Yes,' replied Archibald, looking at his notepad. 'One of our theories was that a gang of Valletta was behind these murders. Prior to that, Inspector Attard had recommended we speak to Don Lorenzo, a Dominican. Being a man of the cloth, the Dominican had many contacts …'

'Good decision, go on.'

Archibald nodded, glanced at the Inspector, then back at his notebook. 'The priest had a good relationship with Ms Anna and her brother Mr Joseph. Ms Anna is the victim found in *Strada*

Vescovo on the 14th of this month. Mr Joseph, her brother, is still missing.'

Inglott nodded. 'Ms Anna is the fourth victim,' he said, fervently.

'The fourth murder case, really. Two victims, the sailors, were found on the second instance – the night of 13th March. That makes Ms Anna the fifth, and …'

'Whitlock, you're off trail,' said Casolani.

Oh! Inspector Attard, I'm already missing you! Archibald nodded as politely as he could. 'Yes Sir. Sorry, Sir. As I was saying … Don Lorenzo told us Ms Anna was seeing someone, before she got murdered. According to the priest, this relationship was her demise. He didn't have a name, unfortunately.' His mind went to the piece of paper inside his room, at Morell's. 'From there, Inspector Attard and myself confirmed our original theory could hold. So, the Inspector suggested we start looking into gangs. He mentioned Mr Calleja and how he often heard of troubling reports about The Falcon's Perch. We …'

'So just like *that*, you decided to arrest Calleja, Whitlock?'

Sorry, Attard. I just can't tell them. Archibald frowned. 'We never had the intention to arrest him, sir. As I explained …' *But are you even listening?* 'We went to speak to him on the evening of the 24th.'

'Yes, right before the murder,' said Casolani, flatly.

Archibald sighed slightly. 'He was the usual bully and thug-like character.' He fixed his eyes on Inspector Inglott. 'He seemed helpful at the time …' *In exchange for turning a blind eye to all the misdeeds that take place at The Falcon's Perch.* Archibald would never agree to that sort of bribery, let alone speak of it with his Superintendent.

The Superintendent had his eyebrows raised. 'And?'

Archibald glared back. 'Unfortunately, we heard screaming coming from the street and there was a lot of commotion. That's when one of Calleja's men came in, reporting the murder.'

'And then you did the last good thing that night - you came to the crime scene. Only until someone told you Calleja was on the run. Why did you chase him in the middle of the night?'

This guy can't be serious … Archibald tapped his foot and pursed his lips. *You told me I could go!* 'There was nothing exceptional on the murder scene. Eyes gouged out, major wound to the temples, no other visible trauma. Then, Constable Caruana came and told us Calleja and his friend were running away from The Falcon's Perch. And with your permission …'

'Fine, Whitlock. I think we heard enough tragedy for one morning.' Casolani leaned forward again, eyeing both of them. 'Gentlemen, now let's discuss the way forward.'

Archibald grimaced. Inglott cleared his throat and nodded.

'This morning, you will interrogate Calleja and see that something good comes out of it. You have less than forty-eight hours. We need to put an end to this mess.'

Archibald bit his tongue. *The devil take you!*

'I don't need to remind you about the urgency and importance of this case,' continued the Superintendent. 'Calleja shot Inspector Attard – one of our best. I *will* see him hang for it. First, I want a confession from him, though. A confession to all these murders. Valletta needs to find peace again.'

Archibald wondered who Casolani's superiors were and what *they* thought about this 'mess'. Did they bully him into finding a solution and the Superintendent was just passing the buck? It was the way of the world, apparently, for those in high rank to scream down at their subjugates. Eventually, the bullying goes down the chain of command, to the lowest rank. Archibald almost smirked at the thought. His superiors in London had sent him here to teach him a lesson, or to get rid of him. His experience was teaching him Malta was no different to Britain. Despite the humour, however, he felt frustrated.

Meanwhile, the Superintendent was still rambling. 'The newspapers have their eyes on this case. So far, we managed to keep photographs at bay. However, the public is now in panic. We have to bring all this to an end, gentlemen.'

'Yes Sir,' said Inglott.

That's all you care about, closing this case. Where's your sense of justice, Casolani? Archibald nodded reluctantly. 'Yes Sir!'

'Inspector Inglott will be leading the interrogation. Constable Whitlock, I'm sure you'll take the opportunity to understand how things are carried out over here.' Nothing about Casolani's voice or expression indicated he was joking.

Archibald gaped. *Understand how things are carried out over here? Calleja shot your best Inspector, for Christ's sake!*

'Is everything clear then, gentlemen?' Casolani ended, glaring at Archibald.

'Yes Sir,' said Inglott, nodding.

'Is something of the matter, Whitlock?'

Archibald thought of Attard. *God, grant me his patience.* He clenched his fists and leaned slightly backwards. 'Everything is fine, Superintendent,' he replied dryly.

The Superintendent waved a hand at them, indicating they could leave. Inspector Inglott got up and walked out. Archibald stood up slowly, and dragged his feet to the exit. With his hand on the doorknob, he stopped. Attard's voice rang inside his head, urging him to remain calm. 'May I have a word, Superintendent?' *I'm not like you Attard, unfortunately …*

The Superintendent grunted and nodded in the affirmative.

Archibald turned to face him. He took a deep

breath and fixed his eyes on his superior. 'I ... with all due respect, Sir. I disagree with your decision.'

The Superintendent didn't even blink. 'Whitlock?'

Archibald bit his lips and tapped his left foot. 'I ... I mean the interrogation ...'

'Close that door, Whitlock.' The Superintendent had his hand raised.

Archibald glared at the Superintendent and did as he was told.

'There, Whitlock. I just did you a favour. Here's another one ... the *last* one for that matter. I do not owe you any explanation when I take a decision. You got me *nothing* in over two weeks - except for a fixation with Calleja and his friend – without any proof of anything. One of Malta's best Inspectors is on his deathbed. Personally, I think you don't have many other options. Besides, you should be *thanking* me you're still here and not on the next ship, back to Britain. If I hear of *one* single act of disobedience or rash decision from your part, Whitlock ... I'll make sure you regret it. Now, get out of my bloody office.'

Whenever he tried, Archibald never managed to remember what happened exactly afterwards and how he got to the interrogation room. A young, dark-haired man sat in a corner; a dark pen in his hand and a thick notepad in front of him. Mr Calleja was manacled to the table. He puffed at Inglott and Archibald as they entered the interrogation room.

Inglott sat in front of Mr Calleja. 'Very well,' he started.

The young man in the corner started scribbling, almost frantically.

Archibald sat down to Inglott's left.

'Do you know why you're here, Saverio Calleja?' Inglott produced a leather-bound book, putting it on the table, between him and Mr Calleja.

Mr Calleja shrugged.

'No problem,' replied Inglott.

Archibald stroked his forehead. *With that tone of voice, Calleja's going to trample you, boy.*

'On the night of the last murder, that is last night, 24th May,' continued Inglott. 'You were visited by Inspector Attard and Constable Whitlock at The Falcon's Perch; your inn, that is. Nevertheless, you tried to run away. The police officers, one of whom is present right here,' Inglott pointed at Archibald, 'commanded you to stop running.'

Now he's being polite to him? Archibald cleared his throat, and glared at Mr Calleja.

The thug didn't hold his eyes on any one of them for too long. He kept rubbing his thick moustache and hopping nervously on his seat.

'You kept running away, however,' went on Inglott, almost in a whisper, 'accompanied by a friend of yours. The officers chased and you shot at one of them.' He paused, leaned forward, and clasped his hands. 'Do you have anything to say, Saverio?'

Sure, why don't you ask him if he wants a cup of tea? Archibald suppressed a frown.

Mr Calleja looked away.

'You were running from the police, right after a murder.'

'That doesn't make me a killer.'

'What were you scared of, Saverio? Why were you running away?'

Archibald rubbed his palms against his knees. *Why do I get the impression you're offering him help, Inglott?*

'I didn't do it.'

'You ran from the police. You shot at a police officer, which is punishable by death. Your actions speak for themselves. You can't possibly think any magistrate will take a liking to your actions …'

'I didn't do it,' insisted Mr Calleja.

Archibald raised an eyebrow. *Where's all your toughness gone now, Calleja?*

'You didn't do it. Right. Do you mean you didn't shoot Inspector Attard? Would you prefer we spoke Maltese? Because you don't seem to understand what I'm talking about. Why did you run away from the police?'

'When that boy was murdered,' Mr Calleja said, in English. 'I was with the Inspector and the Constable, at my inn.' He glanced at Archibald.

'I know that already. And still, you shot Inspector Attard.'

What are you doing, Inglott? We're here to ask him about the murders.

'Now, tell me about your friend.'

'What friend?'

Archibald moved in his seat. Casolani's voice rang in his head. *Not one single act of disobedience, Whitlock. Inspector Felice Inglott will lead the investigation …*

'The one who ran away with you,' explained Inglott.

'I don't know who you're talking about.'

'Saverio, listen to me. I want to help you, believe me. I would, if I could. But you ran away, and you shot an Inspector. What do you think the magistrate will have to say to that? You've earned the right to go before a jury - I'll grant you that.' Inglott chuckled slightly. 'Still, you can hardly escape the noose, at this stage.'

Mr Calleja shrugged and looked down at the table.

'Would your friend be more talkative, if we had him in a cell like you?'

Mr Calleja glanced at Inglott, then at Archibald. 'How would I know?' he shrugged.

'Valid point, Saverio. It would be nice of you to satisfy my curiosity … if only your friend were here.' Inglott winked at the thug, who raised an eyebrow. 'I don't think you killed those people, Saverio …'

Archibald almost fell off his seat. *Am I in a madhouse, or what? Grow a beard, Inglott … what in heaven's name are you doing?* He bit his tongue.

'But your friend did.' Inglott's voice was as stern as the Superintendent's. 'Pity, he runs free while you rot in here.' He closed the file and got off his chair.

Archibald fought against all his instincts and followed Inglott. Not before shooting Mr Calleja one last glare.

'You cannot hold me here forever. You've got nothing to prove your theories.'

Inglott stopped at the door, and turned to look at Mr Calleja. 'I don't have any theories. You shot a police officer, that's a *fact*. Another *fact* is that we have a notorious killer on the loose. This killer happens to be your friend. Constable Whitlock and myself believe you could help us bring him to justice. It would bring you some honour at least, before you faced the noose. But now, you're of no other use, sorry,' he ended, walking out and closing the door behind them.

Inspector Inglott stubbed out his cigar under his foot.

Couldn't you find a bin for that? Archibald looked up at the blue sky. He didn't feel like observing the goings on in *Strada Reale*, this morning. He whiffed at his cigar, and looked at Inglott. 'How hot, I say.'

Inglott nodded idly, but didn't look at him. He wasn't talkative, apparently.

'So, Inspector Inglott. What do you think?'

'It wasn't wise, bringing him in.'

Archibald fought the urge to roll his eyes. 'Mr

Calleja, do you mean?'

Inglott nodded. 'Anyway, he's all we've got now. The Superintendent wants a confession, and I will get it,' he said, winking at Archibald and heading back to the entrance.

Calleja is not giving you anything ... 'You sound confident,' said Archibald.

Inglott stopped and turned to look at Archibald for the first time, since the interrogation. 'Mr Calleja doesn't have much choice. He will get the noose for shooting Inspector Attard. I will hold it against him.'

Archibald narrowed his eyes. *You will hold it against him. Just* you, *all by yourself?* Archibald clenched his fists. 'To what end?'

Inglott looked at him for a while, then sniggered. 'Mr Calleja is a dead man already, whether he admits to anything or not. The Superintendent needs *a* confession, Constable Whitlock. That's why I'm focusing on his friend.'

The Gentleman. Archibald whiffed at his cigar. His mind took him back to the conversation he had stumbled upon last week. Pawlu and the other one had mentioned this Gentleman could silence Mr Calleja. To them, it sounded like quite a feat. Pawlu's friend had feared it wouldn't be too long before they found Mr Calleja on their doorstep, with this Gentleman's help. He was right. Most probably the latest victim was Pawlu's friend himself.

Archibald frowned. This could be Calleja's weakness. This could be what he needed. It meant Inglott wasn't wrong, after all. 'Do you think the G*entleman*... I mean, Calleja's friend,' he whispered, 'is behind all these murders?'

Inglott nodded and shrugged. 'Maybe. We know much less about him than we know about Saverio Calleja. Mr Calleja, however, is harbouring information which may be useful to us. We need to make him talk ... before he walks up the gallows,' he ended, winking and going back inside.

Good luck with that. Archibald walked to the closest bin, stubbed out his cigar and threw it in. This Inglott had a lot of confidence in himself ... and in his interrogation. He pursed his lips and winced under the sun. There was no doubt, the young inspector would resume the interrogation without him. Archibald sniggered. *And Attard thought I wasn't a team player.*

Focusing on Mr Calleja's friend, the *Gentleman*, wasn't a bad idea. But Calleja wasn't giving them any lead. Certainly, not the information they needed and Valletta couldn't wait. *I need to find Pawlu*. He thought about the riddle of the letter found at Mr Joseph's house. *I should have brought it with me, in the first place.* He glanced northeast, towards Morell's. *I could be back here in less than five minutes, if I ran.*

29.

The cool atmosphere inside the Auberge was a relief, compared to the heat outside. He wiped his brow a hundred times between the entrance and right here. He felt his throbbing heart in his head. Archibald took a deep breath and opened the door into the interrogation room.

'Yes, the *Gentleman* did it. He killed them ... all of them.' Mr Calleja looked pale.

Archibald almost gasped, not out of breathlessness though. The young clerk in the corner gaped and blinked at Calleja.

'You made a good choice today, Saverio.' Inglott was back in his seat, opposite Calleja. He glanced at Archibald and winked.

Archibald took his seat to Inglott's left, hoping

no one noticed he was blushing and sweating from head to toe.

'Very well, Saverio. So, you're telling me this … this *Gentleman* is the murderer of Valletta.'

Calleja nodded.

'Did you ever assist him?'

'No.'

'Did you ever *see* him kill, or pluck out the eyes of his victims?'

'No, Inspector.'

'I believe you, Saverio. Unfortunately, however, the magistrate and the jury might not. You're going to have to give me more than your word.'

'I ... it's a long story.' Calleja looked at his feet.

'You have almost forty-eight hours. I can wait.' Inglott folded his arms and leaned backwards.

Calleja glanced at them both, biting his lips. 'Would it guarantee my life, if I told you?'

Inglott winked. 'I'll do the best I can, Saverio.'

Archibald wanted to roll his eyes. *Sure … you will do the best you can, Inglott. All by yourself.* He reached for Mr Joseph's letter inside his breast pocket.

'I … I don't know where to start,' Calleja glanced around the investigation room.

'Let me help you …'

Sure! Archibald sighed slightly.

'You could start by telling me this G*entleman's* name.'

Calleja shook his head. 'I don't know it, sorry.'

Sorry? What about saying sorry for shooting Attard, and beating me close to death? Archibald glanced at the young clerk in the corner. *Yes, this must be some kind of miracle. Better write it all down, mate.*

'I always called him 'the *Gentleman*'. Honest to God.'

Inglott narrowed his eyes. 'How did you and the *Gentleman* meet?'

Calleja looked down again, sighing heavily. 'I … my brother, Giorgio,' he muttered. 'When he … when he passed away, I needed the *Gentleman's* help.'

'The *Gentleman's* help. What does he do, then?'

Calleja shrugged. 'He had helped me and Giorgio start our business, many years ago. Me with The Falcon's Perch, and Giorgio with The Grand Mariner. The legal kind of help, of course.'

'The Grand Mariner ... number 98, *Strada Stretta*?'

Calleja nodded.

'Another inn,' Inglott told Archibald, with barely a glance.

'It was an inn, before … ' Calleja frowned, and looked away.

Inglott raised an eyebrow. 'Before what?'

Calleja shook his head slightly.

Archibald narrowed his eyes. *What got into you, Calleja?* He'd seen criminals lose their confidence before, but not like this. Not when they could get *nothing* in return. Until last night, not only did this man refuse to surrender to arrest but also retaliated with violence. He shot Inspector Attard. Archibald believed in miracles and a change of heart but not to this extent. This was beyond logic and it made him feel uncomfortable. Calleja was up to something.

'Giorgio was my brother,' he was telling them. 'I saw no reason why he would bequeath The Grand Mariner to a third party, after his death. We had started our business together. I …'

Archibald frowned. Calleja was trying to deviate them with stories of wills and inheritance. *He is buying time for his accomplice. I shouldn't even be here. This is a waste of time.*

'Why didn't you consult the authorities, Saverio? It's not an excuse to …'

'I did, Inspector. I mean … the *Gentleman* did, on my behalf. He confirmed I wasn't mentioned anywhere in Giorgio's Will. I had no right to it.'

Inglott chuckled.

Calleja glared back.

'So you went to the *Gentleman* for help, again,' added Inglott.

'I didn't know he was a killer, Inspector!'

He's either a good actor, or he fears us less than he does the Gentleman …

'He had sorted out all the legalities for us, back when Giorgio and I started our businesses. How could I know he had become a murderer?'

You're going to play the victim now? Archibald moved in his seat, leaning forward. 'You said you're not a fool, earlier,' he said sarcastically, without looking at Inglott.

Inglott nodded slightly and cleared his throat. 'You couldn't know. So, what makes you so certain he is a murderer *now*?' he added, straightening in his seat.

Calleja nodded and grimaced. 'I ...'

'You helped him commit the murders, Saverio,' said Inglott, matter-of-factly. 'That's how you know.'

Calleja shook his head fervently. 'Never.'

'You gouged out your victims' eyes, when he was finished with them,' added Archibald.

'No! I shot Inspector Attard, but I never killed anyone in my entire life.' He glared at Archibald. 'You know I speak the truth. I could've killed you last night, Constable Lock,' he ended, heaving. This time, he was neither grinning nor smirking.

Archibald glared back. *You would be running free with the Gentleman friend of yours, if you had.*

Inglott unfolded his arms, clasping his hands casually on his lap. 'How did he do it, Saverio? *Why* did he take out the eyes? Why the sailors? Why Ms Anna? Why the others?' His eyes were fixed on Calleja.

'I do not know, Inspector.'

Inglott sighed, and got off his chair. 'We're done here,' he told the clerk.

Good, go out for a smoke ... of course! Archibald glanced at the clerk from the corner of his eye. The young man was folding his notepad ...

The sound of manacles against the wood of the table startled them. 'Wait,' said Calleja, bobbing on his seat.

Inglott stopped at the door. The clerk fell back into his seat.

'I'm going to sit down, Saverio,' said Inglott, eyes fixed on Calleja. 'Don't make me regret it.'

Archibald rubbed at his eyes. He thought of the sun outside and Attard in hospital. Whatever Calleja was up to, he was playing it very well. *He's buying time. I need to get out of here ... need to find Pawlu.*

Calleja sighed heavily. 'I ... sometime last week, the *Gentleman* told me he found something that could help me take possession of The Grand Mariner.'

'Take possession of The Grand Mariner?'

'*Legally*, Inspector. The *Gentleman* said my brother's Will was ...'

'Yes. *You* were not mentioned in it, Saverio.' Inglott nodded. 'You just couldn't let that inn go, could you?'

'Of course not. It belonged to Giorgio, my brother. Now that he's gone, The Grand Mariner should belong to *me*.'

Inglott grunted. 'Apparently not, Saverio. Your fixation with owning The Grand Mariner led you to kill your own brother.'

'I would never!' Were it not for the manacles, Calleja would be on his feet.

'Not with your own hands, being the coward that you are,' insisted Inglott, calmly. 'That's why you needed the *Gentleman*. You killed your own brother, because having The Falcon's Perch was not enough. How much did you pay him to do it,

Saverio?'

'What are you talking about? My brother was not murdered. He died of ...'

'Tell me something.' Inglott leaned backwards. 'Did you also kill the new owner of The Grand Mariner?'

Calleja sighed heavily and looked at his feet again. 'I wish I had,' he whispered.

Inglott's eyes widened. 'You wish you had. Are you telling me someone else did it for you? The *Gentleman*, perhaps?'

Calleja shook his head. 'No one did. Pawlu ... I mean, the ownership of The Grand Mariner was mine for the taking. He's still alive and luckily for him, I'm locked away in here. I should've killed him when I had the chance. But Filippo ... the latest victim, no. The *Gentleman* killed him.'

Archibald almost fell off his seat. 'Did you just say Pawlu?'

Inglott glanced at Archibald, then back at Calleja. 'Why did the *Gentleman* kill Filippo?'

Calleja shrugged, almost submissively. 'I ... I *never* told the *Gentleman* to kill anyone, Inspector. He has a mind of his own. He's crazy and dangerous. But he told me he had found a way to get me The Grand Mariner. Giorgio's Will ...'

'By killing Filippo?' Inglott chuckled loudly.

Archibald was gaping. *I asked you about Pawlu, Calleja.*

'You're a fool, Saverio,' Inglott went on. 'You knew the *Gentleman* was killing all these people, and spreading terror in our city. And what did you do? Nothing. You just wept over losing The Grand Mariner, which, legally, was *not* yours …'

Archibald rubbed the palms of his hands against his knees and inhaled deeply. It was the best he could do to stop him from jumping off his seat and punch Calleja in the face. 'Inspector Attard and myself asked you about Pawlu,' he said suddenly, interrupting Inglott's speech. 'When we visited you at The Falcon's Perch, last night, you …' He clenched his fists. 'Now you … why didn't you tell us all this before… how could you?' *Did Attard have to take a bullet, for this to come out?*

'Constable Whitlock.' Inglott was looking at him, with those childish brown eyes. 'Please, sit down.'

Archibald looked at him and blinked, then glared at Calleja. 'You're one big, loony, paranoid, do you know that?'

'Constable, please sit down.'

'No wonder your brother didn't give you anything.'

'Whitlock!'

Calleja pulled at the manacles. The boy in the corner screamed like a little girl. 'I should've killed you when I had the chance,' he bellowed at Archibald. 'Uncuff me, you English bastard. I'll make sure not even your mother recognises you when you meet in hell.'

Luckily, Inglott got between them, just in time. He dragged Archibald out of the interrogation room. 'Whatever is the matter with you,

Constable Whitlock?' he said, slamming the door behind them.

Archibald heaved and made back for the room.

'No! Not before you calm down. I'll punch you if I have to.' Inglott was between Whitlock and the door.

Archibald sighed heavily, then ran his hand through his hair.

'Why did you provoke him like that?' Inglott raised an arm pointing to the interrogation room. 'I was getting something out of him. Why did you offend him in that manner?'

Offend him? 'You ... ' Archibald rolled his eyes. 'When Inspector Attard and I asked him about Pawlu, he didn't have anything to say. Why is he so willing to help us now? He's either lying, or ...'

'You know what, Whitlock? I'm sorry for Attard too. *Very* sorry. But that doesn't mean you can ruin this interrogation.'

'Ruin this interrogation?' Archibald raised his arms and turned away. 'This interrogation is already a ... never mind!' He walked towards the exit, away from the interrogation room.

'Where do you think you're going?'

Archibald stopped and turned slightly. 'I need a break. I need some fresh air. Why, are you going to tell the Superintendent, like a good boy?'

Inglott shot him a glare. 'Attard was right about you, you know? You're rash, insolent, and practically insane.'

Archibald inhaled deeply. Banishing the

scolding faces from the past was not easy, especially when it seemed like history was repeating itself. 'If Inspector Attard were here, we wouldn't be in this mess,' he ended flatly, going out of the door and slamming it behind him.

Strada Reale was in its usual state of organised confusion. Men rushed to their destinations before time stole the money only business could buy. Women were in smaller and less regular numbers, giggling under the protection of their *faldettas* or delicate bonnets. The sun was scorching.

Archibald winced. He needed to get to the *Ospedale Centrale* before it was too late. He could ponder about the miserable interrogation later. The city gate out of Valletta was straight on, to his right. From there onwards, he needed help. But as his mother would always tell him - one step at a time. Thoughts of his mother brought back other memories. Memories he couldn't afford pondering on right now. So far, he had managed to suppress them during his stay, here. This morning's scolding from Casolani, however, had rekindled memories to a point he could no longer contain. The *karozzin*'s bumpy ride through Floriana, Valletta's suburb, was not helping. He closed his eyes and wiped his forehead with his handkerchief. When he opened them again, the Chief Superintendent from London sat right in front of him.

'This was no petty mistake, Inspector

Whitlock. You will be held accountable,' he said.

Archibald blinked and rubbed his eyes. The Chief Superintendent was gone, but his voice still echoed inside his head.

'You are not authorised to take such decisions. You're not an Inspector anymore, *Constable*.' The voice beat like a drum in his head.

Archibald closed his eyes and buried his sweaty face in his hands.

'Come in, Constable Whitlock,' the voice went on. 'This assignment is crucial. The island of Malta is facing a dire situation …'

Constable Williams, his best friend, spoke next. 'Do you think you could still understand that strange tongue?'

Archibald took a deep breath.

'This could very well be your ultimate chance of redemption, Archie,' Williams said. 'Please, be careful when you're in Malta.'

'No,' whispered Archibald.

'Sir?'

Archibald jolted. The cabman was looking at him from his seat.

'Is anything of the matter, sir? You look pale, even for an Englishman.' He grinned.

'I'm fine, I'm fine. Where …? Have we arrived already?'

'Of course, sir. L'*Ospedale Centrale* is right opposite, look.' He pointed at the hospital building.

Archibald nodded idly and stepped down the *karozzin*. 'Thank you very much, have a good day.' He paid the driver, put on his hat, and hurried towards the hospital. *I'm here, Attard. Please don't be dead.*

The *Ospedale Centrale* was small, yet as busy as a beehive. Something about its structure gave Archibald the impression it had not always been used as a hospital. He winced at the slight smell of alcohol and decay. 'I'm here to see Inspector Attard, please,' he told the Ward Mistress, showing his police badge.

'*Mi segua, signore*,' she replied, smiling and walking further into the hospital.

Archibald hoped that meant he could follow her and did. He avoided looking around him. He had enough woes of his own. As soon as he saw Attard, however, he froze. His previous feeling of dejection was a drop in an ocean compared to the Inspector's sorrowful state. Attard was pale, thin and frail; like a character out of a horror story. His eyes were closed, but Archibald had no doubt he wasn't having a peaceful sleep.

'Good afternoon, Inspector.'

Archibald jumped.

'I'm Sister Maria. I can speak English.'

Archibald raised an eyebrow. *Alright …* He smiled faintly, then nodded at Attard. 'How's the Inspector?'

Sister Maria sighed. 'He's fighting the fever, Inspector.'

'I'm a …' Archibald sighed. 'Do you think he will …?' He bit his lips and cleared his throat. 'Do you think he'll make it?'

Sister Maria looked at Attard. 'Well, he lost a lot of blood on the way here. The bullet missed his heart by two inches, according to the Doctor. But surgery went well and he managed to remove the bullet without too much more blood loss.' She sighed and pursed her lips. 'The fever, however, cannot break.'

Archibald nodded. 'He looks …' He faltered.

Attard's chest barely rose. If it weren't for a slight flicker of the eyelids, every now and then, he could be mistaken for dead. 'Did he wake up, or say anything?' Archibald said, still looking at his withered colleague.

'No, sorry. He does mumble, sometimes. That's perfectly normal for someone having a fever. He's a fierce fighter, that's for sure. God is with him.' Sister Maria smiled, faintly.

Archibald nodded and walked closer to the bed.

'I'll give you a minute. Call me if you need anything, Inspector.'

Archibald thanked her, then looked back at his dying colleague. 'I'm sorry, man. I'm so …' He sniffed. 'I'm so very sorry.'

Attard's silence made it even worse. He had a neat dressing just below his left shoulder.

'Try not to die on me, man,' he went on, reaching for his handkerchief. 'The investigation is in shambles. Please, don't give up. There's this …' He gave a quick look around him, before continuing. 'There's this young Inspector,' he whispered, wiping his nose. 'Inglott. I don't think he's as half as good as you are.' He let out a light chuckle. 'I ... we got Calleja. Most probably he will face the noose for shooting at you. But I don't think he killed those people, as crazy as it sounds. He's blaming the *Gentleman*, who's a friend of his, apparently.' He sighed heavily. 'Calleja had a brother too, did you know that? He owned an inn as well, or a bar, in *Strada Stretta.* The Grand Mariner, it's called. Apparently, when the brother died, he did not include Calleja in his Will and passed the inn to a third party. And, guess what?' Archibald blushed. 'Do you remember Pawlu and the conversation I eavesdropped in the City? We were on the right track, man! Pawlu is the proprietor of The Grand Mariner. Mr Calleja became furious and keen on owning the property, bah! So, he got in touch with this *Gentleman* again, who – according to Calleja – has figured out a way he, Calleja, can snatch The Grand Mariner from Pawlu. Now it seems Pawlu also had help from a friend. This friend, Filippo ... is our latest victim.' Archibald sniggered slightly. 'Calleja keeps saying the *Gentleman* killed him; like he was out of his control. And that he, Calleja, would kill Pawlu if he ever got the chance.

'Anyway, it's a complete mess and we're nowhere close to ever solving this case ...' He pursed his lips and frowned. 'And I don't know what else to do, man.' He shook his head slowly. 'I ... I left the interrogation room, you know? Because ...' Archibald looked at the ceiling. 'The

Superintendent is so intent on seeing this case closed, man. You should've heard him, saying how we made a mess of this investigation. And Inglott isn't too different, mind you. You used to tell me I need to learn how to work as a team, hah! You should see this Inglott! The interrogation … it's going nowhere, that's why I left. I need to find Pawlu. Calleja is alienating Inglott with these inheritance stories … while the *Gentleman* skips the island. I am going after Pawlu. Hopefully, he knows something about the *Gentleman*. I hope I don't scare him off.' He took out Mr Joseph's letter from his pocket, now all crumpled. 'His friend has just been murdered; should be enough motivation for him to come forward. I was going to pay him a visit at The Grand Mariner.' He folded his arms. 'What do you think?' he ended, stroking his chin.

Attard groaned and mumbled.

Archibald couldn't help wonder what kind of nightmares the poor man must be having. He pocketed the paper again. *God be with him, please.* He walked to the chair beside Attard's bed and collapsed into it. *What am I doing?* He yawned, leaning his head slightly backwards. It was definitely not the most comfortable chair ever …

30.

Rita looked at the inn's sign. The colour of the signage matched the red door beneath. She only knew what they read because Luciana had told her. A moment of sadness crept over her as she remembered Filippo's gift and the inscription she could not read. Her eyes paused on the black cloth pinned to the door; a custom signifying mourning for a relative or acquaintance. Whatever the relationship between Pawlu and Filippo had been, she would find out before the day was over.

'Evening, miss.'

Rita blinked. The stranger just came out of The Grand Mariner. 'Good evening to you too, sir.' She smiled back, casually.

The stranger tipped his hat and disappeared

around the corner.

Her smile faded. It would soon be dark. This evening was her first step towards avenging Filippo's murder. She looked at The Grand Mariner and took a step forward.

The bar was getting busy. Rita walked to a free table, in the corner, close to the old piano. Something was strikingly odd about this bar. Filippo, who apparently frequented this bar often, had just been murdered. Yet there was a different kind of atmosphere to what one would expect after such a terrible incident. Something about the place made her feel at ease. She didn't know whether it was the clientele's gaiety, or the smells coming from the kitchen, behind the bar. Yet, crazy as it may sound, she felt comfortable.

'A glass of water would do just fine,' she answered the servant, who nodded and rushed to the bar to get her some water. Then she looked around, warily. The old, crooked man wasn't there. Rita glanced at the stairs leading to the upper floor. No one went up or down, despite the fact that there was nothing to prevent entry. Luciana, who didn't seem to be here either, had told her The Grand Mariner didn't provide any rooms.

It must lead to the proprietor's private rooms, then … Pawlu's private rooms. Rita bit her lips, then sipped from the glass. She was still not entirely sure if Pawlu, the proprietor of this bar, was the same Pawlu she was looking for. The Pawlu she had glimpsed two days ago, portrayed something different. Maybe, because she had seen him running away from Mr Calleja, or because he was accompanied by Filippo, who was now dead. Whatever the reason, she couldn't quite explain it in words.

'This is to my lost love,' said a man at the far end, beside the bar. The barmaids giggled at him, and some of the clients clapped and whistled. The fellow was short, half drunk and wore a sailor's uniform. Someone brought him a step stool.

'I sing from my heart,' he said, stomping one foot on the stool and brandishing a mandolin. 'This is for you, Carolina. Love of my life and light of my soul.'

The crowd cheered and stamped their feet to the rhythm.

Did they already forget Filippo? Rita sipped at her drink. Her father had always been a terrible singer, particularly when he had a go at the local *għana*. She smiled faintly at the memories of his terrible voice, then looked at the piano to her right. It was dusty and, most probably, kept there only to conceal the weird structure of this particular corner. Although this bar was similar to The Falcon's Perch in structure, it was different in everything else. The Falcon's Perch was gloomier and dirtier. The Grand Mariner, though smaller, emitted an aura of tranquillity, sobriety and mystery.

'Pawlu, there you are,' someone said.

Rita spun her head towards the entrance. The singer stopped and the bar almost turned quiet.

This was the Pawlu she'd seen with Filippo. That was two days ago, when Mr Calleja burst out of this very same place and chased them through the streets of Valletta. Despite the typical dark hair, eyes and thick black beard, his face was blank. He wasn't as tall as Filippo and not as handsome. Rita didn't take her eyes off him as he gave a quick look around, flashed a polite smile, then scurried up the stairs. The atmosphere in the bar returned back to normal the moment Pawlu disappeared upstairs. Rita closed her eyes, leaning her head on her clasped hands.

'It's still too fresh,' someone said. 'It might take a while.'

'They were good friends. Very good friends,' said another.

'I bet we'll be seeing that cloth out there for a while longer,' whispered another.

Rita opened her eyes. *Should I even be here?* She reached for Filippo's gift inside her leather satchel. In her mind's eye she visualised Mr Calleja ... and Filippo's eyeless face staring at the dark sky. She blinked and rubbed her eyes ... unconsciously, she stood up. *What are you doing?* She stopped. The staircase was within arm's reach. *Rita!* She staggered back to the table and sat down languidly.

'Are you alright, missy?'

She blinked. *Filippo used to call me that*. She looked up at the speaker. 'Yes, I'm fine, thank you. I just ...' She blinked. 'Pawlu?' she whispered, before she could contain it.

Pawlu nodded and sat on the other chair near her, at table. 'I see you already know my name.'

Rita straightened, fidgeting with her glass. Pawlu's dark brown eyes were fixed on hers. She looked at the dusty piano standing in the weird corner.

'You wanted to talk, missy.'

How do you know? She looked around. No one seemed particularly interested.

'Shall I get you something to drink? The first one's on the house, missy.'

Filippo used to call me that. She shook her head, timidly. 'I already came this morning.'

There was a half-smile on his face. 'Very honest, I see.' He leaned slightly forward, clasping his hands together on the table. 'I now understand why Filippo enjoyed your company. This meeting has to be short and to the point, however.'

Rita looked at him, then lowered her eyes. She raised a hand to her forehead. 'Sorry, this is so embarrassing, I shouldn't have come.'

'Yet here you are. And it's good that you listen very well. We do not have much time.'

She looked at him. 'Excuse me?'

Pawlu harrumphed and stroked his black beard. 'He spoke highly of you. Filippo ... he mentioned you often.'

'Me?' She blushed.

'Yes. All the time.'

'Is this some kind of joke?'

'You *are* here about Filippo, no?'

'Whatever makes you think that?'

Pawlu straightened. 'I'm the owner of The Grand Mariner.' He said that in quite a boastful manner.

Bloody old crook told you. She scowled at her own foolishness. It *was* a small world, after all.

'Listen, missy. As much as I would love to converse with you …' He looked over his shoulders. 'There are evil powers at play, here. Dangers ...' he whispered. 'Dangers ... even beyond my control, unfortunately. Out of the respect I have for Filippo and how highly he spoke of you, I will answer your questions in the best way I can.' He glanced around again. 'We don't have much time, however.'

He talked to you about me? She made to stand up. 'Look, I shouldn't have come here. Sorry, this was a mistake.'

'Missy. You will not get another chance. Please, stay. I'll answer you the best I can in the little time we have.'

Will not get another chance? She looked around, warily. Some patrons of the bar had their eyes on them, but when Pawlu met theirs they looked away submissively. Rita reached for her cloth *borsetta*. 'Can you read?'

Pawlu shook his head. 'No, missy, sorry.'

She curled her lips. *So how, in heaven's name, do you manage this bar?*

'Filippo used to help me, in that regard,' he said in a low voice, as if he had read her thoughts. 'Yes, he was literate.' He sighed. 'I always told him he was too intelligent to work in a bar. He said he loved it here, though, and wouldn't leave no matter what. Maybe I should've tried harder …'

She raised an eyebrow. 'He worked *here*?'

'Yes.'

Rita shrugged. Luciana, the barmaid from this morning, said Filippo *frequented* the bar often. That woman was odd. 'What did he do?' *What did Mr Calleja want with you two? What got you into trouble?*

Pawlu looked pensive. 'He helped me with book-keeping, stock and writing and reading letters, mostly. He could read and write English, Maltese and Italian. I don't think I'll find a replacement so easily. Filippo was … he was someone you could trust.'

I know. She nodded. The world is such a cruel and unfair place - it takes those who deserve to live and leaves those who deserve to die. This was most probably the closest she would ever get to putting things right. Pawlu was right. She couldn't just walk away from an opportunity to take her revenge. Blushing, faltering and thinking twice was not going to help her get things done. Filippo deserved justice and she deserved the truth. Whatever dangers lay on this path, Rita was sure she had faced worse.

'Who do you think did it?' she whispered, leaning slightly forward.

Pawlu lowered his eyes and remained silent.

'It was Mr Calleja, right? Or the *Gentleman*,

that mysterious friend of his.'

Pawlu narrowed his eyes at her.

'Yes, sir. I know about Mr Calleja, and his friend. I saw Mr Calleja chasing you both out of here, three nights ago. Please ... for the love we share for Filippo. I need to know what got him killed.'

'To what end, missy? So that you kill Mr Calleja?' he said, concern evident in his voice. 'He's caught now. He shot a police officer too, did you know? I doubt he's going to be alive for too long. You got your justice, there.'

Rita frowned. *Not the one I wanted.*

'Besides that. There are things, missy ...'

'Powers beyond my control?' She said, mockingly.

'You wouldn't talk like that, if you knew.'

'Tell me, then. I do not know. Tell me. That's why I'm here, sir!'

Pawlu looked around, then sighed. 'Just pray for the repose of Filippo's soul. That would ...'

'I've abandoned that path long ago,' she replied.

It was Pawlu's turn to mock her. 'Have you, really?'

'Why do you think I'm here, sir? Look at me. I'm a ... I've seen more than enough of the world's darkness and man's evil. So please, just tell me. And I'll be gone before you know it.'

Pawlu shook his head, stubbornly.

'You said you were going to answer all my questions. I might as well leave.'

'Missy. Filippo was an educated man; intelligent and trustworthy. Those virtues are seldom found altogether in one single person.'

'I know who Filippo was! That's not why I'm here,' she harrumphed. 'You told me Filippo mentioned me often,' she said, fixing her eyes on him again.

He nodded solemnly.

'If it weren't for him, I wouldn't even be alive. Now, how do you expect me to carry on without finding what happened to him?'

Pawlu pulled his seat backwards. 'Missy, I think we're done here.'

'Sir, please,' she almost reached out for his arm.

Pawlu relaxed a little.

'Last Sunday,' she went on, reaching for her satchel. 'When I returned to my … I found this, in my room.' She brought out the wooden box and put it on the table between them.

Pawlu smiled, for the first time this evening. 'Filippo made that for you?'

She nodded, then pointed at the inscription on the lid. 'Couldn't you at least tell me what it reads?'

Pawlu sighed. 'I'm sorry, missy. I cannot read and write.'

'I've shared all this with you. I … please, sir,' she whispered, leaning closer to Pawlu's face. 'I'm a … I'm a lady of the night … I cannot go to the police. Why won't you help me? What are you so afraid of?'

Pawlu's face became stern. 'I'm not afraid of anything.' He looked at the bar, and around. 'Wait for me outside, missy,' he ended, standing up and heading for the staircase.

Does he think I'm that stupid?

Pawlu halted and shot her a warning look, as if to say, 'do not follow me'. Maybe it was something about his eyes, or simply her instincts, that obliged her to obey. She put the wooden box back into the satchel and headed towards the exit.

The waning gibbous was veiled by clouds, leaving *Strada Stretta* in complete darkness. Rita was grateful for the two dim lanterns hanging by the bar's entrance. She glared at the black cloth pinned to the jamb of the doorway. In this darkness, it looked like a hand ... trying to reach out to the life and noise inside The Grand Mariner. She shuddered and looked away. She had already been pondering her foolishness when Pawlu appeared.

'You loved him, didn't you?' he said, looking at her.

Rita wasn't sure, but she thought he was smiling. 'Yes,' she whispered.

'As did he.' Pawlu sighed, then shook his head. 'I am not half the man Filippo was, missy, but … ' He reached for something inside his breast pocket. 'This is his share, all he had left. It's yours now.' He handed her a hand-sized, leather pouch.

Rita gaped, pulling her hand back. 'I … sir. Please, I can't. Just …'

'No, missy. Filippo would've wanted *you* to have it, eventually. I hope your love for him is enough against this terrible darkness that's hit the city.'

Rita shook her head. 'No, please. You …'

'You haven't even looked inside it,' he insisted, holding the chinking pouch closer.

'Thank you. But I just cannot …'

'Cannot what, take Filippo's savings? I still own this bar thanks to him. Let him do the same for you, missy. There might not be much, but it's all he had left before … well, you know.'

Rita took the pouch and took a step backwards. 'You're a good man, sir. No wonder Filippo was your friend.' She smiled faintly.

Pawlu shook his head. 'Don't speak of things you know nothing of.'

Rita shrugged. 'I didn't come for money.'

'I know,' said Pawlu, nodding. 'That's why I am giving it to you. Promise me one thing now, missy. Please. That you won't come here again. It is dangerous and …'

'And what?' Rita looked to her left, into the darkness of *Strada Stretta*. 'Sir, I just …' she stopped abruptly.

Pawlu followed her gaze.

Police hats … 'Are they walking towards us?' She narrowed her eyes.

'You need to leave, missy.'

'Pawlu? Stop right there!'

Rita moved out of the way as a group of police officers came rushing towards The Grand

Mariner. They didn't stop at the red door.

'Are you alright, miss?'

She blinked at the officer. Pawlu was gone. She was holding her satchel tight to her chest. She tried to see behind him, but his lantern almost blinded her. 'Yes,' she replied idly, as more policemen swarmed into the bar.

'Pawlu. We're only here to talk.'

'Upstairs, find him!'

The Grand Mariner's sweet noise suddenly turned into a chaotic blend of screaming and yelling. Numerous clients rushed out and were swallowed into the darkness of *Strada Stretta*. Rita pushed herself against the wall opposite the entrance. She tried to spot Pawlu amidst the escaping crowd. All she could see were eyes and mouths wide open, arms raised in panic and feet shuffling across the floor. The weak rays of search lanterns appeared on the open balcony, on the second floor. Police officers' faces, followed by the most random stuff that was being thrown out.

What seemed like only seconds later, a short chubby policeman came out of the inn's entrance. Everything went quiet again.

'What is your problem, miss? The Grand Mariner's closed for good,' he shouted at her, then looked away into the darkness. 'Why don't you go and stuff your nose into some other hellhole, while they last.'

Rita looked up at the bar's sign and the balcony above it, on the right. She pressed her *borsetta* tighter to her chest, nodded to the police officer and made her way to the *Manderaggio*.

31.

Archibald woke up with a start.

He looked at Attard, who still gaped at the ceiling. In the dim light of the candle, he could see his eyes were closed and his breathing shallow. A Sister nurse was cooling his brow with a damp cloth.

'Sorry, I must've dozed off.' Archibald winced and stood up.

'Yes,' she answered, sternly.

He raised a hand to his forehead. 'How is the Inspector?'

'Bad. *Very* bad.'

Italians had a peculiar accent when speaking in English. Archibald held back a grin, until he realised what she had just said.

'His fever is *terribile*,' went on the Sister,

noticing his dismay. 'He ... well. I have to see other patients. I will be back.' She paused and looked downwards. 'I'm very sorry, *signore*,' she ended.

Archibald smiled faintly, and thanked her, then looked at his colleague. His face was as colourless as the pillow beneath his head. The hollow space around his closed eyes made him shudder.

Please God, he's the best chance Valletta has, he prayed, closing his eyes. When he opened them again, Attard was looking at him.

'Whit ... Whitlock!' He coughed.

Archibald almost lost his balance. 'Inspector! Sister ...'

'No! Look at me, list ...' Attard coughed again, harsher this time. 'Just listen. I don't have much time left.'

Archibald leaned downwards. 'What on earth are you talking about! You're fine ...'

'Whitlock. The killer ... he's ...' He coughed again, glancing at a jug of water on the bedside. 'Lips are parched, quick ... quickly now, Whitlock!'

Archibald filled the glass and lifted Attard's head gently. He winced as his dying colleague entered a coughing fit, pinkish water dripping from his mouth. 'Let me call the Sister,' he murmured, eyes wide open.

'No, Whitlock. No. For once in your life, just listen. This ... this ... is your last opportunity to do so ...'

Archibald grimaced. 'Don't speak. You need to rest.'

'I'll have plenty of time to rest when I'm with God. This … this is crucial.' His fading eyes were fixed on Archibald's and his look was as grave as ever.

'Inspector Attard, please! You need to rest. Stop speaking.'

Attard raised his arm hanging on to Archibald's neck. 'Shut your hole!' His hollow eyes moved quickly around, then turned back on Archibald. 'Where is the man who brought me here? The one who accompanied me on the *katalett* here. Where is he?'

Archibald tried to pull his head away. *All this strength on his deathbed …*

'Have you lost your tongue, Whitlock?'

Archibald blinked. 'Who …?'

'The young man with the thick black beard … he accompanied me here …'

Archibald winced as Attard coughed harshly in his face. *Does death smell this awful?*

'Where on earth is he, Whitlock?'

'He … I don't know … I haven't …'

'Find him, damn you! He's our killer.'

Archibald narrowed his eyes. 'He's … who?'

'The young man who waited for the *katalett* with me, you idiot! He's Pawlu.'

Archibald pulled himself backwards, straightening and almost losing his balance. 'Pawlu?'

'Yes, Pawlu.' Attard coughed again. 'Come

closer, you fool. I can barely speak.'

Archibald did as he was told, hoping that the stench coming out of Attard's mouth doesn't reach his nostrils. 'Pawlu ... did you say?'

'Are you deaf, Whitlock?' He coughed again, grimacing and fighting for breath. 'You make me repeat ... I'll make sure I'll haunt you for the rest of my eternal life.'

Archibald couldn't help but grin.

'Pawlu. He told me his name. He's our killer, Whitlock. His voice, his mannerisms. The stuff he told me ... '

Where are you getting all this sudden power from?

'He comes across as someone who cannot handle his grief and guilt anymore. Just like we hypothesised at Morell's. He's our killer, Whitlock.'

Archibald sighed heavily. 'With all due respect, Inspector Attard ...'

'Shove respect up your white arse, Whitlock. There are no pleasantries where I'm going. Listen ...' More violent coughing. 'You need to find him, Pawlu ... he's our killer.'

'But ...'

'Whitlock. Don't go alone. He's powerful, he has ...'

'Inspector Attard, I cannot just ...'

Attard pulled him closer, making him wince. 'Don Lorenzo was right. The devil's behind this. Whatever you do, don't confront Pawlu alone. For once in your life, listen and do as you're told.'

Archibald raised an eyebrow.

'Do not give me that look,' went on Attard, coughing and grimacing. 'I saw it with my own eyes.' He shut his eyes, then opened them again. 'There was this black thing … it was like a cloud hanging around him. It was sucking the life out of him. It couldn't touch me, though. It was …'

'You need to rest, Inspector Attard. You've got a fever.'

'I am dying, Whitlock. But I know what I saw. Pawlu spoke to me on our way here.'

'And what did he tell you?'

'He told me Valletta is in danger. That he should've done something about it sooner. That it's too late now. He said his master told him I wasn't going to make it … that's why I suspect he felt comfortable confessing his guilt with me, Whitlock. He matches our profile, perfectly. We were right on another thing, he has help …'

'From whom?'

'The devil himself, you dotard! We were right, our killer's ashamed and full of guilt. Find him, Whitlock.'

'He's the owner of an inn. A bar, I mean. Calleja …'

'Whitlock.'

Archibald paused.

'Whitlock. You did a great job.' He coughed harshly. 'Now finish it. Pawlu is our man. Valletta is in your hands. You … you did a great job.'

Archibald sniggered. 'Well, if it wasn't for you …'

'Don't waste your breath on me.' He inhaled deeply, then yelled for the nurse.

The Sister was at his bed before Archibald had even blinked. 'This one's leaving us,' she called out.

'Do not go alone, Whitlock. Great job, Whitlock.'

Archibald straightened and moved out of the way, as two more Sisters of Charity swarmed around the dying Inspector. They wet his brow, called his name and went through all the life-saving procedures they were renowned for. Eventually, the Doctor arrived, whatever his name was, only to declare Inspector Eduardo Attard dead.

Archibald crossed himself and uttered a prayer for the repose of his soul.

Pawlu, he thought, heading for the hospital's exit like a lost soul. The Grand Mariner was his best chance of finding the man. With Attard gone, he had to learn to become better at this on his own. Arresting Pawlu would be too hasty, not to mention improbable. Only God knew how Inglott's interrogation had ended and whether Calleja had finally managed to find a way out of execution. Hopefully, he would still face a Judge and jury for killing Attard.

Archibald froze.

Two constables stood at the hospital's exit. They straightened the moment he emerged, glaring at him with eyes that could kill.

'Constable Whitlock. Superintendent Casolani

expects you in his office,' one of them said, lifting his lantern almost in Archibald's face. '*Now.*'

'Follow us please,' said the other.

They were both very young, and he didn't recognise anyone of them. *Sending your youngest pawns after me now, Casolani.* 'Inspector Attard has just passed away, constables,' he whispered, solemnly.

The two constables looked at each other, then one of them cleared his throat. 'You will follow us, Constable,' he said. 'Superintendent's orders.'

Archibald nodded and obeyed, as the two constables led the way. No stars penetrated the thick clouds tonight. Even the waning gibbous was shrouded in thick, dark clouds mourning Attard's passing. Valletta was veiled in a terrifying, almost surreal darkness. Archibald was glad for the constable's lantern, despite how dim it was.

'No carriage, I see?'

'The Superintendent said a good walk will help you think,' replied the constable holding the lantern.

The other one didn't laugh, despite Archibald's sniggering.

There's nothing to think about. He shook his head and walked on. This was going to be just another meeting. The Superintendent was going to yell at him for running away and being irresponsible. For Casolani, Attard's death would barely come as alarming news; something that could be dealt with later. Inglott was going to be at this meeting, undoubtedly, gloating on Archibald's defeat. Then they'd shake hands again, and get on with wasting more precious time on trying to prove Calleja's guilt. Only then would the Superintendent be able to answer his call – obey his superiors – and send him back to London with the case officially closed.

What a mess! Archibald thought as he followed the constables into the silent Auberge d'Auvergne, to the Superintendent's office.

'Sit down,' Casolani ordered, dismissing the constables with a wave of his hand. 'Close the door behind you.' He was writing something in a book.

You don't even have the decency to look me in the eye. Archibald obeyed. *Where's Inglott?*

'Do you know what time it is, Whitlock?'

Archibald reached for his pocket watch.

'It will be Wednesday, in a couple of minutes,' he said.

He re-pocketed the watch. *Get to it, Casolani. Or let me go to The Grand Mariner in peace.* 'Apparently so, Superintendent.'

Casolani put the pen back in its holder, then closed the book. 'I hear you were at the *Ospedale Centrale*.'

Archibald straightened and nodded. 'Inspector Attard passed away, Sir.'

'I know.' The Superintendent's eyes were fixed on his.

Archibald looked at his knees and clasped his hands.

'Do you want *me* to tell you the latest news, Whitlock?'

Archibald looked up a little, then back at his feet. 'Yes, Sir. If that pleases you, Sir.'

'Guess who's made an appearance ...'

Archibald looked at Casolani. *Guess? You really like to waste time …* 'Sir?'

'Come on.' The Superintendent leaned back on his seat, resting his chin on his elbow. 'One guess. Come on, try.'

Archibald cleared his throat. 'I do not know, Sir.'

'Of course you do not. You were at the bloody hospital,' he bellowed, chuckling loudly.

This is all a game to you. Archibald held back a frown, forcing a grin.

'Do you remember Mr Joseph Sultana?'

Archibald looked up, his eyes wide open. 'Yes, Sir. Ms Anna Sultana's brother.'

Casolani waved a hand at him. 'You still have some memory left, at least.'

'When, Sir? I mean, where?'

The Superintendent shrugged. 'You're asking me, Whitlock.' He pointed his index finger at him. '*You* would be telling me this if you hadn't left the Auberge.' He stood up and walked to the window, giving Whitlock his back. 'I'm only going to brief you on the following out of the great respect the Police Force has towards your home country. Also, because it does honour to the memory of Inspector Attard.'

Archibald frowned. *What's that supposed to*

mean?

'One of Inspector Inglott's men found Mr Joseph Sultana. He was on the brink of death, in a gutter, and … well, that's irrelevant and my time is short. We got him here. Inglott questioned him.'

'Sir, Mr Joseph is not in his right state of mind. I need to speak with him …'

'Silence, Whitlock! We are aware of that. Inglott did the questioning. Despite his unstable mind, Mr Sultana's narrative has been crucially essential to this investigation. Do you still remember what happened on the night between the 12th and the 13th of this month?'

Are you mocking me? 'Of course, Sir. Mr Joseph Sultana woke his entire neighbourhood in the middle of the night, claiming …'

'Inglott has managed to construct the events that transpired on that terrible night, following his questioning of Mr Joseph. Apparently, the murderer himself visited Mr Joseph. Did you know that?'

Inglott has discovered this now? Archibald smirked.

'Did I say something amusing, Whitlock?' Casolani was no longer facing the window, but glaring at him.

'No, Sir.' *Though Mr Joseph reappearing … that is interesting!* Inglott was one lucky fellow to be at the right place at the right time.

'Mr Joseph,' went on the Superintendent, returning to the window.' He told Inglott that he crossed the murderer right on his doorstep, that night. Apparently, the murderer was messing with their letterbox, right by the door. Sultana claims this dark-haired, bearded fellow asked him to let him inside. Sultana refused. The man, a fool, if you ask me, told him his name. It's Pawlu. He also told Mr Joseph that he was the owner of a bar in *Strada Stretta*, The Grand Mariner. He ... is anything of the matter, Whitlock? You look pale all of a sudden.'

Archibald took a deep breath. 'No, Superintendent, he lied. 'Everything's just fine. I'm just ... amazed. I mean, Mr Joseph was believed dead.' *Good Lord!* Suddenly, the chair felt so comfortable.

'Apparently,' went on Casolani, clasping his hands behind his back, 'this Pawlu insisted on getting inside Mr Joseph's house. Mr Joseph kept refusing. He recounts Pawlu kept insisting he wanted to talk to him about Ms Anna, his sister. But our dear Mr Joseph was adamant on not letting him in. Because, and I'm quoting here: "*my sister always told me not to let strangers in after dark.*" Well, Pawlu didn't give up so easily. Neither did Mr Joseph. Thanks to Inglott's skill and insistence ...'

Of course. Everything's thanks to Inglott, the inspector who just happened to get so lucky and find Mr Joseph ...

'Mr Joseph told us that Pawlu admitted to killing his sister. And that's when all the havoc started and *Strada St Ursola* was woken from its sleep. You know the rest. You were called to visit Mr Joseph's house after he ran away from the scene, on the morning of the 12th.'

Archibald nodded.

'Of course, Inglott's first impression was these could all be madman's fantasies. We compared Sultana's description of Pawlu against the owner of The Grand Mariner, in *Strada Stretta*, it matches perfectly.'

'What about the letterbox? What was … Pawlu fidgeting with?'

The Superintendent gasped. 'Oh, yes. That one. Well, Mr Joseph kept saying Pawlu had a letter in his hand, during this whole mayhem.'

'We found nothing,' Archibald lied, promptly.

'I know that. Inglott and his men are raiding The Grand Mariner, as we speak. Mr Calleja still claims he's innocent and that the *Gentleman* is responsible for all this. I'll still see him hang for killing Attard.' He grinned. 'It's only a matter of time before we find whatever proof we need against the *Gentleman*. In the meantime, however, Pawlu is our top priority, now.'

Archibald instinctively got off his chair.

'Where do you think you're going, Whitlock?'

He paused at the door and cleared his throat. 'I am …'

'You're dismissed from the case. That's what you are. Now sit down.'

He had to hold against the jamb of the door. *I'm … what?* 'Beg your pardon, Sir?'

'Have you gone deaf? I'm sending you back to

London. Now sit down.' Casolani walked to his desk, sat down and opened the book again.

Archibald wiped his brow, blinked and staggered to his chair. He didn't sit. 'Sir,' he started, but faltered. The Superintendent's office was shrinking, its colours fading. His senses were getting dim, like the candle on Casolani's desk. The ground shook and he clenched his fists around the back of the chair. 'But sir …' His lips were dry, his throat parched.

'There will be no more of that, Whitlock. Just sit down, while I write this. You are to head straight to Morell's, for tonight.' He stopped and fixed his eyes on Archibald. 'And remain there until Inspector Attard's funeral, which should take place in the coming days. After that, you will be catching the very next ship to London.' He turned his attention back to whatever he was writing. 'I recommend you spend the next few days pondering on the terrible mistakes you committed on this case. You're young and have plenty of time to learn.'

Archibald inhaled deeply. His chest felt heavy. His heart was in his mouth. *I still have plenty of time to learn? You want me to believe that you care.* 'Sir, with all due respect …'

The Superintendent harrumphed. 'No, Whitlock. I said I will have none of that. Do I have to repeat in all languages? Sit down and be quiet, for Christ's sake! I need to finish writing this, then you can leave for Morell's.'

Archibald cleared his throat. 'I need to speak

with Mr Joseph, Sir.'

Casolani slammed the palm of his hand on the desk. 'Enough, I said. One more word from you and you'll find yourself on the way to London before the sun is up. Am I clear?'

Archibald nodded. *Why are you doing this? What have I ever done to you?* Maybe it was better to be in Attard's place, right now; enjoying eternal rest. The man had done his duty and died serving his country. Was there a better way to present yourself in front of the Lord? Archibald shuddered at the thought. Besides, The Grand Mariner was being raided while he sat here. For a moment, he almost wished Pawlu would escape. Inglott was a lucky fellow, that's all he was. And Attard had been right again, even after his own death. Seems like, in this country, having good contacts was *very* important. Someone had found Mr Joseph and reported it to Inglott. Archibald grimaced, wondering where he would be right now if Attard hadn't been shot. This 'someone' would've most probably reported Mr Joseph's appearance to Attard, instead. *And we'd surely not be sitting in this office.*

'Good,' murmured Casolani, closing his book and standing up. 'You're dismissed, Whitlock,' he ended, grabbing his hat and walking to the door.

Archibald nodded, got up and walked out of Casolani's office.

'To Morell's, Whitlock,' he said firmly, seeing him out.

'Yes, Sir,' replied Archibald. *If only there was a way I could just blend into the shadows.* This city was full of them, with its narrow lanes and flickering lights. Then he'd be able to hop from one dancing, black shade to the next. He would be able to get to The Grand Mariner without being seen or followed. He smiled faintly; he still had the imagination of when he was eight. Maybe the Superintendent was right - there was still a lot for him to learn. Irrespective of whatever Casolani, Inglott or anyone else said, he was short of one thing - time. He could not afford to waste any time. The Grand Mariner was raided and all the proof against Pawlu found.

But I'm a doubting Thomas, he thought, heading out of the Auberge with a faint smile. *I will not believe unless I see things with my own eyes!*

32.

Archibald looked over his shoulders, heaving and wiping his brow.

He had skulked out of Morell's and through *Strada Stretta* without being followed. *The Grand Mariner*, he read, narrowing his eyes. *And no one left to guard the entrance.* Apparently, his luck had not run out yet. Still, the darkness was more terrifying than he cared to admit. He shuddered and took a step closer to the door. *Number 98 ...* The door was ajar and no light or sound came from within. He glanced around. *Lord, help me.* He pushed the door slightly and walked inside.

The place immediately brought back images of The Falcon's Perch. The building's structure was almost identical. One large open plan with a bar to the left. As his eyes got used to the darkness, he noticed a staircase on the opposite side of the room. The layout was very similar to The Falcon's Perch. Most of the chairs were far out from the tables, which could mean recent unwanted activity. Other than that, there were no further signs of any brawling. A bulky piece of furniture lay in the corner, to the right. He walked towards it, blinking in the dark. It was a piano. Behind it, in the corner, there was a form of landing and a … Archibald gaped.

A trapdoor, instead of the ground. The constable aimed his pistol with one hand and used the other hand to lift the door. A stench of damp, musty air hit his nostrils.

You missed this, Inglott. He couldn't help but grin.

Resting the door of the hatch against the wall, he forced himself down the stairs, through the gap in the ground. He felt his way down the hole, through the darkness.

On the ground floor it was dark, but the darkness underground was indescribable. A tiny ray of light came through the guttering on the ceiling. Archibald half hoped the street above was *Strada Stretta.* When his eyes got used to darkness around him, he looked about and made out the shadow of an oil lamp. *God, help me, please,* he prayed, fidgeting with the lamp in the dark.

Archibald fumbled with the lamp and almost knocked it over. He finally lit the wick and the flickering flame gave life to shadows dancing on the walls. A multitude of bottles and containers lay on the shelves covering most of walls in the cellar. Archibald moved the lamp to his left ... He raised his free hand to his mouth, as if to stop himself from letting out a cry, his eyes widened.

A naked male corpse lay on a stone ledge. It was facing upwards; the eyes were taken out. Archibald sniffed, frowning at the realisation that the stench in the air should be more than just damp. The cellar should be suffocating with the stench of rotten flesh and decay. Against his own instincts, he walked closer. Apart from the empty eye sockets, the rest of the body was intact. In another scenario, Archibald could've easily mistaken it for someone asleep ... if it were not for the gouged eyes. It looked like someone in their thirties.

Still no trace of any smell ...

There was an opening, which he hadn't noticed before, between the foot of the stairs and this wall. A pile of books lay scattered on a wooden table there. Archibald hovered his candle over the books, narrowing his eyes at the different sizes, hues and level of wear and tear. Most of the titles were in Latin or Greek. One almanac contained more drawings than words. Archibald's eyes feasted on all the complex mathematical diagrams it contained, most of which depicted astronomical tables and lunar phases. Another book, *Lord Byron's Cain: A Mystery*, was open on a page, with a huge letter F painted on it.

A murderer with intellect, but no murder weapon, thought Archibald, grabbing another tome and frowning at the title. *Liber Iuratus Honorii … whatever that means.* He looked over his shoulder at the corpse, crossed himself, then put the book on the table.

A low thump made him jolt and instinctively aim his pistol at the corpse. *Come on Archie, you're not a child.* Narrowing his eyes at the entrance, he tip-toed towards the foot of the stairs. The sound of fidgeting grew clearer. *God, let it be rats*, he prayed, taking the stairs.

The ground floor was as quiet and as dark as he left it, save for a dim yellowish light coming from the opening at the foot of the stairs. The sound of footsteps above made him almost drop the lamp.

Well, climbing up the stairs was still better than going down, he thought, as he made his way upstairs. He wished he didn't need to breathe. *Why can't you just be a rat …*

At the top of the stairs, he clenched his fist tighter around his pistol and aimed at the landing. The room was huge, with two door-sized windows overlooking *Strada Stretta* below. A man stood next to one of the apertures; it was a balcony. A lantern stood on the table between the two windows, its light barely reaching the stranger's face. There was no other light in the room.

'Constable … it's good to finally meet again,' he said, picking up pile of papers and putting it down next to the lantern.

Archibald aimed a shaking pistol at him. Attard had been right. This was the same young man who had offered to wait for the *katalett* when Attard was shot. His voice was familiar.

You're the one I eavesdropped ... 'Pawlu.'

The stranger sniffed and stroked his thick beard.

'You're under arrest for the murder of Ms Anna Sultana and the other murders in Valletta.'

'You know my name. That's ... comforting. Judging by how horribly you and your comrade know the rest about me. By the way, how is he, Inspector Attard?'

Despite the flickering lights, Archibald could see Pawlu's eyes were on him. 'You're crazy if you think this is funny, sir,' he said in the firmest voice he could muster.

'Funny? I actually think it's very sad. He died, didn't he? The master was right.' Pawlu walked to the balcony. 'Pity. He was one of Malta's best.'

God, give me a steady hand. Archibald cocked his weapon. 'Put your hands where I can see them, Pawlu. It's over.' He shoved away his thoughts about Inglott's incompetence for later. This was no time for rivalry. 'The blood of the victims demands justice ...'

'Save me your dramatic poetry, constable. I'm a simple man from Rabat; I'm not a city man.' Pawlu leaned against the railings of the balcony and turned to look at the Constable. The moon's rays shone on his dark face; his eyes showed concern. 'The city is in grave danger, Constable. You need to hear me out, if you want to save it.'

Archibald chuckled. 'Hear you out? You killed six people. I have you right here. All I need to do is take you to the Auberge. It's over.'

Pawlu gestured with an open hand. 'I only killed Ms Anna, poor thing. And Ġlormu … but he kind-of deserved being killed.'

'And the corpse in the basement? That makes it seven.'

Pawlu raised an eyebrow. 'The corpse in the basement …' He sighed, then blinked. 'No. That one must be Luigi. Listen, Constable, you're getting it all wrong. Please, just hear me out.' He got off the rail and took a step towards Archibald.

'Don't even try, man,' said Archibald, pointing his pistol. 'Put your hands where I can see them.'

'Had you done your job well, we wouldn't be having this conversation. And The Grand Mariner would still be blooming with light and life.'

Archibald had to fight an urge to shoot him, straight between the eyes. 'Shut your hole, Pawlu.' He steadied his hand holding the pistol firmly. 'You're coming with me, to the Auberge.'

'Please, listen to me.'

'Do you think I'm a fool?'

Pawlu sniggered. 'What I think is irrelevant. There is no time.'

'You'll have all the time you need, before the judge and jury.'

'The judge and jury? Bah! You don't get it,

Constable, do you? There's someone else behind this.'

Archibald nodded. 'And you're going to help me find him. Now put your hands where I can see them.'

'*Him*?'

'The *Gentleman*, of course.'

'What *Gentleman*? It's a woman, Constable. I thought you knew that.'

'A woman?' Archibald couldn't help but chuckle.

'See,' went on Pawlu, clapping his hands against his thighs. 'That is the problem with society, Constable. Everybody speaks of progress and knowledge and scientific advancement.' He looked at the lantern, as if he was seeing a vision. 'In less than a century from now, however, the world will be full of artificial light. The cities will be blooming with this ... sparkling thunder, and cultures will mix and mingle like a hotchpotch. Knowledge will be at a climax, but despite everything ...' He sighed and looked out of the balcony. 'Despite all that light, humanity will still be shrouded in darkness. There will always be darkness and shadow ... for as long as there's light.'

'You're quite dramatic, for one who just asked me to save my poetry for another place and time,' said Archibald, frowning. 'Still, you're mistaken if you think I'm going to scour the city for a woman,' he said, smirking.

Pawlu looked at him and sighed. 'Well, I hope

you're ready for more gruesome murders then, Constable. Because she's crazy, man. I never thought it would get to this. She's become so obsessed not to let anyone near me, apparently. That's why she killed Rosaria and then Filippo. She's paranoid! *Very* paranoid! The others were just a means to an end.'

Archibald grimaced. *He must really think I'm crazy ...* '*You* killed Filippo, or had the *Gentleman* do it.'

Pawlu raised an eyebrow, then let out a chuckle. 'Oh, you mean *Mr Calleja's* Gentleman. That has nothing to do with this ... I mean, not directly anyway. They're both fools, that's all. Mr Calleja wanted to see this place burnt to the ground because he couldn't take it from us.' He glared at Archibald. '*You* helped him accomplish his dream, really, when you raided this place.'

'If you stole this place from his brother, then ...'

'I didn't steal anything. Mr Giorgio Calleja was an honest, hard-working man. You wouldn't believe they were brothers. Mr Giorgio gave us a life. But his brother ... Bah! I'm glad Saverio Calleja is facing the noose. There's still some justice in this world, at least.' He paused a little, fixing his dark eyes on Archibald again. 'Still, neither Saverio Calleja nor his *Gentleman* killed Filippo. *She* did. Because she's insane, man. She thinks everybody's going to hurt me, or take me away from her, or ... I don't know. She wasn't always like this, you know? I think all those books ...'

I think I should take you to the asylum, not the Auberge. 'Why the eyes, Pawlu?'

Pawlu paused, then looked away.

Archibald straightened the arm holding his pistol. 'I've been in the cellar, Pawlu. You've completely lost your mind, do you know that?'

Pawlu sighed, and looked at him. 'I've heard you cannot know whether you're crazy. What I know for certain, however, is that you're a stubborn police officer. And you're really going to regret it, one day.'

'Like you regret killing Ms Anna Sultana?'

Pawlu narrowed his eyes and folded his arms. 'I saved her from Luciana.'

'Of course, the lady killer,' said Archibald in a sarcastic tone. 'Did the lady killer make you do it? Do you know Mr Joseph, her brother, survived your nightly visit? Not only, but he's going to be your demise. Justice prevails, you're right.'

Pawlu smiled slightly. 'I'm glad to hear Mr Joseph is alright.'

Archibald raised an eyebrow, then reached cautiously inside his pocket. 'Feeling guilty won't save you,' he said, throwing the crumpled piece of paper at him.

Pawlu stared at him for a while, then stepped forward and picked up the paper. 'This ...' He uncrumpled it and sighed. 'I cannot read, constable.'

'That's the letter you dropped at Mr Joseph's and Ms Anna's house, after you had ...'

'I know what it is.'

'Keep it. It'll be the only thing you will take with you to the grave, Pawlu. Now, hands where I can see them. I won't say it again. You're coming with me,' he said, winking and smirking.

'I'd rather die first,' he said sternly, unfolding his arms and giving his back to the Constable.

Archibald shook his head. 'You should've considered that before you killed all those people. You have till the count of three.'

'I'm the best chance you have at finding Luciana, do you know that?'

'The lady killer again? Fine, whatever. That's why you're coming with me to the Auberge. One…' *Come on man, give up.*

Pawlu sniggered. 'Luciana is still on a killing rampage. And there is no way in heaven you'll ever find her as long as the sun's light hits the world.'

The sun's light hits the world? You've lost your sanity, that's all I know. 'Two.'

Pawlu took a deep breath. 'Wait for the new moon. Then stop Luciana and stop the murders,' he said. Then leapt off the balcony.

Blast you, no! Archibald pulled the trigger.

Pawlu toppled over the rail.

For a second, Archibald was sure he saw blood spatter in the moonlight. He rushed to the balcony. Gaping faces peeped from behind closed windows.

Someone screamed. A dog barked in the distance.

Pawlu, owner of The Grand Mariner, lay splattered in a crimson puddle, in front of the red door.

33.

She looked at the building she had once called home.

Eleven days had passed since her mother cast her out. In those eleven days, Rita had wept, contemplated suicide, met Filippo, and seen him dead … It felt more like eleven *years*. She had been through hell and back! Back with a treasure.

She looked down, smiling at the clinking *borsetta* next to her hip. Her father used to tell her, sailors often travelled far and wide, beyond Maltese waters to find hidden treasure.

'Most of them get lost, poor fellows. Never to return,' he would tell her, that smile beaming on his reddish face.

'Who tells their story, then?' She would ask.

His eyes would shine. 'You're a very

intelligent girl, my daughter,' he would say.

She doubted how intelligence could ever land someone in the situation she was in. Like the sailors and their ships, she had gotten lost at sea. Had descended into the deepest and darkest abyss and drank from the chalice of bitter wine. The journey had almost destroyed her. But, she returned, safely. Not entirely sound, but safe, nevertheless. Every ship needed repairs; some repairs took longer than others. Despite all the turmoil, however, she was *home*.

She survived.

Not the same for Pawlu, the murderer of Valletta.

Pawlu and the *Gentleman* were partners in crime ... or so the police claimed. Word on the street was the *Gentleman* shot Pawlu two nights ago, throwing him off the balcony of The Grand Mariner and killing him.

One of the murderers of Valletta, killed on his own property. Rita found it almost satirical when compared to Filippo's honourable death. She had met the man, just a few hours before he was apprehended and indicted. She had sat at his table; he had not given her the impression of being a killer. Then again, that was the *only* time she ever met him, and she wasn't the brightest penny in the fountain.

The *Gentleman* ... well, she had almost been expecting that. He used to silence Mr Calleja and carried the aura of dread and fear wherever he passed. Killing Pawlu, his partner in crime, barely came as a surprise. What *was* surprising, however, was how Mr Calleja was not part of this murderous gang. Still, he was facing the noose for shooting and killing a police officer. It was not the kind of justice Rita had in mind for him, but it would suffice.

She had not come to the *Manderaggio* and so close to home simply to waste time pondering Valletta's murderers. Some challenging days awaited her if mother didn't take her back in. Only God knew what life had in store for her at The Falcon's Perch, now under new management. But before she took that ship and sailed the seven seas, she tried her luck back home. She could land on other treasures, but she had to deliver this one, first.

Oh, Filippo. How I wish you were here. Rita glanced around, wincing in the afternoon sun, then reached for the bag of coins. She had set aside some money for Victoria and made sure it was stored safely away. *Hopefully that slut didn't trick me … oh, Filippo, if only you were here.* She blinked and shuddered. Those were thoughts she could not afford having at this time. She pulled the strings of her bonnet and tightened it around her head. She crossed the street - her heart was thumping and her legs shaking - she knocked … and waited.

'Yes?'

The door creaked open. She had to stop herself from gasping as her sister peeped through the narrow opening.

'Is Mrs Formosa at home, please?'

Lucia frowned at her. 'Who asks?'

Maybe it is for the better, that you do not recognise me, dear Lucia. 'Could I speak with her, please? It will only take a minute.' *How good it is to see you again.*

Lucia narrowed her eyes.

'Oh, yes! Beg your pardon. Sorry, tell her it's Isabella.'

Lucia nodded and disappeared behind the door.

Rita looked around her warily, hunching her shoulders and covering her face behind her bonnet best way she could. She had wrecked her brains planning which was the best day and time to come here. Still, the urge to run away was stronger than she imagined. Yet, seeing her sister's delicate face and hearing her sweet voice again, had already made her effort worthwhile. As for the rest, she would find out soon enough.

'How may I help you, miss?'

Rita jolted. 'Good afternoon, Mrs Formosa.'

'To you too. Miss Isabella …?'

Rita nodded. Against all her instincts, she kept her head down. *Oh, ma …* 'I can't be long, Mrs Formosa. I came to deliver what is yours.'

'Mine?'

'I'm only a messenger, Mrs. It's a …'

'You thought I wouldn't recognise you?'

Rita forgot the money and looked up. Their eyes met. 'I'm … you must …' She mumbled.

'How could you come here, Rita?' Her

mother's voice was almost hoarse.

Rita's shaking didn't improve. 'Ma, please,' she said in a trembling voice.

'Why are you here?'

Rita sighed. She had looked *both* the murderers of Valletta *straight* in the eyes, yet couldn't bring herself to keep looking into her mother's. 'I'm here to ask for forgiveness. And, to give you this.' She handed her the heavy bag.

Her mother's eyes widened as the bag clinked. She was going to say something, then closed her mouth and shook her head.

'Ma, I did …' She let out a short sigh, and looked at her feet. 'I did it for you and for Lucia.'

'My wages have always sufficed,' replied her mother, flatly. 'And if they don't, it's not good reason enough to sell your …' She cleared her throat. 'You come begging for forgiveness … with *that*?'

'They're all my savings. They're yours now.'

Her mother took a step backwards. 'They're the fruits of your sin that's what they are. What have you done to my daughter? Did you take me for some kind of fool? Accepting money you earned by eating from the devil's table and laying in his sinful bed? Away with you.'

'Ma, please …'

'Begone from my doorstep, disrupter of peace!'

She lowered her bonnet. 'Ma, it's me, Rita!'

'You're not my daughter, you shameful being. You servant of the devil. Begone, now! Before I call the Lord's servants upon you.'

Tears flowed uncontrollably down Rita's cheeks, and despite the blazing sun, she trembled and felt cold. 'You cannot possibly think that, let alone say it …'

Her mother turned pale, and started to wail. Familiar faces glared from behind the doors and windows of the *Manderaggio*. The same faces that for many years had nodded and smiled at Rita were now peeping curiously and eavesdropping. Now, they glared at her, as they did to harbingers of bad news.

'Ma, please. I did this for you. For Lucia, please,' she said, over her mother's loud cries of fright and despair.

'Begone! Begone!' shouted her mother.

Lucia appeared behind the door, her eyes wide. 'Rita?' A faint smile was forming on her face.

Rita looked at her younger sister and smiled back.

'No!' Their mother stepped between them. 'Begone! Leave my family alone,' she yelled at her.

Rita clenched her fists and bit her lips. *Why, God, why?* She could taste salty tears on her lips. How could this be the same woman who had loved her, Lucia, and their father? *It seems like we both don't recognise each other anymore,* she thought, wiping her soaked eyes and giving her mother her back. 'Take care of Lucia,' she ended, before crossing the street and rushing out of the

Manderaggio.

'She thinks you are possessed by the devil.' Victoria narrowed her eyes.

Rita sighed and shrugged.

They were standing in the doorway at The Falcon's Perch. Victoria was on her fifth glass of whiskey this evening; she was in one of her talkative moods. Rita just wanted to languish in her bed and cry her eyes out. Blaming it on the terrible heat, she wished Victoria a good evening and rushed inside.

In a matter of weeks, Mr Calleja, the owner of The Falcon's Perch, would be walking to the gallows. Yet the atmosphere at the inn hardly changed. Not that Rita felt sorry for him, of course. Still, it amazed her how indifferent people could remain in front of this grim reality. The clients didn't seem to care, as long as The Falcon's Perch gave them what they were looking for. Maybe it was true, the world was changing; or maybe it was just the attitude of the clients who frequented The Falcon's Perch. Rita didn't know which was the case.

What she did know, however, was that Filippo was gone. And that there was probably no chance of her ever returning home again. *How in heaven's name do you expect me to help my family, now?* She hadn't prayed to God for a long time. Her father used to tell her that God loved man beyond any measure. Rita sniggered at the thought. Despite all her best efforts to redeem herself, God seemed intent on punishing her severely for straying away flagrantly from His path.

She opened the door to her room and walked inside. It smelt of sex, alcohol and opium. After downing the glass of water from last night, she sank into her bed and closed her eyes.

The Falcon's Perch felt safer without Mr Calleja roaming about, ready to bully her at every turn. That was surely one turn in her favour. She thought of the *Gentleman*. *Most probably, he's on a ship to Britain*. She opened her eyes and looked at the ceiling. *What did he want from Filippo, anyway? Why kill him …* and *Pawlu?*

A knock at her door made her jump.

'Who is it?' She flew off the bed, tugging at a braid in her hair.

'It's me, Rit. Victoria.'

With Mr Calleja gone and a new management still underway, the employees of The Falcon's Perch were enjoying a luxurious sense of freedom. Most of all Victoria, going round everybody, gathering and spreading gossip like wildfire.

Rita rolled her eyes. 'Oh, come in.'

'I've got it,' said Victoria, closing the door behind her.

Rita jumped to her feet.

'Do you still have the payment you promised?' Victoria reached inside her cloth *borsetta* and produced Filippo's wooden box.

Rita's face flushed. This morning's events took a toll on her and she had forgotten all about

Filippo's gift. Victoria had promised her she knew somebody who could read the script on the wooden box … for a fee.

'What does it say?'

'Well, darling. It's just your name. Rita,' replied Victoria, shrugging. 'I'm sorry, darling.'

Rita gaped, then flashed a smile. 'That's … that's lovely,' she said, grabbing Filippo's gift box from Victoria's hands and heading towards her bedside. *Oh, Filippo … you found out my name!*

'There's more.'

Rita paused and turned to look at Victoria.

'Open it … no. No, not from there, look. Let me show you.'

Rita reluctantly surrendered the box to Victoria, glaring and ready to pounce at any moment. 'What is it?'

'The bottom opens … look here. He showed me. You just have to …' Victoria fidgeted with the base of the rectangular box for a while. 'Aha! There you go,' she said, slipping out a thick piece of parchment from within.

Rita took it.

'Gently, Rita!'

'What …?' Rita unrolled the paper. 'What is this, Victoria?' She pursed her lips and frowned. *I'm such a simple woman …* She blushed.

Victoria carried a grave face. 'My contact, he told me …' She looked at the door, narrowing her eyes. 'You should probably not tell anyone about this, Rita.'

Rita raised an eyebrow.

'My contact,' she whispered. 'He says this looks like an official document of some sort. It's written in Italian. But ... ' She sighed, reluctance in her voice. 'He says it is incomplete, so it couldn't have been stolen from the public registry.' Victoria sniggered at Rita's blank expression. 'He says you could very well be in possession of a forged document, Rita. Or, well ... one that was still in the making. Incomplete, I mean.'

'A forged document? This looks very neat and genuine. The handwriting, I mean.'

'That's why it's called forgery, Rita! It's a skill. It's more than just knowing how to read and write. What did you *really* know about this Filippo, Rita?'

Rita laughed. 'Excuse me?'

'It's not funny, Rita. Not if you could read the contents.'

'Can you?' Rita grinned slightly.

'Of course I cannot! But my contact can. And he did.' Victoria paused.

'Tell me, then. What does it say?' *Why, of course* ... 'I'll give you double what I promised.'

Victoria's eyes shone, then she composed herself. 'It's an incomplete forgery of a Will.'

'A Will?'

'Yes, Rita. It is about the ... The Grand Mariner. This is *the* inn where one of Valletta's murderers was found dead.'

I know where The Grand Mariner is. And it's a bar, not an inn! Rita pretended to look surprised.

'What does it say?'

Victoria's eyes widened. 'You are either fearless, or foolish, my dear Rita. It says Mr Giorgio Calleja, the previous owner of the place, bequeaths The Grand Mariner to Pawlu … and somebody else.' Her face looked genuinely grave.

Rita looked at her blankly. 'Somebody else?' She looked down at the paper. *Oh, Filippo, how I wish you were here …*

'Rita, the document is incomplete. As I already told you, the forgery is incomplete. That means, whoever was forging it either had to stop, or … God knows what. There are a lot of things missing. Look ...' She took the parchment gently from Rita's hands and pointed at the foot of the page. 'There should be the names and signatures of the Notary, witnesses and the person making the Will, right here. But it's completely blank.'

Rita looked at Victoria. 'How do you know all this?'

Victoria grinned slightly. 'I have to admit I don't. That's why we paid my contact, didn't we?'

I *paid him, not you!* Rita smiled faintly at her and nodded.

'As I was explaining, he told me there are signs of another name, because there is the letter L. Just L, on its own.'

'So, Mr Giorgio Calleja bequeathed to more than one person?'

Victoria shook her head and rolled her eyes at Rita. 'This is a forged document, Rita. Most probably, Mr Giorgio Calleja didn't even have a Will, or it mentioned other people. Whoever was creating this document needed to have ownership of The Grand Mariner for them to pass on to Pawlu and whoever L is. Or, he was just paid good money to do it for them.'

Rita glared at her. *You can't possibly think Filippo did this?*

Victoria handed her back the letter and took a step towards the door. 'Listen, Rita. Whatever it is, and whoever wrote it … it is illegal! Not to mention that Pawlu is also the name of one of the murderers of Valletta. He owned The Grand Mariner before his partner in crime killed him. So please, do yourself a favour and just keep it hidden, if I were you. I'm keeping my mouth shut, of course.' Her eyes scanned the room, then fell back on Rita's.

Fine, I get your point. 'Here's your payment. Twice over, as promised. For your information … and your silence.'

Victoria's eyes gleamed as she grabbed the lump sum of money. 'Better take care of yourself, Rita …'

As if you care.

'Filippo might not have been the man you thought he was, after all. I mean, he gave you a box with a Will hidden inside it. A *forged* Will naming one of the murderers of Valletta and his property.'

You're disgusting … just take the money and leave me in peace.

The forged Will didn't bother her, really. It was, most probably, a part of some unresolved matter between people who chased after power and the riches of this world. Filippo might've been involved in this cobweb of intrigue - Pawlu and the *Gentleman* too. Till they all got burnt. She felt sorry for Filippo, though he had always needed a beating to help him grow up. Life's experiences hadn't made it in time to teach him and now he was dead. She was sure he hadn't put the document at the bottom of the wooden box by mistake. He needed to hide it somewhere safe. And what was safer than giving it to a lady of the night, who no one knew she even existed? If this is what it took to buy Filippo's secret, she was more than willing to do it. The rest of the money would go to her younger sister. Even though she still had to figure out how, under heaven and earth, she was going to do that.

I am a lady of the night, that's all.

She was not going to fall for the trap which Filippo himself had fallen into. Wills, power, money, politics ... those worlds belonged to the upper classes of society. She was little Rita, owner of the night. The Falcon's Perch was her new ship, steering through stormy seas that raged around the ever-changing world. The only treasure she had lay hidden beneath her bed. She was going to bequeath it to her family. Figuring a way how, was her next adventure.

Her next journey. Her current destination.

With Filippo, Pawlu, Mr Calleja and the

Gentleman all out of her way, there was nothing to stop her.

34.

Stepping into Hastings Gardens, after all this time, brought back various memories. Most of them were of silent but pensive strolls, pondering on the Lord's will. Leaving the parish of Mdina had been far from easy. Valletta, back then, had seemed like a huge beast he would never be able to tame. So, for the first couple of weeks he was serving in Valletta, Hastings Gardens had been a place where Lorenzo found solace; like a second church.

That was nine years ago, only one year after the tragedy at the Manduca's household. Lorenzo understood, now, why the Lord had brought him to Valletta nine years ago. *Oh, Thy Divine Wisdom!* He narrowed his eyes, trying to pierce the darkness.

The waning gibbous shed a mist-like, silvery veil over the Gardens. He almost found the ambience alluring. He had never been here in the dark.

The witching hour ... he shuddered, reaching for his pocket watch. It was exactly three o'clock and for a moment, he regretted not getting a lantern. *Where are you, Luigi?*

The police said one of the killers was shot by another, the so-called *Gentleman*. The dead one, Pawlu, was the owner of that terrible inn: The Grand Mariner. As if anything worthy ever came out of *Strada Stretta.* Pawlu was the same wretched fellow who had murdered Ms Anna Sultana. Thanks to Mr Joseph's sudden re-appearance, his sister's killer had been brought to justice. Pity, Inspector Attard had not survived to see this through. Lorenzo felt sorry for him. Malta had definitely lost one of its best.

As for the British Constable, rumour had it someone spotted him coming out of The Grand Mariner the night Pawlu was shot. Lorenzo couldn't care less; the English Constable was an imbecile, of that he was sure. No wonder the police hadn't yet figured Luigi was this *Gentleman* and apprehended him.

He sniggered. He had thought of telling them, of course, until he learnt Inspector Felice Inglott was now in charge of the investigation. *From the frying pan and into the fire*. Lorenzo harrumphed. This Inglott was an insolent, big-headed twit, if there ever was one.

No.

The Lord had brought Lorenzo to Valletta nine years before, in preparation for his great mission. The city was far from safe yet, but Luigi stood no chance against God and his ministers on earth. The police might as well stuff their noses in their dusty tomes of bureaucracy and civil law and lose themselves looking for their *Gentleman*.

With these thoughts and his chest held high, the priest walked into Hastings. If Luigi was planning to taunt him, he couldn't cower. He walked to the closest parapet, the one overlooking Manoel Island across the water. The gargantuan silhouette of Fort Manoel always fascinated him. Carved out of Maltese limestone, the star-shaped fortress had offered a vantage point to the Knights. Now, it served as a military base for the British forces. Lorenzo smiled faintly, remembering his childhood dreams of becoming a soldier.

Then he felt it. That same eerie feeling of being watched. It felt exactly like it did two weeks ago, when he was walking out of Valletta. His smile faded and he looked over his shoulders. *Even though I walk through the valley of death, I will fear no evil.* Luigi was watching him. 'Thou art with me; Thy rod and Thy staff, they comfort me,' he prayed, giving his back to the Fort, hundreds of yards away.

The priest jolted and turned, his hand to his mouth. That odd feeling just struck him again. He narrowed his eyes, looking into the darkness which seemed ready to engulf him, since the moon's rays hardly lit up the Gardens. Lorenzo glanced around; his throat felt dry, his limbs numb. No cricket chirped, no leaf moved.

And that dreaded feeling hit again.

Please, Lord. Anything but not that …

He stood there, for what seemed like hours; barely breathing, with his back against the parapet. He'd rather fall off into the sea, than fail to see Luigi coming towards him.

'Don Lorenzo.'

The priest jumped. It came from his left, where a row of benches stood facing the panoramic view. Lorenzo walked towards the benches, wishing he had, at least, brought a candle. A tall, slender figure sat on one of the benches. The stranger lifted their head in an almost noble-like manner.

Lorenzo raised an eyebrow. 'Excuse me, Miss. I didn't mean to disturb.' *How did I just assume it was a he?* He blushed. Her clothes were lower class, yet something about her emitted an aura of pride, usually present in the upper classes of society. Lorenzo was about to turn back the way he came, but halfway there he froze. *Those dark, round eyes, and the thick, straight, black hair …* He turned to look at her again, wincing in the dark. *Sitting up so straight, so noble.*

'Good evening, Don Lorenzo.' Her eyes were on the panorama. In the darkness he could make out a faint grin on her face.

That voice! He could blame the darkness for

playing tricks on his eyes, but not on his ears. *She can't be!* He narrowed his eyes at her. 'Maria Isabella?'

The woman turned her head slowly to look at him.

Lorenzo took a step backward. 'Aren't you supposed to be ...?' He faltered. Luca had been found dead, *not* his sister.

'Dead?'

Lorenzo gulped. Those dark eyes, glistening like orbs in the moonlight.

'My name is Luciana.'

Luciana? No ... Lorenzo turned as pale as the moon itself. Maria Isabella Manduca would be in her thirties today; this woman looked exactly like her. He wasn't sure he could feel his limbs anymore. 'You look like someone I ...' He inhaled deeply. 'Listen, Miss. You must leave. It's not safe for a lady to stay here, tonight.' *What is she doing here in the middle of the night, anyway?*

'Aren't you here to meet someone, Don Lorenzo?'

Lorenzo stopped. *Who do you think you're talking to like that, woman?* He took a deep breath and glanced around, grateful for the darkness. 'How do you know my name?' *Is this some witchery of yours, Luigi, conjuring images of the dead?*

The woman turned to look at Fort Manoel in the distance, giggling lightly. 'You still don't believe...'

'Stop this, Luigi. In God's name, I command

your witchery to stop.'

The lady raised an eyebrow and looked at him. 'Luigi?'

Lorenzo sighed heavily, looking around Hastings again. Then said, 'Miss. With all due respect. I believe ...'

'Exactly! What do you believe, Don Lorenzo? Come sit, let's talk. I've been waiting for this moment ever since I saw you, the Monday before last.'

Oh Lord. 'Where is Luigi? Where is your evil master?'

The woman shook her head slightly. 'Luigi is dead. I killed him with my own hands. It was fun, gouging his eyes out, if you really must know.'

Lorenzo's jaw dropped. 'You ...?' He couldn't help but snigger, despite what he was hearing. 'Miss. Luigi, he's ...' *The letters were signed by L ...*

'Listen, Miss. Whatever bet you made with your friends for coming here, you won it. Now please, look, just leave. It's dangerous for you, to be here. You have my blessing, you can leave. I will say a prayer for you too, if that's ...'

The woman threw her head back and laughed hysterically. 'Is it that difficult to believe a woman is behind the murders of Valletta? Well, we live in a dark age, so I don't blame you entirely, Lorenzo. Just give humanity a couple of decades more ...' She fixed her eyes on the priest, tapping the empty seat next to her. 'In a hundred years' time, women will have the right to vote and form part of parliament. Why, we'll be working as hard as you men!'

Against every instinct and fibre in his body, Lorenzo walked to the bench and sat beside her. He fixed his eyes on the view, his clenched fists resting on his lap. *Lord, be my light and my guide.* He could hear her breathing; she smelt of fresh flowers. *What kind of witchcraft is this?*

'I know you wanted to save Valletta,' she said, in her delicate yet noble voice. 'I will give you all the answers you seek, in exchange for your help.'

You will give me what? 'I will speak with Luigi, woman. Your master,' he said, struggling not to smack her insolent face. 'You are dismissed.'

The woman giggled. 'Are you deaf, Don Lorenzo? I don't remember you being deaf. Luigi is dead. My master … I really don't think that's a good idea. He deems your faith unworthy and would have you killed, as I explained in the letter.'

Lorenzo's heart skipped a beat. He closed his eyes and wiped his brow. *Oh Lord, please*. Remaining seated was a struggle.

'Luigi, was my friend,' she said, sighing. 'A lowborn, from Rabat. Are you sure you don't remember him, Don Lorenzo? We were always running around Mdina together.'

Lorenzo shook his head slightly. 'Do you know how much your family looked for you, after that night?'

'You recognised *me* immediately.' She giggled. 'You're a man, I don't blame you. It's only natural. I half expected you to recognise Luigi from his eyes, though.'

Lorenzo turned his head slightly towards her. 'His eyes?'

'Luigi's eyes. The ones I gave you last Saturday.'

Lorenzo took a deep breath, remembering the incident near the Chapel of the Bones. So many things happened since then; it seemed like a long time ago, not just a week.

'Forgive me,' she said. 'I did not expect your reaction. You look well, though.'

'Are you mocking me?'

The woman giggled again. 'Look, I think we started on the wrong foot. You came here expecting to meet somebody else, while I was a bit too forward … Let's start all over again. Ask me whatever you wish, Don Lorenzo. I'll answer you.'

The priest gulped and forced himself to look at her. *God, she looks exactly like Maria Isabella.* 'What happened in Mdina, that night?'

She smiled. 'Luigi and I always wanted to leave. My parents never even accepted our friendship. Besides, being a woman, I was not going to inherit anything. Mdina had nothing to offer, and the world is a big place … Anyway, Luigi was of the same idea.'

'You tried to run away with a lowborn, and got caught.'

'Yes we had tried, more than once. See? You remember!'

'I had heard something,' he whispered. 'Had

no idea it was you. Your parents, God bless them, managed to keep the rumours quiet. They loved you, Maria Isabella. Your father, he's …'

She sniggered. 'My name is Luciana now. It derives from *lux*, which means light. My Master gave it to me. He said all our names must follow the Greatest Master's name; the angel of light.'

Lorenzo cringed. 'Lucifer,' he said in a low voice.

'Anyway, to answer your question… Luigi and I finally managed to run away. I came across Nikola that night, though we really became family only some years later, in Valletta. You know him by his new name, Pawlu. Pawlu managed to see me despite my Master's Veiling, that night. The man had True Faith, though I don't think he ever realised it. My Master says it only takes True Faith to pierce his Veiling. True Faith actually pierces all my Master's powers and tricks. But, do *you* have True Faith, Lorenzo?'

The priest scowled at her. *Oh, St Michael, defend us in battle and in the struggle which is ours against the Principalities and Powers.* 'Pawlu had faith?' He tried to snigger. 'Pawlu's a murderer. Who do you think you are?'

She flashed a grin. 'Do you really believe it's the body of Christ, when you raise the Host during Mass, Don Lorenzo? Do you really believe it is *His* blood, in that goblet? I think you just got so used to the ritual, Lorenzo, you don't believe in it any longer. That's what I think about you. Your lack of belief is very dangerous, you know?'

Lorenzo blinked. This had to be some kind of bad dream. He never doubted he was dealing with a servant of the devil, but this … He sighed deeply and closed his eyes. 'We were talking about the night Luca was … found dead,' he said, staring at the floor.

Luciana nodded. 'Yes. I killed him,' she replied, matter-of-factly.

Lorenzo gaped. 'You? Your own brother, Maria Isabella.'

'My name is Luciana,' she looked at him.

He fought the urge to look away. 'Why?'

She looked at Fort Manoel in the distance. 'I was not going to inherit anything.'

'You couldn't just …' The priest inhaled deeply. 'Your parents loved you. They didn't deserve such tragedy.'

'The Lord and Lady Manduca loved Luca and no one else. He was the son they'd always wanted. They would pray day and night, until the Lord granted their wish.'

'He was your brother, Maria Isabella. Your family!'

'My name is Luciana. Pawlu was my brother,' she said, coldly. 'Mr Giorgio Calleja was my family. The Grand Mariner was our home. And it was taken from me.'

Lorenzo opened his mouth to say something, but stopped short. He had spent a lot of his physical, mental and spiritual energy to find the killer. He had walked and run through the entire city to save it. *From a woman? From Maria Isabella?*

This can't be real. 'Maria Isabella …'

She got up, almost suddenly. 'My name is Luciana now.'

Lorenzo looked up at her. 'Why am I here? Are you going to kill me?'

She grinned. 'I brought you here because you're a hypocrite, Don Lorenzo. You do not really believe in what you preach. Your faith is mere routine and ritual, a manipulation of those around you. You do not have True Faith.'

'Is that also why you killed Ms Anna and all the others?'

Luciana raised an eyebrow. 'When Mr Giorgio Calleja passed away, he bequeathed The Grand Mariner to Pawlu. Luigi never accepted the situation, and tried to get rid of him in many ways. Even Saverio, Giorgio's brother, tried. Nobody gets between my family and me.'

'You killed Luca, your own brother. You had a family and you ran away from it.'

Luciana smirked. 'Luigi got between Pawlu and me, as did Rosaria and Filippo. As for Ms Anna, Pawlu killed her for the same reasons, I suppose. The rest … they were for the Veiling. Means to an end.'

The Veiling? Lorenzo narrowed his eyes. 'The Veiling?'

Luciana nodded. 'As long as the light of the sun hits the earth,' she looked at the waning gibbous, 'our Master grants us the ability to become one with the shadow.'

Lorenzo followed her gaze, frowning at the

moon, then glared back at her. 'In exchange for your soul.'

Luciana sniggered. 'In exchange for the eyes of the victims, Don Lorenzo,' she said, matter-of-factly.

The priest shuddered. *Disgracing the victims by taking out their eyes ...* 'Are you going to gouge out my eyes, too?'

She looked at him as though she was actually considering it. 'Not if you can help me, no. Besides,' she said, looking upwards. 'The new moon is in five days' time, so it wouldn't be worth it. The Veiling only works when there's light from the sun. Ironical, isn't it, that the light strengthens the shadow.'

Lorenzo wanted to die. *No! I won't become a victim to some devil's ritual.* 'Help you? Why would I help the murderer of Valletta?'

Luciana giggled again. 'Because if not, I will kill you.' She reached into a pocket in her skirt and produced a fist-sized stone.

The priest gasped. *It can't be!* His heart skipped a beat as he glimpsed the symbol painted on the stone. *The Murderer's Mark! God, help me please. Not like this.* 'The Murderer's Mark.'

'Yes, the Mark of Cain. Cain had received it for killing his brother, Abel, in the beginning of time. Personally, this is my favourite mark, so Master let me inscribe it on my killing implement.'

Lorenzo fought the strong urge to stand up and run. *Can't show her I'm afraid, lest she launches some wicked devil after me.* 'How could I possibly help you, Luciana?' Maybe going along with her madness was his only way out. *Forgive me, Lord Almighty.*

Luciana grinned and returned to sit next to him. 'The person who killed, Pawlu, he …'

'It was the *Gentleman*. He's …' Lorenzo stopped short.

If the *Gentleman's* accomplice was right here, sitting next to him, that meant the City's intellect was truly misled. The infamous murderer wasn't a man, after all.

I failed. Lorenzo wasn't sure he could breathe anymore.

'Good. You're finally seeing the light, Lorenzo,' went on Luciana, in a mocking tone. 'I brought you here because I really wanted to meet you, after all these years. That was my intention, originally. I never believed they would kill Pawlu, though he was a bit of a foolhardy, at times. That night, I couldn't protect him because I was focused on you, beneath St Michael's statue. I need to find who killed him. So now, *you* …' She pressed her index finger against his chest. 'You, are going to tell me who did it.'

Lorenzo stiffened. He wished he could reach for his watch to check the time. They must've been at this conversation for at least an hour. He looked at the waning gibbous. Dawn was still far. He needed more time.

'I don't know, Maria Isabella.'

'My Master was right, then. You really are of no use to me. And you keep calling me that name too …' She got off the bench. 'Maybe, it *is* actually time for you to go and meet my Master. Like all his fellow angel brothers, he takes a fancy for hypocrites. You can hear his wings flapping with eagerness, every time I grant him a victim. Did you know the Fallen Angels reserve a special torture chamber in Hell, just for the likes of you, Lorenzo?'

I knew the devil was behind this … Lorenzo winced at the image of hellish fires forming in his mind. He tried to get up, but couldn't his legs. *Lord Almighty …* He pushed against the bench with his arms, but he had no strength. It felt as though he was trying to push a rock with a feather. *Lord … oh Lord, no, please, Lord!* He looked around frantically. 'Enough of this witchcraft,' he shouted.

Luciana threw her head backwards, letting out one of her hysterical laughs. 'Lorenzo, the good thing about the coming century, is that people will no longer believe in the likes of me or you,' she said, glaring at his Dominican robes. 'And people like me will thrive in power and wealth. Now, let's be done with this,' she ended, throwing the stone into the air and catching it again.

'Wait, wait, Luciana. Please!'

She raised an eyebrow.

'Look. Everybody believes the *Gentleman* is the other murderer of Valletta, now that … that Pawlu is dead. They're all wrong. You were good, you were great. Nobody even has a clue, as to who the real murderer is.' *Lord, forgive me.* He cleared his throat. 'I … I heard that Whitlock, I mean, I heard that Constable Whitlock shot him.'

'Constable Whitlock? Sounds like an Englishman to me.'

Lorenzo nodded fervently. 'Yes, he is. London sent him to assist the local police to help solve … well.'

Luciana wasn't smiling anymore. 'You're saying an Englishman shot Pawlu?'

Lorenzo nodded. 'Ask your Master, I'm not lying.' *Oh Lord, forgive me!*

'Don't mock *me*, Lorenzo.'

He winced and cowered. *Lord, forgive me*. 'I am saying the truth. I'm sure of it. Whitlock shot Pawlu.' *Lord, I don't want to die.*

'Who told you this?'

'Rumour has it … I heard it through the grapevine and during Confession. A man named…'

Luciana raised her hand. 'You really *are* a hypocrite. The Seal of Confession binds you with an ancient vow; you of all people should know that. You cannot divulge your penitent's secret, not even to save your skin.'

Lorenzo gaped. *What am I doing here, sitting and being told what to do by this woman?* He tried to get up again, but the force holding him down had only strengthened. He must be having a nightmare. He'd soon wake up, smile, drink a cup of tea and go out on the streets of the City in search of the real murderer. On second thoughts, maybe, this time, he should just leave it in the hands of the police.

'London will pay dearly for this,' went on Luciana, fidgeting with the stone.

Lorenzo winced. *Forgive me Lord.* He looked up at her. *Oh God!* The look on her face needed no interpretation. Her dark eyes shone and the way she smirked at him … *Forgive us our trespasses, as we forgive those who trespass against us …* Lorenzo trembled.

How could he expect the Lord to save him from hell, when he failed to save Valletta? He deserved eternal torture; for being deceived by a woman, to say the least. His whole life appeared in front of him. When had he ever forgiven those who trespassed against him? When had he ever been humble? Never! Instead, he had almost spent his entire life using the Word of God to manipulate others. For example, he never cared about Ms Anna, when it was evident she was being led astray by Pawlu. It was more convenient for him to sit back and condemn her to the devilish road she had taken, at the time.

'I should've killed you at the Chapel of the Bones,' Luciana was saying, her left fist tight around the marked stone. 'My Master was right, Lorenzo, you are a hypocrite.'

Lorenzo closed his eyes and winced, hunching his shoulders. *I failed.*

The last thing he felt was the crushing of bones in his temple; he heard hysterical laughter and the sound of flapping wings.

Epilogue

London, two years later

Archibald woke up with a start.

'Good Lord,' he whispered, sitting up and reaching for the oil lamp beside his bed. This was the fourth or fifth time, this week, he was having these nightmares. It wasn't so cold, so he couldn't blame the chill. He got out of bed, lit the lamp and walked to the window. He hated waking up this early. Downing a glass of water, he returned to bed. The face of Superintendent Casolani appeared before him the moment he shut his eyes.

No. Archibald opened his eyes, harrumphed and stared at the ceiling.

It had been more than two years ago, since he

was in Malta.

He shut his eyes and the image of Casolani returned.

They were in his office. Archibald sat opposite his desk. The Superintendent was growling; spitting and uttering words Archibald never even knew existed. Meetings with Casolani often made you age before getting out of his office. But, this was no ordinary meeting. It was short and snappy. Not because the Superintendent avoided bombarding Archibald. On the contrary, he made sure to list out all of Archibald's bad decisions through the entire investigation. He was blamed for both Inspector Attard's and Pawlu's death. Archibald should not have shot him off the balcony of that cursed inn. There was no discussing how Archibald was, in fact, trying to stop him from committing suicide. The disappearance of the *Gentleman* from Valletta was Archibald's fault, as well. He was also blamed for Don Lorenzo's death, when he was found in Hastings Gardens, on the same morning Archibald left the island. The meeting ended with Archibald storming out of the office. Obviously, the Superintendent had compiled all the required paperwork in advance and by the afternoon, Archibald was on the first ship back to London.

In time, he would've dealt with his pain. His human side would forever be curious to find out how the whole case was eventually resolved – if it ever was. He would've healed, some day. After all, part of him was convinced that the

Superintendent and Inglott had not yet solved the case by the time he left. Time would've helped; Archibald would've come back and got busy with being a constable in London, again.

He would have.

If only he hadn't been welcomed with *that* infamous letter the moment his feet touched British soil, again. That letter requesting his presence at the Chief Superintendent's office, the very same day he arrived.

Archibald sighed and bit his lips, remembering the scene.

'Pick up your stuff and get out of here. You're expelled from the constabulary,' the Chief had said, handing him the official letter of dismissal.

Archibald didn't need to read it to know its content. It spoke of disobedience, imprudence and all those heavy words superiors often use to belittle their inferiors. After the incident, he often told himself they were just words on a piece of paper. But, the consequences of those words were far reaching.

Home was home and he had missed it … somehow. The District of Whitechapel had not seen a good day for decades and finding work in the area was like finding a needle in a haystack. Archibald felt he was lucky when the owner of the Ten Bells, in Church Street, let him work behind the bar. It sure felt ironical, to say the least, but it was better than dying in the gutter.

Thoughts of the gutter brought back vivid images of Malta. The narrow streets of Valletta, with their limestone structures blazing under the sun. The eyeless corpses and their mutilated faces … Archibald opened his eyes, scowling at the ceiling. *Not a good way to help yourself sleep.* He shut his eyes and forced his mind to think about the events of the previous day – anything but Malta, really.

Before he knew what was happening, he found himself back in Valletta. It was dark, and he was walking down *Strada Vescovo*. Don Lorenzo appeared from behind the corner that crossed *Strada Stretta*, to the left.

'Archibald Whitlock,' he frowned at him with hollow eye sockets. 'It's an ancient power!'

Archibald lowered his head and took a right turn.

'Archibald Whitlock, where are you going?'

Archibald quickened his pace until he could not hear the priest's cries anymore. He rushed through *Strada Stretta,* allowing the shadows to engulf him.

'Constable Whitlock.' A familiar voice called.

Archibald raised his head. The street was empty and quiet.

'Here, on the door,' the familiar voice whispered.

Archibald looked to his left and jolted. The red door of The Grand Mariner was ajar. A shadow of a man was on the door, slithering to the jamb and onto the wall, towards Archibald.

'Why can't you all just leave me in peace?' Archibald blinked, taking a step backwards.

The shadow was coming off the wall, and taking shape, turning into a body. Archibald gasped and tried to run away, yet his feet felt heavy. The figure was now a complete man, in the flesh; he was no longer a shadow. His dark face stared blankly at Archibald, his eyes wide open. His thick black beard quivered on a breeze that Archibald could not feel.

Pawlu!

The man nodded. 'The Veiling,' he whispered.

I killed you.

Pawlu nodded and took a step closer to Archibald. 'I warned you! The Veiling protects her, and there's no piercing it, unless it's new moon.'

'Leave me alone.'

Pawlu's face looked sad. 'The light gives life to the shadow.'

'You're dead. This is not happening,' whispered Archibald, trying with all his might to run away.

Pawlu took another step forward.

Hysterical laughter broke out in the air. Archibald winced and cowered, looking everywhere.

Pawlu sighed sadly. 'She's coming. I tried to stop her. She's coming.'

Archibald's eyed widened. 'No! Anything but that ...'

The hysterical laughter was deafening.

Archibald covered his ears and closed his eyes. 'No, please. Anything but this! Please *stop*!'

The laughter just got louder and louder ... the piercing sound of laughter was making the ground shake.

'She's here,' were Pawlu's last words, before he disappeared into thin air.

'No!' Archibald pushed himself towards the red entrance. *Can't look back, no cannot look back.*

The laughter got louder and closer.

No, please, no. Archibald's skull started cracking, his eyes dripping blood. *No!* He knew what was happening. *Not the voices, please, stop!*

The laughter sounded like the bells of hell, growing louder and louder. And then, the voices came. A multitude of harrowing screams, filling the air with agony and despair. Ash landed on his lips, decay caressed his nostrils and darkness covered his bloody eyes. Archibald tried to reach for the knob on the entrance, yelling as it turned into a wall.

The hand ... no, no. Please God, no!

That skeletal grip was on his shoulders.

No, please, I beg you! He felt his head turning. *I'll do anything, please God. Please, Lord.* His neck cracked. He tried to close his eyes. *I'll do anything, please ...* Tears of blood trickled down his face. It was useless trying to shut his eyes or stop his head from turning. Her eyes were on him, piercing through his soul. He wept, in vain. She was grinning and laughing.

The wailing voices stopped, followed by his heartbeat.

'No!' Archibald woke up with a start.

Weak rays of the sun entered the room and landed on his bed.

Good Lord … He was sweating, trembling and breathing heavily like he had just run a mile. *Heaven and earth!*

A knock at the door startled him.

'Brought you the newspaper, Mr Whitlock.'

Archibald sighed. 'Thanks Ms Agnes.' He closed his eyes and buried his head in his hands. *God … please. Make them stop.* In the morning, any nightmare felt conquered. But, in the realm of sleep they were very real. The nightmare about Valletta was always the same. Somehow, during the dream, he could never remember what was going to happen next. Even though the events followed in perfect sequence. *Strada Vescovo*, Don Lorenzo and Pawlu - taking shape from a shadow. And then … Archibald gulped.

Just thinking about the hysterical laughter and the voices gave him goose bumps. Out of all the people he had met in Malta, a woman he'd never even seen was making him beg for his life. Pawlu had tried to make him believe a woman was behind the murders. Archibald didn't even remember what the villain had called her. Maybe these nightmares where as a result of the fear of the unknown - this 'lady' was tormenting him without even having met her. It was embarrassing, to say the least. Malta and the Maltese had affected him much more than he'd ever care to admit.

Shrugging and getting off the bed, he staggered towards the newspaper beneath the door. The front page didn't help to brighten his mood. He grimaced. *Good God!*

Another murder in the district. No ... two!

He sighed heavily, skimming through the article. He tried his best to let go of his Malta experience. He desperately wanted to leave all the tragedies behind. Similar to the never-ending nightmares of Valletta, there seemed to be no ending to the murders in Whitechapel. The District saw a lot of murders. Homicides were almost a weekly occurrence, to be exact. However, the Press described these as somewhat different and 'horrific'.

Aren't all murders 'horrific'? Maybe, some more than others. Archibald shut his eyes and frowned. No wonder he was having nightmares; blood and gore followed him everywhere - even at home, it seems.

The first victim was found on a Friday - 31st August. She was a prostitute, by the name of Mary Ann Nichols. A week later, another prostitute by the name of Annie Chapman, was also found dead. Now, three weeks later, these *two.*

'Elizabeth Stride and Catherine Eddowes,' he read, biting his lips.

Unlike the murders in Valletta two years ago, these followed a pattern. So far, the victims were all ladies of the night. They were all found in the early hours of morning, with serious wounds to the throat, chest and abdomen. Ripped open … putting it mildly, they were slaughtered like pigs.

Jesus Christ! Archibald scowled at the newspaper. It was horrific! Eddowes was found only forty-five minutes after Stride. The police still seemed to have no clue as to what, in heaven's name, was going on. *Not dissimilar to what happened in Valletta.* Archibald sniggered at his own impulsive instinct of comparing the two scenarios. He wasn't a constable anymore, but his knack for investigation came so natural. His investigative streak was not going to die anytime soon, anyway. *What if the Gentleman, from Valletta, survived and skipped the island …* Archibald blinked.

What on earth was crossing his mind?

Harrumphing, he threw the newspaper onto the worn piece of furniture he used as a desk. He was skilled at carrying out investigations and more importantly, he loved it. But of what use were one's talents if superiors didn't recognise their skills? Archibald looked out of the window at the grey dawn. He had tried, with all his might and had failed. *Will I ever learn to let go?* He sighed and made for the wardrobe.

Life was a bitch! One could say that, judging by what was happening to these prostitutes. However, all things being equal, he wasn't doing too bad. *Archie, now you're a barman, just like Pawlu. Maybe, one day, you could own the bar … who knows?* It wasn't a bad thought, after all. It was certainly better and more real than chasing phantom murderers through the alleyways of Whitechapel! For the time being, he had to learn how to let go. *Let go of the past*. He started putting on his clothes. Now, *you're a barman, act like one.*

'The present is a gift, Archibald.' His mother's voice echoed in his head. 'Always pray to God, not for justice, or for wealth and similar vanities. Pray to God for Him to grant you Peace, Archibald. And Peace comes from accepting your situation, whatever it is. Live it. It's a gift. Live it, Archibald, with all your heart, body and soul.' She would caress his head and hum a lullaby to help him go to sleep.

Archibald wasn't too sure he would be able to follow his mother's advice, but smiled at the thought of her.

***

Luciana looked at the empty street. The shadows danced around her, caressing her soul.

My soul ... she smirked.

The Catholic Church said, people like her, who sold their soul to Lucifer, would forever be tormented in the fires of hell. She didn't really care, as long as her Master walked by her side. *He* had saved her from the greatest hell of all. Ten years ago, when no one else cared, *he* had been her saviour. He had given her the Veiling. It had protected her, more than her parents ever did. It had given her power over everything and everyone. A few years later, she heard that her mother had joined the Creator of the Universe.

Presuming she was welcomed in Heaven ... she sniggered.

Irrespective of how unjust and how narrow-minded the Creator's way of thinking was, Luciana was pretty sure He would punish her mother, severely, for always having preferred her brother over her.

Love is fair and treats everyone equally. Otherwise it is not love at all. Luciana smiled faintly at the slight chill she always got whenever she remembered her Master's teachings. She closed her eyes for a second, her mind drifting back to that night, ten years ago. She would never forget the look of peace on her brother's face as he slept. He was not entitled to that peace, he had stolen it from Luciana the moment he was pulled out from their mother's womb. Stealing a piece of bread was acceptable, but stealing unconditional love was inexcusable.

I hope you're burning in hell with your mother, Luca. Luciana looked at the waning gibbous, and flashed a grin. The Veiling had helped her get to this foreign land - the land of Malta's oppressors - the land of Pawlu's killer.

Thoughts of Pawlu made her wince. She had warned him not to trust anyone; changing his name wasn't enough. Why did he have to be so stubborn and believe The Grand Mariner would be a safe haven? Hadn't he, like her, been through enough to realise how untrustworthy and deceiving people could be?

Luciana harrumphed in the darkness.

If he *had* seen it or if he *had* known, he would definitely not have fallen for Rosaria's beauty. Nor would he have fallen for Filippo's pretences of intelligence. He would still be alive and Luciana wouldn't need to be here, in this sunless land, seeking to avenge his murder.

Anyway ... Luciana glared at the wall to her right. She liked the fact that, thanks to the Veiling, she had no shadow. She looked at the moon again, remembering what her Master had promised her on the first night, just before she sacrificed Luca. She was going to become like the moon reflecting the sun's light onto the world.

An emissary of a great power, she smiled faintly, quoting her Master in her mind. *A victor of darkness and shadow, empowered by the light itself.* Luciana looked down at the tome in her hands. *Liber Iuratus Honorii* ... the book title itself had a nice tone to it. A melodious intonation the world would never understand. The crimson script almost shone in the moonlight. Indeed - the world would never understand. Neither would the poor bastard who killed Pawlu; he would never see her coming. Malta had failed, and Britain was going to pay for it.

And in all this chaos and confusion, I remain the victor. She laughed hysterically. *I am invincible.*

A note by the Author
may contain spoilers

(not to be read before Novel)

For clarity's sake, this is purely a work of fiction. All names, characters, places, events and incidents are either the product of the author's imagination, or used in a fictitious manner. Any similarity to actual persons, living or dead, or actual events is purely coincidental.

For those readers who are interested in knowing which elements are of historical fact and which aren't, Superintendent Casolani, Prior Massimo Gauci and Inspector Ġio Felice Inglott all held respective positions in the late 19th century.

The street names are all authentic for the period in which the story is set. Today, most street names still stand but they are translated to Maltese. Most buildings were replaced, possibly as a result of two World Wars. If any are still standing, their purpose has changed. Morell's Hotel, in *Strada Forni*, stood until World War II, when it collapsed during an air raid. Nowadays, St Albert's College stands instead of this Hotel.

The Falcon's Perch and The Grand Mariner were both inspired by real venues in *Strada Stretta*, though the names are fictitious. The former is abandoned and in a run-down state. At the time of writing, the latter is being renovated into a public bar.

L'Ospedale Centrale, in Floriana, is now the General Police Headquarters. The Auberge D'Auvergne in *Strada Reale*, which collapsed during World War II, was replaced by a new building in 1965. Nowadays, this building hosts the Courts of Justice. The Chapel of Nibbia fell to an aerial bombardment in 1941, although the Crypt of Bones survived and is now in a cordoned off area, in the car park of the Evans Building in Valletta. *Café de la Reine* has changed slightly through the years; there is still a popular cafeteria under a different name.

Hastings Gardens has seen structural changes, thanks to maintenance and refurbishment but it still stands in the very same great location, where one can enjoy a unique view in peace and quiet. Fort Manoel, which is situated on Manoel Island in Gżira is visible from Hastings Gardens. The Fort has been restored to its original grandeur.

The newspapers and book titles mentioned throughout the novel are all authentic, though they have been used fictitiously and entirely to the author's imagination.

About the Author

From a very young age, John always had a passion for writing, especially in English. From the days of creative writing at school, through the various attempts at novel writing in his early teens, John's passion for writing grew and matured over time.

His efforts paid off. In his mid-twenties, John published *Tales from Alrais* and *The Downfall of Pride* (both available on Amazon). John was always obsessed with writing a historical fiction novel, until he began forming and working on the idea of *City of Shadows*, back in 2014.

Born in Malta, John lived in Birkirkara until he was 10, when he moved with his family to Ħamrun. He is now married to Justine and lives in Pembroke (still Malta). He is working on his next book and frequently blogs on *johnnaudi.com*

Follow John on *facebook.com/johnnaudiauthor* or *twitter.com/john_naudi*

23632430R00261

Printed in Poland
by Amazon Fulfillment
Poland Sp. z o.o., Wrocław